Saturnalia

SATURNALIA

Lindsey Davis

Century · London

Published by Century in 2007

1 3 5 7 9 10 8 6 4 2

First published in Great Britain in 2007 by
Century
Random House, 20 Vauxhall Bridge Road,
London, SW1V 2SA

www.randomhouse.co.uk

Addresses for companies within The Random House Group Limited
can be found at: www.randomhouse.co.uk

The Random House Group Limited Reg. No. 954009

A CIP catalogue record for this book
is available from the British Library

Hardback ISBN 9781846050343
Trade Paperback ISBN 9781846050350
UK Trade Paperback ISBN 9781846051753

The Random House Group Limited makes every effort to ensure that the papers used
in its books are made from trees that have been legally sourced from well-managed
and credibly certified forests. Our paper procurement policy can be found at:
www.randomhouse.co.uk/paper.htm

Mixed Sources
Product group from well-managed
forests and other controlled sources
www.fsc.org Cert no. TT-COC-2139
FSC © 1996 Forest Stewardship Council

Typeset in Bembo by SX Composing DTP, Rayleigh, Essex
Printed and bound in the United Kingdom by
Clays Ltd, St Ives Plc

To Andrew Wallace-Hadrill with thanks for help and support over many years from the British School in Rome

PRINCIPAL CHARACTERS

The ignoble Didii	– see Didius family tree
The noble Camilli	– see Camillus family tree
Nux	a nut, but never thrown
Galene	a nursemaid, who wants to be a cook
Jacinthus	a cook, who wants to be anything else
Apollonius	a wine waiter, who expects nothing
★Vespasian Augustus	Emperor for the duration
★Titus Caesar	Emperor-for-the-Day, who wants to do good
Ti Claudius Laeta	a scroll secretary ⎫ all vying for
Ti Claudius Anacrites	Chief Spy ⎬ the magic
Momus	a slob ⎭ bean
The Melitan brothers	field operatives, found wanting in all departments
★Q Julius Cordinus G. Rutilius Gallicus	a bunch of names to watch
M. Quadrumatus Labeo	whose house is less safe than he thinks
Drusilla Gratiana	his wife, taking her own medicine
S. Gratianus Scaeva	her brother, a martyr to catarrh
Phryne	a loyal old retainer (not to be trusted)
A boy flautist	silent or silenced?
Hired medical experts:	
Aedemon	offering Egyptian empiricism (purges)
Cleander	offering Greek pneumatism (rest)
Mastarna	offering Etruscan dogmatism (the knife)
Pylaemenes	offering Chaldean dream therapy (twaddle)

Zosime	offering charitable outreach for Æsculapius (free)

⋆A Very Important Prisoner   on the run
⋆Ganna   an acolyte, on the loose

The IV Cohort of vigiles:
L. Petronius Longus   watching his drink intake
M. Rubella   a tribune with a fine pair of pins
T. Fusculus   a man of many words
Scythax   a doctor, offering no hope (and wonky stitches)
Sergius   the big softie

Legionaries, recalled from leave:
Clemens   an acting centurion
Cattus   his servant, not taking much part in the action
Scaurus, Gaudus, Sentius,
Paullus, Gaius, Lusius, Minnius,
Granius – and there is always
one called Titus
plus lentullus   the dopey one

Dora & Delia (but not Daphne)   professional ladies with a bucket of bones
Zoilus   a ghoul, available for hire

A full supporting cast of Praetorian Guards, vigiles, narks, quacks, vegetables, runaway slaves, priests, priestesses, stewards, door porters, members the German community in Rome, including:
Ermanus   the sexy one, who likes partying
plus an Elderly Vestal Virgin

⋆denotes real person

Extract from the Family Tree of Marcus Didius Falco

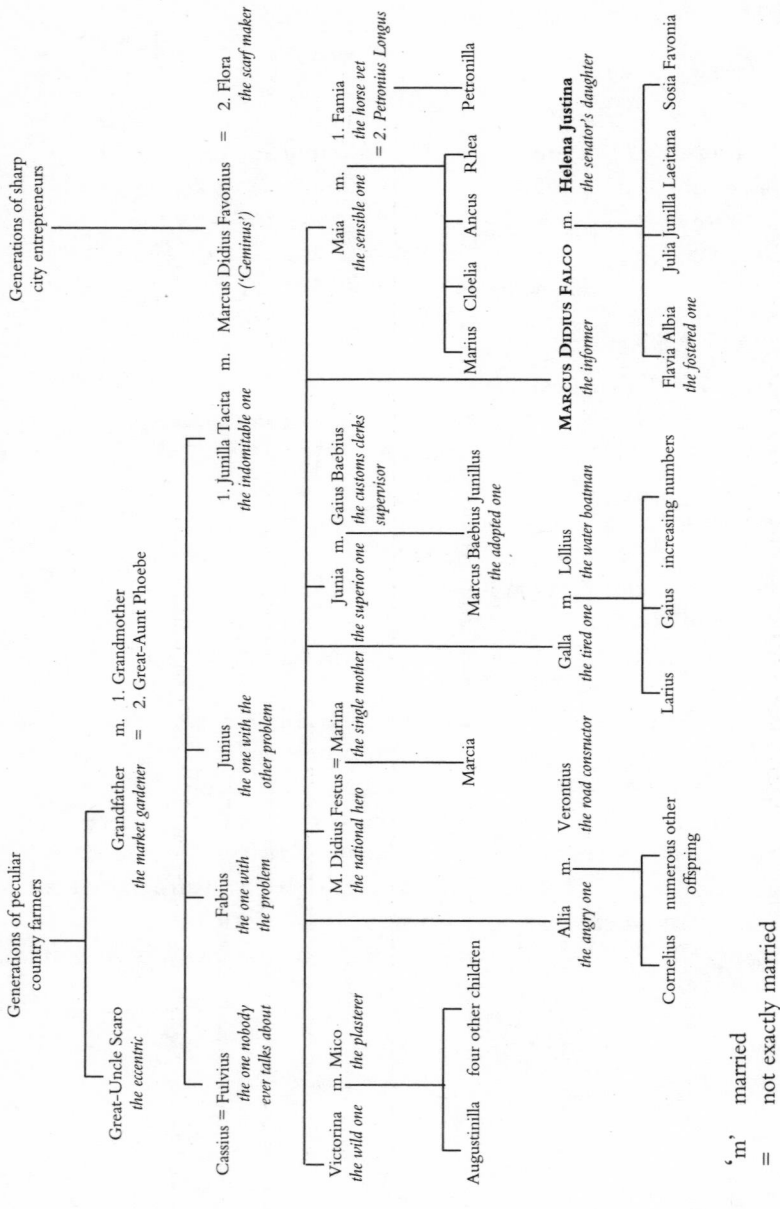

'm'   married
=   not exactly married
?   unknown, never mentioned in public, or a matter of speculation

Extract from the Family Tree of the Noble Camilli

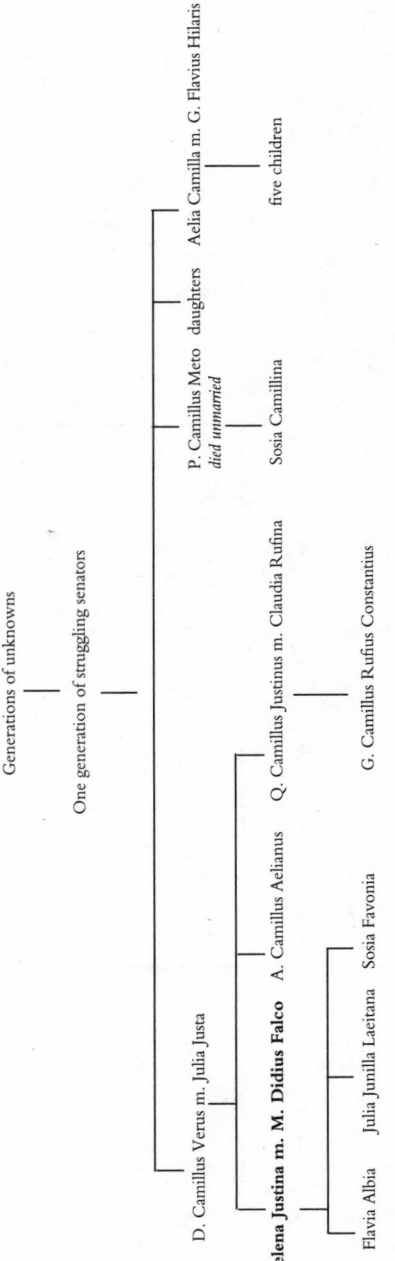

Generations of unknowns

One generation of struggling senators

D. Camillus Verus m. Julia Justa

P. Camillus Meto   daughters   Aelia Camilla m. G. Flavius Hilaris
died unmarried

Sosia Camillina

five children

A. Camillus Aelianus

Ielena Justina m. M. Didius Falco

Q. Camillus Justinus m. Claudia Rufina

G. Camillus Rufius Constantius

Sosia Favonia

Flavia Albia   Julia Junilla Laeitana

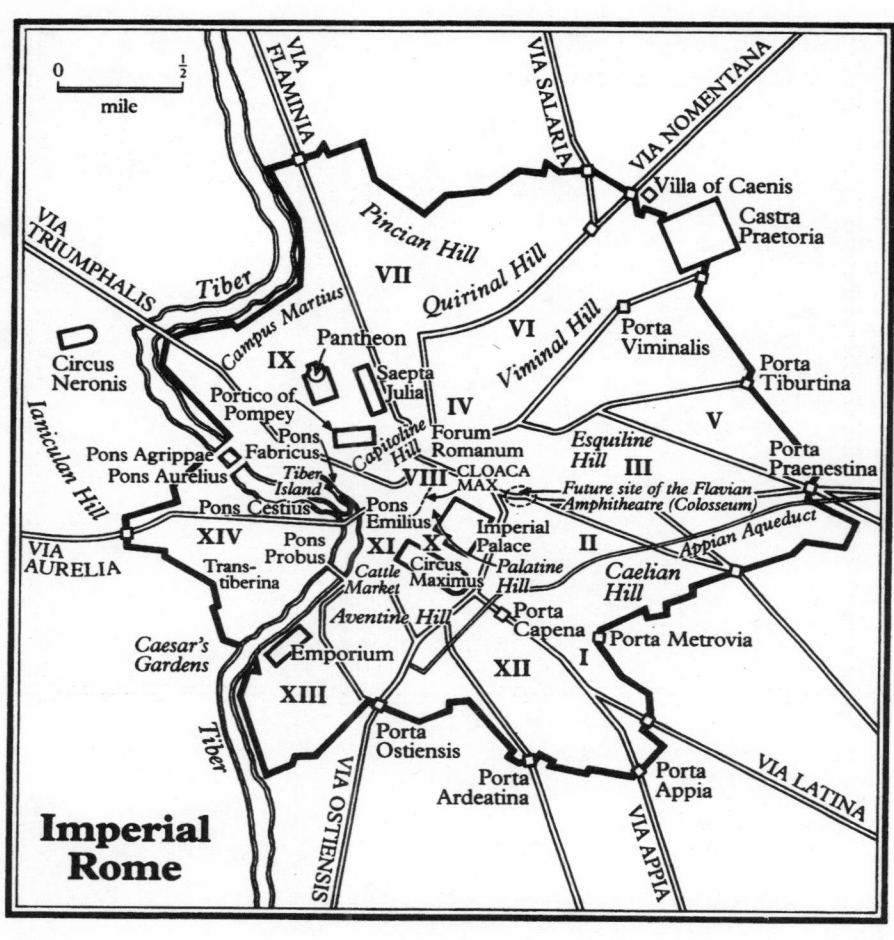

Imperial Rome

Jurisdictions of the Vigiles Cohorts in Rome:

Coh I	Regions VII & VIII (Via Lata, Forum Romanum)
Coh II	Regions III & V (Isis and Serapis, Esquiline)
Coh III	Regions IV & VI (Temple of Peace, Alta Semita)
Coh IV	Regions XII & XIII (Piscina Publica, Aventine)
Coh V	Regions I & II (Porta Capena, Caelimontium)
Coh VI	Regions X & XI (Palatine, Circus Maximus)
Coh VII	Regions IX & XIV (Circus Flaminius, Transtiberina)

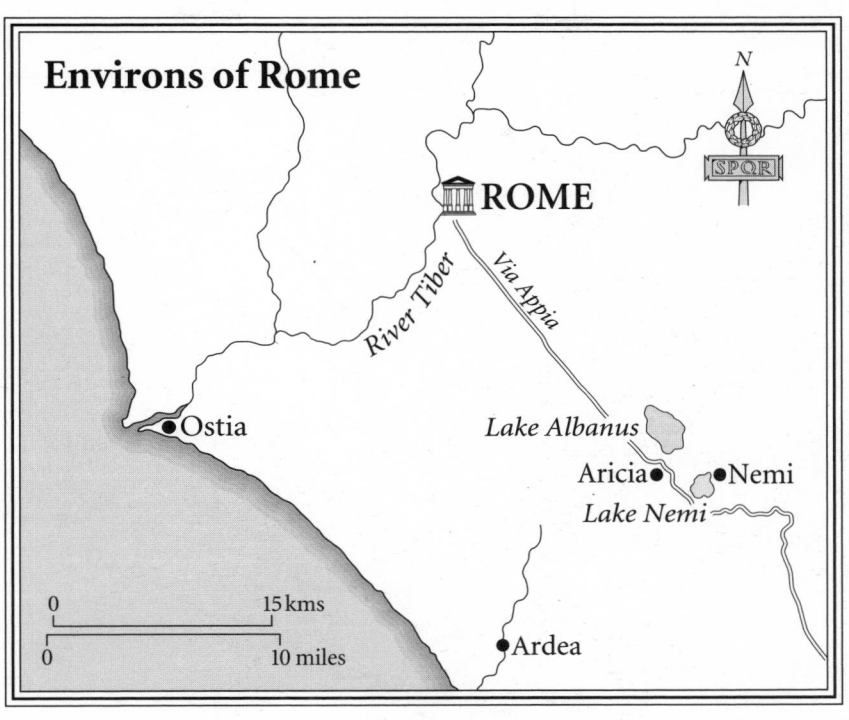

Environs of Rome

N

SPQR

🏛 **ROME**

River Tiber

Via Appia

●Ostia

Lake Albanus

Aricia● ●Nemi

Lake Nemi

0   15 kms

0   10 miles

●Ardea

Extracts from the Hippocratic Oath

I swear by Apollo the healer . . . I will use my power to help the sick to the best of my ability and judgement; I will abstain from harming or wronging any man by it.

I will not cut, even for the stone, but I will leave such procedures to the practitioners of that craft.

Whenever I go into a house, I will go to help the sick and never with the intention of doing harm or injury . . .

ROME: DECEMBER AD76

=====

If there was one thing you could say for my father, he never beat his wife.

'He hit her!' Pa was spluttering; he was so eager to tell my wife Helena that her brother was guilty of domestic violence. 'He came right out and admitted it: Camillus Justinus *struck* Claudia Rufina!'

'I bet he told you that in confidence too,' I snapped. 'So you come bursting in here only five minutes later and tell us!' Justinus must have gone for a bribe to reinstate himself. Once Pa had sold the culprit an exorbitant 'forgive me darling' gift, my parent had rushed straight from his fine art warehouse at the Saepta Julia to our house, eager to snitch.

'You'd never catch me behaving like that,' he boasted self-righteously.

'Agreed. Your faults are more insidious.'

There were plenty of drunken male bullies in Rome, and plenty of downtrodden wives who refused to leave them, but as I licked the breakfast honey from my fingers and wished he would go away, I was glaring at a much more subtle character. Marcus Didius Favonius, who had renamed himself Geminus for reasons of his own, was about as complicated as they come. Most people called my father a lovable rogue. Most people, therefore, were bemused that I loathed him.

'I never hit your mother in my life!'

I may have sounded weary. 'No, you just walked out on her and seven children, leaving Mother to bring us up as best she could.'

'I sent her money.' My father's contributions were a fraction of the fortune he amassed in the course of his dealings as an auctioneer, antique dealer, and reproduction marble salesman.

'If Ma had been given a denarius for every foolish buyer of flaky Greek "original statues" you conned, we would all have dined on peacocks and my sisters would have had dowries to buy tribunes as husbands.'

All right, I admit it: Pa was right when he muttered: 'Giving money to any of your sisters would have been a bad idea.'

The point about Pa is that he could, if it was absolutely unavoidable, put up a fight. It would be a fight worth watching, if you had half an hour before your next appointment and a piece of Lucanian sausage to chew on while you stood there. Yet to him, the concept of any husband *daring* to hit a feisty wife (the only kind my father knew about, since he came from the Aventine where women give no quarter) was about as likely as getting a Vestal Virgin to buy him a drink. He also knew that Quintus Camillus Justinus was the son of a respectable, thoroughly amiable senator; he was my wife's younger brother, in general her favourite; everyone spoke highly of Quintus. Come to that, he had always been *my* favourite. If you overlooked a few failings – little quirks, like stealing his own brother's bride and backing out of a respectable career so he could run off to North Africa to grow silphium (which is extinct, but that didn't stop him) – he was a nice lad. Helena and I were both very fond of him.

From the moment of their elopement, Claudia and Quintus had had their difficulties. It was the usual story. He had been too young to get married; she was much too keen on the idea. They were in love when they did it. That is more than most couples can say. Now that they had a baby son, we all assumed they would set aside their problems. If they divorced, they would both be expected to marry other people anyway. They could end up with worse. Justinus, who was the real offender in their stormy relationship, would certainly lose out, because the one thing he had acquired with Claudia was joyful access to her very large fortune. She was a fiery piece when she needed to be, and her habit nowadays was to wear her emeralds on every occasion, to remind him of what he would lose (apart from his dear little son Gaius) if they separated.

Helena Justina, my level-headed wife weighed in, making it clear where her sympathies would lie. 'Calm down, Geminus, and tell us what caused poor Quintus to be in this trouble.' She tapped my still-excited father on the chest, to soothe him. 'Where is my brother now?'

'Your noble father has requested that the villain leave the family home!' Quintus and Claudia lived with his parents; it cannot have helped.

Pa, whose children and grandchildren rejected all forms of

supervision, especially from him, seemed impressed by the senator's bravery. He assumed a disapproving air. From the biggest reprobate on the Aventine, this was ludicrous. Pa gazed at me with those tricky brown eyes, running his hands through the wild grey curls that still clustered on his wicked old head. He was daring me to be flippant. I knew when to hold my peace. I wasn't mad.

'So where can he go?' A curious note of hysteria squeaked its way into Helena's voice.

'He told me he has camped out in your uncle's old house.' The senator had inherited this property next door to his own. I knew that house was currently empty. The senator needed the rent, but the last tenants had left suddenly.

'Well, that's convenient.' Helena sounded brisk; she was a practical woman. 'Did my brother say what caused him to lash out at dear Claudia?'

'Apparently,' my father's tone was lugubrious – the old bastard was enjoying every moment of this – 'your brother has an old girlfriend in town.'

'Oh "girlfriend" is putting it far too strongly, Geminus!' I gazed at Helena fondly and let her commit herself: 'I know who you mean of course – Veleda is her name –' All Rome knew the past history of this notorious female – though, so far, few people realised she and Quintus had ever been connected. His wife must have heard something, however. I guessed Quintus himself had stupidly told her. 'Quintus may have met the woman once,' Helena declared, trying to reassure herself, 'but it was a long time ago, long before he was married or had even heard of Claudia – and anything that occurred between them happened very far away!'

'In a forest, I believe!' Pa smirked, as if trees were disgusting.

Helena looked hot. 'Veleda is a barbarian, a German from beyond the frontier of the Empire – '

'Isn't your sister-in-law also from outside Italy?' Pa now produced a leer, his speciality.

'Claudia comes from Hispania Baetica. Absolutely civilised. An utterly different background and position. Spain has been Romanised for generations. Claudia is a Roman citizen, whereas the prophetess – '

'Oh this Veleda is a *prophetess*?' Pa snorted.

'Not good enough to foresee her own doom!' snapped Helena. 'She has been captured and brought to Rome for execution on the Capitol. Veleda offers no hope of romance to my brother and no threat to his wife. Even Claudia at her most sensitive should be able

3

to see that he can have nothing more to do with this woman. So what in Hades can have driven him to hit her?'

A wily look appeared upon Pa's face. People say we are alike physically. This was an expression I had certainly not inherited.

'It could be,' my father speculated (knowing the reason full well, of course), 'because Claudia Rufina hit him first.'

II

Saturnalia was a good time for a family quarrel; it could easily be lost among the seasonal rumpus. But not this quarrel, unfortunately.

Helena Justina played down the incident for as long as Pa stayed around. Neither of us told him any more gossip. Eventually he gave up. The minute he left, she pulled on a warm cloak, called up a carrying chair, and rushed off to confront her brother at their late uncle's empty, elegant house by the Capena Gate. I did not bother to go with her. I doubted she would find Justinus there. He had enough sense not to place himself in a losing position, like a doomed counter on a backgammon board, right where furious female relatives could jump on him.

My darling wife and mother of my children was a tall, serious, sometimes obstinate young woman. She described herself as 'a quiet girl', at which I openly guffawed. Still, I had heard her describe me to strangers as talented and of fine character, so Helena had good judgement. More sensitive than her outward calm revealed, she was so upset about her brother she failed to notice that a messenger from the imperial Palace had come for me. If she had realised, she would have been even more jumpy.

It was the usual washed-out slave. He was underdeveloped and rickety; he looked as if he had stopped growing when he hit his teens, though he was older than that – had to be, to become a trusty who was sent out alone on the streets with messages. He wore a crumpled loose-weave tunic, bit his dirty nails, hung his lousy head, and in the customary manner, claimed to know nothing about his errand.

I played along. 'So what does Laeta want?'

'Not allowed to say.'

'Then you admit it is Claudius Laeta who sent you to get me?'

Out-manoeuvred, he cursed himself. 'Fair do's, Falco . . . He's got a job for you.'

'Will I like it? – Don't bother answering.' I never liked anything from the Palace. 'I'll fetch my cloak.'

We buffeted our way through the Forum. It was packed with miserable householders, taking home green boughs for decoration, depressed by the inflationary Saturnalia prices and by knowing they were stuck with a week when they were supposed to forget grudges and quarrels. Four times I rebuffed hard-faced women selling wax candles from trays. Drunks were already littering the temple steps, celebrating in advance. We had nearly two weeks to get through yet.

I had worked on imperial missions before, usually abroad. These jobs were always terrible and complicated by ruthless scheming among the Emperor's ambitious bureaucrats. Half the time their dangerous in-fighting threatened to ruin my efforts and get me killed.

Though designated a scroll secretary, Claudius Laeta ranked high; he had some undefined oversight of both home security and foreign intelligence. His only good point, in my opinion, was that he endlessly struggled to outwit, out-manoeuvre, out-stay and do down his implacable rival, Anacrites the Chief Spy. The Spy worked alongside the Praetorian Guard. He was supposed to keep his nose out of foreign policy, but he meddled freely. He possessed at least one extremely dangerous agent in the field, a dancer called Perella, though generally his sidekicks were dross. Up to now, that had given Laeta the upper hand.

Anacrites and I had occasionally worked together. Don't let me give the impression I despised him. He was a festering fistula of pestilential pus. I treat anything that venomous only with respect. Our relationship was based on the purest emotion: hate.

Compared with Anacrites, Claudius Laeta was civilised. Well, he looked harmless as he rose from a couch to greet me in his highly painted office, but he was a silken-tongued twister I had never trusted. He saw me as a grimy thug, though a thug who possessed intelligence and other handy talents. We dealt with one another, when we had to, politely. He realised that two of his three masters – the Emperor himself and the elder of Vespasian's sons, Titus Caesar – both had a high regard for my qualities. Laeta was far too astute to ignore that. He held on to his position by the old bureaucrat's trick of feigning agreement with any views his superiors held strongly. He only stopped short of the pretence that hiring me had been his recommendation. Vespasian could spot that sort of creep.

I was quite sure that Laeta had managed to find out that the younger princeling, Domitian Caesar, had a deep-running feud with me. I knew something about Domitian that he would dearly love to expunge: he once killed a young girl, and I still possessed the evidence. Outside the imperial family it remained a secret, but the mere fact that such a secret existed was bound to reach their sharp-eyed chief secretaries. Claudius Laeta would have buried a coded note in some scroll in his columbarium, reminding himself to use my dangerous knowledge against me one day.

Well, I had information on him too. He schemed too much to stay in the clear. I wasn't worried.

Despite this plotting and jealousy, the old Palace of Tiberius always seemed surprisingly fresh and businesslike. The Empire had been run from this fading monument for a century, through good emperors and debauched ones; some of the slick slaves went back here for three generations. The messenger had dropped me off almost as soon as we entered through the Cryptoporticus. With barely a wave of a spear from the guards, I wound my way up into the interior, through staterooms I recognised, and on into ones I could not remember. Then I hit the system.

An invitation was no guarantee of a welcome. As usual, working through the flunkeys was a frustrating grind. Vespasian had famously abandoned the paranoid security Nero used to protect himself from assassination: now, nobody was searched. It may have impressed the public; I knew better. Even our most lovable old emperor since Claudius was too shrewd to take risks. Power draws lunatics. There would always be one crackpot ready to run amok with a sword in the perverted hope of fame. So as I sought Laeta's office I was pushed around by Praetorian Guards, held up while chamberlains consulted lists upon which I did not feature, stuck alone in corridors for hours, and generally driven crazy. At which point Laeta's tidily dressed minions had let me in.

'Next time you want me, let's meet on a park bench!'

'Didius Falco! How pleasant to see you. Still frothing at the mouth, I see.'

Arguing was about as useful as demanding a recount of your change in a busy lunchtime food bar. I forced myself to simmer down. Laeta saw he had nearly pushed me too far. He caved in. '*So* sorry to keep you waiting, Falco. Nothing changes here. Too much to do and too little time to do it – and a panic on, naturally.'

'I wonder what that can be!' I implied I had private information about it. I didn't.

'I'll come to that –'

'Keep it brisk then.'

'Titus Caesar suggested I talk to you –'

'And how is the princely Titus?'

'Oh – wonderful, wonderful.'

'Still screwing beautiful Queen Berenice? Or have you dreamed up some stratagem to whisk her back to her desert and avert embarrassment?'

Nursemaids must give a potion in babies' little pottery feeding bottles, one that makes aristocratic Roman males hanker after exotic women. Cleopatra had worked her way through enough Roman top brass. Now Titus Caesar, like me a handsome lad in his thirties, was an amiable prince who ought to be marrying a fifteen-year-old pretty patrician with good hips so he could father the next generation of Flavian emperors; instead, he preferred to dally on purple cushions with the voluptuous Queen of Judaea. It was true love, they said. Well, it must certainly be love on his part; Berenice was hot stuff, but older than him, and had a terrible reputation for incest (which Rome could cope with) and political interference (which was bad news). Conservative Rome would never accept this hopeful dame as an imperial consort. Astute in all other matters, Titus stuck with his no-brain love affair like some bloody-minded teenager who had been instructed to stop smooching the kitchen maid.

Bored with waiting for an answer, I had lost myself in these gloomy thoughts. Without any obvious signal, Laeta's minions had all melted away. He and I were now alone and he had the air of a sword-swallower at the high point of a trick: *'Look at me; this is terribly dangerous! I am about to disembowel myself . . .'*

'And there's Veleda,' said Claudius Laeta in his polite bureaucratic accent.

I stopped daydreaming.

III

'Veleda . . .' I pretended I was trying to remember who she was. Laeta saw through it.

I took a free couch. Relaxing at the Palace always made me feel like an unpleasant grub that had crawled in from the gardens. We informers are not meant to spread ourselves on cushions stuffed with goose-down, embroidered in luminous silks with imperial motifs. I had probably brought in donkey dung on my boots. I didn't bother to check the floor marble.

'When Titus suggested you, I looked at your record, Falco,' Laeta pointed out. 'Five years ago, you were sent on a mission to Germany to help batten down any persisting rebels. The scroll box has been mysteriously weeded – one wonders why – but it's clear you met Civilis, the Batavian chief, and I can work out the rest. I presume you crossed over the River Rhenus to negotiate with the priestess?'

Back in the Year of the Four Emperors, when the Empire had collapsed in bloody lawlessness, Civilis and Veleda had been two German activists who tried to free their area from Roman occupation. Civilis was one of our own, an ex-auxiliary, trained in the legions, but Veleda opposed us from alien territory. Once Vespasian assumed the throne and ended the civil war, they had both remained trouble-makers – for a while.

'Wrong direction,' I smiled. 'I went across from Batavia, and then worked south to find her.'

'Details,' sniffed Laeta.

'I was trying to stay alive. Formal negotiations were difficult when the rampaging Bructeri were after our blood. No point ending up decapitated, with our heads hurled in the river as sacrifices.'

'Not if you can make friends with a beauteous blonde at the top of a signal tower, and then borrow her boat to sail home.' Laeta knew all the details. He must have seen my 'confidential' report. I hoped he did not know the facts I had omitted.

'Which I did, very fast. Free Germany is no place for a Roman to linger.'

'Well, things have moved on –'

'For the better?' I doubted it. 'I left both Civilis and Veleda grudgingly reconciled to Rome. At least neither was intending any more armed revolts, and Civilis was pinned down in his home area. So what's the problem with the buxom Bructeran now?'

Claudius Laeta balanced his chin on his hands thoughtfully. After a while he asked me, 'I believe you know Quintus Julius Cordinus Gaius Rutilius Gallicus?'

I choked. 'I've met parts of him! He wasn't using that whole scroll of names.' He must have been adopted. That was one way to improve your status. Some wealthy patron, with a desperate need for an heir and not much judgement, had given him a step up in society and a double signature. He would probably drop the extra names as soon as he decently could.

Laeta pressed out a pitying smile. 'The estimable Gallicus is now Governor of Germania Inferior. He's gone formal.' Then he was an idiot. The six-name wonder would still be the same anodyne senator I first met in Libya when he was an envoy surveying land boundaries to stop tribal feuds. I had since shared a poetry recital with him. We all make mistakes. Mine tend to be embarrassing.

'As I recall, he's not special.'

'Are any of them?' Now Laeta was being chummy. 'Still, the man is doing an excellent job as governor. I don't suppose you've kept up with developments – the Bructeri are active again; Gallicus crossed over to Germania Libera to put a clamp on that. While he was there, he captured Veleda –' Using *my* map of where she was holed up, no doubt.

I was annoyed. 'So it made no difference at all that – acting on Vespasian's orders – I promised the woman there would be no reprisals once she stopped her anti-Roman agitation?'

'You're right. It made no difference.' Still pretending we were friends, Laeta showed his cynicism. 'The official explanation is that since the Bructeri were threatening the stability of the region again, it was presumed she had *not* stopped stirring.'

'Alternatively,' I suggested, 'she and her tribe have had a falling out. When the Bructeri put on war gear nowadays, it is nothing to do with her.'

There was a pause. What I said was correct. (I *do* keep up with developments.) Veleda had found herself increasingly at odds with her countrymen. Her local influence was waning, and even if he thought he needed to put down her fellow-tribesmen, Rutilius Gallicus could have – *should* have – left her alone.

He needed her for his own purposes. Veleda was a symbol. So she stood no chance.

'Let's not haggle, Falco. Gallicus made a brave foray into Germania Libera and legitimately removed a vicious enemy of Rome –'

I finished the story. 'Now he's hoping for a Triumph?'

'Only emperors have Triumphs. As a general, Gallicus will be entitled to an Ovation.' Same deal as a Triumph, but a shorter procession: done on the cheap. Even so, an Ovation was rare. It marked extraordinary civic thanks to a general who had courageously made war in unconquered territory.

'Mere terminology! Is Vespasian promoting this? Or just Rutilius' friend at court – Domitian?'

'Is Gallicus on good terms with Domitian Caesar?' Laeta was playing disingenuous.

'They share a deep admiration for horrible epic poetry . . . So is Germania Libera and all its nasty, violent, Rome-hating, wolf-skinned inhabitants, now part of the Empire, thanks to heroic Rutilius?'

'Not quite.' Laeta meant, not at all. After Augustus lost the three Varus legions in the Teutoburger Forest seventy years before, it was obvious that Rome would never be able to advance safely beyond the River Rhenus. Nobody knew how far the dark trees extended east, or how many ferocious tribes inhabited the vast uncharted zones. I had been there briefly; there was nothing for us. I could see a theoretical risk that the hostile tribes would one day come out of the woods, cross the river and attack us, but that is all it was: theoretical. There would be no advantage to them. So long as they stayed on their side, we would stay on ours.

Except when a self-aggrandising general like Rutilius Gallicus felt obliged to embark on a crazy adventure, to add lustre to his piss-poor status at home . . .

Disapproval was flavouring my saliva. Not only was Rutilius an idiot, Claudius Laeta was a fool for the glint of respect he was showing the man. Put policy in the hands of such dimwits, and you could hear the gods guffawing.

'We still have in place our old decision not to advance territorially beyond the river.' Laeta was so complacent I wanted to pour ink from his silver stationery set all over his pristine white tunic. 'Nonetheless,

there is a tricky area opposite Moguntiacum –' That was a large base
we had, halfway down the Rhenus. 'The Emperor was content for
Gallicus to consolidate the area for safety. When he goes back –'

'Goes back?' I shot in.

Laeta looked shifty. 'We never publicise movements of governors
when they are outside their provinces –'

'Oh, he's stolen a mid-term break.' They all did it. They had to
check up on their wives at home.

Laeta carried on doggedly: 'That's the problem, you see, Falco. The
problem with Veleda.'

I sat up. 'He brought her back to Rome?' Laeta merely closed his
eyes longer than usual and did not answer me. I for one had known
for weeks that Veleda was here; I had sailed back from Greece early,
just to head off any trouble with Justinus. 'Oh, I see! Rutilius brought
her back to Rome – but *you are not admitting it*?'

'Security is not a game, Falco.'

'I hope you'd play better, if it was.'

'The governor, very sensibly, preferred not to leave such a high-
ranking, sensitive captive behind. The risks were too great. A woman
prisoner in an army camp is always a focus for unrest, even pranks that
could get out of hand. Without Gallicus to impose an iron grip, her
tribe could have tried to mount a rescue. Rival tribes might have tried
to assassinate her; they are always at each other's throats. Veleda might
even have escaped independently.'

The list of possible crises sounded like an excuse in retrospect. Then
the subtle way Laeta failed to meet my eye alerted me. Dear gods. I
could hardly believe what must have happened: 'So, Claudius Laeta,
let me be quite clear: Rutilius Gallicus brought the priestess back to
Rome with him – for "safety" – then he let her escape *here*?'

Veleda was a stupendously influential barbarian, a famous enemy
who once rabble-roused a whole continent into revolt against Rome.
She hated us. She hated everything we represented. She had united
northern Europe while we were preoccupied with our leadership
tussles, and at the height of her activity she nearly lost us Batavia, Gaul
and Germany. And now, Laeta was telling me, she was on the loose,
right inside our city.

IV

Claudius Laeta pursed his lips. He had the sorrowful expression of a top official who is absolutely determined his department will not be blamed for this.

'Is it *your* problem?' I murmured mischievously.

'Chief Spy's remit,' he announced firmly.

'Then it's everybody's problem!'

'You are very frank about your differences with Anacrites, Falco.'

'Someone has to be open. That fool will do a lot of damage if he isn't stopped.'

'We believe him to be competent.'

'Then you're nuts.'

We were both silent. I was thinking about the implications of Veleda's escape. It was not that she could launch a military attack here. But her presence right in Rome was a disaster. That she had been imported by an ex-consul, a high-ranking provincial administrator, one of the Emperor's favourites, would damage public confidence. Rutilius Gallicus had been stupid. There would be outrage and dismay. Belief in the Emperor would shrink. The army would look pitiful. Rutilius – well, few people had heard much of Rutilius, except in Germany. But if word got back there, the effect on the province of Germany could be dangerous. Veleda was still a big name on both sides of the River Rhenus. As a so-called prophetess, the woman had always caused a frisson of terror that was out of proportion to her real influence; still, she had summoned up armies of rebels, and those rebels had wreaked havoc.

'Now she's free in Rome – and you've sent for me.'

'You have met her, Falco. You will recognise her.'

'As simple as that?'

He knew nothing. Veleda was of striking appearance: the first thing she would do was dye her hair. Most Roman women wanted to go blonde, but one visit to a cosmetic pharmacy would have Veleda well disguised.

'You may charge a premium.' Laeta made me sound mercenary. He ignored the fact that he himself received a big annual salary – plus bribes – plus pension – plus legacy, if the Emperor died – whereas I was stuck with whatever I could claw together on a freelance basis. 'This is a national emergency. Titus reckons you have the skills, Falco.'

He mentioned the fee, and I managed not to whistle. The Palace saw this as an emergency all right.

I took the job. Laeta then told me the background. It was worse than I thought. Missions from the Palace always were. Not many were as bad as this, but as soon as I had heard Veleda's name I had known this particular fiasco would be special.

Rutilius Gallicus had arrived back in Italy several weeks ago, was debriefed at the Palace, caught up with the news in the Forum and from his noble acquaintances, then swanned off north to Augusta Taurinorum, where his family lived. That's right up close to the Alps. I mused that his background should have given him sympathies with the barbarians in Germany; he had been born and bred right next door to them. He was practically German himself.

I had met his rather provincial wife, Minicia Paetina. She did not take to me. It was mutual. She had attended the poetry recital Rutilius and I once gave together, where she made it clear she thought me a plebeian upstart, unfit to wipe her fellow's nose. The fact that our audience openly preferred my snappy satires to his endless extracts from a second-rate epic did not improve Minicia's attitude.

The audience were no help, in fact. Rutilius Gallicus had invited Domitian Caesar as his guest of honour, whereas I was supported by cat-calling members of my Aventine family. From memory, Anacrites had been there, too. I could not remember whether this was in the ghastly period when he tried moving in on my sister Maia or the even worse episode when everyone thought the Spy had made himself my mother's gigolo.

Helena Justina had been polite to Minicia Paetina, and vice versa, but we were generally glad when the Rutilii went home. I could imagine the kind of stiff Saturnalia they were now about to enjoy at Augusta Taurinorum. *'As a special treat, we can all wear informal tunics at dinner, instead of togas . . .'*

'There's no chance Rutilius will cut short his leave and pop back here to sort out his mess?'

'No chance at all, Falco.'

As for Veleda, Laeta said Rutilius had brought her to Rome, where she was ensconced in a safe house. She had to be put somewhere. Burying her in a prison cell for the next couple of years, until Rutilius reached the end of his tour as governor, was not an option. Veleda would never have survived the dirt and disease. No point having a famous rebel die of jail fever. She must be kept fit and looking ferocious for the triumphal procession. A bonus would be to claim she was a virgin; by tradition she would be formally raped by her jailer just before her execution. Rome loves that kind of smut. So no one would want any dewy-eyed junior jailers falling in love with her and comforting her in the cell, let alone prankster sons of consuls bribing their way in for a quick thrill on the straw.

Priestesses always call themselves virgins. They have to clothe themselves in mystery. But Veleda had had at least one fling in the past. I knew who she had had it with too. Why do you think she gave us the boat?

'Tell me about your so-called safe house, Laeta.'

'Not *mine*!' I wondered whose. Would Anacrites have fixed it up? 'All necessary checks were carried out, Falco. There were rigorous measures in place. Her host is absolutely reliable. She gave us her parole as well. It was perfectly secure.' Officialdom's usual excuses. I knew how much they meant.

'So it's incredible, is it, that she somehow got out? Who was the lucky host?'

'Quadrumatus Labeo.' Never heard of him.

'Who was in charge of security?'

'Ah!' Laeta's immediate enthusiasm for the subject told me *he* was in the clear. 'That's an interesting point, Falco.'

'In Palatine argot, an "interesting point" is generally a complete rat's arse . . .' I squeezed Laeta until he admitted the mess: Rutilius Gallicus had brought Veleda home with an escort of troops from Germany. Then confusion set in. The legionaries assumed that they had handed over responsibility to the Praetorian Guard; the soldiers all expected to bugger off to brothels and winebars for three months until they had to take Rutilius back to Germany. Nobody told the Praetorians they had acquired the magic maiden.

'So, Laeta. Who *should* have told the Praetorians? Rutilius himself?'

'Oh he has no remit in Rome. And he is a stickler for propriety.'

'Of course he is! So the stickler jumped into a carriage and rushed north, with his Saturnalia presents stuffed in the luggage box . . . Did Titus Caesar know Veleda was here?'

'Don't blame him. Titus may be nominally commander of the Praetorians, yet he does not issue orders of the day. His role is ceremonial –'

'He'll certainly give a ceremonial bollocking to the Guards who watched her flit!'

'Don't forget, Falco, it is supposed to be a secret that she ever arrived.'

'So if it's a secret, did anyone notify Anacrites?'

'Anacrites bloody well knows now!' muttered Laeta tetchily. 'He has been assigned responsibility for finding her.'

This was worse than I had thought. 'Then I repeat: did he know before?'

'I have no idea.'

'Get away!'

'I am not privy to security policy.'

'But you're privy to the balls-up! Next awkward question then: if Anacrites has oversight of the recovery operation, why are you commissioning me? Does he know I'm to be involved?'

'He was opposed to it.' I could have guessed that. 'Titus wants you,' said Laeta. His voice dropped uncharacteristically. 'There are some odd circumstances surrounding the woman's escape . . . exactly your sort of thing, Falco.' Afterwards I knew I should have pursued that straight away, but the hint of flattery diverted me, then Laeta cunningly added, 'Anacrites believes his own resources will suffice.'

' "Resources"? Is he still using Momus, and that dwarf with the enormous feet? And I may know what Veleda looks like, but *he* hasn't a clue. He won't spot the woman if she steps on his toe and steals his arm-purse . . . Presumably, the troops Rutilius brought across from Germany to guard her on the journey all saw her? They should be able to recognise her. Has anyone thought of recalling them?'

'Titus. Titus cancelled their leave.' Titus Caesar could think in a crisis. 'They are yours.' Laeta quickly pushed a scroll of names at me. 'Anacrites wants to use the Praetorian Guard. Actually, we couldn't find the whole escort for you – some must have gone to see their mothers at the back of beyond – but these ten men and their officer have been told to report to your house tomorrow, in civilian clothes.'

These must be the ones who were so unlovable their mothers refused to have them home. 'I must tell my wife,' I sneered, 'that she has to entertain ten disgruntled legionaries, who have been robbed of their home leave, in our house for Saturnalia.'

'You'll have to pretend they are your relatives,' said Laeta, nastily. He thought he was insulting my family. He had not met my real relatives; nobody could be as bad. 'The noble Helena Justina will undoubtedly cope. She can charge us for their keep.' That wasn't the point. 'I imagine your young woman's domestic accounting is immaculate. The men have specific orders to behave politely . . .' Even Laeta tailed off, foreseeing the kind of domestic strife that now awaited me.

'During a festival devoted to misrule? Laeta, you're an optimist!' Glancing at the names on the list, my heart sank even more. I recognised one of them. Rutilius Gallicus must be the kind of bright commander who instinctively picks his most useless men for the most delicate tasks. 'Right —' I braced myself. 'I need a full briefing on Veleda's host at this so-called safe house, your Labeo character.' Meekly, Laeta proffered another prepared scroll. I made no attempt to unravel it. 'What's my target completion date?'

'End of Saturnalia?'

'Oh flying phalluses!'

'My dear Falco!' Laeta was now smiling slyly, 'I know you will see this as a race against time, a challenge to beat Anacrites.'

'And that's another thing: I don't want to be pissed about by him. I want the right to overrule him. *I* want command of the exercise.'

Laeta pretended to be shocked. 'Can't be done, Falco.'

'Then I'm out.'

He had anticipated trouble. 'I offer you one concession: *Anacrites* will have no right of command over *you*. He keeps his normal reporting line; you remain a freelance. You will work to me, of course, but you are nominally acting direct for Titus Caesar. Will that suffice?'

'Have to. I don't want bloody Anacrites getting his debauched hands on the priestess before me —' I grinned salaciously. 'Claudius Laeta, I *do* know what she looks like, remember: the priestess Veleda is a beautiful girl!'

═══════

V

A genuine virgin was waiting on my doorstep when I returned home. That did not happen often now. In fact, I had always preferred my women to possess a degree of experience. Innocence causes all kinds of misunderstandings, and that's even before you get tangled up with your conscience.

This one told me her name was Ganna. She was late teens and tearful, and she begged me to help her. Some informers would have palpitations just thinking about this. I invited her in politely and fixed myself up with a chaperon.

I had never acquired a doorman. Ganna's scared rap on our dolphin knocker had been answered by Albia, our foster-daughter, who was scared of very little except perhaps losing her place in our family. Orphaned as a baby in the Boudiccan Rebellion in Britain, Albia was now also late teens and lived with us, learning to be Roman. With fierce defence tactics against any young woman who looked like a rival, she had commanded Ganna to stay outside. Then she forgot to mention to Helena Justina that a new client had called.

A young female client who was tall, lithe and golden haired . . . I knew I would enjoy telling my friend Petronius Longus about Ganna. He would be jealous as all Hades.

I made sure I told Helena straight away. I had put Ganna in quarantine in the small blue salon where we saw unexpected visitors; there was nothing to steal and no back way out. Nux, our dog, sat by the door as if on guard. Nux was really a crazy, friendly, frowsty little mutt, always keen to give visitors a guided tour of the rooms where we displayed valuables. Still, I had told Ganna not to make any sudden movements, and with luck she had failed to spot Nuxie wagging that disreputable tail.

Outside in the corridor with Helena, I applied a concerned expression and tried to look like a man she could trust. Helena's chin was up. She looked like a woman who knew exactly what kind of fellow she had married. In an undertone, I sketched in a rapid résumé of Laeta's brief. Helena listened, but she seemed pale and tense; she had a slight frown between her dark, definite eyebrows, which I smoothed away with one finger gently. She said she had failed to find her brother. Nobody knew where Justinus was. He had stormed out that morning and still not returned home. Apart from the one sighting by Pa at the Saepta Julia, Justinus had disappeared.

I hid a smile. So the disgraced Quintus was managing to evade confrontations.

'Don't laugh, Marcus! It's clear that his quarrel with Claudia was serious.'

'I'm not laughing. Why spend money on a very expensive present for Claudia, yet not hand it over?'

'So you are as concerned about him as I am, Marcus?'

'Of course.'

Well, he would probably turn up here this evening, blind drunk and trying to remember in which seedy wine bar he had left Claudia's present.

We marched in on Ganna.

She was perched on a seat, a thin, hunched figure in a long brown gown with a plaited girdle. Her gold torque necklace subtly told us she came from some predominantly Celtic area and had access to treasure. Perhaps she was a chieftain's daughter. I hoped her papa did not come looking for her here. She had ice-blue eyes in a sweet face, upon which an anxious expression was making her look vulnerable. I knew enough about women to doubt that.

We seated ourselves opposite her, side by side formally like a husband and wife on a tombstone. Stately and brisk, with her best agates nestling on the rich blue gown that covered a wonderful bosom, Helena led the conversation. She had worked with me for the past seven years and regularly handled interrogations where my direct participation would not be respectable. Widows and virgins, and good-looking married women with predatory histories.

'This is Marcus Didius Falco and I am Helena Justina, his wife. Your name is Ganna? So where do you come from, Ganna, and are you happy to speak our language?'

'I live among the Bructeri in the forest beyond the great river. I speak your language,' Ganna said, with the same slight sneer Veleda had had when she made the same boast five years ago. They learned from traders and captured soldiers. The reason they learned Latin was to spy on their enemies. They enjoyed the way their Latin startled us. 'Or would you rather speak Greek?' challenged Ganna.

'Whichever is most comfortable for you!' countered Helena, in Greek – which put a stop to that nonsense.

As a supplicant, Ganna was fiery but desperate. I listened, watching her in silence, as Helena drew out her story. The girl had been Veleda's acolyte. Captured with Veleda, she had been brought here as her companion to give an appearance of propriety. According to her, Rutilius Gallicus had told them they would be honoured guests in Rome. He had implied they would be treated as noble hostages, like princes in the past, who were taught Roman ways, then returned to their home kingdoms to act as friendly client rulers. This was the explanation for placing the women in the safe house, with the senator Quadrumatus Labeo, a man Gallicus knew. They were there for some weeks, then Veleda overheard that she was really to end up paraded in chains in a Triumph and ritually killed.

'Very distressing for her.' Helena thought intelligent women should have foreseen it.

'You call *us* barbarians!' scoffed Ganna.

Like Cleopatra before her, Veleda was determined not to be made a spectacle for the Roman crowd. I muttered to Helena, 'Luckily the Bructeri have never heard of asps.'

Ganna said Veleda had made up her mind to escape immediately – and being both determined and ingenious, she did so. She went alone. It was very sudden. Ganna was left behind; in the hurried investigation that followed, she was terrified to learn that the Chief Spy intended to interrogate her, probably using torture. She took advantage of the confusion at the Quadrumatus house and also ran away, not knowing where she could find her companion or how to survive in a city. Veleda had told Ganna that there was one man in Rome who might help them return to the forest, giving her my name.

I like to be thought of as a man of honour – but returning these women to the wild woods a thousand miles to the north would be harder than Ganna seemed to realise. For a start, the logistics would be appalling. But I had no intention of allowing either to go back to the Free German tribes, carrying yet more stories of Roman duplicity. Even if I could manage it, if the truth came out here, I would be a traitor, crucified by a high road and damned to the memory.

There was more. With extra tears and entreaties Ganna wrung her hands and beseeched me to help with a desperate problem. She wanted me to find Veleda before harm befell her –

'This is a very serious request,' I said gravely. Helena Justina glanced across sharply. I always loved having duplicate commissions, if they came with a double fee. 'And for a private informer, perhaps it is inappropriate.' Helena shot me another sarcastic glare.

It did not stop Ganna. She was determined that I was the man for the business – for much the same reason as Laeta had been: I knew Veleda. Ganna believed that would make me sympathetic towards her missing companion, for whom she expressed worse anxieties. With more of those entrancing tears running down her pale face from her delicate blue eyes, Ganna said that ever since Veleda had arrived in Rome, she had been suffering from a mysterious illness.

Veleda was sick? That really was bad news. Captives who are destined to adorn famous generals' Ovations are not supposed to pass away from natural causes first.

It was bad news for me too. 'Abate the fee' was the Flavian emperors' motto: I would lose the extremely generous reward I had been promised by Titus Caesar if, when I produced Veleda, she was already dead.

I told Ganna I was obliged to work for money and she assured me that she had it to give. She left her gold torque as a surety. I say 'left' because I quickly moved her out; I was uneasy about keeping her at our house. Apart from Albia's hostility, there was the coming problem of ten disgruntled brutes from the German legions. They would know who Ganna was and might report us to the authorities for harbouring a fugitive. Helena knew nothing about them yet, so I kept quiet about the soldiers.

I persuaded my mother to take in the blue-eyed forest virgin. Ma was suffering badly from cataracts; although she hated needing a guide around her own kitchen, she was in so much trouble with her vision, she admitted she could use help. Ganna knew nothing of Roman domestic procedure now – but by the time my mother had finished with her, she would. It amused Helena to think of her one day returning to the wilds of Bructeran territory, able to make an excellent pounded green-herb dip. In Free Germany, she would never be able to find the rocket and coriander to show off at the tribal feast, but she would spend the rest of her life dreaming of Ma's eggwhite chicken soufflé . . .

I wanted Ganna kept somewhere under my control. Apart from the fact that it would salt her away from Anacrites' clutches, I was not fooled by the tears and hand-wringing. This young lady clearly had something she was not telling us. Ma would keep her under strict guard until either I found out the secret for myself, or Ganna was prepared to tell me.

I was right about her hiding something. When I discovered just what she had omitted from her story, I saw why. She should have known I would find out, though. I was going to the Quadrumatus house next day.

VI

The day opened on a cool, crisp morning with a bite in the air that would make your lungs hurt if you had anything of a cold. Most people in Rome did. It was the time of year when a visit to a public library was orchestrated by coughs, sneezes and snorts as constantly as the rattle of snare drums and riffle of flutes at some dimly lit dinner party where your millionaire host's parting presents would include the pretty serving boys. If you didn't have a wheeze when you started the day, you would catch something by your return. I had to walk along the Embankment towards the meat market, where some snotty stallholder was bound to catch me with his filthy spittle as I passed.

I was visiting a senator with consular connections, so I had dressed to a high standard. I was wearing a good woollen cloak, with oily waterproofing, my current best boots, which were leather with bronze tags on the laces, and a seductive Greek Mercury's hat. All I needed was wings on my boots to look like a messenger of the gods. Beneath this striking outer ensemble was a triple layer of long-sleeved winter tunics, two of them almost unworn since the last laundering, a belt with only three buckle-holes ripped beyond use, an empty money purse attached to the belt and a second money purse, half full, hidden between the second and third tunic to thwart any thieves in the Transtiberina. If I wanted to pay for anything that cost more than a bruised apple, I had to show off my privates as I fumbled through these layers of clothing to reach my cash. The swanky outerwear was not because I am impressed by senators, but because their snobbish door porters inevitably reject anyone who looks remotely faded.

I was an informer. I had spent seven years tracing stolen art, helping hapless widows manoeuvre themselves into legacies their ruthless stepchildren coveted, pursuing runaway teenagers before they got pregnant by handsome delivery boys, and identifying the blood-soaked killers of nagging mothers-in-law when the vigiles were too busy with fires, chicken races and arguments about their pay to bother. While carrying out this fine work for the community, I had learned all there was to know about the arrogance, awkwardness, ineptitude and prejudice of the bloody-minded door porters of the city of Rome. That was just the ones who decided at first sight they disliked my chirpy face. There were also plenty of sloths, gossips, drunks, petty blackmailers, neighbourhood rapists and other scallywags out there, who were just too busy with their personal careers to let me in. My only protection was to find out that a porter was having a passionate affair with the lady of the house so I could threaten him with revealing all to his jealous master. It rarely worked. In general the debauched mistress couldn't give two figs whether her antics were known, but even if she was terrified of exposure, the door porter was usually so violent the betrayed master would be scared of *him*.

I had no reason to think Quadrumatus Labeo had a porter who fell into any of those categories, but it was a good stroll to where he lived so as I loped along I amused myself with the lore of my craft. I liked to keep the brain active. Especially in cold weather, when my feet were so cold from tramping the travertine that thought became too tedious. The last thing an informer needs is to arrive for a big interview with his once-incisive mind frozen like a snow-sorbet. Preparation counts. No point in meticulous planning of penetrating questions if you lapse into a coma as soon as they give you a warm welcoming drink. The best informer can be lulled into uselessness by slurping an insidious hot wine toddy with a lick of cinnamon.

Don't drink and delve. Hot toddy after a long walk goes straight to the bladder, for one thing. You'll never persuade the guild treasurer to admit he defrauded the funeral club so he could take three girlfriends to Lake Trasimene, if you are absolutely bursting to relieve yourself.

Quadrumatus Labeo lived outside the city on the old Via Aurelia. I trotted out of Rome through the Aurelian Gate, and kept going until I found a finger post with red letters announcing that the right estate lay up the next carriage drive. It took less than an hour, even in the dead of winter when days are short so the hours into which they are divided are also at their shortest.

I supposed his home's location was what had made Quadrumatus attractive as a potential host for Veleda. He had an isolated villa on the western side of Rome, so she could be brought up from Ostia and slid into the house without passing through any city gates and without too much attention from nosy neighbours and tradesmen.

There was one significant disadvantage. The priestess was the responsibility of the Praetorian Guard. I considered it critical that the Praetorian Camp lay outside the city too – but on the eastern side. The captive and her minders were thus separated by a three-hour walk across the whole of Rome, or four hours if you stopped for refreshments. Which, in my opinion, you would have to do.

That said, there was not much wrong with the place. Since Quadrumatus was a senator, he had a decent boundary thicket to stop sightseers watching his summer picnics in the grounds. These grounds were stuffed with shady stone pines and much more exotic specimens, jasmine and roses, topiary that must have been maturing since the time of his grandfather the consul, dramatic long canals, miles of triple box hedges, and enough statues to fill several art galleries. Even in December, the gardens were awash with groundsmen, so intruders looking for a priestess to snatch would be spotted long before they reached the house. If intruders came on foot, they would be weary anyway. I was, and my home was well placed for this adventure. I had only had to stroll along the Aventine embankment gazing at the muddy, swollen Tiber, nip across the Probus Bridge and head out through the Fourteenth District, the Transtiberina, which is the roughest part of Rome so you don't linger. I had passed the Naumachia on my left, the imperial arena for mock sea battles, then the Baths of Ampelidis on the right, and met the old Via Aurelia – which travels into Rome by a shorter route than I had come on, passes the station house of the Seventh Cohort of Vigiles, and crosses the Tiber at the Aemilian Bridge, close to Tiber Island. I mention all that because as I surveyed the house on arrival I was thinking, I bet the old Via Aurelia was the way Veleda fled on her escape.

The Villa Quadrumatus lacked imposing steps, though it had a white marble portico that fully made up for that, set with very tall columns on a circular centrepiece, covered by a pointed roof. Pigeons had behaved disrespectfully on the big finial. It was too high for the household slaves to get up there on ladders and clean off the revolting guano more than once a year. If the steward was safety conscious, he probably made them build a scaffold when they had to do it – which I guessed was when they held their annual party to celebrate the master's birthday and invited half the Senate for a feast at which, undoubtedly, they had a full orchestra and a troupe of comedians, and served their own vineyard's Falernian specially brought up from Campania in ten ox wagons.

You see their style: Veleda, fresh from the dark forests of Germania, had been placed where she could witness the cream of Roman society in all their insane wealth. I wondered what she made of it. In particular, what she made of it once she realised these ostentatious persons would also one day be holding a glamorous garden party with two hundred guests, to celebrate the Ovation where *she* would be humiliated and killed . . .

No wonder the woman took her chance and escaped.

The door porter did not fail me. He was a thin Lusitanian in a tight tunic, with a flat head and a pushy manner, who spurned me before I had spoken a word: 'Unless you are expected, you can turn around and leave.' I gazed at him. 'Sir.'

My cloak, being my smart one, hung on a big brooch with a red enamelled pattern, on one shoulder. I threw the material back over the other shoulder in a nonchalant gesture, barely tearing any threads of the cloak. This enabled him to see me stick my fists in my belt. My grimy boots were planted apart on the washed marble. I wore no weapons, since going armed is illegal in Rome. That is to say, I wore none the door porter could see, though if he had any intuition he would realise that there might be a knife or a cudgel somewhere, currently invisible yet available to whop him with.

I had my civilised side. If he was a connoisseur of barbering, he would admire my haircut. It was my new Saturnalia haircut, which I had had two weeks early because that was the only time the decent barber at my training gym could fit me in. The timing suited me. I prefer a casual look at festivals. On the other hand, there was no point investing in a cripplingly expensive snip, with a slather of crocus oil, if porters still sneered at my locks and slammed the door.

'Listen, Janus. Let's not get off on a bad footing unnecessarily. You just go to your master and mention that I, Marcus Didius Falco (that's as in respected imperial agent) am here on the orders of Titus (that's as in Caesar) to discuss something *very* important, and while you (that's as in unmitigated ning-nong) are off on your errand, I'll try – because I am a generous man – to forget that I would like to tie your scraggy neck in a double clove hitch knot.'

Titus' name worked like a love charm. I always hate that.

While the porter disappeared to make enquiries, I noted that there were two very large cypress trees in four-foot pots like round sarcophagi, one either side of the twelve-foot-high double entrance doors. Either the Quadrumati liked their Saturnalia greenery to be *very* sombre, or there was another cause: somebody had died.

M. Quadrumatus Labeo, son of Marcus, grandson of Marcus (a consul), had a bulbous shape hung about with a flowing long-sleeved robe, embroidered all over with lotus blossoms, which carried unexpected hints of Alexandrian decadence. I reckoned the pharaonic cuddler was worn for warmth; he was of straight deportment otherwise. A couple of enormous gold rings forced him to hold his hands rather stiffly so people would notice the metalwork, but his general manner was austere. His personal barber kept his hair clipped like a boxer, shaved him until his cheeks were the colour of crushed damsons, then splashed him with a light orris water.

I knew from prior enquiries at the Atrium of Liberty records office, his family had been in the Senate for at least three generations; I had been too bored to trace them any further back. It was not clear how this family had acquired their money, but I deduced from their home situation they still owned pleasant quantities. Quadrumatus Labeo could well have been a jovial fellow who kept his household in stitches with his witty stories, but when I first met him he was preoccupied and looked nervy.

The reasons for this emerged straight away. He was accustomed to business meetings, which he probably chaired with dispatch. He knew who I was. He told me what I needed, without waiting for questions: he had accepted Veleda into his house as a patriotic duty, though he was reluctant to have her for long and had intended to make representations for her removal (which I fancied would have been successful). They had made her comfortable, within reason, given that she had once been a ferocious enemy and was now a captive with a death sentence. His house was large enough to hide her away in a self-contained suite. There had been minimal contact between Veleda and his family, though his gracious wife had extended the courtesy of taking mint tea with the priestess in the afternoons.

He regretted that Veleda had overheard details of her fate from a visitor. (Of course this indicated that visitors *had* been allowed to gawp at her.) If he or his staff could assist me in my investigation of her disappearance, they would do so, but on the whole, Labeo would prefer to forget the whole ghastly incident – insofar as that was possible. His wife would never get over it. The entire family would be forced to remember Veleda for the rest of their lives.

There were some odd circumstances, Laeta had warned me. Ganna had

27

said nothing, but I had sensed her keeping things back. I had a grim feeling. 'What happened, sir?'

Sometimes interviewees waffle; sometimes they conceal the truth. Sometimes they just don't know how to tell a story straightforwardly. Quadrumatus Labeo was an exception. He wasted neither my time nor his. His manner was restrained, but his voice was tight: 'When Veleda escaped, she murdered my brother-in-law. There is no doubt she was responsible. His decapitated body was lying in an enormous pool of blood; the slave who was first on the scene has had a mental breakdown. My wife then found her brother's severed head in the atrium pool.'

Well, that explained the funereal cypress trees. And I could see why Laeta and Ganna had omitted this detail.

VII

I had walked through the atrium when I arrived, but now I knew it was a crime scene I asked Quadrumatus Labeo to show me again. While we stood on the marble-clad edge of a twenty-foot basin of water, I took out my note-tablet and stylus. I sketched the scene and indicated with an arrow where the head was found. Behind me, the Lusitanian porter ogled from the narrow, curtained corridor that led in from the entrance door; seeing his master, the lanky creep busied himself looking officious. Ahead, beyond the pool and the square spacious hall with its scatter of plinths bearing pompous fat-faced busts, I could see an enclosed garden. Clipped box globes and a fountain in the form of a clam shell. Two stone doves drank from the shell. A real dove currently perched on one of the stone ones, cooing for crumbs. Classic.

Not many beauteous patrician atria have severed human heads staring up from their water features. The head was gone now, but I could not help imagining it.

'When did it happen?'

'Ten days ago.'

'*Ten days?*'

Quadrumatus looked abashed momentarily, then became petulant. 'I was not willing to have strangers barging about my home, upsetting my family even further, until we had gone through the nine days of formal mourning. I am sure you understand that.'

I understood all right. Veleda had now been on the run for too long. The trail, if I could ever even find it, would be stone cold. This was why Laeta hadn't told me about the murder. I would have spurned the job.

'I'll be discreet.' My reply was curt.

At my feet, clear water lapped almost imperceptibly against black and white marble. The atrium pool, peaceful beneath a classic square rain-hole up in the elegant roof, contained a small base upon which danced a floral female deity, in bronze, about a foot and a half high.

She looked cute, but I knew my father would have said it was a bad statue. The drapery was too static to be interesting, and the flowers were badly moulded.

'We had to drain the cistern below completely, afterwards,' complained the senator, talking of a water storage basin that must be fed from the atrium pool. His voice was low. 'None of my staff wanted to volunteer . . . I had to supervise closely in person. I needed to be sure it was done thoroughly.'

I was still angry, so I said, 'You wouldn't want to end up drinking your brother-in-law's gore.' Quadrumatus shot me a swift look, but did not rebuke me. Perhaps he realised the position on the ten-day delay. With his rank, he must have been an army officer and he would have held civil posts where he needed to handle crises. Now he ran who knows what kind of property portfolio, with who knows how many interlinked commercial businesses. I could tell from his neat, calmly behaved slaves, he had basic efficiency. When you are dealing with an idiot, you see it in his staff's expressions.

'Was any weapon found?'

'No. We assume she took it with her.'

'Did Veleda come here with companions?'

'A girl – Ganna.'

'Yes, I know about her. No one else? And did the priestess have any visitors while she stayed here?'

'My orders forbade that.' Did he mean the orders he had issued, or orders that had been issued to him by the Palace? Both, I hoped. 'Her presence was, as I am sure you know, Falco, a state secret. I only agreed to give her houseroom on that basis; I could not have tolerated disruption and public curiosity. We are a very private family. But to my knowledge, nobody attempted to see her.'

'And tell me about your brother-in-law, please.'

'Sextus Gratianus Scaeva, my wife's brother. He lived here with us. He was a young man of exceptional promise –' Inevitably. I had yet to meet a senator who described his relatives in any but glowing terms – especially ones who were safely dead. Given that most relatives of senators are talentless buffoons, a cynic might wonder.

'And before Gratianus Scaeva died so tragically, what were his connections with Veleda?'

'He barely met her. We held a couple of formal family dinners to which the woman was invited as a courtesy; she was introduced to him. That's all.'

'No infatuation on one side or the other, a flirtation that you might have been unaware of at the time?'

'Certainly not. Scaeva was a man of spirit, but we could always rely on him for proper behaviour.'

I wondered. The Veleda I remembered glowed with lustrous assurance. We had looked at her and gulped. It was more than a queenly figure and pale gold hair. To win the trust of suspicious, belligerent tribesmen took special qualities. Veleda made the Bructeri believe fighting Rome was their only destiny; moreover, she persuaded them they had chosen this for themselves. She used strength of mind and strength of purpose. She was cloaked in an aura that went way beyond the fake mystery of most fortune-tellers and charlatans. She was brilliant, enthralling – and, when I met her, she had been desperate for intelligent male conversation. If she had been a prisoner for months, she would have been desperate again.

Veleda had been quick to share her thoughts and dreams with a 'promising young man' when *we* provided one. The young man I saw vanish up her tower with her had cast aside 'proper behaviour' without thinking twice. I did warn him to watch himself, but he rushed at the chance to be close to her.

Afterwards, Justinus had carried the pain of leaving Veleda behind for five years, and I saw no reason to think he would ever be free of her. So had Scaeva been captured in the same subtle spider's web?

Quadrumatus Labeo had finished with me, whether or not I had finished with him. His dream interpreter had arrived.

'Nightmares since the murder?'

The senator looked at me as if I was cracked. 'Such consultations aid rational thinking. My man calls daily.'

So the dream therapist governed his every act. I kept my gaze neutral. 'And did you consult him about whether to allow Veleda to stay here?'

His expression sharpened. 'I assure you, Falco! I maintained scrupulous security.'

I took that as an admission.

The dream therapist had a cold. He was wiping his nose on the sleeve of his star-spattered knee-length tunic as he brushed past me, heading after his dignified client to the inner sanctum. We were not introduced. I would know him again, though. He looked straight from the Chaldees, right down to the long hooked nose, peculiar cloth head-dress and air of having caught a disease from over-friendly relations with his camel. As exotic enhancement, he wore soft felt slippers with curly toes that had foully moulded themselves to the shape of his feet; he was a martyr to bunions, by the look of it.

His name was Pylaemenes. The house steward told me. To my surprise the slaves here seemed indifferent to the man; I had reckoned they would be hostile to an influential outsider – especially one of distinctly foreign appearance whose robe hem needed tacking up but who was probably paid zillions.

'We are used to all sorts,' shrugged the steward, as he took me to find the slave who discovered the body.

This was a distraught waif of about fifteen, now trembling in the corner of his cubicle, hugging his knees. When I entered the bleak compartment, a typical slave cell which he shared with another, he showed me the whites of his eyes like an unbroken colt. The steward picked up a thin blanket and draped it over him, but it would clearly slide off again.

As a witness the lad was useless. He would not speak. It looked as if he did not eat. If nothing was done soon, he was a lost soul.

What could anyone expect? The steward had told me about him. He had been a cheery, useful teenager who then found himself alone in a room with a headless corpse. Born and bred a house slave in a home of refulgent luxury, where the owners were obviously civilised people and he was probably never chastised by more than wounding sarcasm, this was his first meeting with crude death by violence. Pools of still-warm, spreading blood, in one of which he had accidentally stepped, had horrified him out of his wits.

He was the flute boy. His double flute sat on a ledge in his cell. He had gone to entertain Gratianus Scaeva with music while the young master was reading. I guessed he would never play again.

'Does Quadrumatus Labeo have a personal doctor? Someone should take a look at this lad.'

The steward gave me an odd look, but said that he would mention it.

Next, I was taken to meet Drusilla Gratiana.

The noble Drusilla was a typical senator's wife: an ordinary woman in her forties who, because she was descended from sixteen generations of senatorial stiffs, believed herself exceptional. The only thing that made her different from a fishwife slitting open fresh-caught mullet was her spending budget.

32

Drusilla Gratiana had papery skin, a suspicious expression, a twenty-five-thousand sesterces pearl necklace bestowed on her by Quadrumatus, four children of whom one daughter was betrothed last month, a troupe of pet dwarfs, a corn warehouse she inherited from her uncle, and a drink habit. Some of this I had extracted from the steward, the rest was obvious. She was draped in red–purple silk, which two pale maidens kept tidy while a seventy-year-old wardrobe mistress constantly supervised. My mother would have made a friend of this black-clad crone. Her contempt for me was immediate. I did not imagine the malignant attendant had seen Veleda as an ornament to the household either.

'We are expecting Cleander,' barked the wrinkled and beady-eyed creature. 'You'll have to be quick!'

I ignored her. I addressed her mistress direct in a cool, calm voice that was meant to establish my credentials as a man of refined manners. It irritated all the women in the room. 'Drusilla Gratiana, I offer my condolences on your brother's dreadful fate. I regret any disturbance I have to cause to your household. But I must confirm exactly what happened, so I can bring the perpetrator to justice.'

'As Phryne says: be quick then!' Mistress and maid worked as a team. Just my luck.

'Who is Cleander?'

'My lady's doctor.' I was told this by the black-clad Phryne, angrily of course.

The noble lady and her freedwoman were bound by thirty years of complicity. Phryne had decked out Drusilla Gratiana as a bride; she knew all her secrets, not least where she kept the wine flagon; there would be no bumping Phryne out of the way. She was owed too much. She wanted to control Drusilla; she would stick around.

I cleared my throat. 'I'll try to be brief, then . . . Were you close to your brother?'

'Of course.' Apart from the fact that Drusilla spoke rather dreamily, with a husky toper's voice, that told me nothing. Gratianus Scaeva could have lived with his sister because they were devoted or because he was a social liability who needed to be kept under tight control. The relationship between the siblings could have been anywhere on a spectrum between incest and outright loathing. Nobody intended me to find out.

'Yes, I assumed that – because he lived with you. Was he your only brother, by the way?'

'I have two others and two sisters. Scaeva happened to be

33

unmarried.' So now I had it: of his five married brothers and sisters, Drusilla Gratiana had the richest spouse and the most comfortable home. Gratianus Scaeva knew how to sponge.

'Not found the right girl yet?'

Drusilla gave me a nasty look. 'There was nothing wrong with him, if that is what you are implying! He was only twenty-five and perfectly normal, though not strong. He would have been a wonderful husband and father; all that has been taken away from him.' I won't say she cried. It would have spoiled her careful face makeup. Besides, I was a lout and she was too proud to give way.

I wished I had brought Helena Justina for this. Even the old bag in black would have been impressed by her.

'This is bound to be painful, but I need to ask about how you found your brother's head, please.' Drusilla Gratiana whimpered and looked faint. Phryne shuddered, making a big show of it. 'Was there any particular reason why you went into the atrium, or were you just passing through normally on your way somewhere?' With a struggle, Drusilla gave a slight nod that indicated the latter. 'I'm sorry. This is unacceptably hard for you. I won't ask you any more.'

I was only being amenable because my interview was ended anyway: the damned doctor had turned up. I knew who he was from the stuffed satchel of medicaments, the piqued frown, and the bustling manner that told his patients they were being charged by the minute by an exceptionally busy specialist who was much in demand.

'Who is this low fellow?'

'The name is Falco. Didius Falco.'

'You look like a slave.'

His arrogance smelt like a fisherman's fart, but I was not in the mood for nit-picking.

Drusilla Gratiana was already stretching out on a couch. There were some female invalids with whom I would happily play doctors and nurses. In this case, I left.

Some informers get to deal with buxom young female slaves who carry the titbit trays and yearn to make free with male visitors. My name is Didius Falco, and I end up with implacable old freedwomen: Cleander had shooed her out, making it plain that however intimate she was with Drusilla, he would not accept an underling at his consultation.

I now needed to be shown where the torso was found and hoped to be led there by the house steward – but once she had been turfed out of the consultation, Phryne took over supervising me.

'What's wrong with your mistress?' I enquired as we walked.

'She suffers with her nerves.'

'And that was her doctor. What's his name again?'

'Cleander.' Phryne disliked him. In view of his snooty attitude towards her, it was understandable.

'He's a Greek?'

'He's a Hippocratic pneumatist.'

Sounded like he was a charlatan. 'And does he attend the whole family? I thought Quadrumatus Labeo sees Pylaemenes?'

'Pylaemenes is his dream therapist. His *doctor* is Aedemon. He is an Egyptian,' said Phryne, who had grasped my line of questioning. 'An Alexandrian empiricist.' Another quack.

'Drusilla Gratiana said her brother was not strong. Who looked after him?'

'Mastarna. Etruscan. A dogmatist.'

As she grew more terse, I took the hint and kept quiet until we came to a prettily decorated salon. It must have been thoroughly cleaned up; there was no sign now of the reported pools of blood. Gratianus Scaeva had been found on a reading couch; it had since been replaced with a different one. There were goat-footed marble side tables, display cabinets with a selection of bronze miniatures, lampstands, a couple of cedarwood scroll boxes, rugs, cushions, a hot wine dispenser, pens and ink, and in short, more pieces of furniture and knick-knacks than my mother had in her whole house – but no clues.

We walked back to the atrium, where I said, 'I did not want to upset your mistress, but I have another question. Was anything found in the water, other than her brother's head? Were there any weapons or pieces of treasure, for instance?'

Phryne looked at me wide-eyed. 'No! Should there have been?'

I was taken aback by her reaction, but I had probably startled her with my reference to barbarian rites.

At my request she then walked me to the suite Veleda had occupied. This was a very large villa. The Quadrumati were not sharing much of their domestic life with their house guest. They had kept Veleda so far away from the rest of them she could have been in a different dwelling.

Her quarters had been comfortable. A couple of rooms, furnished in the same basic style as the rest of the house, though lighter on luxuries. She and Ganna had shared a bedroom, each with her own well-furnished bed. They ate in a small private dining room. A reception room with seating gave on to an enclosed courtyard when they wanted fresh air. They had been attended by a slave, on a daily rota to avoid any danger of suborning. When the family were not using their musicians and poetry readers, these had been sent along to provide entertainment – though Drusilla Gratiana had never allowed the priestess use of her troupe of dwarfs.

Life would have been lonely but tolerable. As imprisonment for a condemned person, this was more than humane. But once Veleda heard of her intended fate, her isolation would have given her too much scope for brooding.

'Veleda was unwell, I hear. What was wrong with her, Phryne?'

The malevolent retainer cackled. 'We never found out. Feigning, probably.'

'Did any of the family medicos take a look at her?'

'Certainly not!' Phryne was outraged at the suggestion that a physician who had touched one of her sacred charges should finger the sickly barbarian.

'So she was left to make the best of it?'

'By no means, Falco. When she started complaining –' The freed-woman emphasised her belief that Veleda was a self-pitying malingerer – 'Drusilla Gratiana kindly arranged for Zosime, from the sanctuary of Æsculapius, to attend her. My mistress even paid for it!'

So these noble folk had had three personal doctors, plus a dream therapist, on call and visiting daily – all of whom could presumably be relied on for confidentiality – yet for Veleda they brought in a completely different person, an outsider, from a charitable shrine that took care of dying slaves.

'Zosime is female? So . . . Women's troubles?'

'Pah! *Headaches!*' Phryne snorted, with a sneer that would have shattered glass.

VIII

I had seen enough, and scoffed at enough, to keep my head reeling as I stomped home.

On the way I did a check: I went straight up the Via Aurelia to Tiber Island, where at the shrine I asked to see Zosime. She was out on calls, and nobody was sure when she was likely to return.

'What's it about, Falco?'

'I'd rather not say.'

This search would be tricky. Since Veleda's presence in Rome was a state secret, and her absconding was such an embarrassment, I would have to pretend she did not exist. It would be awkward. Still, I like a challenge.

When I played coy, the receptionist at the Temple of Æsculapius merely nodded. The shrine attendants accepted any story; they were used to hard-hearted citizens dragging in worn-out old slaves they could not be bothered to feed any more, and pretending they just found these sorry specimens wandering in the street. No sick slave was turned away. This was the only truly charitable temple in Rome, the only hospital. Treatment was free; the temple survived on donations and legacies. Most of their patients arrived only when they were past saving, but even then, after they had been allowed to die as gently as possible, the hospital conducted and paid for a burial. Way back when I was a very poor informer, I used to think that one day they would be doing it for me . . .

Hey ho. Time for lunch.

I hoofed on over the Fabrician Bridge to the Theatre of Marcellus, then turned down the left bank past the meat market and the corn dole station. By the Temple of Ceres there was a commotion: a posse of Praetorians were throwing their weight about. Big bullies, they were unmissable in their scarlet cloaks and crested helmets. All of them came with a filthy attitude. This was the result of encouraging long-term legionaries, sad men who loved the army too much, to volunteer for special duties. The minute they put on their shiny moulded breastplates and took their personal oath to the Emperor, the Guards were in Elysium. No danger; double pay; a soft life in Rome, instead of being stuck in some dire province – plus the chance to behave like utter bastards every week.

'Name?'

'Didius Falco.' I kept silent about my profession, let alone my current mission.

They grabbed me, pulled off my elegant hat, peered in my face (breathing with a whopping gust of garlic), then threw me aside like a dirty duster.

'What's the commotion for, boys? Surely Vespasian is not reduced to claiming the pauper's corn dole? He gets good rations at the Golden House, and can eat them beneath the revolving ivory ceiling in the fabulous octagon –'

'Push off!'

I was a man. They were not interested in me. I knew whose orders they must be following, and why. Anacrites had sent them. They were only assaulting women – which in that area was foolish, even in the cause of a national emergency. The beef-butchers' wives are neither pretty nor polite. Despite the December chill, the ladies of the Cattle Market Forum were all barefoot and bare armed. They had strong husbands with bloody cleavers who could manhandle dead oxen – but these sturdy women did not ask their men for assistance; when the Guards tried to 'inspect' them, they weighed in with fists, teeth and feet fearlessly. The Guards' bravado was slipping.

'Looking for someone special, officer?' I enquired (wondering how the Praetorians dealt with not mentioning Veleda) – but blood from a split lip was despoiling his bright breastplate and he was already exasperated. I hopped off without waiting for an answer.

As I marched quickly up the embankment, something struck my neck with a vicious sting. A cobnut bounced on the pavement. When I turned back, a small boy ran away, giggling. We still had ten days of this menace to endure. *Io Saturnalia!*

More of our national treasures were loafing truculently outside my house. These shiftless wastrels were the soldiers Titus had assigned to me. They looked as bad as I was expecting. I rounded them up from various flower stalls and wine counters where they were ogling pretty garland-sellers and begging for free drinks. I knew without asking that Albia must have locked them out and in this instance I did not blame her. They were bandy-legged ex-marines from the salty First Adiutrix legion, an emergency outfit Vespasian had put together in a hurry, who were currently stationed at Moguntiacum on the Rhine. Camillus Justinus had been a tribune in the First for a time. Not a prestigious posting. 'And you lads were the travel escort for she-whom-we-do-not-name? Bad luck.'

'Oh, Veleda was all right, Falco.'

'No, soldier – I mean, bad luck: now you are taking orders from me!'

As they looked at each other warily, I opened up with my key, and led them indoors.

Helena Justina was waiting in the entrance hall, a tall, tart young woman in three shades of blue wool, with ear-rings that shouted not to annoy her. Hiding behind her, Albia was terrified of the soldiers. The acting centurion in charge of them was already inside, chatting up Helena Justina as if she were a wine-seller, while she glared at him stonily. Nux was hiding behind Albia, though when I came in the dog ran out and barked loudly, before scurrying into retreat again.

Head high and bursting for an altercation, Helena cried, 'Marcus Didius! Welcome home.'

Her tone was enough to make the boys of the First shuffle closer together nervously. Even the centurion stepped away slightly. He stopped short in wondering if he dared bully the householder and quickly adopted a respectful hangdog mode. How wise.

I kissed Helena's cheek formally, looking deep into those fabulous brown eyes with mischief and lust in equal measure.

Helena Justina managed to remain calm. 'This is Clemens, an acting centurion. He has explained about the soldiers.' I held her closer than a senator's daughter expects to be clutched, while in close view of a bunch of surly legionaries; then I smiled at her with so much affection she blushed. 'Marcus Didius, I am quite happy living in a very large house with a very small staff.' She tried to wriggle free surreptitiously. I held on. 'I will even entertain – with only a small staff – large numbers of relatives over the Saturnalia period. Relatives who make no contribution, and most of whom are yours. But – darling – I do now find myself wondering exactly *how* I am to manage here, if eleven –' Helena kept my accounts and business records. Believe me, she could count – 'hungry soldiers are to join us for the festival.'

'Twelve,' stated Clemens. 'I've got a little servant who will be along presently.'

'Twelve!' exclaimed Helena, in a voice that would unman Hercules.

I released her and turned to Clemens. 'As you see, my wife – the most hospitable of women – is delighted that you and your men are to join us.' A couple of soldiers sniggered. I folded my arms. 'Here's how it will work. Everyone in my household – right down to my dog – will be treated with respect, or the whole bunch of you will be hog-tied and thrown off the Probus Bridge. Two soldiers and the acting centurion's servant will be on a roster daily to assist the noble Helena Justina. They will escort her to market – take handcarts – and help bring home provisions as she directs. They will work in our kitchen, under her supervision. Helena, sweetheart, all soldiers can make bread and scrub vegetables.'

'Don't you have a cook?' asked Clemens. He looked amazed. He was also worried; a true soldier, on making camp he thought first about his rations.

'You will meet Jacinthus,' I assured him, smiling.

Jacinthus was new. I had had him a week. He was one of two slaves I had recently forced myself to buy, aiming for a last-minute Saturnalia discount as the markets prepared to close for the holiday. The other acquisition was Galene, who was to look after my children. Neither slave knew anything, but they had both appeared clean and fit, which was better than most specimens on special offer in December. Julia (aged three and a half) and Favonia (aged twenty-one months), were teaching Galene Latin, and how they wished to be looked after with late bedtimes and rewards of sweetmeats.

'Jacinthus,' Helena explained, with her neck as stiff as a javelin, 'will no doubt produce exquisite pork loins in fig sap sauce one day. His baked quince will be a legend all over the Aventine. Women I scarcely know will beseech me for his recipe for mushroom bread . . .'

'Once he has learned his craft?' Clemens caught on fast. He would fit in here. You needed nifty footwork and a clear head.

'Exactly. In the meantime, Jacinthus spends his time asleep.'

Clemens shot me a look as if he could guess which partner had purchased this treasure. He did not know it was my fifth attempt to buy us a cook. Sleeping was better than cooking, if Jacinthus cooked like his predecessors. All had been sold back at a loss within a month. 'I dare say my boys can help you wake him up,' offered Clemens. His tone had a pleasantly ominous timbre.

A small, shy voice now made itself audible: 'Hello, Falco. I bet you don't remember me!'

The soldier's name was Lentullus. Last time I saw him he was a raw recruit in his first posting in Germany. His most distinguished act on our expedition had been swinging on the tail of a giant bull while I tried to cut its throat with a small knife as the creature attempted to kill the rest of us. The youth had courage, but of all the ragged failures in all the least victorious legions, Lentullus was the daftest, silliest, clumsiest and untidiest. He had no idea. He had no luck either. If there was a large hole, with a great notice beside it saying *Don't fall in here; this means you, Lentullus!* Lentullus would home in and tumble head first down the hole. Then he would wonder why he had been so unlucky. Any legion that included him had no hope. Sometimes in nightmares I heard his off-tune voice croakily singing an execrable and obscene ditty called the Little Mess-tin Song. I woke up shaking. It wasn't the Mess-tin Song that brought me out in a sweat.

'I bet I do remember,' I answered him. 'Have you learned to march yet?'

'No, he bloody hasn't!' muttered Clemens, with feeling.

I already had a queasy-gut feeling. My house had been turned into a scene from some mythical nightmare. Then Helena smiled grimly and told me that my mother-in-law was in our best reception room in a foul mood, and wanted to speak to me.

'That's funny about you remembering,' burbled Lentullus. He had never known when to shut up. 'Because Veleda told me she remembered me too! I was hoping that if we all came to Rome, I'd see you, Falco – and the tribune too . . .'

The 'tribune' was Quintus Camillus Justinus. And while I was sure that the affable Justinus would be delighted to meet up with Lentullus again, my next task was to ensure that Julia Justa, my mother-in-law – a forthright woman, whose hearing was almost as good as my mother's – did not overhear that there was a soldier in my house who could tell her just what her favourite son got up to, back in the forest with Veleda.

IX

Had the soldiers not known more than was convenient, I might have taken them as an escort. I did try swinging into the room like a lad who had nothing on his conscience. Twenty years of practice should have taught me such a performance was ridiculous. My mother-in-law wanted somebody's liver chopped and fried – and the warm bread was already being sliced open to receive mine. She was accompanied by her daughter-in-law, Claudia Rufina, and if the rocks didn't finish me the whirlpool would.

The noble Julia Justa, wife of the most excellent Decimus Camillus Verus, was a Roman matron with the full rights of a mother of three children, an affiliate of the rites of the Good Goddess, the benefactor of a small temple in Bithynia and a confidante of one of the older, plainer, more prickly tempered Vestal Virgins. She ought to have expected a quiet life of luxury. Given that her husband tried to dodge his responsibilities, both her sons ignored suggestions to settle down respectably and her daughter had married an informer, Julia looked depressed. Only her little grandchildren gave her hope – and one of those was now at risk of being whisked away to Baetica by his angry mother.

Julia Justa owned outfits in all the colours in the fullers' dyeing range, but had chosen to come in crisp white robes that blazoned she was not in the mood for nonsense. These garments were held in place, as she swept up and down our salon, by exquisite jewellery. Julia's necklace, ear-rings and head-dress were heavy with Indian pearls of memorable size and lustrous good quality. Perhaps, I thought, this was an early Saturnalia gift. Probably, then, the gift of her younger son's extremely wealthy wife, Claudia Rufina. She was the only one in the family with real money, and the Camilli – though diffident people – were desperate to keep her married to their son.

Julia was venomous and sleek. Claudia enjoyed her wrath. While Julia prowled, Claudia sat very, very still. Claudia – aflame in saffron – had swapped her own favourite heavy emeralds for enough gold chains to shackle a complete set of galley-slaves. Clearly she wished her absent husband Justinus could be set to rowing on a trireme bench, under the lash of a *very* sadistic overseer.

'Ah Marcus! You have bothered to return!' Useless for me to say I had been working. I could not admit what I was working on, in any case. I had a nasty feeling they might know.

I managed to nip in close enough to plant a kiss half an inch from the mother-in-law's well-groomed cheek, but abandoned greeting Claudia. She was a tall girl with a habit of leaning back to look at people down her long nose. Justinus was also tall, so whenever they quarrelled they were able to do it eye to eye in a satisfactory manner; perhaps that had encouraged them. She had nice teeth and by the look of things would be gnashing them the minute her husband was named.

'You know where he is, of course?' Julia accused me.

'Dear Julia Justa, I have no idea.' She gave me a long, hard look, but was an intelligent woman and knew I did not waste effort on lies. Not with her. In a ghastly way, she trusted me; it made life very difficult. 'Quintus saw my father, Favonius, at the Saepta Julia this morning, I believe, but he has been nowhere near us here today or yesterday.' I turned to Claudia. 'Do you want to tell me about what happened?'

Pa had said Justinus hit her, but there were no visible wounds or bruises. I was familiar with the evidence of wife-beating, from many a sad soul I knew when I lived up on the Aventine and from plenty of battered witnesses I met through my work.

'We had a quarrel,' stated Claudia in a tight voice. 'As I am sure you know, Marcus Didius, this was nothing unusual.' With compressed lips, Claudia stared at me for a moment. She was a proud girl; it hurt her to say it openly. .

'This was a *particular* quarrel?'

'Oh yes!' Oh dear! 'The woman Veleda is in Rome. Quintus is extremely agitated. I cannot bear it any longer. I told him if he attempts to see her, I will divorce him and return to Hispania Baetica. He has to choose. We cannot possibly continue as we are —'

Claudia was close to hysterical. I glanced at Julia Justa then suggested she go and help Helena deal with the soldiers. Julia glared but took the hint.

After she left, Claudia sat down on a couch, went into a short sobbing session which she ended of her own accord, then blew her nose, and sat up straight to discuss things. She had always been practical. It simplified the crises.

'How did Quintus come to hit you, Claudia?' Best to get this dealt with.

Claudia blushed. 'It was nothing. Just stupid. I was so furious and frustrated I must have accidentally knocked into him and he reacted instinctively.'

I had been told similar by many an abused woman, but in this case I believed her. Abused wives don't wriggle with embarrassment. 'You lashed out and belted him, he swiped you back, neither of you meant it? And then,' I said gently, 'both of you were terribly shocked. He couldn't cope, so he fled?' Claudia was staring at the ground. 'Look, I heard about it from my father. Quintus went to buy you a present to apologise – he was horrified and ashamed . . . ' Claudia was starting to look more cheerful. I didn't fool myself; she was probably just happy to hear of Quintus being ashamed. 'Was the baby in the room?'

'No.'

'Well, at least he didn't see the riot.' I gave her a grin. 'You're a dangerous woman! And don't blame Quintus; he has been taught by army trainers to react to an attack . . . It won't happen again. If it did, you would both have to worry – but it won't.'

'It certainly won't happen if he never comes home,' snarled Claudia.

'So you *want* him to come home?' I demanded pointedly. She fell silent.

The narrow double doors of our pleasant turquoise salon slid apart quietly; Helena came in, closing the doors again behind her back and leaning against them momentarily. She had probably been listening outside.

I wondered where her mother was. The thought of the noble and elegant Julia Justa showing a group of inept soldiers where they could set up their campbeds was piquant. She would do it without a qualm. Julia was competent, much more competent than the lads would expect. I lived with her daughter, so I knew how the Camilli had been brought up.

There had been plenty of past affection between Helena and Claudia. Even so, Helena came to sit by me. I knew her loyalty was to her brother rather than his wife.

This was the predicament of the foreign bride, when things went wrong. Even if the people among whom she had made her new life were taking her part, she could never entirely trust them. My common origins made me different and I could sometimes comfort

44

the girl, but Helena would always be one of the Camilli. Justinus had been in the wrong more than once, and he was going to make a fool of himself over Veleda if he possibly could, but his wife would struggle to find allies. She knew it too. She also knew it was her own fault she had married him, and if she gave him a divorce notice everyone else would blame her.

Claudia Rufina was isolated in Rome. Her family, such as it was, lived far away in Corduba. Her parents were long dead; her younger brother had been murdered; her grandparents were very elderly. I was not even sure the old couple were still alive. She had had one close friend out in Baetica, a young woman called Aelia Annaea, but Aelia had stayed at Corduba and also married. Although they presumably wrote to each other, their relationship must have altered. For one thing, having announced that she intended to marry Camillus Aelianus (whom her people at home all knew because he had had a posting there), Claudia Rufina might have felt some reserve about telling them later that she had switched to his brother, Camillus Justinus. At the time, Claudia thought Justinus was more handsome than his brother and more fun. That was before she discovered just how much fun lay in his past.

'Tell me what happened in Germany.' Claudia was addressing me. Even Helena turned towards me expectantly; Claudia immediately noted that.

'It's pretty straightforward.' I kept my voice level. 'The Emperor sent me on a mission to persuade two bitter opponents of Rome to make peace. They were Civilis, a one-eyed Batavian turncoat who had served in the legions, and Veleda, a priestess who was stirring up hatred against us from a remote location in the forest. She lived in Germania Libera, where Rome has no remit, so that part of our trip was extremely hazardous. Quintus came over with me, as you know. We got into trouble – bad trouble. Most of my party fell into the hands of Veleda's tribe, the Bructeri, who loathe Rome. They were going to kill us. Quintus and a couple of others, who had escaped their clutches, came to rescue us. While the warriors were feasting and working themselves up for the massacre, Quintus had to win the priestess' confidence. He argued our fate with her for many hours; eventually he persuaded her to let us go. I don't know – and frankly, I don't care – just how he won Veleda over. We owe him our lives. It was the most difficult and dangerous thing he had ever done, and it affected him deeply.'

'He fell in love with her.' Claudia was wooden.

'We were only there for a night.'

'That's long enough!' murmured Helena. I glanced at her, curious.

'He only spoke with the priestess, as far as I know.' Both women thought I was lying. Mentally, I stuck with the strict truth: Justinus never had confessed to me that he slept with Veleda. Of course we all made assumptions. His behaviour afterwards made everything damned obvious. Besides, we all wished we had had the chance . . . 'Whatever Quintus did, was in the service of Rome.' That pompous declaration won me no friends. 'Obviously Veleda is a charismatic woman – that is how she controlled her tribesmen. And Quintus must have admired her. We all did. For him, it was the big adventure of his youth. He will never forget. But Claudia, he then came home to Rome and settled down to a normal Roman life. He married you because he loved you –' His wronged wife's expression stopped me.

Claudia Rufina was a fatalist. 'Loved me? I dare say he did – but it was never the same, was it? And now Veleda is in Rome.'

I tried not to comment. Helena said quietly, 'Please Claudia, you must not mention her in public.'

Claudia's voice was dull. I had to bend forward to catch what she was saying. 'If this had never happened, we might have managed. If she had stayed in the forest, we might have been all right. I thought Quintus and I had remained friends through all our problems. We were bound to one another by love for our son.' Tears wound their way down her pale cheeks, unheeded. I hate to see a tough woman demoralised. 'It is no use,' she whispered. 'He has gone to her. I cannot hold him any longer. I have lost him now.'

X

W hy is it that bad behaviour by one male gets all the rest of us into trouble?

Both Helena and her mother were polite women but strong-willed. They told me that I was expected to find Justinus, and I heard myself promising to do it. Unless he was already with Veleda, I really wanted him to stay missing. Keeping them apart was my best chance. If Justinus learned of my search for the priestess, he would attach himself to me – and not with a view to solving problems diplomatically. He would use me to find his forest sprite – and I knew he wouldn't be intending to give her back to the authorities.

My aim was to hand her in immediately. That is, immediately I had ascertained whether she did hack off the head of Quadrumatus' brother-in-law. That niggled me. It was not in character. And I owed her something for saving my life. If Veleda had *not* killed Scaeva, I would not let the authorities – or Scaeva's family – dump the crime on her just because it was convenient.

According to Claudia, Justinus had denied making any contact with the priestess since she came to Rome. If that was true – and he was usually too transparent to lie – then as far as I could see, there had been no opportunity for the pair to collude before Veleda did her flit, and little opportunity since. Without a pre-arranged rendezvous, she would never find him. And now he had vanished from home, she had no hope of fixing such a rendezvous. Or so I hoped.

Maybe they had found one another and were now together?

No. Not feasible. Not unless they had already been in contact somehow.

Never mind where Veleda had gone – where had *he* gone? *Why* had he gone? The element that made no sense was his buying a present for Claudia, as if he intended to crawl back home apologetically. Could he have run into the priestess among the monuments south of the Saepta Julia as he made his way home, and they had done a bunk? No. Too much of a coincidence.

A cynic might have suggested he had actually bought the gift for Veleda, to reinstate himself – but Pa would have sniffed out a subterfuge. Pa thought it was a genuine peace offering. Justinus had been horrified at hitting Claudia. Besides, when he and Veleda had been together in the forest, it was love's young dream; their relationship was far too ethereal to include the kind of bribery husbands and wives adopt in daily life. If Justinus went rushing to Veleda, he would fly headlong on swansdown wings of love, without any basic planning.

I sent one of my nephews to obtain from my father a description of the purchased gift. Gaius, the runner, was also to tell Pa to ask around among his cronies at the Saepta and the Emporium for sightings of the missing man. Or indeed, sightings of the gift. Pa would love this. He adored pretending he was some kind of expert with a brilliant set of contacts, whereas I was an incompetent amateur. If he discovered anything, I would have to endure his crowing, but there was just a chance Pa would come up with results.

At home the pressure was truly on. In search of peace, I myself went to a wine bar up on the Aventine. I did not expect to find Justinus in this bolthole. As a place to drink it held very few attractions. But the waiter was amiable and the clientele, many of whom had something to hide from wives, mothers or taxation officials, respected other people's privacy. Until the First Adiutrix soldiers discovered it – as they were bound to – I could brood there alone.

Well, I took the dog. Walking Nux was always a good excuse to get out of the house.

Flora's Caupona was no longer run by Flora, who had died, probably worn out by twenty years of living with my father. Previously given by Pa to this mistress of his as a little business where she could earn hairpin money (a business which kept her busy when she might otherwise have taken unwelcome interest in what *he* was up to), for about twelve months now Flora's had had my elder sister Junia as its hopeless proprietress. In the evening Junia was safe at home with her aggravating husband and her rather sweet deaf son; every day at sundown she would leave the caupona in the capable hands of the waiter, Apollonius, then everyone relaxed.

The bar was situated on a corner, as the best bars are. It had the usual two counters with crazy-marble tops, into which were set big pots containing sinister stews in anaemic hues, thickened with what seemed to be a mix of lentils and pavement dust. As the lukewarm pots fermented, from time to time half a gherkin or a lump of turnip would pop up through the slime, then softly sink to its death.

Awnings provided shelter in winter, when most topers sat miserably inside at a couple of wonky tables. Three wormy shelves on a wall held earthenware beakers. A clutch of amphorae leaned askew beneath them, around the bottom points of which Stringy, the caupona cat, curled his emaciated body. Stringy's diet, being the food at Flora's, was slowly poisoning him. The waiter (who always ate at the other caupona, the one across the street) either presided with lugubrious formality or lurked in a back room, where I knew he often read Euripides. When that happened it was bad news. He went off into another world and nobody could get served.

Tonight Apollonius was out among the clients, with a cloth over one arm. I had known him since he was an infant teacher; as a wine-bar waiter he still applied his skills to quell rowdies and to explain simple arithmetic to confused people who could not work out whether he had diddled their change. As I arrived that night, he was telling a drunken vegetable stall holder, 'I think we've all heard enough from you. Sit back on the bench and behave!' I felt I was seven years old again. The drunk did as he was told. I hid a smile.

Apollonius greeted me with a silent nod, then provided a dish of seeping chickpeas, which I ignored, and a cup of red wine, which I tried. 'I'd like your opinion of that, Marcus Didius.'

I noticed that instead of the normal thin crowd, tonight Flora's was warm and full of customers – all crushed in, hoping for free samples. The rest of them eyed me jealously.

'Junia experimenting with a new house wine?' I took a longer swig. 'Oddly enough, I can't taste anything wrong with it.'

'Oh it's not for here,' Apollonius hastened to calm my unease.

'That's reassuring. This caupona has a proud reputation for serving only the most disgusting rotgut on the Hill. People like to know where they stand, Apollonius. Change for change's sake is never welcome!'

Apollonius beamed. He had a quiet, intelligent sense of humour. This is always refreshing (and unexpected) in an intellectual. 'Trust me. We have no intention of destroying the traditions of the establishment. Rotgut remains the house speciality.'

'So what slippery travelling salesman offloaded this palatable gem on my dear sister?'

'We are testing it on a few favoured customers. Junia plans to provide this wine for the vigiles, at the Fourth Cohort's annual

49

Saturnalia drinks party next week. She has been awarded the much-coveted contract as their official caterer.'

I whistled. 'What kind of bribe did that take?'

'I believe their tribune was impressed by her prospectus and sample menus,' returned Apollonius stiffly. He had a certain loyalty to Junia, as his employer, and managed to remain civil even after I guffawed. 'So what do you think, Falco?'

'I think it's all right.'

He took the hint and gave me more. 'It's called *Primitivum*.'

The vigiles would like that.

I quaffed a couple of drinks, then prepared to go home.

I didn't bother to enquire after Justinus, and I was not supposed to mention Veleda so I dutifully avoided that subject too. Some of you may wonder why I went to the caupona. I found no clues, searched out no helpful witnesses, turned up no bodies and announced no public appeals for informants to come forward. I accomplished nothing for the case and a pedant would argue there is no reason to describe the scene. But these are my memoirs, and I shall include damn well anything that interests me.

I was paid by results. So long as I was getting the results, my methods were my own affair. You do your job, tribune, and leave me to mine.

If it makes you feel better, let's say, a good informer who is under pressure sometimes finds it useful to take a few moments of private reflection after a busy day.

'Petronius Longus is back,' said Apollonius, as I paid up.

Well, there you are. That was a result.

=====

XI

'What are you buying for Mother?'

Maia, the most ruthlessly organised of my sisters, was working on a list. A stylus was pushed into her dark curly hair, and her big brown eyes were glaring at a waxed tablet where various relatives' names had been assigned tasteful (but economical) gifts.

'Maia, the best thing about being married is that at last I can leave my mother's Saturnalia present to somebody else. Helena knows her duties. It saves Ma having to grit her teeth over one more manicure set that she doesn't need since five people bought one at the last minute from the same stall for her birthday.'

'Tell Helena she can do bath oils. There won't be duplicates. I had a brilliant idea – I'm clubbing together with the others to pay for an eye doctor. Galla and I are paying for the left eye operation, Junia and Allia are getting the right.'

I raised an eyebrow gently. 'Discount for the pair?'

'Special one-time-only offer – two for the price of one on his low-interest instalment plan.'

'Does Ma know?'

'Of course not. She'd run off to the country. Don't you let on, Marcus.'

'Not me!' Personally, I thought another set of ear-scoop and tweezers was safer. I knew what would be involved in the cataract operation; I had investigated cures when the white scales appeared and Mother first started bumping into the furniture. I'd like to be there when my four sisters explained to Ma how she had to endure some quack pushing cataracts aside with a couching needle. The girls would probably expect me to be the heavy who held our mother down while it happened. 'In case you're wondering,' I said to Maia, 'I could use some extra weight training sessions from Glaucus at the gym.'

'You're getting a new note-tablet,' sneered Maia.

I was still trying to think up ways to suggest I already owned enough notebooks to write a Greek novel, when Petro came in. He appeared to have woken from a nap, and was now gearing himself up for an evening shift on duty. This involved winding on leather wrist bands, rubbing his eyes a lot, and belching.

Petro had been out-stationed at Ostia for most of the summer, but with typical skill had wangled a move back to Rome just in time for the big festival. He and Maia, who had been living together for just over a year, were renting half a house three streets from the vigiles' Aventine patrol house. They needed plenty of room, with Maia's four growing children, Petro's daughter who was staying with them for the holiday, the cats he always allowed around the house, and young Marius' exuberant dog; Arctos had to be kept in a room away from the cats, who tyrannised him and raided his bowl. Nux, who was his mother, had gone in to see Arctos when we arrived.

Despite the way he tolerated his mangy cats, Petronius Longus had been my best friend since we were eighteen. We were both born on the Aventine, though we really met up when we knocked into each other in the recruiting queue and were jointly assigned to the Second Augustan legion. We survived our nightmare posting to Britain only by comforting each other with tall stories and drink. As we both threw up in the boat on the way over there, we already realised we had made a mistake; the subsequent horrors of the Boudiccan Rebellion only confirmed that. We got out of the army, no one needs to know how. Now he ran criminal investigations for the Fourth Cohort of vigiles, while I ran a private enquiry business. We were both damned good at what we did and we were on the same side in fighting life's filthy surprises. Now he had finally settled with Maia, after yearning after her for years, and for both their sakes, I hoped it lasted.

'Io, Marcus!' Petro thumped me on the shoulder. He enjoyed festivals. He knew I hated them. I gave him the gloomy scowl he expected.

He was taller than me, though not enough for it to matter, and broader. As a vigiles officer, he had to be. When the arsonists and other villains weren't attacking him with fists and knives, the ex-slaves he commanded were giving him almost as much trouble. He handled it. Petronius Longus could handle most things except the death of a child or an accident to a pet cat. In our time, I had seen him through both. He had stuck by me in bad situations too.

'What are you working on, Marcus?'

'I am not allowed to tell you,' I complained solemnly.

'Well, spit it out at once then, lad. I won't pass it on.'

'That a promise?'

'Same as the one you must have given somebody . . .'

'I gave my oath to Tiberius Claudius Laeta.'

Petronius grinned broadly. 'The big poppy at the Palace? Well that's all right; it doesn't count.'

Trust a public servant to take a realistic view.

In a few taut sentences I summed up the mission for him.

There was a reason why I was bringing Petronius into my confidence. I explained – though to him it was perfectly obvious – that with the whole of Rome to search and no clues, I stood little chance of finding Veleda, let alone both Veleda and Justinus, aided by only a handful of lackadaisical legionaries from Germany.

'This stinks.' He sounded calm.

'Surprised?'

'It's one of your jobs, you idiot. You're going to need our help as usual.'

'It's a rat's arse,' I agreed quietly. 'In which, as you so rightly notice, it differs from my usual commissions by not one digit of linear measurement. That Veleda is on the loose in Rome, and has been for over ten days, is a State Secret of some delicacy –'

'Everyone's heard about it,' scoffed Petro. He let out another belch; he claimed this kept him fit. Maia just glowered. They were like an old married couple; although both had been previously hitched to other people, most of us thought these two should have been sharing a bed from the start.

I carried on: 'Anacrites has been put in charge of an official hunt, using the Praetorians –' This time Petronius really swore. 'Right! If the Praetorian Guard, fired up with Saturnalia drink, find Veleda, she'll become a new, and ghastly, festival game.' The vigiles would not be delicate with her either, but I left that to his imagination. Petro was well aware that his cohort was composed of roughs and toughs; in truth he was proud of them. 'And the common people are terrified of barbarians invading the citadel, so they will tear Veleda apart.'

Maia, who had been silent and apparently absorbed in her Saturnalia list, looked up and inserted in a caustic tone, 'That is nothing to what Claudia Rufina will do if she catches her.' Petronius and I both winced.

'Give me a description to circulate,' Petro offered.

'I'd like this to be kept from your tribune, you know.'

'Be realistic, Falco. Rubella needs to know – and what's more, so do his oppos: you need this to be given to *all* the cohort tribunes because Veleda could be anywhere. She may know that you live on the Aventine and Justinus lives by the Capena Gate, but in what? – nearly two weeks – she hasn't come looking for either you or him. So by now she could be hiding up in any of the districts – assuming she *is* hiding up, and not being held by some bastards against her will somewhere.' I was protesting, but he stopped me. 'I can put it forward as a game the tribunes will all like: "find the lost prisoner first, to annoy the Praetorians". They will do it, and be discreet.'

I could see this would work. In theory the Praetorian Prefect looked after the Emperor, the Urban Prefect looked after the city by day, and the Prefect of Vigiles controlled the Night Watch; according to their rulebook, the three forces worked in harmony. In fact, there was serious rivalry. Bad feeling went back at least as far as when Emperor Tiberius found himself under threat from the usurper Sejanus, who had the loyalty of the Praetorians. Unable to trust his own imperial guards, Tiberius had cunningly used the vigiles to arrest Sejanus. The Praetorians now liked to pretend it had never happened – but the vigiles never forgot.

'You could also whisper to the Urban Cohorts why their big brothers are stonking all over the city; the Urbans will defend their patch.'

'Unfortunately our lot are not talking to the Urbans either. But I'd thought of that,' said Petro.

Of course if it became known that I had brought in the vigiles on a confidential, entirely Praetorian matter, my position would be . . . difficult. I decided I would deal with that if the issue ever arose.

I could now trust Petronius to put in place a city-wide search for the priestess. He understood that it needed to be an observation and reporting back exercise, nothing too visible. For all we knew, Veleda might have assembled a support group; they could be armed and plotting trouble. We also had to avoid causing general alarm.

I asked Petro for advice on where to start looking myself.

'The obvious way to disappear,' he said, 'is for her to get a job in some backstreet bar.'

'Not feasible. She's never been in a city. She's never lived as a free woman anywhere. We call her a barbarian, though she's more sophisticated than you would expect – yet she'll stick out as a stranger. She's always held a position of respect among the tribes; she's been tended and protected – she lived at the top of a signal tower, for

54

heavens' sake – so she won't know anything about normal life. She probably couldn't live alone unnoticed, even in her own country –'

'Does she have any money, Falco?'

'Probably not. She should have been stripped of her valuables. Perhaps some jewellery. I can ask Pa to put the word out in case she tries to sell anything.' Ganna should be able to tell me what Veleda possessed. Anything worthwhile would find its way to the gem stalls at the Saepta Julia. 'I am told she wants to get back to Free Germany. It's the wrong time of year to travel and the alarm is raised. Unless she makes contact with sympathisers who are willing to help her, she can't even pay for the journey.'

'So she has to go underground.' Petro was thinking. He ticked off people I should contact. 'The German community in Rome.'

'Is there one?'

He shrugged. 'Traders. Must be. Your father should know, from colleagues at the Emporium.'

'Aren't traders by definition friends of Rome?'

'When were traders friends of anyone but themselves?' Petronius was cynical. 'Traders come from all over the place, you know that. They have no qualms about making money from their nations' enemies. Aliens can get here. There's probably some tight little nest of Bructeran barterers right under our noses, if we knew where to look. But don't ask me.'

'No handy list of Free German interlopers?' Petronius ignored my jibe about vigiles' lists. They kept one for informers, and I knew my name was on it. 'I can't think what the Bructeri would have to sell in Rome.'

'People come here to buy, Falco.' He was right there. He thought of another unpleasant group to search: 'Then assuming your priestess is destitute, she might find a refuge among runaway slaves.'

'And how,' I asked sarcastically, 'do I find them, given that their wronged masters have failed to do so? Aren't they invisible on principle?'

'Plenty out there. Doorways. Under the arches. A large colony sleeps rough among the tombs on the Via Appia.'

'I thought the necropolis was haunted by ghosts?'

'Be bloody careful if you go there!' Petro warned. He did not offer to accompany me, I noticed. 'There's one more place. She is a priestess – you could try looking in temples.'

Oh thanks very much. It must have escaped his notice how many of those there were in Rome.

One of his cats crept into the room. The beast could tell I was a dog man, so it smugly came straight for me, purring. Petronius started grinning. I was already flea-bitten after Stringy at the caupona, so I made my excuses rapidly and went home.

XII

My house seemed suspiciously quiet. It spoke of recent ructions. I didn't ask.

Helena and I sat in the kitchen and organised ourselves a quiet supper. We had the last of today's bread, some cold fish, olives and soft cheese. I scrutinised her carefully, but she seemed at ease. Being landed with the soldiers, in the run up to Saturnalia, failed to faze her. The truth was, Helena Justina liked a challenge.

From a corner of the room, our new cook Jacinthus watched. If he had seemed upset by us invading his territory, we would have let him choose the food and serve us, but he was indifferent. So we took over the scrubbed table where he was supposed to prepare things, I fetched a jug of white wine which we two kept to ourselves, and we carried on discussing the day as we always had done, cook or no cook. I had worked on occasions with various partners, including both of Helena's brothers. The person I most enjoyed working with was Helena Justina herself. Non-judgmental, aware and intelligent, she had understood my approach and my routines pretty well from the first time I met her. Ever since, she had been my confidante. She would help me chew over ideas, where possible she would accompany me to interviews, she researched backgrounds, worked out timescales, often came up with solutions. Importantly, she took charge of my finances. The best informer in the world is useless if he becomes insolvent.

'Everything all right, sweetheart?'

'We organised ourselves.' Helena managed to combine reproof about the soldiers' sudden arrival with acknowledgement of my good manners in asking. She knew what most husbands were like; she had been married before me, for one thing. So gratitude just took precedence over complaint. 'The legionaries have taken over the ground floor rooms. They made a few complaints at first, but you will have noticed they are all in their quarters now, rather chastened.' I raised my eyebrows but Helena did not bother to elaborate. 'Clemens has complained about the damp; I told him the Tiber floods us every spring and suggested they might like to leave before then . . . At least we don't have the sewers backing up in our house. I've heard there's a terrible stink three doors down and everyone there has fallen ill.'

'We don't have backing-up shit,' I explained, 'because in all the time he lived here –' which must have been twenty years – 'my skinflint father never paid for a connection to the Cloaca. It *looks* as though our privy empties into the city sewer system, but I suspect our waste just runs into a big cesspit out back.'

'Well at least there is a cesspit,' Helena replied brightly. 'More cheese, Marcus?'

We ate in silence, thoughtfully. Any minute now we would start talking about my mission. I could see Jacinthus out of the corner of my eye, still staring at us. As he was a slave it was easy to ignore him, but perhaps I'd better not. He was lean and dark, about twenty-five. I had been told by the dealer when I bought him that his previous owner simply wanted a change of face around the house. I did not trust the story. I wondered where Jacinthus originated. Like the majority of slaves, he looked Eastern and not at all German. I supposed I should dig into his background a bit more, if we were to speak freely in front of him.

'You had a visitor this evening, Marcus. A woman called Zosime.'

'From the Temple of Æsculapius? I didn't expect her to seek me out, or I would have briefed you, sweetheart.'

'Naturally!' Helena was wry. Once again, her right of complaint went unspoken: I was a thoughtless swine and she was supremely tolerant. In some homes, reaching this happy solution would require a large purchase of jewellery. I wiped away olive oil with my napkin then kissed her hand in a relaxed admission that I didn't deserve her. I kept hold of the hand temporarily, holding her long fingers against my cheek and considering just how lucky I was. A quiet moment passed between us.

'So tell me about it. What did Zosime want?'

Helena pulled back her hand so she could pick at the dish of olives. They were small chewy black ones, marinaded in garlic and chervil. 'She's a woman in her fifties, I'd say – once a nursing assistant, now calls herself a doctor, presumably experienced. She looks after female patients at the temple, ones who have gynaecological problems.'

'So was she called to see Veleda because the priestess had a complaint of that sort?'

'Well, Zosime says in her opinion Veleda had nothing like that at all and the Quadrumati sent for her because she was recommended by one of their other doctors. Veleda was suffering from some general illness, with bouts of fever and terrible headaches. In fact the pain was so bad, Veleda was begging for that terrifying surgery where people have a hole drilled in their skull –'

'Trepanation.'

'Someone had told her a Roman surgeon could carry it out. Veleda had convinced herself it would relieve the pressure in her head.' Helena shuddered. 'It seems drastic. She must have felt desperate – even though by then she knew she was doomed to die anyway.'

'There may be no escape from the public executioner, but patients have been known to survive trepanation,' I said. 'Many don't – naturally, surgeons keep that quiet. What was Zosime's suggestion to help her?'

'Zosime works on gentle principles, what she calls "softly, safely, sweetly". It goes back to ancient Greek theories, the Hippocratic tradition, and involves treatments based on a combination of diet, exercise and rest. Zosime was not really given a chance to try this out, though. She prescribed a sensible regime, but was discouraged from visiting again.'

I was startled. 'The Quadrumati locked her out?'

'Nothing so crude. But she took the hint and stopped attending.'

'Was Veleda happy with her?'

'Zosime thought so. But it was obvious to her that Veleda was not a free agent.'

'Had Zosime been told that her patient was a prisoner?'

'Not directly.'

'You think she knew?'

'I think she's very shrewd,' Helena said.

'And could she have seen Veleda again, after Veleda escaped from the house?'

'Possibly. I didn't ask. How could I, without revealing things that are supposed to be kept secret?' This time, Helena's tone did contain a slight suggestion that the awkwardness of the mission was my fault.

'All right, go back a bit: why did Zosime think she had become unwelcome at the senator's house?'

'I had the impression there might have been conflict with one of the other doctors you told me are employed by the family. She muttered something about Mastarna, and used the phrase "damn fool dogmatist". I pressed her on that –' Helena could be stubborn in interrogations. She saw me smiling and threw an olive at me. I opened my mouth and it went straight in, for which I gloatingly took the

59

credit. 'Well, your mouth's big enough, Falco! . . . It seems to have been Mastarna who was encouraging Veleda towards trepanation. Zosime was circumspect in talking to me – perhaps because she is a woman, venturing into what male doctors believe is their special territory – but it's clear she felt Mastarna had not bothered to carry out a proper diagnosis, but was dead set on radical surgery.'

I pondered this theory. 'Do you think that after Zosime left, this crazy knife-man persuaded Veleda to have the trepanation after all, that he drilled out a circle of her skull and managed to kill her with the procedure – so somebody has hidden her body to avoid political embarrassment?'

'Zosime did not suggest it.'

'If she stopped visiting the house, she wouldn't know. She may never have dealt with the kind of devious people we meet.' I was now thinking back to my interviews that morning with Quadrumatus Labeo and his wife, trying to decide whether they could have been hiding such a cover-up.

'Was Mastarna one of the doctors you met today?' Helena asked.

'No, I just saw the senator's dream therapist – Pylaemenes, a crack-pot Chaldean – then I had a surly encounter with Cleander, who came to tickle up the wife with his cold Greek fingers.'

'You're being lewd, Marcus.'

'Who, me? Cleander once taught Greek theory to Zosime, but that doesn't make him enlightened; he's an arrogant swine who looks down on mere mortals. Presumably he's in medicine for the money, not from charitable feelings. I can't imagine he was connected to the Temple of Æsculapius for long. Now what else did the witchy freedwoman say – dark, forbidding Phryne – the senator has a tame Egyptian, who I suppose feeds him ground crocodile bones, and yes: then there's Mastarna – Mastarna, she told me, used to look after the dead man. So Gratianus Scaeva was in the hands of the keen surgeon Zosime quarrelled with.'

Helena slowly munched a slightly stale bread roll. I said she liked a challenge. I had seen her test her teeth on hard crusts before, in the same way that my mother always made out it was her maternal lot to endure leftovers and inedible scraps. 'So,' Helena asked me eventually, when her jaw tired of this punishment, 'what is the significance of Scaeva's doctor in this household of hypochondriacs?'

'The answer will probably depend,' I said, 'on whatever link we find between Veleda and Scaeva. Who really killed him: whether it was, or was not, Veleda. And why? Was there any connection between the death of Scaeva and the timing of Veleda's escape – other than her taking advantage of panic and commotion in the house?'

'His head was cut off,' Helena commented, in surprise. 'Are you suggesting that somebody other than Veleda carried out that particularly Celtic act?'

'Could be. I never saw the body; of course it's cremated. I'd like to ask Mastarna if he carried out a professional examination when his patient's corpse was found. There could have been other wounds, wounds that were inflicted first. Who would bother to check? There's a man with his head cut off, so you assume that is the cause of death . . . But I shall keep an open mind. He could have died some other way, then Veleda's presence in the house gave someone the idea to blame his death on her.'

'Somebody with a very cool nerve!' Helena commented. 'Even if Scaeva was already dead, I imagine it takes courage to decapitate a corpse.'

'You're right. The tribes do it in the heat of battle, and they do it to their enemies which must be an encouragement . . . Maybe, when I find an opportunity,' I said, 'I should find out what enemies Gratianus Scaeva had.'

Helena pulled a face. 'He was a young man. Was he the type to have enemies?'

I laughed bitterly. 'Well born, well off, well thought of . . . I was told he was a perfect character – so trust me, fruit; he's bound to have been a right bastard!'

XIII

Next day began with a visit to my father at the Saepta Julia. My runner, Gaius, had failed to report back, but I found him with Pa at the family antiques warehouse. Gaius had completely forgotten about my questions, and was absorbed in negotiations to sell Pa various statuettes he had stolen from temples when I took him on our tour of Greece. Pa was in his usual battered old folding campaign chair; Gaius was lounging like a prince in a stationary litter that had a five-foot-high gilded armchair. Most of the carrying poles looked sound, but the chair was very worn.

'He's got a good eye,' beamed my father approvingly.

'Oh he knows when to commit sacrilege. Gaius is a little tyke; he could have got us all arrested if anyone had noticed him looting ritual offerings.' Luckily, in the family tradition, Gaius could bluff his way out of trouble. He was around sixteen, with a curly rug of black hair just like my father's (and mine), and currently had the air of one born to sprawl under a regal canopy as if being carried to his banker's by a team of eight Mauretanian bearers. 'Now look here, Father, I sent this chancer to you with some important questions –'

'No, just look at this –' Pa held up a tiny model of a womb. Some patient cured of a tumour or infertility had donated it gratefully to the gods at Olympia, Corinth or Athens, only to have Gaius swan along and swipe it. 'This is quite a rarity.' Pa noticed Gaius taking too much interest, so dropped the praise before my nephew tried to negotiate an improved purchase price. 'Difficult to sell because of the religious connection . . .' Gaius raised his eyes to the ceiling; he recognised devious backtracking.

'Uncle Marcus will vouch for the provenance.'

'No, I'll vouch for you being a bad boy who has no respect for ancient sites, Gaius!'

'Don't be so stiff-necked,' ordered Pa. 'Give the lad a bit of encouragement. He's shaping up really nicely; I need Gaius, since *you* refuse to take an interest in the family business.'

Groaning, I managed to extract from my father a description of the silver ear-rings Justinus had bought to mollify Claudia. I told Pa to look out for Justinus, the ear-rings, or a lost-looking woman of German extraction whose name I was not allowed to mention.

'Oh you mean Veleda? Everyone is talking about her being free,' said Pa.

'Is there a finder's fee?' Gaius demanded, voicing what my father would have put to me had he got in first. Instead, Pa, ever the hypocrite, pretended to tut at the greed of modern youth.

'The reward is a clear conscience.'

'Not enough!' snorted Pa, and Gaius nodded.

'Doing your duty to preserve the Empire –'

'Bugger that for a game of soldiers,' sneered Gaius. This time Pa did the seconding.

Not long afterwards I was in the Emporium, trying to track down German traders. The Emporium was the long stone building on the banks of the Tiber, which ran from near my present house southwards along the shipping lane, almost to the city boundary. There were unloaded all the best commodities, brought in from worldwide sources, to be sold in Rome. It was a wondrous hubbub of sights, sounds and smells, where tight knots of dealers and double-dealers fixed the rates and the outlets for artwork and marble, precious woods and metals, spices, gemstones, wines, oils, dyes, ivory, fish products, leather, wools and silks. You could buy a barrel of fresh British oysters in saline for your dinner party, peacock fans to decorate the dining room while you ate them, a handsome slave to serve the meal, and a sarcophagus to hold your corpse after you discovered the oysters had not survived the journey safely. The item prices were tempting – until you added in the dealers' premiums, luxury tax and the costs of transport to your house. This was if you managed to get in and out of the building without having your purse stolen.

My father, in whom snobbery flared high, had declared there would be no *importers* bringing local wares from either Roman or Free Germany, though I would find plenty of *exporters* sending fine Roman products to deprived provincials. He was only slightly wrong. Following his directions, I did track down a few sad purveyors of Rhenish hides, woollen coats, and even decorated terracotta bowls, but most of the negotiators who were here from the north were sending luxuries back home. Where they were selling, their dinnerware was good (Helena and I already owned a similar set from

Gaul), but as they were passing off the stuff as coming from the well-known factory sites at Arretium, the prices here were Italian and there was no cost benefit.

The men I interviewed wore heavy trousers and tunics, with cloaks fastened on one or both shoulders. Some had brooches in intricately twined Celtic patterns; others fixed their garments with fibulae whose gold filigree was much more Mediterranean, and occasionally ancient. They had been trading with Rome for generations – and probably trading with Greece long before that – whereas they had been trading *in* the city here for maybe only thirty years, since the Emperor Claudius introduced German allies into the Senate and, while fighting the prejudice of his peers, tried to welcome tribal leaders to Rome and Roman society. This group were mean-eyed capitalists from the west bank of the Rhenus who did not want peace on the east bank because it posed a direct threat to them financially. Theirs was the usual self-serving of commerce. They wanted to remain sole suppliers of Roman goods to their own area. Sharing the trade with Easterners did not appeal. They were very quick to label the east-bank tribes as barbarians.

I probed delicately how they had felt about Veleda. I was chancing it here. Rebellion was a sensitive subject in Europe. Even on the western bank, which had been in Roman control for a long time, there were those who had sought independence not so long ago when they thought Rome was vulnerable. But if these men had felt any sympathy with Veleda back then, they knew better than to show it now.

Laeta's injunction to secrecy made it impossible to ask whether they would help Veleda if she came to them as a supplicant. I could see a risk that her well-known hostility to Rome might arouse anti-German feeling generally, if the public heard she was in our city. If that happened, maybe the traders would turn against her for causing them problems. Insofar as they would talk about her, they claimed that Veleda had always denounced them as collaborators and they denied that there had ever been any possibility of an alliance across the river.

This was bosh. I knew that before Vespasian stabilised the region recently, there had been contact, of which some was very violent but much was friendly. I did not trust the traders, therefore; and since they obviously wondered why I was questioning them, it was fair to say they did not trust me.

I got nowhere. Since I had to disguise my purpose, I had expected nothing better. I did obtain one useful piece of information: how to find a particular group of Germans who had lived in Rome for decades. The traders sent me to them with sardonic expressions – and I knew why. They were hoping their notorious fellow-countrymen would do me physical damage. In fact, they probably thought I was about to be bent into a mystical Celtic knot with all my protruding bits neatly tucked in.

The group I went visiting had shrunk to a grim little enclave: I had tracked down the neglected remnants of Nero's legendary German bodyguard.

I was among elderly men giving off a strong odour of the dangerous past. Those were sour times, and these were sprawling old bullies, nostalgic for a culture that no longer existed. Why had they remained in Rome? Probably to avoid disappointment if they returned to their own land and discovered that it was now populated by neat Roman towns where citizens carried out Romanised occupations in a Roman ethos. Even the farmers and country manufacturers brought in their produce to sell at our kind of market in our style of urban forum. Across Europe, fewer and fewer people lived in roundhouses. Tribal culture was dying. Upper and Lower Germany were filled with industries making equipment for the legions. Beer was losing out; vineyards were spreading ever northward.

Originally the bodyguard must have numbered around five hundred. Some had died, some had drifted elsewhere, yet a hard core stayed on, dreaming of the good old days as fighting men do. Now they were pushing pension age – had they been given pensions. From their shabby dress and faded energy I deduced that public handouts for these one-time palace servants were few. In Roman politics during the mad days of the Julio-Claudians, loyalties had tended either towards Nero or Claudius; political advancement had depended on alliances made with one or the other; and Vespasian was a Claudian supporter. When Nero died and he came to power, fortune finally stopped smiling on these men.

It was thirty years since their heyday. They had not so much run to seed as decayed into compost. I found a mildewed huddle of about fifteen, teasing out a flagon or two at their regular lunch club. A withered Ubian waiter, who must have served their bread and blood-sausage for forty years, tottered away to fetch extra wine that I paid for, muttering what sounded like bitter Ubian curses under his onion-flavoured breath. The old warriors regarded me with greater toleration, aware that few people nowadays would stand them a warm toddy on a cold morning, but even they failed to reach my classification of 'friendly'.

I seemed to remember that in the old days the German bodyguard had been selected for size. Now the big men were stooped in the shoulder but their once-giant frames supported heavy bellies. They looked truculent. I had had a fight with another group of these bullies a few years ago and it had been vicious. These were older now and might not be able to catch anyone who ran away very fast, but if you stumbled as you tried to escape, they could kill you just by rolling on you – and I was pretty sure they would do it. When the drinkers banged down their metal cups with their fat fists, the reverberation shook sheets off the washing lines three streets away. It was deliberate. Nero's bodyguard had always been violent and uncontrollable. Nowadays they were lazy old slobs and their blond plaits had thinned out to sad wisps, but they were still off-putting.

They did not like me either.

Once again I was hamstrung by my order to keep Veleda's name out of my enquiries. And once again, I thought I saw expressions in the watery blue eyes of some here which said they knew exactly why I had come to question them.

As a lead-in, I asked whether they had had a visit recently from the Praetorian Guard. This elicited a loud burst of laughter and boasting about how they bettered the Praetorians. I joked chummily that the Guards were having a bad week, and we settled down pretending to be allies. It was temporary.

The Praetorians, never famous for subtlety, had come right out and admitted they were looking for someone, a woman from the old guards' home country. I asked if they had had any visits from anyone like that, and they responded rudely that they wouldn't tell me if they had. They must have spurned the Praetorians with the same derision. While this meant that the Praetorians, and Anacrites, had failed to get ahead of me, it also meant that all of us were getting nowhere.

The Germans continued drinking the wine I had paid for, pretty well ignoring me. I considered them. Enough had been said for me to suspect that in general they would show no sympathy to a woman. Veleda's fall into captivity would be an excuse to ignore her. Since they spent their time bemoaning the loss of the old days, they were also antagonistic to the younger generation that Veleda represented. I asked if they had sons; a few did, but they were serving in the legions and I guessed that if those soldiers ever came home, there would be distrust and family arguments.

I wondered which side of the River Rhenus these warriors originally came from. They could even be a mixture of tribes. Although Nero was best known for using this Rhineland protection force, it had been instigated earlier, by Augustus; other emperors and generals had employed them too. Vespasian had stopped that; now the Emperor was meant to be the Father of his Country, utterly loved by his people. Rule by threat had given way to rule by coercion. While bad emperors would continue to be set upon and stabbed, we all pretended the public were devoted. It had become embarrassing to employ foreigners for imperial protection, because that implied that the Father of his Country could not trust his own.

Suddenly one of the bleached braggarts produced a coin from his bosom. As if he sensed that I was mentally condemning his brothers and him as outdated, he flattened it on the boards in front of me. Typical of imperial propaganda, it showed Nero on a box, addressing three figures in military dress, whom I deduced must be members of his German guard. 'We are history, Falco!'

'You must be very proud,' I said, pretending to be overawed. I would have felt uncomfortable surrounded by this number of manicure boys at a public bath house. These overweight monsters made me nervous. I had been aware of men coming and going in the low-roofed hall where we were squashed. They could be taking messages, summoning reinforcements. I could no longer see the Ubian waiter. Perhaps someone had recognised me from that fight I had had with the others from their group five years ago. Perhaps somebody had remembered how on that occasion, I had laid out several men who were selling themselves as hired muscle at the house of a certain Atius Pertinax; they fought viciously, but I had left them dying in the road . . . It was time to leave.

I thanked them for their co-operation and made good my escape. I walked away from the area purposefully, though not so fast as to let anybody watching know I felt nervous. I thought I had managed it safely. I knew the bastards had loathed me but I thought they had let me go.

Only as I slowed down and started to relax did I sense that I had been followed.

XIV

Being tracked was always dangerous. I never underestimated the risk. Whether it was general muggers emerging from unlit alleys, hoping to follow some lump of off-guard after-dinner flab and snatch his purse along with his fine linen banquet napkin, or whether it was thugs trailing me specifically for reasons connected with a case, I treated them all as potential killers. Never ignore the half-seen shadow you try to convince yourself was nothing; you may very well end up with an assassin's knife sliding under your ribs. That cart being driven erratically in a road where carts don't normally deliver may have a driver who is planning to run you down. The faint noise overhead may be a heavy flowerpot falling down accidentally – or a pot someone has pushed over with a view to crushing your head. It may be three men dropping down on you from a balcony.

'Hey, Falco!'

Even before I pinpointed them, I knew I was being hunted by Germans. I had recognised the accent. Not the ex-bodyguards. The voice belonged to a younger man. At the breathy shout from my left, I spun around and checked my right. Long practice.

No one rushed me. Two quick steps had me with my back against a house wall. As I scanned around, I pulled my knife from my boot.

My mind raced. I was in the enclave between the Fourth and Sixth Districts. The High Lanes. Not as elegant and lofty as they sound. Somewhere close to the Porta Saluta, named for the Temple of Salus, or well-being. About to be very unhealthy for me.

I knew nobody in these streets. Had no idea where the nearest vigiles station was. Could not rely on local stallholders. Was unsure of the configuration of local lanes and back doubles, if I had to make a run for it . . . I identified the Germans. Several, and they looked tough.

People were about. A woman stood outside a shop with two young children; she was gazing at produce – knives? cushions? pastries? – while the little girl tugged her skirts, whining to go home.

Businessmen were arguing lazily but long-windedly on a corner. A slave wheeled a handcart laden with cabbages, pretending not to notice when he dropped one and it rolled away. Two dogs stopped sniffing each other and stared at me. Only they had spotted my sudden movement and sensed something interesting was about to occur.

In the brief pause, one of the dogs walked over to the lost cabbage, which was still slowly rolling, and put his nose down to it as the vegetable teetered on the edge of the kerb then toppled down into the gutter. The cabbage gave a lop-sided lurch, and covered itself with muddy water. The dog licked it, then looked up at me, his curiosity on the wane. The other dog barked once, just making a point about who owned the street.

My heart was pounding.

'Hey, Falco!'

Taller than me by several inches and heavier by many pounds, three fair-haired men in their thirties stood in a loose group a few strides away. They had seen my knife. They looked faintly sheepish. I refused to be fooled.

'Hello. I am Ermanus,' offered the spokesman. He smiled at me. I did not smile back.

They were well built with heavy bellies; they looked raffish and untidy, but much harder than the old slugs I had been talking to earlier. These large boys went to the gym. If you punched those paunches, your fist would bounce off solid flesh, too fat, but supported by muscle. The black leather straps holding in their guts would barely give, and the metal studs in those workmanlike straps and five-inch belts would break your knuckles. If you hit these men, you would only have yourself to blame. They would fight back – and they would have had practice. Their biceps were bursting below their short, taut tunic sleeves. They had calves like military gateposts.

'You're Falco?' Ermanus now almost sounded tentative. Not true. In case anyone failed to find him frightening, dark blue patterns in woad wreathed all over his arms. His comrades were equally menacing. None of them wore cloaks, despite the cold. They wanted everyone to see how hard they were.

'Don't come any closer!'

'We just need a word . . .' Every landlord's enforcer, every master villain's back-up gang, every curmudgeon with a cudgel I had ever encountered said that. *We just need a word* . . . Dear gods, when would the world's brutes change their script? It was ridiculous when what they all meant was: shut up, don't call attention to us, just give in and lie down in the road quietly while we kick you insensible. Most of them were illiterate. Holding a conversation was the last thing any of the bastards really had in mind.

I shifted my balance. 'You stay right there. What do you want?'

'You've been talking with our old fellows.'

'I was talking. Your old fellows were unresponsive. What of it?'

'Was it about a woman?'

'It may have been.' Or it may not. Or maybe I am not allowed to say. Thank you, Laeta, for putting me in this stupid position. Let me know how I can make *you* look like an idiot some day.

'From Germania Libera?'

I wondered if the heavyweights were lusting after her – but I was starting to suspect that was the wrong scenario.

'I am searching for a woman from Free Germany, yes. Can you give me information?' I looked at them. They looked at me. 'If I find her – and find her quickly – there may be a reward.' If I really did find her, I was confident Laeta would pay whatever I had to negotiate. He would have to. I would not hand her over until he covered any debts.

'She came calling on the old fellows.' They were not after a reward. It all emerged without prompting. 'Someone had told her they were from her region and she begged for assistance. They refused to have anything to do with her.'

'Do you know where she went afterwards?' No. 'You followed me – why not follow her? She used to be beautiful.' I was picking up hints now that the fabulous priestess held no appeal for Ermanus and his muscular pals. 'When was it she came calling? And this is important – what was her condition?'

'A week ago. She was desperate. And she said she was ill.'

'*Very* ill? Enough to mention it – so how ill?'

'The old fellows thought she was playing on their sympathy.' First Phryne, the old freedwoman at the Quadrumatus villa, now her compatriots; either Veleda was faking, as Phryne suspected, or she had terrible luck when she sought help. I hoped she was not genuinely sick. I could not afford to have her keeling over from a neglected disease. Rome has its moral standards. We care for our special prisoners right up to the moment when we execute them.

'What did you think?' They shrugged. Total uninterest. I pressed them for further information, but they were stringing me along, trying to keep my attention; trying, I realised with foreboding, to detain me. I was starting to think this was a soft kind of ambush.

'Well,' I said. Best not to feel too outraged by the situation I now suspected. 'Thank you for telling me she turned up. It lets me know she had not found help at that stage. There was no need for you to try and scare me witless, creeping up like that.'

'We like the look of you, Falco. We know some people who are having a party tonight –' I had prised the truth out of them. 'Music, good food, entertainment – there will be drinking a lot, and playing around . . . Much fun. Much relaxation. Want to come along?'

I had a good idea what kind of party this relaxing hop would be. I understood now. The Rhineland fun-lovers with the leatherwork and studs were just looking for a new playmate.

'Sorry, blue eyes.' I tried to let them down gently. 'I don't get out much to orgies these days. I'm married, and I need to be at home. I have to ensure the wife doesn't get the taste again for her old wild ways.'

'There will be women!' Ermanus promised, while his two friends nodded, still begging me to change my mind. 'Hot women, Falco!' An alarming vision hit me of what kind of women would associate with these fruity party-lovers. There would be animal furs. People wearing tails. Skimpy costumes that ended where clothes ought to start. I wondered if they would have pastries in the form of male genitalia and drinks made with poppy sap. There were bound to be pornographic lamps.

I could hardly bear to say it: 'Don't tell me – it's a nymphs-and-satyrs party!' They looked amazed that I knew. 'Too much for me, Ermanus. My sciatica holds me back these days. It's always good to be wanted – but no, thanks!'

I walked on, still aware of being followed – but now only by three wistful gazes.

XV

Dear gods, I hadn't been invited to a nymphs-and-satyrs party since I was seventeen. The only time I plucked up the courage to go to one, my sister Victorina (who had organised it) inadvertently let out the secret, so all our aunts turned up. As a result it was not quite the occasion Victorina had hoped.

Feeling old, I carried on home. Lunch with the wife. To whom, though I told her all about the traders and the ex-bodyguards, I somehow made no mention of my newfound happy friends. Still, I could tell Petronius. Or perhaps not. He would want the address of the party 'for security reasons'.

Helena Justina had had a useful, though frustrating morning. She had started by providing Clemens with a map of the city, which she divided into segments for his men to search. Since none of them had ever been to Rome before, she tried to show the soldiers where they were in relation to the map: 'You would think that would be easy,' raged Helena, 'since we live beside the river − I had marked the river in blue ink, and put a big cross by our house so they could find their way back . . . I could tell they didn't understand it. Juno, I don't know how legionaries survive on campaign!'

'A tribune tells them where they are,' I explained gravely. 'They are given orders when to march, and when to stop, and when to eat, and when to sleep, and when to fart and when to blow their nose.'

'They will never find Veleda.'

'Even if they do, darling, will they find their way back home with her?'

'I notice *you* didn't involve yourself in telling them anything, Marcus.'

Quite right. I had met legionaries before.

'Maybe we'll never see them again,' growled Helena hopefully.

'They will be home for supper,' I said. 'Will there be any?'

Luckily there would. After the map episode, Helena had worn

herself out further taking two soldiers and Jacinthus, our sleepy so-called cook, to market for provisions. I had exempted myself from that task too, again with foresight. As I had promised her, the two soldiers then proved themselves perfectly happy left in the kitchen with big knives, pans and buckets, preparing food. With a strange kind of patience, they were showing Jacinthus how it was supposed to be done. He just stared, as po-faced as ever. Galene, however, our other new slave, had abandoned the children and was watching, entranced, everything the soldiers did. When I looked in, she was examining a long curl of apple peel. Gaudus was elbow deep in pastry, complaining that our milled flour was gritty, discussing the virtues of cinnamon (if you could afford it), and arranging for Galene to escort him to the local baker so he could get his pies baked. Scaurus was searing meat in a pannikin and did not wish to be disturbed.

A tray had been made up with our lunch on it, so I grabbed the tray and carried it to our dining room. Obviously we householders were expected to set an example by eating formally. How formally was a surprise: slices of cold meat had been laid out with military correctness on a serving platter, decorated with neatly halved eggs; each knife was set at a thirty-degree angle on a folded serviette with a bread roll; there were six black olives per person, plus two gherkins; the water jug had been buffed like a lady's hand mirror.

Helena calmed down grudgingly. We found the children. Julia was playing farms with Favonia's little horse-shaped pottery feeding bottle. Favonia was gnawing the leg of a stool. In her own room, our foster-daughter Albia was laughing as she read through a letter; I had no idea who her correspondent was, but if a teenaged girl has a smile on her face instead of the normal filthy scowl, in my view you think yourself lucky and leave well alone. Helena acquired a thoughtful expression, however, rubbing her forehead abstractedly with the back of her hand, like a woman who already has enough to cope with. I grinned reassuringly. As usual, that made her look more anxious.

'Where's the dog?'

'Hiding. Probably in your bed.'

Helena and I then assembled with Albia and the children in the dining room, though we did not start to eat. Helena sat silent, and I knew why she was uncomfortable.

'Something is not right here, Marcus.'

'Too perfect. They are taking us for idiots.'

'I'll go –'

'No, leave it to me. I'll deal with it.'

'Oh I love it when you play-act as the father of the family . . .'

I went back to the kitchen. Nobody heard me coming, so I found them all stretched out on benches, ensconced with mounded bowls of double rations, clearly set in for a siesta they expected to extend all afternoon. A flagon that did not contain water slid its way back on to a shelf and looked innocent, just as I entered. I pretended I had not noticed. Gaudus, for one, was sharp enough to know I had seen it.

'Now look here. In our house we don't have "them and us". I run a benevolent democracy. Our slaves are loved and part of our family; so are army visitors. Helena Justina and I would like to implement a slight adjustment, therefore: Galene and Jacinthus, Gaudus and Scaurus, either you four come and join us decently for lunch, or I'll have to bring the tray right back and the rest of us will come down here.'

Four pairs of hostile eyes stared back at me. I stood my ground and told them to collect cutlery. They knew I was on to them.

I was a Roman. Just as Helena kept the keys to the store-cupboards – which from now on, she really would have to hold in a bunch on her belt – I was the master: father of all the household, priest, judge and king. I would not allow ganging-up in the kitchen. There were damn good reasons for running an establishment the Roman way: it prevented riot and bankruptcy.

We all had lunch very pleasantly together as a family.

Helena warned me afterwards, we must ensure that none of those four won the bean to be King-for-a-Day at Saturnalia, or they might retaliate with more misrule than we could handle. I returned a genial smile. I was king all the other days. And I myself was determined to allocate that bean.

XVI

Helena needed rescuing from domesticity. I told Galene to watch the children, and Albia to watch Galene. Albia agreed readily; she was a born tyrant. We showed Gaudus where the local bakery was; I reckoned that if Galene took him she would be pregnant before the pies coloured in the oven. I was barely coping with ownership of my first generation of slaves; it would be some time before I could face the idea of a dynasty.

I had warned everyone we would be back in half an hour, though we were planning to bunk off for longer. (Next time I would imply I was going out for ages, but then return unexpectedly after ten minutes . . .)

Suddenly I understood why there were so many suspicious masters. I also understood why they were bad-tempered; I hated the slaves and the soldiers for putting me – a fair-minded, friendly, relaxed character – in that position.

Helena and I stood on the Marble Embankment and slowly inhaled the cool December air like captives drinking in the fresh breath of freedom. Then we set off together on foot for our next enquiry. Always thinking ahead, Helena had persuaded Zosime from the Temple of Æsculapius to give directions for finding Mastarna, the physician Zosime had quarrelled with, who had looked after the young man Gratianus Scaeva until somebody segmented him.

Knowing only that Mastarna lived 'somewhere by the Library of Pollio', it took us a while to identify his house, though I knew that area well and found an apothecary nearby who told us where to go.

'Presumably you have dealings with him.' I like to find out a few facts in advance.

'Not that one. I always thought Etruscans favoured roots and shoots. You know – gathering herbs by moonlight, pounding bulbs, assembling folklore potions.'

'Mandrake and religious magic?'

'Bloody dogmatist.' The apothecary spat. It was an insult rather than for medical relief. 'All he wants are scalpels and saws. I need the ones who prescribe ointments and laxatives. He'll always have idiots with too much money pleading for him to slice bits off them, but how am I to earn a living? Give me a decent empiricist prescribing purges any day. I may as well live near the beast market as across the alley from Mastarna. At least then I could hope the real butchers would give me free oxtails . . .'

He was still maundering on when we shuffled away and knocked on the doctor's door, keeping our backs to the complaining apothecary in the hope he would not follow us over there. Mastarna was out, but his housekeeper said he would be back soon, and we could wait. She was a short, wide little bundle with her girdle right under her bulging bust, who faced the world with her left shoulder forward, squinting at us with her wall eye. I started to wonder if Mastarna was one of those sinister medical men who collect freaks. He certainly collected fees. He lived in a small but beautifully decorated apartment on the good side of a quiet street. He possessed much desirable furniture, which meant he earned more than I did. His whole house reeked of terebinth resin, however; I thought ours, always smelling of young children, rosemary hair-wash and grilled meats, was healthier.

When he came home, he was impeccably groomed and elegantly turned out. All I knew of Etruscans was that my own nose, which plumb-bobbed straight down from my forehead with no bumps, was reckoned to show that Etruscans had lurked in the Didius pedigree somewhere about the time of the last Carthaginian war. From tomb portraits that had passed through my father's none-too-legitimate auctions, I had gleaned a picture of reclining men and women in rather Greek poses, with slanted eyes and cheerful smiles. Mastarna had none of that strange pointy-eared elfin look. He was as wrinkled as a roof gargoyle. When I asked, he said he came from Forum Clodii, but he looked more Roman than I did and sounded like a swanky lawyer lying his head off over some writ in the Basilica. His tunic was pristine and he wore a toga over it. The toga was meticulously pleated; he was so pleased with the effect, he kept it on at home, and it stayed on even after he learned we were not prospective patients who would need to be impressed.

He had a goatee beard. That pigeonholed him for me. The apothecary had been right to curse him.

'It is so good of you to see us without an appointment. I hope you don't mind us calling.' I let Helena do the softening up. Before I could interrogate him fairly, I needed to get over my irritation with his beard. 'Didius Falco is investigating the disappearance of Veleda – we can mention her openly to you, since I believe you knew she was staying at the Quadrumatus house. Inevitably, in view of the timing, my husband has to consider the sad death of your late patient.'

No shadow passed behind Mastarna's eyes, yet I knew he would refuse to help us. His reply was smooth and meaningless. If he was diagnosing a splinter in your finger, he would be just as bland. I wouldn't trust this man to mop up vomit – not that he would. He thought himself well above that level of patient care.

'I am loath to ask his grieving relatives about him,' I joined in, speaking firmly. 'But since it appears that the priestess killed him, I need to investigate Scaeva, and any possible relationship he had with her. As he was your patient, you must have known him as well as anyone.'

'A delightful young man.'

Such clichés were what I would expect from a pomposity with goat's whiskers. 'Why did you attend him? What was his illness?'

'Sniffles and –' Mastarna cleared his throat slightly – 'sore throats. He suffered badly from catarrh in winter.'

'Do you mind if I ask how you treated him?'

'Patient confidentiality –'

'He's dead, Mastarna; he won't sue. Being run down and suffering from an extension of childhood illnesses does not usually constitute a family secret anyway.' It did not normally lead to decapitation either, but this was not the time for bedside wit; Mastarna lacked any sense of humour. 'What did you do for him?'

Mastarna was clearly annoyed, but he merely said, 'These are seasonal disorders. Difficult to cure.'

Helena leaned forward, a stylus poised over a note-tablet between her long fingers. 'I believe you belong to the dogmatic school?'

Such a question, from a woman, surprised Mastarna. 'We diagnose scientifically. We study the human body through research and theory.'

'Research? You approve of dissection of corpses?' Helena had raised a contentious subject. Mastarna's expression immediately became veiled. 'Did you dissect Scaeva?' I nearly choked. I was supposed to be outspoken, but Helena could be outrageous. I wondered if she had gleaned this background knowledge from Zosime. Not necessarily: Helena was quite capable of rushing to a library, while I had been mooning at Flora's Caupona yesterday, and reading up the major schools of medical thought with a scroll in one hand while she tucked the children into bed. She was addressing the doctor with an expression full of reasonable sweetness, while she posed her brutal questions: 'I wondered if the family might have allowed an autopsy, since somebody had already begun the process . . .'

Mastarna looked savage. But again his tone stayed level: 'No, I did not carry out a post-mortem examination on Gratianus Scaeva. Nor did I seek to do so. Cutting up corpses is illegal, young woman. Apart from a short period, in Alexandria, it always has been.' He made Alexandria sound a pit of depravity. That would be news to the learned liberals at the world's greatest library.

I was pretty sure that Scythax, the Fourth Cohort's vigiles doctor, had more than once conducted anatomical research using the remains of dead criminals, but I refrained from saying so. When the criminals had been thrown to the lions, not much of their corpses remained for Scythax to play with anyway.

It was my turn to tackle a frog in my throat. 'Tell me, Mastarna: did you attend Veleda too? She's on the run, and it is important for me to gain some idea of her physical condition.'

'The woman was hysterical, in my opinion.' Mastarna sounded curt. I saw Helena bristling. Unaware of it, Mastarna carried on condemning himself. 'Hysterical in the medical sense. I diagnosed a classic case of "wandering womb" –' I had heard Helena raving against doctors who dismissed all female ills as neurotic, and she particularly loathed the Greek idea that women's organs moved around their bodies, causing a kind of suffocation and hence a hysteria that explained any female symptoms, whether piles or athlete's foot. Her set face was eloquent: *to suggest that a woman with a headache has her womb between her ears proves that the doctor has decayed matter where his brain should be . . .* 'The woman refused to succumb to an internal examination.' As Helena visualised Mastarna offering to subject Veleda to a vaginal groping, no doubt conducted with a crude expanding metal uterine probe, she took a deep angry breath –

I intervened quickly: 'I believe Veleda had asked for trepanation. Was it your suggestion?'

'Trepanation was not carried out.'

'Were you willing to do it?'

Mastarna seemed evasive. 'It never came to surgery.'

'But you had discussed it with her?'

'Not in person. Trepanation is a tradition in German communities, I understand – though I cannot believe it is often successful among unskilled barbarians. Veleda had asked whether any of the doctors who attend the Quadrumatus family possessed the necessary knowledge. Cleander's discipline forbids surgery; he was unwilling to attend a barbarian in any case. Aedemon is less snobbish but follows a theory that all illness is caused by putrefaction and can be addressed with chants and amulets, with purges, astringents and laxatives . . .' Mastarna's lip curled in contempt. 'Carried out to excess, that can be more lethal than the knife. I do on occasion conduct drilling to relieve pressure in the head –' He paused. 'But not this time.' He seemed uncomfortable. Maybe he thought I would criticise him for considering dangerous surgery on a state prisoner.

'So what happened?'

'Another practitioner was called in.'

'Cleander recommended her? Zosime. Her methods sound much less radical than skull-boring.'

'So I believe.'

'Still, you and she had a disagreement about the appropriate treatment?'

Recovering his confidence, Mastarna passed off the quarrel with Zosime as unimportant. 'There can be many approaches to ill health. All or any of them may work. Zosime was trained by my colleague, Cleander. His regime and mine are antipathetical.'

'But Zosime was not permitted to attempt her gentle regime?' Helena said.

Mastarna seemed reluctant to admit this, unaware that Zosime had told Helena she had been given the hint to abandon Veleda's care. 'It was an issue between her and the patient. Then, of course, the lady from Germany removed herself altogether.'

'Patient choice,' I commented. It was clear from Mastarna's expression he thought that kind of licence was a bad thing.

The thought crossed my mind that if Veleda had trusted Zosime and wanted to continue with her suggested gentle treatment, after her escape the priestess might have traced the female doctor to the Temple of Æsculapius. When we left Mastarna, irritated by more unsatisfactory answers from that suppurating smoothie (Helena's definition), I considered making our way home via Tiber Island. It would have meant a detour. And I reasoned that if Zosime had been willing to own up to further contact with Veleda, she would have confessed it to Helena when she came to our house yesterday. So late that afternoon, I tracked down Clemens and the soldiers on search duty; I dispatched them to do a room-by-room search of the temple and its hospital buildings. If Veleda was there, they would recognise her – or I hoped they would. I had warned them always to be aware that she might have changed her appearance. They were not to manhandle women with the rough treatment I had seen the Praetorians using, but they were to check carefully for height and eye colour, neither of which could be altered.

They did not find her. As Helena pointed out, if she ever had been at the hospital after her escape, then as soon as questions started to be asked, she would have been moved elsewhere. It was generally thought that runaways who could demonstrate they were seeking refuge from brutality were helped to disappear. If the staff sympathised with Veleda's predicament, she could have been whisked off by the same escape route.

After the search, we let it lie. I had no evidence at this stage that would justify either leaning heavily on Zosime or threatening the administrators.

It had been a busy, though mainly unproductive day. I was ready for a quiet night in, planning my next moves. This was where, on a normal enquiry, I would have welcomed a case consultation with one of the Camillus brothers. It would be a good ploy on a winter's night. We could have sat around a warm brazier munching almonds and apples, with a glass or two of table wine, and Helena would steer us towards sensible conclusions while we men tried to duck the issue . . .

No chance of that. Aelianus was in Greece – and I was about to hear very bad news about what had happened to our missing Justinus. It began when we were greeted on the threshold by Albia, in tears.

'Marcus Didius, something terrible has happened – I've been searching for hours but I can't find the dog anywhere. Nux has run away!'

XVII

'You are joking, Albia? You cannot seriously mean, not only do I have to search for a missing murder suspect, and my missing brother-in-law – but now I must waste yet more time and effort looking for a *dog*?'

'*I* cannot go; you do not let me roam outside.' That never stopped her when she wanted to buy cinnamon cakes.

Albia spent a lot of time imagining she was a princess, among whose accessories was a noble hunting hound, a role she crazily assigned to Nux; the little dog just let her get on with it. Albia loved Nux. Nux returned the favour. To the rest of us my pet was a scruffy, often stinky bundle, whose matted, multicoloured fur nobody would willingly investigate closely. Nux was friendly and full of life, but she had no pedigree. She had adopted me. She came from the streets and saw me as a soft touch. She was right, too. Nobody who had a choice would let Nux into their home. I took in the dog, and later I took in Albia, because their lives at the time were even worse than my own. Besides, in both cases, I blamed Helena. She wanted to believe she was in love with a generous person, a benefactor of the oppressed. She had willed me to do it. Both times.

'Poor Nuxie was upset when the soldiers came, Marcus Didius.'

'Have the bastards mistreated her?'

'No, but she doesn't understand why they are all in her house.'

'She'll come home of her own accord.'

'How can you be so *heartless*? The streets are wild with revellers – she will be terrified!'

Infected by Albia's agitation, both my children began wailing. Julia and Favonia, two fine little tragic actresses, were clutching Nux's favourite toys and looking piteous. Needless to say, I soon found myself promising to go out and find the lost doggie. Trusting young faces beamed at heroic Papa, expecting miracles.

Albia came with me. I think she suspected I would bunk off to a wine bar. (No, sweetheart; that was last night.) Eventually, when we had walked all the local streets and alleys, feeling like fools as we called the dog's name, I got sick of being jumped at by revellers in fancy dress who then ran off whooping. I marched to the vigiles' patrol house, and asked to see Petronius. Albia stuck with me, glaring balefully.

'Petro – I want you to tell the men to look out for my dog, please. *Don't say anything!*'

Petronius Longus eyed up the situation; saw I was being supervised; saw that this was not my own idea. He revelled in my discomfiture. 'You mean, Falco, my hard-pressed lads are to ignore all the arsonists, plotters, market-trashers, temple-defilers, robbers, rapists and heartless killers –'

'I said, don't say anything.'

'What – not even, *I hope you've come to collect your dog?*'

XVIII

Nux had been recaptured by Petronius himself. He had spotted her slinking up an alley, covered with mud and worse. Fortunately the vigiles keep a plentiful cache of water. Now washed and fluffed up prettily, my dog had established herself as a guest in the all-night galley that kept the men supplied with hot rissoles and mulsum. She had her snout in a bowl of delightfully rich broth and did not want to come home. She wagged her pert tail when she saw us. Nux did not believe in guilt.

'Oh you naughty girl; they've been spoiling you!' Albia was entranced.

None of Petro's cohort were likely to pass up the chance of showing a bright young woman around the *excubitorium*, their local outstation here in the Thirteenth District, so I had to wait with the dog while pumping engines sprayed water all over the yard and long ladders were rushed to imaginary blazes; then even the cells were opened up so Albia could look in wide-eyed at that evening's bunch of really stupid drunks who had thrown nuts at the watch.

While I waited, lolling in the doorway of Petro's office so I could keep an eye on Albia and prevent any malpractice, Petro took delight in telling me there had been no progress in the surreptitious search for Veleda. 'Your trail is cold, Falco.' I thanked him courteously.

The lads had led my foster-daughter into the depths of their equipment store, so I had to saunter over there. Of course they would be stupid to try anything on with her – but in their eyes, once presented with the opportunity, they would be stupid *not* to try. They were all ex-slaves, all with a hard attitude; they needed it to do their job. Left to themselves, they would have my teenager bemused on a pile of esparto mats in ten minutes, wooing her with a private demonstration of their ropes and fire axes – then luring her into other things.

Albia could look after herself. Still, best to avoid that situation. If

83

the alarm sounded, we did not want half the duty fire response group to be doubled up in pain after a kneeing from a lass who was far more streetwise than she looked.

I gave the girl the wink that it was time to go. Always alert, she took the hint, thanked the men sweetly, and came with me.

We had crossed the yard, waving to Petronius, who saluted us satirically. As we approached the big double-gated exit, Fusculus came in. He was Petro's best officer, increasingly rotund, cheery and totally imperturbable. '*Io*, Fusculus! How goes it with the king of nipping and foisting?' Fusculus loved lore and cant. If a criminal activity lacked technical terms to describe it, he would invent some.

Now he squinted at me, unsure whether these were real variations he ought to know; his eyes showed suspicion, though he rallied fast. 'All posy-posy on the Via Derelicta, Falco.' While Albia stared in puzzlement, I let him chatter happily. 'Is that dog yours? She's a ferrikin!'

'Right up there with the champions of fragonage,' I agreed. I was so glad to have found Nux so easily, I had stopped being sour. The way my mission was going, to have found any missing person, even a lost pet, was a bonus.

'A woozler,' nodded Fusculus approvingly. I think that was one of his coinages. But you never knew with this dictionary dabbler. Canine woozling could be traditional among totters' lurchers. Romulus might have owned a woozler, queen among beasts around the antique shepherds' folds . . . No, probably not. I bet my Nux was scared stiff of wolves. '– I'm glad I've seen you, Falco.'

'I'm honoured to bring joy to you, my dear Fusculus.'

He went with the joke. 'It's a pleasure to be in the company of a civilised man. Top-pigeonhole in life's columbarium –' Eventually even Fusculus grew tired of playing weird man's bluff. 'Dear gods, I do maunder on, don't I? What a wonk.' I raised my eyebrows as if in great surprise. His friendly face wrinkled with fun, then sobered. He was, despite the soft-sponge impression, a rather good vigiles officer. Astute and with an eye for detail. Good in a fight too. Petronius Longus knew how to pick them. 'I gather you're searching for somebody, Falco?'

'Apart from the lost dog? – Nasty but handsome barbarian lady. I believe, with a very bad headache.'

'Oh don't give up! You can work your charm on her.' Albia shot me a sharp sideways glance. Fusculus carried on blithely, as if unaware of the damage he had just done to my domestic reputation. He knew all right. 'But I don't mean the priestly pullet.'

'There's Justinus too; you know him. We work together. He's missing. My brother-in-law, the mild one.'

'Well, I'm glad it's not the vicious one.' This time Albia bridled; she seemed to have a latent admiration for Aelianus. Not all that latent sometimes. When they were together they tended to gang up like starlings.

'No, Aulus is in Greece. I've only one of them to worry about. He hasn't been seen for two days now.'

Fusculus now lowered his voice. 'I've just come from a recce. Heard word of a possible.'

I stiffened. 'Straight stuff?'

'Partially reliable. Seventh Cohort.'

I fumbled to recall the cohort delegations. 'Seventh – that's the Fourteenth district and . . . the Ninth?'

'Transtib and Circus Flam,' said Fusculus. 'What a hotchpotch – the immigrant quarter over the river, and all the public monuments around the Field of Mars. Includes,' he said, gently tapping his pug nose, 'the Saepta Julia.'

'Right! Justinus was last seen at the Saepta.'

'You have a fit then. The Seventh are indignant that a man was lifted from their patch. You know we're all taking strop from the bloody Praetorians? Pushing their way in all over the shop –'

'Hunting my barbarian.'

'So that's why they're at it!' He gave me a look. I didn't react. I was used to taking blame for other people's messes. 'Well, they hijacked a mark who could be Justinus two days ago, as you say, in the Saepta. The Seventh think the Guards must have been following him. They let him carry out his business and he seemed to be heading homeward. They jumped him just by the exit next to the Pantheon, and had him away like a flea up a barmaid's skirt.'

'Was he doing something the Palace grandees objected to?'

'Nothing at all, I heard.'

'No official explanation then?'

'Nobody asked them. Would you do it?'

I tried to look like a hero. 'If I suspected a miscarriage of justice, I might politely enquire.'

'Nuts, Falco! The Guards dragged him off, no questions asked. The Seventh keep a finger-man permanently at the Saepta, and he saw it all. Happened in the proverbial flash. Most people noticed nothing.

For the Guards,' admitted Fusculus grudgingly, 'it was professional . . .
Mind you, your fellow dropped his arm-purse in the scuffle. Now I
know who he was, I wonder if he dropped it non-accidentally.'

'A signal? Who has it?'

'The Seventh's nark. Name of Victor. You'll find him most days
lurking in the Saepta, *not* looking inconspicuous . . . Or just ask anybody there to point to him. They all know Victor. As an undercover
operative, he's rubbish. Bloody Seventh! Incompetent whosits.'

Fusculus was enjoying himself, insulting his rivals. I felt more
benign towards them. The Seventh Cohort (Transtiberina and Circus
Flaminius) might not meet the exclusive professional standards of the
glorious Fourth (Aventine and Piscina Publica), but so far they were
the only people who had given me a lead.

'Were all those words ones I need to learn to be a Roman?' Albia
asked, as we walked home. She had waited a while before she spoke,
aware that I was glumly lost in thought. The streets were dark and
fairly quiet now; I was watching out for trouble, as I always did, but
that only accounted for half of my preoccupied air.

'Definitely not, Albia. You don't want people thinking you are
eccentric.'

There was a pause. 'Is Fusculus eccentric?'

'Not him. Rock-solid character.'

'What about you?'

'I'm a total grozzle.'

Another pause. 'Oh no, Marcus Didius. I'd say you're a woozler!'
Albia decided forcefully. '. . . So are they real words?'

'Words are real if other people think they understand their
meaning.'

'What do those words mean then, Marcus Didius?'

'Albia, I have no idea.'

We walked along in silence for a while. The Aventine is packed with
temples. We had come past the great dominating bulk of Diana on the
Aventine, high on the main part of the hill, and were heading down
via Minerva, Liberty and Juno the Queen. As we then jumped down
the Stairs of Cassius with Flora, Luna and Ceres away on our right, we
were almost on the Embankment, by the Probus Bridge. Nearly
home. Before it was too late, Albia asked her real question: 'So will
you have to ask the Praetorian Guard why they arrested Quintus?'

'I shall ask, certainly. But not the Guard.'

The girl waited. When she got tired of that she demanded, 'Ask who, then?'

'The man who gave them their orders. But I won't tell you who. You don't need to know.'

For another short moment Albia was silent. She was a bright young woman, my foster-daughter from Britain. There were many things I had never explained or discussed with her, yet she had picked them up from fragments of conversation, almost from facts that Helena and I had left unsaid.

We walked maybe another five paces, sauntering to accommodate the pace of Nux, who had to sniff every inch of the pavement. Finally, Albia stated quietly, *'Anacrites!'*

Then Nux stopped dead; she looked up at us both, with her ears right back, and growled faintly. Even my dog loathed to hear the name of the Chief Spy.

XIX

I suppose it is possible that someone, some well-meaning woman with an exceptionally soft heart, for instance, might wish that the Fates could provide Anacrites with a happy life. A freedman now, he must have been born in slavery – though to me, the concept of normal birth and Anacrites was a contradiction. I'd say he was dragged howling from the belly of a sea monster, one of those horrors and portents that are regularly catalogued in the *Daily Gazette* for the delighted terror of the squeamish. It was just too upsetting to think that around about the time when that maniac emperor Caligula was sleeping with his sisters, some poor little pasty-faced seamstress in the imperial household had been forced to endure birth pangs, only to find she had inflicted Anacrites on the suffering world. Now his mother had gone wherever old palace retainers go, remembered only perhaps by a bleak memorial slab. Jupiter knows who his father was. Such records are rarely kept for slaves.

He could have been happy. If contentment had been in his nature – instead of the restless, seething envy that kept him fidgeting – Anacrites could have relaxed and enjoyed his achievements. He now held a respected high office under an emperor who seemed likely to last; he was flourishing. People will shower presents on a Chief Spy (being bribed by members of the public is one way a spy can identify who has something to hide). He owned a villa on the Bay of Neapolis that I knew of; and probably more real estate elsewhere. I had once heard that he had a lavish place on the Palatine, an old republican mansion that came with his job, though he never invited anybody there. That might have to be handed back one day, but he must have invested personally in property in Rome. How much movable treasure he had salted away was anybody's guess. I was sure it existed. He had advised my mother on investing her savings, so he knew about banking – though he did not know enough, for he had nearly afflicted her with fatal losses when the Golden Horse Bank crashed so spectacularly two years ago. Ma had escaped disaster, although that was through her own nous and bloody-mindedness, not a result of tips from him; perversely, she still believed he was a financial marvel. Or so she said. I sometimes wondered if she saw through him after all.

Anyway. A good Roman has a generous nature, so I concede that he may have had a fan club. It did not include me.

What I knew of Anacrites was that he couldn't run a harvest picnic, yet some idiot had placed him in full charge of spying in Rome. He also meddled in global intelligence. He and I had once worked together successfully, on a tax-collecting exercise in connection with the Great Census. Apart from that, he had several times deliberately put me in a position where I was nearly killed. He had terrorised my sister. He had attached himself to Ma and clung on, like a repulsive parasitic leech with a mouthful of needle teeth. When Helena was being charitable, she said he was jealous of me for my talent and for the life I led; when she was honest, she admitted he was dangerous.

He also had a secret that could damn him. I kept his secret, so far avoiding blackmail. Sifting the dirt is informers' work – but we don't always sell our nuggets straight away. I was saving up for a real emergency. Now Anacrites had Justinus, but I would aim for a solution without cashing in my precious information. One day Anacrites and I were going head to head; I knew that as well as I knew I was right-handed. The fatal day had not yet come. When it did, I would need everything I had on him.

This left me with only one tactic: I would have to be nice to the bastard.

I took Albia home, dumped the dog, tickled the wife and kissed the children. Julia and Favonia fell on Nux with happy squeals, though they failed to acknowledge that their father had fulfilled his promise like a hero. I told Helena I would have to miss dinner, left Albia to scare her with the explanation, and went out again.

I stomped tetchily back to the Probus Bridge, made my way past the Trigeminal Portico to the Vicus Tuscus, and climbed up to the old palace that way. I ate a bad pancake *en route*, which gave me indigestion; I had gobbled it, irritated at having to abandon the delights of dinner at home. By the time I reached Anacrites' office, with its unnerving smells of his clerk's discarded lunch, ink, expensive hair lotion and old antiseptic ointments, I was so overwrought at the thought of exchanging pleasantries, I was ready to sock him as I came through the door.

He was out. That made me even more angry.

89

★

I managed to find Momus. He carried out exercises for the spy network, but was also an old contact of mine. I liked to think he admired me, and that he thought much less of the Chief Spy. He had once been a slave-overseer, and I did wonder if in his past life he had encountered Anacrites or members of his family; I had asked that once, making a joke of it, but you don't get palace freedmen to give away much on the subject of their previous existence. They all pretend slavery never happened. They can't, or won't, remember it. I don't really blame them.

'Momus! Still working in Anacrites' filthy unit? Still slogging it out for that cretin we all despise?'

'Still here, Falco.' He gave me a look, from bleary eyes, their eyelashes stuck together with seepage from some long-term infection. His ills probably had a sexual origin, a hangover from his perks when organising slaves. Momus was big-bellied and bald, a slapdash slob who rarely went to the baths. He wore a tunic that had not been laundered for weeks and hard boots for kicking people. These days it was an empty threat; he had grown too lackadaisical to make the effort. He still yearned to torture the helpless, so just amused himself imagining pain. 'If anyone else accused me of working for Anacrites, I'd grab them so hard I'd pop their eyes out . . .'

There were moments I pitied Anacrites. Not only was Claudius Laeta constantly plotting to subsume the intelligence service into his own spider's web the next time secretariats were reorganised (as they were on an annual basis), but here was Momus looking on jealously, always hoping to see a big Corinthian capital fall off a column and crush the Spy, so he could inherit his post. Some of Anacrites' own field agents were light on personal loyalty as well.

'Sorry!' I said.

'You will be! What are you after?'

'Who says I'm after something, Momus?'

'You're here,' he answered. 'Given how you hate him, that's a bloody big clue, Falco! Don't tell me – you want him to release that young purple stripe he's holding?'

'Quintus Camillus Justinus, a senator's son. Well guessed. Where's the bastard put him?'

'If I knew that,' said Momus, 'I wouldn't be able to tell you, Falco.'

I could possibly disprove that statement by handing over money; Momus followed life's simple rules. 'If you really don't know, I won't bother bribing you.'

'Keep your money.' Like many corrupt men, Momus was fair.

'Well then. His office is empty. I can't even thump that pointless grubby-toed clerk he has. Save me from boiling over with frustration – I know he has a fancy house; where can I find it?'

Momus leaned back and laughed gustily. I asked him what was funny, and he said the thought of me putting on a dinner-wreath and a pleasant face to go round for an evening drink and toasted nuts with Anacrites.

XX

I didn't have to strain my face looking friendly; Anacrites was not at home.

With directions from Momus, I had found his house. It was typical of those old, expensive places that infrequently survive on the Palatine, perfectly placed with a view of the Forum just above the Vestals' House. Once owned by names that are famous in history, these houses are now used as grace-and-favour payoffs for important officials. High walls obscured much of the view inside. The house stood on just enough land to allow carefully positioned pine trees in front of any windows people might see into. Most windows had closed shutters anyway. The property looked tended and occupied, yet it lay almost in darkness. I had the impression there would never be anyone about, no sign of household slaves even by day. But it would be well supplied with staff. Some would be for security. They would react first, and ask who you were when you regained consciousness.

I managed to force my way in through double gates and knocked heavily at the front door. An obviously enormous dog began to bark somewhere indoors. Nobody answered for a long while. Then eyes looked out through a grille and a man's voice told me the master was not at home. That was probably true. Anacrites would be so surprised someone had come to visit him, he would have me dragged indoors at once.

I contemplated lurking in a gateway opposite until the Spy was brought home in a litter, then jumping out and giving him a nasty shock as he fumbled with his door-key, but it was a cold night. For all I knew he had a woman somewhere and would stay out with her. More likely, he would wind up back in his office, brooding alone – though his return there could be at any hour. Now, he could be enjoying himself at an imperial banquet; he pretended to be unobtrusive, but he liked to socialise. The thought of him nibbling snacks somewhere warm and hospitable while I tramped the dark streets on a blind errand killed my best intentions. I lost the heart to persist.

I had made an effort; before I left the Palace, I had left a cryptic note on his desk: *'Something to tell you – MDF.'* This might not set the Spy's pulse racing, but he would eventually turn up at an inconvenient moment to discover what I wanted; when I used to work with him, I had seen his curiosity boil over. The harder he pretended to be indifferent, the sooner he jumped up and rushed to investigate. It indicated lack of confidence in his own judgement. Some of us can toss an annoying note in the rubbish pail, then forget it.

No chance of that for Anacrites: Momus would also make sure he knew I had been there, and would delight in being mysterious. Anacrites always thought Momus had been put on the same corridor so he could report on him to his superiors, or to watch him for Claudius Laeta. Momus encouraged this fear by giving himself increasingly dark titles such as Inspector of Audit Inspectors. (This also upset Internal Audit, a body that assumed inflated rights and privileges under Vespasian, whose middle-class father had been a tax inspector.) Everyone but me failed to notice the salient fact: Momus was a lazy hound, whose sole aim as a government employee was to hide from notice and do absolutely nothing.

They were all paranoid at the Palace. Knowing what I did, most of them were right.

Tomorrow I would probably have too much to do; tonight there was nothing else I could achieve. From Anacrites' house, I set off for home, cursing this waste of effort and time. It was typical of the Spy to thwart me. Typical that he did it without even knowing that I was trying to find him.

It was now late. I walked quietly, keeping to the centre of the street, checking dark entrances and looking carefully down alleys as I passed. The wintry air tingled with cold. There must be snow up in the hills; sometimes ice creeps a long way down from the Alps and along the Apennines, sheeting on the edges of the lakes. Blizzards can occasionally gust as far south as Sicily. Tonight the sky was clear, making it even colder. More light filtered down from the stars high above than from lanterns, though thin cracks of lamplight showed around the edges of ill-fitting shutters. People were quiet. We had a lull in the run-up to Saturnalia, as everybody braced themselves for the real festival. Mostly I seemed to be alone.

It was too cold for burglars and street-muggers, though you can never entirely rely on that. At times I heard hurried footsteps as determined drinkers made their way to bars, or slower footfalls as they left. Family businesses that would normally show lights all evening had their folding doors pulled tight across. Furniture-makers and copper-beaters had finished work early. There were very few builders' delivery carts. This was no time to discover a leaky waterpipe or to lose half your rooftiles; nobody can get any work done over Saturnalia, and that isn't because frost ruins mortar. Most trades in construction had already closed down for an extended holiday. Other deliveries seemed equally slack. Instead I could hear ghastly a cappella drunks serenading themselves in wailing caupona choirs. It robbed me of any desire to stop for a drink.

I had been forced to take a long route. Anacrites' billet lay at the far end of the Forum, so I had to trek home around the Circus Maximus. I chose to trudge across the valley at the apsidal end, which lay closest, aiming to turn towards the river once I made the far side. Going from the Palatine to the Aventine is a real pig. The monumental racetrack completely blocks your way, and I happened to know that climbing in and walking the length between two great empty banks of seats at night was a great jape only for the young and crazy. I was far too old for dodging night-watchmen. Being somewhere I was not supposed to be no longer held a thrill. I had had to do it too many times in the normal course of my business.

Negotiating the arches of the Aqua Marcia and Aqua Appia, I was so near the Capena Gate I took the opportunity to call in on Helena's family. I could boast I was pursuing their lost person by both day and night. As I cut away from main highways on my short detour to the senator's house, which lay close to the aqueducts, I came down one dark sidestreet where I sensed trouble. I had thought I heard some-body scuttle away as I turned around the corner. Then I stumbled over a pair of legs. I jumped back, with the hairs standing up on my neck.

I was going for my knife, but paused. The figure on the ground lay too still. This did not feel like an ambush, but I made sure no accomplice rushed out of the darkness to rob me. Gingerly, I stretched out one leg and moved rags aside with a toe. The man was dead. I could see no signs of foul play. A stinking vagrant, too rank to inspect closely, had succumbed to cold and hunger, curled up in misery against the bay tree outside some householder's forbidding door.

I listened: silence. If I ran into the vigiles, I could report the corpse. Either they would cart it away routinely or the householder would discover the deceased tomorrow and inform the relevant aedile that something unpleasant needed to be cleared from a respectable street. Another pauper, another runaway slave, another inadequate had lost the fight to survive. Fleas would be hopping off him, searching for a new host, so I kept well back.

I eased my tense shoulders, listened once more, then walked on. At the end of the street I turned back. A fellow-traveller, cloaked and hooded, appeared from the far shadows, leading a donkey. Unwilling to delay longer when I could offer no help, I slipped into my own patch of shadows and moved off again without speaking.

The Camillus door porter was a long-headed loon with a tiny brain and a truculent attitude, whose main delight in life was turning away legitimate visitors. He took his time answering my knock, and then claimed nobody was in. This was traditional. He had known me for six years now, knew I was a regular visitor, knew I was married to Helena. I asked this Janus politely if he could give me some idea how many more aeons I had to endure before I gained rights of entrance. The insufferable squit played dumb.

I was just threatening to beat him so he would recognise me next time, when he was rescued by the senator. Decimus Camillus had heard the commotion and came out in his house slippers to let me in himself. This spared me from having to decide what I would tell Julia Justa and Claudia Rufina, and more importantly, what at this stage of uncertainty I would *not* tell them.

However, I relayed to the senator everything I had found out.

He said, 'That's not much!'

I said, 'Thanks for the vote of confidence.'

The Camillus family lived in the more run-down of a pair of houses, spacious by my standards but cramped when compared with most senatorial homes. The senator and I walked quickly, like conspirators, through the black and white tiled hall, where the faded dado had at last been given a repaint, this time in a rather hot orange. Unwise, I thought. I said nothing, in case the senator had chosen it. We ended up in his tiny study, overlooked by statue busts and high shelves of book canisters. Richer men keep their scrolls in ornate silverware; Decimus had wood, but it was delicately scented cedar-wood and the fittings were smart. Unlike many an aristocrat, I knew he read the scrolls. His children had grown up welcome to take and read anything they chose; Helena still came back on raids when we needed to research, and I too was allowed borrowing rights.

I cleared a space among the untidy documents, finding a stool hidden beneath the mess. 'It's a tricky situation, sir. The Praetorians were seen arresting your son, and my private information is that Anacrites – who is attached to the Guards, of course – is currently holding him. I take it no one has informed you? Well, that's illegal for starters. You have to decide whether you want to go straight to Vespasian, and make indignant protests. As the Emperor's old friend, as a member of the Senate, and just generally as the father of a free Roman citizen, you can demand an immediate audience.'

We were both silent. Decimus gazed at me. He was tall but stooped, his hair thinner and greyer than when I first knew him; both age and family troubles had taken their toll. 'I see you really want me to wait, Marcus.' He often looked as if he disagreed with my methods, but we rarely fought over it.

I had never shown him fake respect. I told him bluntly, 'I'd like to interview Anacrites first. Find out his game. If that fails, then we have the heavy option.'

'You think the man is dangerous.'

'I think I'd like to remove every hair on his body, using the slow singe method, then baste him with honey and leave him tied up by a hornets' nest.' It would be at a time of my choosing, however. 'He makes a bad enemy. Rationally, therefore, it would be best to extract Quintus without making Anacrites feel he has been publicly over-ruled.'

'Is Quintus being harmed?' His father tried not to be specific. In prison the risks were starvation, disease, buggery by fellow-prisoners, beating by the jailer, nibbling by rats, chafing of chains, fear, and professional torture.

I tried to ignore the thought that I could not find Anacrites tonight because he was in some dank cell, watching as inquisitors applied their painful techniques to Justinus. 'A senator's son? One to whom Vespasian once promised rapid social advancement? What do you think, sir?'

'I won't be happy until I have him home, Marcus.'

'Well, give me half a day. If I haven't got him back by noon, you go and raise havoc on the Palatine yourself.'

'If you do get him back, I may raise havoc anyway!'

That was how we left it. It was late now, and I could see that the senator was put out, so I did not even stay for a drink with him.

I climbed back over the Aventine, this time making my way past my mother's apartment. To my surprise, she still had a light showing, so I went up. It was possible she was entertaining Aristagoras, a ninety-year-old neighbour who had set his sights on her. If so, it was time the flirtatious old bastard tottered back to his own roost and let Ma go to bed.

I let myself in. Every Roman mother's boy is allowed to keep a latch-lifter to the place where he was brought up; every Roman mother hopes one day he will come home again.

Even with Ma's sight failing, everywhere was spotless. I moved gently through the door curtain, and straight into the kitchen. The usual frugal lamp was supplemented by a candelabrum Ma brought out for favoured visitors. Someone was sitting at the big table, with his back to me. He wore a subtle oyster-coloured tunic, decorated with grey and purple braid that must have cost more by the yard than most families had for their weekly food bill. Black hair was combed back on to his neck, where it curled in oily spikes as he hunched over a bowl from which rose wafts of Ma's delicious leek broth. There would be none for me, because the cauldron was already washed and upended on a workbench behind my mother. She herself was sitting with her hands folded on the table.

'Who's that?' squawked Ma, pretending she was unable to make out who had come in. 'Marcus! Is that you creeping about to frighten me?'

Her guest turned around quickly. He was nervous. That was good.

I stared into those pale eyes – noticing for the first time ever that while one was a watery grey as I remembered, the other was a light hazel. I let him worry for a moment, then smiled at him. I knew how to make it look sincere – and I knew that would cause him more anxiety. 'Fancy finding you here – *Io,* Anacrites!'

XXI

'*I*o, Falco!'

'I've been looking for you.' I sounded like a bailiff.

'I got your note . . .' So either the crazy workaholic had been to his office after I was there, or some frightened minion had hotfooted to him with my message. A mad thought struck that maybe he had been there all the time when I went to the Palace, hiding behind a pillar, secretly observing me. Now he had come here to worm out what I wanted before he approached me. What kind of inadequate asks your mother first? As if he knew what I was thinking, he coloured slightly.

'You've got more than my note.' I kept my tone light but ominous.

'Why don't you come in decently?' demanded Ma. That would stop me making the Spy squirm round to look at me over his shoulder. He was on a bench that was pulled tight under the table, so movement was hindered. I was standing, so I could dominate the bastard.

'I'm fine, Ma.' Anacrites was clutching his spoon like a toddler, tantalised by the half-eaten bowl of leeks. 'So you still come to visit my mother, Anacrites?'

'Anacrites is a good friend to a poor old woman.' Ma's usual note of reproof made me sound like a bad son. Since I would never over-turn this myth, I did not bother trying. 'I only wish everyone took so much trouble . . .'

'Just bringing Saturnalia greetings,' he excused himself wanly. 'Why did you want to see me, Falco?'

'You need to do some quick talking, old mucker.' The endearment was fake. I kept smiling. He started to sweat. A severe blow to the head several years ago had left Anacrites with a permanently damaged skull and a tendency to panic at times of tension. He suffered headaches and a changed personality as well. And although I had brought him unconscious to my mother to be nursed back to life (which was how he knew her, and knew her well enough to get free broth), he could never trust me to maintain the insane generosity that had once saved him.

I came into the room and moved around the table. Anacrites tried to relax. 'I've taught you nothing; never sit with your back to the door.' He dropped his spoon. I bent and kissed my mother's cheek like a good boy. She glared at me suspiciously. 'Now then, Anacrites, what do you mean by arresting Camillus Justinus?' I demanded.

'You haven't!' cried Ma. I perked up as he took the arrows. 'What's he done? He's a lovely boy!'

'Some palace mistake,' I told her.

Anacrites was glowering. 'State business,' he bluffed.

'State incompetence,' I snorted back. 'Young Camillus is a free Roman citizen. No one may lay hands on him.'

Anacrites was about to make his favourite boast, that he could do anything because he was the Chief Spy – but he paused. I was invoking the law. It was forbidden to imprison a citizen; being chained breached a free man's rights. Quintus had the right of direct appeal to Vespasian if he was manhandled, and for wrongful arrest he could claim massive compensation. Anacrites' official budget wouldn't cover that. 'This is an issue of the highest security.' His voice became haughty. 'When the barbarians threaten, sometimes liberties must be suspended.' He added insincerely, 'I don't like it any more than you do, Marcus.'

I had never allowed him to use my praenomen. Sitting in my mother's house with his sly snout in a foodbowl did not make him part of my family.

'The barbarians are cosy in their forest. One woman is your supposed "threat". She must be frightened and we know she's feeling ill. Some terrorist! Never forget,' I warned him, staring at his head suggestively, 'that I know where your weakness is.' His right hand went up; he brushed back his hair as if to protect his once-holed skull, though he must be aware I had not been referring to his wound. My mother shook her head at me reprovingly. I grinned at her; if my laddish brother had grinned like that she would have turned coy, but it failed to work in my case. I never learn. 'Now then, old fellow; you and I are old compatriots, especially after Leptis –' Leptis Magna, where Anacrites had put himself outside the law, was my big threat. 'I just warn you, Justinus' father is intending a personal appeal to his old friend Vespasian. I've managed to put off the senator until tomorrow, but if you want to keep your job, produce your captive before then.'

'Impossible –'

'Better to give him to me voluntarily.'

'Falco, I can't –'

'You are the Chief Spy; you can do anything you want.' He moved restlessly, as I enjoyed myself. Irony is the informer's friend. Spies may be devious, but they have to take themselves seriously. 'Anyway, what in the gods' name do you want him for, Anacrites?'

The Spy glanced at my mother. Ma jumped up at once, crying huffily, 'Oh I know when I'm not wanted!' She swept away into her bedroom; its door had been rather firmly closed until now. I had been hoping Ma had hidden Ganna, Veleda's acolyte, in there to stop Anacrites seeing her. It was two days since I left the young girl in Mother's charge and I needed to check up on her, but it was impossible with the Spy here.

'I wouldn't dream of upsetting your mother. I know she is discreet,' Anacrites muttered apologetically. I knew she was bound to be listening. Rushing from the room – and then getting her head against a door to eavesdrop – was an old trick. 'Junilla Tacita is the best of women. I never forget what she did for me.' I never forgot what she did for him either. And my own stupid part in it.

I swung myself over the end bench where my mother had been sitting, so I could gaze at him directly. There was a vegetable knife on the table, which I played with to worry him. 'Well, now you've upset her feelings, let us get on with it! Is arresting Camillus a misguided ploy for finding the priestess?'

'He knew her in Germany.'

'I knew her too. Why don't you arrest me? That way at least you gain something: you won't have the embarrassment of me finding her before you do.'

'Justinus had intimate relations with Veleda,' Anacrites insisted. How in Hades did he find that out?

'Five years ago, perhaps. Now he is a married man and a father, and but for your interference, he would have forgotten her. Instead,' I said heavily, 'you have rekindled any loyalty he had for the damned woman.'

'He is in love with her,' Anacrites sneered.

'No he's not. He told me at the time.'

'He lied to you.'

'He lied to himself,' I said easily. 'He was a boy, that's what boys do. Time moves on. The fact is, he did not know Veleda had been placed in that stupid "safe house", the Quadrumatus villa' – I hoped Anacrites himself had selected it. I took a chance. 'He has not contacted her –'

'You don't know that!'

So Anacrites didn't know either. 'Take my word. When your ridiculous goons arrested him, he was attempting a reconciliation with his wife.'

'His wife,' sneered Anacrites, 'who believes that her husband is leaving her to pursue his forest love.'

'She's wrong,' I replied lightly.

There was a silence. Anacrites could no longer bear to be kept from his cooling broth. I expect Ma had told him to eat it up quickly while it was good. As he tucked in, I waited. From time to time I stabbed Ma's knife on the board in front of me. Once I picked it up by the old bone handle, and aimed a throw at Anacrites, as if unconsciously.

With the issue of Justinus' release still unsettled, the Spy decided to enrage me by discussing foreign policy. I refused to play. Eventually he turned to foreign women. Ignoring his own Eastern looks and Greek forename, he had the ex-slaves' common snobbery: *he* counted as a true Roman, but all other foreigners were second-class invaders. Anacrites asked about Claudia Rufina; he knew she came from Baetica. The fool must have the innocent girl on some blacklist. 'Why is Camillus Justinus – who, as your mother said, seems a "lovely boy" – so obsessed with foreign women?'

'I wouldn't call him obsessed. He has a perfectly normal devotion to his wife's money. Common enough. Rome is full of wealthy provincials, and poor senatorial families need helpful alliances. Justinus and Claudia are close. He always liked her.' They flirted. They giggled together. He stole her from his brother... 'They are both devoted to their baby son.'

'He was fascinated by the priestess first –'

'Mars Ultor! You're the one with the obsession, Anacrites. That was absolutely normal too. Veleda was mysterious, beautiful, powerful – and he was a very young man, inexperienced, who was flattered when she took an interest. Any one of us was ready to jump on her, but he was handsome and sensitive so she chose him. What counts is that once he left Germany, Camillus Justinus believed he would never see her again.'

'Anyway, why not dabble? Barbarians can be tamed, I believe,' Anacrites suddenly suggested crudely. 'To benefit the Empire, maybe every citizen should keep one in his household.'

Albia. How did he know who lived in my household? Why had he bothered to find out? What was he implying or threatening?

★

I took a deep breath, hiding it. 'Let's get to the point, Anacrites. We are working on the same side to find Veleda.'

'So what, Falco?'

'Tomorrow the Emperor will make you surrender your prisoner. You know me and I know you; I'm saying as a friend, give him up now. His father will keep him out of trouble. Or I'll stand parole myself.'

Anacrites went rigid. Weak men are ridiculously stubborn. 'I need him.'

'What *for*?' I roared. 'He knows nothing!'

'That's not why I want him.'

My heart lurched. 'I hope you have not harmed him.'

'He is in one piece.' The Spy's lip curled. Now he was making me seem crude.

'Why then?'

'It's the kind of scheme you would come up with yourself, Falco.' Helena always said this idiot wanted to be me. The concept sickened me. 'I'm using him as my entrapment device.' At last I was forcing him to come clean. I should have known his plan would be ludicrous and unworkable. 'To lure Veleda out of hiding: Camillus is my bait.'

I lost my temper. 'If *I* can't find where you've stuck him, how is she supposed to do so? It won't work! You would need him to co-operate and her to be stupid. How are you planning to bring this off, Anacrites? *Tie Quintus to a post in a clearing by himself – then let the woman hear him bleat?'*

XXII

I was so angry, I stormed out.

There was no chance of searching the endless rooms at the Palace, but I went to both prisons, the Tullianum where foreigners under suspicion were held, and the Mammertine political cells, sometimes called the Lautumiae. Anacrites had always favoured the latter. This damp hole was where Veleda would end up on the day of the Ovation, if we caught her. For various reasons that I preferred to forget, I was no stranger there myself. Informers can find themselves in bad places. Hazard of the job. Normally it's temporary.

Hazards had brought me to grief so often in the past, the jailer even remembered me. 'I can't tell you who's in the holding cell, Falco. Security. You know the rules.'

The rules were simple: it took more money to bribe this righteous public servant than I had on me that evening.

'Can't you take credit? Let me write an IOU.'

'Sorry, tribune. Been caught out that way before. You wouldn't believe the so-called respectable people who don't know how to honour a promissory note!'

Since my banker would have left the Forum long ago, I had to give up.

I went home. It was now extremely late. When I crashed in, I heard the low murmur of soldiers' voices as the troops waited up to report to me on their latest day's searching. I knew they would have discovered nothing. We were all on a fool's errand.

Clemens and one of the others looked out as I stomped upstairs holding a pottery lamp. They thought I was drunk. I didn't care what they thought. I *needed* a drink, but I was not going to confirm their views by getting one. None of us spoke.

All my family were in bed. Even the dog, curled up in her basket, barely tolerated me patting her. She humphed and turned away, letting me know I was a disreputable stop-out. Neither of my children stirred when I looked in on them.

Always anxious if I was out so late, Helena Justina was awake. As I undressed and had a cursory wash, I gave her a stripped-down version of the night's fruitless efforts. Helena sat in bed, with her glowing hair spread over her shoulders, hugging her knees. She knew how to listen. I tried to continue grousing, refusing the lure of a spirited woman who could be wonderfully peaceful in the presence of the stressed. Her calm wore me down.

'I did my best.'

'You always do, Marcus.'

'And it's never good enough.'

'Don't denigrate yourself. You're tired, you're cold, and you had no dinner —'

'And I've a dirty great blister refusing to burst on my toe.'

'Do you want me to salve and bandage it, darling?'

'Don't fuss. I don't want tenderness and care. I'd rather suffer and look tough.'

'You're an idiot, Falco. Come to bed and get warm.'

I went to bed, intending to get warm the lively way. I fell asleep.

As I lay in her arms, I was faintly aware that Helena stayed awake long afterwards. She lay still, but her eyelashes were fluttering against my arm. Helena was thinking. If I had been less weary, I could probably have worked out where those busy thoughts were going. Then I might have worried too.

Some time next morning I groaned and retreated under the bedcover, refusing to wake yet. For a moment I believed I was back in my old bachelor apartment in Fountain Court, where I could lie in all day and nobody loved or liked me enough to notice. I cared more about myself nowadays. My habits were decent, though I still enjoyed living controversially. And sometimes, when a mission was going nowhere and I had had a punishing day, I took time off to recover. That was when solutions sometimes came.

Dimly, I had heard Helena asking me to keep an eye on the children because she was going out. Well, I generally allowed that. I was a liberal husband and I had taken on a single-minded, independent wife. She had made me happy. I accepted that keeping a happy woman required time, the regular hire of a carrying chair with bearers, and permission to go where she liked so long as no aediles arrested her. She could shop, gossip with her friends, argue with her mother, argue with *my* mother, visit galleries and public libraries. She could walk in parks or make offerings at temples – though I advised against both, since public gardens are sordid places, haunts of rapists and rabid dogs, while temples are even more disgusting dives, used by purse thieves and pimps.

As a partner I was tolerant, affectionate, loyal and house-trained. She lived on a loose rein in all respects. However, there was one area where I thought I deserved to be consulted.

I did not expect Helena Justina to lean over me exuding a fug of her favourite perfume, amidst the tinkle that I recognised belatedly as her best gold ear-rings with the three rows of tiny spindle-whorls, to kiss me goodbye – knowing I was lost to exhaustion – and then to sail off on a visit to Titus Caesar. Without saying where she was going.

Titus had had his eye on her once. She knew how I still felt about that.

Finding myself fully awake about an hour afterwards, I suddenly remembered properly that heady scent of *malabathron* and those tuneful ear-rings – not to mention the innocent way she had murmured 'I'm just going out, darling' . . .

I shot out of bed, conducted a lightning ablution and pelted downstairs.

I was formally dressed. '*Toga*, Falco?' chortled the acting centurion, Clemens, acting amazement. He was leaning in a doorway with his arms folded. '*Running* in a toga?'

'Seems like everybody's going to the Palace today!' commented Lentullus. So they all knew where Helena Justina had gone.

Lentullus was teaching my daughters to march up and down the hallway, bearing new little wooden swords. I recognised the wood (I had been saving it to make a pantry shelf, one day, in about ten years' time.) Lentullus, babysitting? Julia and Favonia dumped with a legionary? I knew what that meant too. Helena had not just taken Albia to make her look respectable, she had commandeered the new nursemaid, Galene, as well. And *that* meant, Helena Justina thought that if she saw Titus Caesar without me, she seriously needed chaperons.

Dear gods. And I had nearly let this feckless, faithless woman rub ointment on my sore toe.

XXIII

'You'll never catch her now!' sneered Clemens. 'She's long gone, Falco.'

I declared it would be a gallant gesture to escort my lady home after her royal interview. It sounded feeble, and if I did set off for the Palace I knew my doubts would grow worse with every step I took. Titus Caesar was commander of the Praetorians, and thus in control of Anacrites. Helena was right. She stood a good chance of persuading Titus to free her brother – perhaps better than her father trying to work on Vespasian. The Emperor tended to leave his subordinates to operate as they chose; he would avoid counter-manding Anacrites unless the Spy was very clearly in the wrong. Titus always boasted he enjoyed doing daily 'good deeds'; Helena would persuade him that generosity to Justinus was classic Roman virtue. Would a man of virtue (a species I distrusted) want classic repayment, however?

'Helena Justina seemed anxious, Marcus Didius. Something to do with a relative, is it?' I refused to respond to this blatant curiosity. When I demanded to know why Clemens was hanging around at home instead of out on the search for Veleda, he suggested I might need company. He didn't mean at the Palace; it seemed I was going somewhere much more unsavoury. 'Man came to see you last night, Falco. Petronius, would it be? Big stiff with a sneer on his face, said he was in the vigiles.'

Like me, and like all ex-soldiers, Petro believed the recent military intake was shoddy. Recruits were rubbish, officers were second-rate, discipline had deteriorated and now that Petronius and I were no longer defending the Empire, it was remarkable its entire political structure did not disintegrate.

I concede that in our day we had the Boudiccan Rebellion. On the other hand, once the legions got to grips with her, Queen Boudicca was eliminated without a trace. Unlike Veleda, she was not now scampering around Rome, gazing at the sacred monuments while she plotted acts of terror right at the foot of the Capitol and made us all look fools.

'You could have told me before! What's his message, Clemens?'

'Our woman has been spotted talking to vagrants.'

'Did he say who? Or where the sighting happened?'

'No, Falco – Oh, I think he mentioned it was on the streets at night.'

'Very specific!'

If I had known this, I would have got up and done something about it several hours ago. Even Helena had not seen fit to pass on this message. She knew about it though: 'Helena Justina,' said Clemens, citing her name with exaggerated respect, 'said be sure to take back-up, if you go out interviewing rough people.' He was making me sound a wimp, in a way that Helena would never have done; she knew I could look after myself. 'Helena told us you will go to find the runaways that your friend told you about, on the Via Appia.' This was Helena subtly reminding me what Petro had originally said. 'Daytime would be best, when they are all sleeping up among the tombs; you'll lose them when they come into the city scavenging at night.' I felt my mouth tighten. 'And she doesn't want you bringing any parasites or skin diseases home, so please go to a bath house afterwards. She's left your oil and strigil out.'

Now I wished I could have done this early enough to have then dropped in at Titus Caesar's boudoir when I stank of tramps and could give the imperial playboy lice.

'Anything else?' I asked Clemens in a nasty tone.

'I've ordered horses,' he responded meekly.

I hate horses. If he did not know that already, he soon worked it out.

I should have known any plan devised by an acting centurion would be a time-waster. Clemens had thought it was clever for us to leave Rome by the Ostia Gate, pick up the mounts he had arranged – which were not horses but donkeys; I could have told him that – then ride right around outside to the south of the city. It was a long way. It was the lazy way, too, and it took far longer than briskly walking across, which is what I would have done, left to myself. Only my abstraction caused by Helena being with Titus let Clemens bamboozle me into this crazy scheme.

Clemens brought a soldier who had not crossed my path and annoyed me yet, Sentius. I had asked for my old comrade Lentullus;

apparently he had to stay with the children, on Helena's orders. I thought twice about leaving my two precious ones with the clumsiest legionary Rome possessed, but Helena had a knack for choosing unexpected nursemaids. I ordered Lentullus to remove the wooden swords because I did not wish my tiny offspring to turn into frightful martial types who would be mocked by social poets: galumphing gym-frequenters, the shame of their parents, who would never acquire husbands. Lentullus just said, 'Well, they're happy and it's keeping them quiet, Falco.' I was only their father. Overruled, I left him to it.

Sentius was a tight-lipped, terse type, who viewed me with brooding suspicion. I thought he was trouble too. He was too big for a donkey and had staring eyes. He spent most of the morning eating an enormous almond pastry. Meanwhile Clemens kept digging into a bag of seeds and pine kernels, which he never offered round.

At least fretting about the wife, the children, the route, these companions, and the fact that I had had no breakfast stopped me losing my temper over the beast I was supposed to be riding. I had been given the truculent one with mange, who kept stopping dead.

It was past noon when we reached the Appian Way necropolis. The houses of the dead stretch out from the city for several miles along the ancient highway. Packed tombs line the worn cobbled road to the south between stately groups of umbrella pines. Occasionally we saw funerals taking place. There would be more cremation parties after the festival, when Saturnalia indulgence and violence had taken its toll. People usually came out here at holiday time to feast with their dead ancestors, but chilly weather and dark nights must be putting them off. Mostly the road was empty and the lines of rich men's mausoleums looked deserted.

As we slowed our mounts when we started to look for vagrants, we pulled our cloaks tighter across our chests, burying our ears in the fabric. We all became morose. It was a cold, grey day, a day for things to go badly wrong with no warning.

None of us had brought swords. I had not even thought about it, because weaponry was forbidden in the city. My automatic failure to carry had lacked forethought. Wandering between these isolated tombs in bad light was a dangerous idea. This was a situation where we were asking to get hurt.

At first it seemed that Petronius must be wrong. We saw no sign of people living rough. We had all heard stories of successful beggars who were so good at their craft they became millionaires; beggars who treated importuning as a business and worked from secret offices; beggars who went home in a litter every evening, rid themselves of their rags and filth, and slept like kings under tapestry coverlets. Perhaps all beggars were like that. Perhaps Rome, where good citizens are generous benefactors, really had no homeless people. Perhaps in winter rich, kindly widows sent all the vagrants on holiday to airy seaside villas where their hair was trimmed, their sores were cured and they listened to improving poetry until they suddenly reformed and agreed to be trained as sculptors and lyre-players . . . Romancing, Falco.

Starting near the city, we began a systematic search through the great variety of monuments. Most were close to the road, giving easy access for funerals, though space was tight and some had had to be built at a distance from the highway. Round ones were favourite but rectangles and pyramids were there too. They came in all designs, some small and low but many higher than a man or two-storeyed, with a lower chamber for the dead and an upstairs for the family to hold feasts. They were in weathered grey stone or different coloured brick. Some were in the form of ovens or pottery kilns, indicating the trades of their dead owners. Classical architecture, pilasters and porticos marked the resting places of cultural snobs; no doubt the urns that contained their burnt relics were of fine marble, carved alabaster or porphyry. Some tombs had religious decorations; others carried statues or busts of the deceased, sometimes accompanied by one of the gods.

Clemens found the first remains of a campsite. Blackened undergrowth showed where a small open-air fire had once been, probably for days on end. The ashes were cold. Broken amphora shards and a sodden old blanket with a distinctive smell convinced us this was not simply the remains of a formal cremation or of a family memorial party held outside a mausoleum. We continued searching and gradually came across more indications that Petro was correct. Locked chambers had had unpleasant rubbish deposited around them, especially in the entrance area. Ancient tombs which were no longer visited by relatives of the dead and newer ones with the doors recently broken in contained evidence of rough sleepers. Some had been used as lavatories. The worst were sordid after being used for both.

Starting to recognise the signs, we trod carefully near doorways. We held our breath before stooping to look inside open tombs. We poked at discarded clutter only with sticks, and we held the sticks at arm's length. We were wary of enclosures where rats might be foraging.

Clemens made the first sighting. He called out, and pointed to a thin figure, some way off, loping away from us. It was probably a man, dressed in patches, hunched double and carrying a bag of some sort over one shoulder. Whether or not he heard us shout, he kept going and was too far off for us to chase him.

The light faded. The day closed in. At the rate we were going we would soon need torches, which we had not brought. To cover more ground, we split up; Clemens took one side of the highway, Sentius the other. I went up ahead some distance, tethered my donkey to show where I started, then moved forward by myself on foot. Intent on searching as far as I could that day, I kept up a good pace. I glanced inside any tombs which had ready access; checked quickly around the back of all those I passed, whether open or locked; kept going steadily. Clemens and Sentius were supposed to pick up my mount in due course, then move on past me so we worked in relays.

They never caught me up. I covered the ground faster than they did. Informers learn to be meticulous without wasting time. This was no area to hang about. Just because the road and the tombs seemed deserted did not mean they really were. You need not believe in ghosts to be aware of an unseen presence. We were all being watched, undoubtedly. I was just waiting for the moment when we found out who it was and what they wanted.

At one chilly monument, a whimsical pyramid, a flight of tiled steps led down into a pitch-dark interior. I could not bring myself to step past the creaking door; irrational fear that it would slam shut behind me held me on the threshold. I had grown so nervous in that lonely place I shouted out, 'Is anybody in there?'

Nobody answered, but my call had been heard. As I turned on the steps, heading out of the tomb, I was suddenly accosted. With a wild but silent movement, someone – or something – all in white reared up above me on the mausoleum roof. This restless ghoul was hooded, jerking its wrists above its head as if jangling spectral bangles. I was so startled, my foot slipped on damp vegetation and I fell heavily. Then the figure continued its wild dance, letting out a high ghostly cry.

XXIV

The cavorting spectre slowed its rooftop dance.

'*Hoo! Hoo!* Are you alive or dead?'

'I'm bloody well not happy!' I sat up awkwardly in agony. I had twisted my ankle as I slid on the tiled steps. 'Stop jiggling about.'

'*Hoo-oo* are you?' The faint, papery voice sounded like a bat-squeak.

'Name's Falco. Who in Hades are you?'

'In Hades, out of Hades . . . Flitting bodiless and airy . . . the unburied dead.' Someone around here had read too much Virgil.

'Suit yourself.' I was in no mood for paranormal crackpots. When in pain, I tend towards the pedantic. 'Tell me, spirit, whose corpse do you represent?'

'I used to be called Zoilus.'

I closed my eyes. I was a sensible man. I had an urgent job to do. The Furies must really be bearing a grudge today, if the spiteful ones – sorry, ladies, the kindly ones – had stuck me here, talking to a ghost.

Wincing, I forced myself upright. I took a few hops to firm ground, where I tested my ankle. Somehow, the spirit of Zoilus had jumped down from the tomb; he bobbed up in front of me. He was still waiting for me to react in fright, and I still wasn't having it. Twilight had descended. By some trick he could have learned in a theatre, he seemed unearthly, wavering around me, his shifting white robes luminescent; only a pale orb that was almost without features lurked in his hood where his face should be. This ghost was light on his feet. In fact he did not seem to have any feet. He had mastered a smooth glide as if he floated several inches off the ground.

'*Hoo! Hoo!* Give me the fare for Charon!' So that was his game. I felt better for knowing. His squeaky tone was wheedling now, like any human beggar. 'Help me pay the ferryman, master.'

He had gone to more trouble with his story than most supplicants do, so I fetched out a coin and promised him the fee to cross the Styx if he would tell me whether he had seen a barbarian woman roaming friendless and solitary like him. He let out a shriek. I jumped. 'Death! Death! Bringer of death,' wailed the pallid sprite – rather pointlessly, if Zoilus was already deceased.

Could he know about the decapitation of Gratianus Scaeva? Had the murder at the Quadrumatus villa become the latest hot news among the shades in Hades? Had Scaeva's soul rushed there after his violent death, indignantly protesting? Were the bored spirits now flocking together to hear this news, all twittering with faded voices in Pluto's underworld forum – by Pluto, why was I messing about on a lonely road all day, when I could just ask this spook to help me out: get him to ask Scaeva's ghost, *Hoo-oo did you in then?*

I offered the coin. He did not take it. Whether unburied dead or simply restless, half-demented human, Zoilus darted away from me, rapidly executing that liquid glide backwards. Then he vanished. He must have jumped behind a tomb, yet it seemed as if he folded himself up and slipped into the very air, becoming bodiless and invisible. I called out. Nobody answered.

He had left me for a reason. As he slithered away into nothing, at last I encountered the runaway slaves. A scatter of them rose from the ground silently around me. I looked frantically for Clemens and Sentius, but they were nowhere. I was alone and unarmed, with dusk closing in. Zoilus had been more of an irritation than a threat; now that he was gone, I yearned for his crazy presence.

I had new companions, and I was even less happy. As the dark figures gathered in number, I remembered Petronius' sombre words of warning. If these beings could scare off a ghost, or a man who believed he was a ghost, I had reason to feel genuinely frightened.

XXV

There was no point in this errand if I now simply gave them the nod and escaped on my way. I took the initiative. I walked up to the man who looked mildest-mannered and, not getting too close, I addressed him. After a long pause while he assessed me, he agreed to talk.

The refugee I had chosen had once been a slave, trained as an architect. He had worked for a master he liked, but on the master's sudden death the heirs sold him off to a new owner, a coarse, violent bully, from whose house he had fled. The runaway was quiet, educated, spoke both Latin and Greek, presumably could read, write, calculate and draw, and had once run projects: giving instructions, controlling the finances, getting things done.

Now he was destitute and alone. I thought he carried the aura of the dying.

When I met him that evening, he was about to walk into Rome, seeking food and any available shelter. He carried a light, loosely rolled blanket. His world was desolate and secret. If he were to be apprehended and identified as a runaway slave, the finder had twenty days to return him to his master, or else be liable to prosecution for theft of another man's property: valuable property, in view of this slave's education. If a finder returned such lost property to his master, a good reward might be paid. If the finder failed to return the slave, he would be swingeingly fined.

'Can you seek refuge anywhere?'

'In a temple. Then – if, while clinging to an altar, I can persuade them to believe I was seriously ill-treated – I may be sold on to a new master.'

'With all the risks.'

'With all the risks,' he agreed, dull and defeated.

After he first ran away, he had managed well enough for a time. A vagrant who lived in a deserted building had let him share shelter, but he woke one night and the other man was trying to rape him. He escaped from that only with difficulty, and was badly beaten up. Then he struggled on his own. He begged, he searched for scraps, he slept under bridges or in doorways in the city. Beggars he met around a brazier under an aqueduct one night gave him wine, either too many swigs on an empty stomach or the liquor was doctored. They battered him senseless and stole everything he had. He had ended up naked, wounded and terrified.

Now we moved. Unwilling to stand still in one place any longer, he began restlessly walking. I followed. He kept talking in torrents, as if his story needed to be told before he vanished from life altogether. He shifted about; perhaps movement eased his aches or made him forget the pangs of hunger.

He told how he had found refuge in a public park. Two men who lived in a broken handcart under an oleander bush helped him recover and find a new tunic. I gathered they probably stole the tunic for him. Barefoot, he survived, but had lost his confidence, and came to live here outside the city, nervous that if he stayed anywhere in Rome he would be set upon while he slept. He had found occasional work hawking clothes-pegs or pies, but it was a poor living anyway, then the middleman who organised the street-tray sellers took most of the profits and, knowing their workers were desperate and outside the law, cheated them whenever possible. The refugee's wild appearance and dirty clothes, such as they were, prevented him getting other work. When he had had a stroke of luck and found some money in the street, he bought stolen goods to sell on, but was even cheated by the thieves, who had shown him attractive vases but swapped them secretly and passed him worthless bundles instead, so he lost the cash he had found and felt betrayed.

Out here, he slept up by day, then roamed in the city. At night, everywhere was more dangerous – above all, there was the risk of being arrested by the vigiles – but there was more rubbish to scavenge and less chance that some 'respectable' citizen would spot him and turn him in. Suspected runaways were hauled before the Prefect of Vigiles, their descriptions were circulated, and their old masters had the right to reclaim them. All options were bad. Once a runaway was restored to a bullying owner, harsh beatings and other cruel treatment were inevitable. If no one came forward, a runaway would become a public slave; that meant back-breaking construction work, cleaning latrines, or crawling into cramped, smoky hypocausts to clean out ashes. It could even lead to transportation to the mines. I knew about slavery in the mines. Few survived.

This man was on a downward spiral. Starvation and cold were killing him, helped by lack of joy and loss of hope. He was thin. His complexion was grey. He had a bloody cough that would take him out in months. I told him to go to the Temple of Æsculapius, but he rejected that for some reason.

'You know they look after slaves?'

'Oh they come around and tend people on the streets.' He spoke in an odd tone, as if he despised the temple's staff. Clearly he had no trust in kindness. Whatever you think of architects, he must have been rational once to have done the job for his first master. Deprivation had stopped him thinking; he could no longer help himself. It almost seemed as if he no longer wanted to.

I gave him a little money. He hesitated, proudly, then snatched it and jabbered with gratitude embarrassingly; his thanks were so excessive, I suspected him of mocking me. Then I asked him if he had seen Veleda. He said no. I could not decide whether I believed him. He offered to take me to meet other people who might know something about her. I was heading into danger with him, but once again I had to accept the offer rather than have a wasted journey.

So I let myself be taken away from the road, to rising ground where a crazy group of homeless outlaws existed in a secret world. A lolling signboard said the land belonged to owners called the Quintilii, but it was not used for farming and no buildings stood there. It was well placed to be developed into an out-of-town villa, but instead was a haven of lawlessness and destitution.

The smell hit me first. It crept across the grass, but once it caught my nostrils I could not be rid of it. Even in the open air, the stink of a dedicated tramp stops your lungs. The only stench more clinging is that of a decomposing corpse.

Men and women congregated here, though there was little to choose between them visually. They were dark, shapeless bundles, either half naked or wearing many impenetrable layers of clothing, with knotted ropes around their waists. Some were plainly mad, others purposely behaved like madmen, intending to terrify. They skulked in filthy rags, one with a half-missing lop-sided hat. Their eyes were dull, and either downcast to the ground, or staring so wildly I tried not to meet their manic gaze. One man had a pipe. He could only play one note, which he did in loathsome monotony for hours. A couple paraded in slave collars defiantly: metal neck-restraints which had been put on them to show the world that they were runaways. One dragged around a mighty bundle of clanking chains. A pair of perpetual inebriates, with loud, hoarse, raging voices, roared tuneless drinking songs to the waking stars.

As my eyes grew accustomed to that haunt of lost souls, I realised that more figures lay around their circle, completely motionless. Some had constructed cocoons to sleep in, like burial mounds. There they lurked, never stirring, giving themselves up to complete exhaustion or drunkenness on the cold ground. Some were guarded by emaciated dogs, which looked equally far gone.

My nameless companion made me sit apart on a log, while he took it upon himself to be my ambassador and went around the group, asking them about Veleda. I watched him at this task for a long time. While I sat there, trying to remain inconspicuous, from time to time someone stood up and shuffled off into the twilight. Impossible to tell whether it had anything to do with me. They could be ambling away on their own tragic business, or seeking reinforcements. I felt I was in a dreadful trap, yet I had to face it out. If Veleda really had been seen talking to one of these people, this was my only chance to find out about it.

Eventually the man I had met first came back.

'They want money.'

'They can have what I have – if they tell me what I want to know.'

'They want the money first.'

'And then they'll run away.' I made myself sound tolerant. 'Look, I realise your situation. I understand the dangers you all face, especially if you let unknown people make overtures. I promise, I have no intention of turning you in to the vigiles. Have any of your friends seen the woman?'

He tried a different ploy. 'They are frightened to talk.'

'No harm will come to them.'

'They know who you mean,' he offered, tempting me. Something about the way he spoke made me sure now that he was unreliable. He had been persuaded to plot against me. I would learn nothing. I needed to escape.

I stood up. 'Which of them has seen her, then?'

'I have to be the spokesman!' returned the ex-architect quickly. His voice rasped from his sickness and now he openly had the liar's attitude. However civilised he had once been in a previous life, he had given himself up to this circle. He lived by their rules, which were non-existent. He had lost any morals. I had no claim on the man. I never had. I had never reached him during our earlier conversation. I could not pressurise him; for that to work, people have to be afraid or covetous. This ragged creature was doomed and knew it. He possessed not the slightest shred of what makes an individual his own man. Only seeing himself as one with these other desperate souls, a faint bond indeed, gave his current existence any form. They were brutal; he, who had once fled an owner's degrading behaviour, now shared their brutality.

I sensed the others watching us. I sensed the undertow of threat.

Then all at once someone rushed me. Before I could brace myself, fists laid into me violently. I felt indignant – then very angry. I hit out, gathering myself to fight back professionally, but was felled by a great blow across the neck and shoulders from a man wielding the log I had been sitting on.

I knew they would batter me, but they had urgent business first. I lost my cloak, tunic, purse and belt before I had time to curl up and struggle. I kicked out – and that made them kick me. But my assailants were so intent on robbing me, it saved me from more serious damage. Those who did stamp or hit were hampered by others, struggling to drag the clothes off me and fighting one another for these treasures. Somebody pulled up my left arm in the air, wrenching painfully at the plain gold ring Helena bought me when I was raised to the middle classes. I clenched my fist and landed a left hook on a face. People swarmed on my legs, trying to unstrap my boots. I bucked hopelessly and twisted like a netted fish.

Abruptly the situation changed. Shouts came out of what was now darkness, over where the road must be. The whole crowd let go of me and ran, not to escape, but downhill towards the newcomers. Shrieking, they swooped off in one excited flock, like sightseers who heard a parade coming. Whoever had shouted could be heard hurriedly riding away.

The moment I was left alone, I dragged myself upright and hobbled away from the clearing on trembling legs, with my unfastened boots flapping. There was no chance of catching up with Clemens and Sentius, or whoever had been on the road. But I hoped somehow to escape. If the runaways caught me again, I faced a fatal beating.

I was alone now in this wild place. I stumbled to the road. There were no mausoleums near me. When I heard the vagrants swarming back towards me, I had only one option. I flattened myself in a shallow drainage ditch. My heart was pounding. Although it was now dark, with the complete blackness that envelops open country, I still felt convinced they would be able to see me here. Like wild creatures, they could probably sense their prey at night.

Any moment they would find me and attack me. I would die in this ditch. I thought of my children. I thought briefly of Helena, though she was always with me anyway. I hid in the ditch, wondering how long death would take.

XXVI

I was so certain of discovery, I nearly leapt to my feet and prepared to go down fighting. But the vagrants astonished me. They shuffled past on the road, in ones and twos, obviously now all hobbling into Rome. It was their normal nightly migration. I had been sure I faced trauma and terror, but they had the attention span of sparrows. Starvation and drink had frayed their brains. Once I moved out of their vision, they had forgotten me.

For a long while, I lay still. One last follower came along, running in odd starts, then pausing and muttering to himself. His language was vile. He was full of hate; it was unclear why. Obscenities poured from him fluidly and so profusely they became meaningless. It was the man with the flute. He began to play his only note, over and over. I waited with my eyes closed, feeling that his monotonous serenade was aimed directly at me. I supposed I could deal with a single opponent if I had to fight him, but the energy he put into cursing, and then blowing, was fierce.

I thought of that other flautist: the terrified young boy who discovered the body at the Quadrumatus house, the musician who would never raise his tibia to his lips again. Slaves don't only run from beatings. The flautist was well treated there, yet a fright like that could yet make him flee from home as the vagrants here had done; he was too fragile to last in this environment. I hoped he stayed whimpering in his cell.

Silence descended. Chilled and light-headed, after a terrible day with neither food nor drink, I ventured to sit up and with clumsy fingers strapped my boots properly. I felt stiff when I stood upright, but I was otherwise mobile and free. Tentatively, I set off walking. Soon I stopped taking care, but walked at a steady pace along the Via Appia. Occasionally I misplaced the road in the dark and meandered off the edge of the paving, but on the whole I found the solid surface and by now the winter stars were faint above me, telling me the way to Rome.

Eventually I thought I saw firelight. I would have made a detour to avoid a confrontation, but two things stopped me. By the light of the flames, I could see that whoever was having a picnic had set up their cauldron right next to the donkey I had left behind; he was still tethered exactly where I had positioned him as a marker for Clemens and Sentius. At this time of night on an open road any presence worried me. But I could hear women's voices, so I took a risk.

Any thought of controlling the situation collapsed as I reached the bonfire party. One of the figures seated on the ground reached out, threw something on the blaze, then the flames shot up several feet higher, turning a curious metallic shade of green. Dear gods. I had now stumbled across a pair of practising witches.

Too late. They had spied me and were calling out a cheery greeting; escape was impossible. I didn't believe in witches, but I knew how they operated. If I ran for it, they would change shape at once and soar after me on huge black wings, talons at the ready . . . I despised such lore, but by this stage I was so light-headed I was not prepared to test the truth of it.

Well done, Falco. Up to your best standard. I just hoped the worst the old mothers were up to out here was collecting herbs. Somehow I thought otherwise. Cuddled between them, this quaintly dressed couple had what was quite obviously a bucket of old bones.

The spell-mixing hags were wizened and wrinkled, though after the violence of the runaways they seemed less threatening. I apologised for disturbing them; I admitted I was unsure of coven etiquette. The old women were at once sociable and welcoming. 'Sit down! Have a bite.'

Although I was starving, nothing would make me accept a ladleful from their battered cauldron. Human ears and the testicles of unhygienic animals were not my favourite cuisine. But I sat down with them – rather abruptly; I was about to collapse. 'I'm fine, thanks. The name's Falco, by the way. I'm a private informer. What do I call you ladies?'

'Our real names, or our professional ones?' Without waiting for an answer they owned up to Dora and Delia. I didn't ask whether those decent Greek appellations were their working pseudonyms. 'We are witches,' one boasted proudly.

'He's not an idiot, Delia. He can tell that by our equipment.'

The enormous battered spoon with which they were stirring their thick black mixture was tied with a fillet of purple ribbon. Lying on the ground in the firelight I could see feathers and odd wisps of wool. A wooden figure boded ill for someone. A tiny model clay puppy, with a squelchy substance stuffed in each hollow eye socket, seemed destined for the magic broth. They had a metal disk, which bore symbols I preferred not to have deciphered. Dora was clutching a square bag made of old sacking, in which I had no doubt she kept offensive ingredients.

I forced myself to look impressed. 'Shouldn't there be three of you?'

'Daphne couldn't come out. She had to mind her grandchildren.'

'And what's in the pot?' I quavered.

'Dung and little piggies' do-dahs mainly. Marinaded for seven nights. Beetles and blood. A pinch of lizard never does any harm. We like to use a lot of mandrake root. You have to grind it very fresh. Pulling it up by moonlight can be a bit of a fiddle, but once you get the knack, it's worth it on results.'

'Scorpion? Mare's urine? *Toads?*' I quavered.

'Oh yes. You can get a good smear up with toad-spawn.'

The Emperor Augustus, that spoilsport busybody, had tried to eliminate witchcraft. Unusually, his method was to persuade court poets to portray witches behaving horrendously. Legislation by literature. Organisation by ode. Those imperial creeps, Horace and Virgil, both rushed to suck up to their emperor. Horace wrote a revolting poem about a boy who was buried up to his neck in the ground by filthy witches, beside a bowl of food he could not reach, and starved to death so his enlarged liver could be used in a love potion.

'Got a girlfriend? We can knock you up a quick philtre while our main brew simmers,' Dora offered.

'I don't go in for love potions. Why lure lovers by secret spells? I prefer women who fling themselves upon me out of heartfelt lust . . .'

'Get a lot of that, do you?' sneered Delia, though her sarcasm was mild.

Something moved close by and I started.

'That's only Zoilus – he won't hurt you.' When Dora told me, I recognised the pale shadow that had crept up close unnoticed. The ghoul was jerking his arms like wings, holding up his pallid garments on pointed fingers. The witch turned towards him and let out a cry: 'Leave us alone or I'll bake you in a curse cake! Bugger off, Zoilus!' At once, the unburied man-bat swooped off obediently.

Conversation flagged. Exhaustion had taken hold of me; I was sinking. I dared not nod off, or I might be transformed into something; it was bound to be one of the animals or birds I loathed. 'I enjoyed your green fire. Can we have another quick burst?' I asked. Maybe someone would see the light and come to rescue me.

'Oh, green fire is totally outmoded, darling. Delia only does it to calm her poor nerves. Bats' eyes, now; bats' eyes never go out of fashion. Tricky, though; ever tried making a bat keep still long enough to pull its eyes out? And bones of course.' Dora rattled her bucket. 'Bones,' she repeated thoughtfully. 'Can't get them so much nowadays. Modern cremation methods sadly don't help us, and the bereaved relatives generally break up any big bones so the ashes will fit those awful streamlined urns. Cheapskates.'

'No it's just overcrowding,' Delia said. 'They all want to save space because they're running out of shelves in the tombs, darling. Only neat little urns will fit.'

'Tragic!' agreed Dora, morosely twisting locks of her hair in her filthy fingers. The braids appeared to be wound with rags instead of the traditional snakes. I refrained from asking about it. She was bound to bemoan the impossibility of getting hold of serpents nowadays and I knew I would fail to keep a straight face.

Our firelit social gathering was ridiculous, but I never entirely lose sight of a mission. Since we were all on good terms, I asked Hecate's sisters whether they had ever come across another woman with infernal aims: I told them as much as I could about Veleda.

'Don't know her. We never mingle in society much,' pouted Delia. She had a good hooked nose, though something about it made me wonder if it was glued on for the occasion. Women dress up to go out on the razzle in their own ways . . .

Dora had the warts. She also had the second sight. 'You'll regret getting involved with that one, dearie!'

'Believe me, I already do. Well, if you do run into her, try to resist any claims of sisterhood. Don't trust her; she's trouble. Just find me and tell me.'

'Oh we will!' they assured me, insisting that they were both completely patriotic. This was like talking to a pair of elderly aunties who had been sipping at the festival wine since breakfast. They reminded me of several of mine. I had been at weddings where the conversation was much crazier than this.

'You know everyone, don't you?' I suggested. Well, they knew

Zoilus, of the unburied dead. He was hardly a social conquest to boast of. 'Have you ever come across people from the Temple of Æsculapius while you've been wandering around with your bucket of bones? I understand they go out ministering to the homeless at night.'

'That's what they call it!' Dora huffed. 'Pottering up lanes, looking for sleepers in doorways and offering them herbal infusions they don't want – A man started it, years ago, but some woman does all the work nowadays.' She went off into a private rant: 'What most people don't understand, Falco, is that when you pop into the apothecary for a purge powder, all you get is only the same as we offer – but without the benefit of incantations. They are amateurs. We're specialists. They use exactly the same ingredients. It takes mystic preparation to produce a decent medicine . . .'

This complaint went on for a long time. I needed to get away.

I asked if I could have the donkey. The witches were disappointed to learn that he was mine, but soon became anxious that my time had overrun at the hire stables and I might have to pay a penalty. Apparently they had been hoping to kill the mangy beast, flay him, and use various dried pieces in their spells; however, theft was not their style and as soon as they realised I had a legitimate claim they helped me climb into the saddle. I felt a moment of anxiety, thinking they might grope me. But I did them wrong. Delia and Dora were far too gracious to indulge, even when tempted by a man wearing only a skimpy undertunic because his other clothes had been stolen.

I offered what money I still had as a reward for their honesty, but they refused all payment.

The donkey would not budge when I told him to walk. Dora tapped him on the nose with the cauldron ladle. She uttered one word in an extremely ugly language; he whinnied and shot away so fast, I nearly catapulted off. I called breathless goodbyes as Delia cackled. The donkey had left a good pile of dung behind; Dora was engrossed in collecting it into her sack.

I clung to the reins and gripped with my knees, yearning for my lost clothes to keep me from freezing. I didn't care too much about the lack of dignity, though I admit I was showing more than is usually considered proper for a ride across town.

After his retraining with the ladle, the donkey trotted along so efficiently that soon I saw the familiar outline of the Appian Gate. The long nightmare was ending. I was going home.

XXVII

Surprisingly, by the time I walked into my house, I had encountered no further adventures. I was cold, starved, bruised, dirty, stinking and disconsolate. Normal, some would say.

Helena Justina, wearing a house-gown and with loose hair, was talking to Clemens in the hall. She looked anxious even before she saw me arrive in only my underwear. I gave her a brisk report: 'Robbed, knocked over, tramps, ghost, witches, learned absolutely nothing. *Left alone to die!*' I snarled at the centurion, who looked scared, though not scared enough.

I grabbed my washing equipment and a clean tunic, whistled up the dog, spun on my heel and went back out again. I hoped I had caused a sensation and left panic in my wake. Nux pattered along beside me, as if this was an ordinary evening walk.

I enjoyed a long steam in our nearest bath house. The facilities were basic, aimed mainly at dock workers, the stevedores who unloaded goods on the riverbank and became filthy doing it. None were around at this time of night to disturb my gloomy thoughts, so I was calmer when I returned to the changing room and found Helena waiting. She eyed me warily.

Nux had been guarding the original clean garment I brought out; Helena supplied extras. She helped dry me and pull tunics over my head. Better still, she silently handed me a bread roll stuffed with sliced sausage, which I devoured in between adding warm layers of clothing. Sitting on the bench, I then worked at my finger where the vagrants had tried to screw off my equestrian ring. They had failed to remove it, but had left my knuckle badly swollen. With spit and persistence, I managed to remove the ring before it became fatally embedded. Then I filled out my previous abbreviated story for Helena. She kicked her heels angrily against the stonework of the bench, though she could see I was unhurt and even regaining my good temper.

'Clemens and Sentius claimed they "lost" you. They say they spent a long time looking for you, Marcus. They only arrived back just before you did.' I bit my bread roll, growling. 'Chew thoroughly. There are gherkins.'

'I know how to eat.'

'And if you took advice, you might avoid indigestion.'

She was right, but I burped at her rebelliously. Then, after a moment, I went over to a fountain and drank plenty from the low gurgle of icy water. It would revive me, and help the food down. Helena watched, sitting with her long hands linked on her girdle, as dispassionate as a goddess.

There was still no one about, so we stayed there. The bald door-keeper peered in a few times, glaring at Helena for intruding in the men's dressing room. He shook the greasy money-bag that hung on his twisted belt, but when we ignored this half-hearted plea for a bribe he gave up and left us to it. We could talk here. At home, there would be endless interruptions.

I went over everything that had happened, although there is a special short version – even of the truth – that a man tells his loved one.

'No need to be worried, fruit.' Helena accepted the reassurance, but she leaned her head upon my shoulder. Her great dark eyes were closed, to hide what she thought. I nuzzled her fine, soft hair, breathing in the delicate scent of the herbs in which she washed it. I was trying to kill today's foul memories. I had shed the strange musty odours of the witches, but the rank smell of the vagrants would be with me for days; it seemed to infuse my own pores, even after fanatical oiling and scraping with my curved bone strigil.

Sometimes when Helena Justina had been frightened for my safety, she let fly with rampaging rebuke. When she was really scared, she said nothing. That was when *I* worried.

I wound my arms around her, then leaned my head back on the wall, relaxing. Helena settled against me, enjoying the relief of my return.

The doorkeeper looked in again. 'No funny business!'

He was a complete menace. We took the hint and left.

Only as we were walking slowly home, trailed by Nux who was fastidiously sniffing every kerbstone, did Helena mention Titus Caesar.

'Oh! Titus, eh?... Note that I didn't ask.'

'But he was on your mind. I know you, Marcus.' Helena kept me waiting as long as she could. I thought she was being mischievous, but she was annoyed with her princely pal. The imperial do-gooder had done no good at all for Quintus.

'Off day, was it?' I asked, all innocence.

'Don't sound so annoying!'

'Touch of a cold? His corns chafing him?'

'He was in a dismal mood. Apparently – and this is a secret – Titus and Berenice have agreed that they must part.'

'Ouch. Not the best moment to approach for a favour.'

His infatuation with the Judaean Queen was absolutely genuine. When his father became emperor, she had followed Titus to Rome, in the blissful hope that they would live together. After openly sharing quarters at the Palace long enough to affront the snobs, it seemed they had now accepted that it could never be. This was probably the worst moment to remind Titus Caesar of another young man who had fallen for a beautiful barbarian.

Heartbroken but stolidly conscientious, Titus had nonetheless heard Helena out. Then he summoned and quizzed Anacrites, while she was allowed to listen. The Spy regaled Titus with his coruscating scheme to use Justinus to entrap Veleda. On hearing this plan from Anacrites (whom I wouldn't trust to keep a pet rat), Titus reassured Helena that her brother was safe and well treated.

'So my darling, while you fumed, did Titus Caesar make Anacrites confess where the prisoner is held?'

'No,' Helena said, sounding short. 'Anacrites – patronising swine – asserts it is best if our family do not know.'

I snorted. 'So – as I asked the idiot Spy myself – how is the lovelorn Veleda to notice the handsome bait he's put out for her?'

'Oh there's a devious plan,' scoffed Helena sarcastically. 'Listen to this gem: the Praetorians have put up a personal notice in the Forum. You know the sort: *Gaius from Metapontus is hoping his friends from abroad will see this and find him at the Golden Apple in Garlic Street.*'

'Ridiculous!' I chortled. 'Everyone knows Gaius from Metapontus is a stifling bore, and his friends try to avoid him. In fact, now he's in Rome, they have all sailed off to the Maritime Alps in a boatload of fish-pickle – '

'Be serious, Marcus.'

'I am. The Golden Apple is a dump; anyone who stays there is dicing with ruin –'

Helena admitted defeat and played my game: 'While Garlic Street is well known as a thieves' kitchen, even though it's not as bad as

126

Haymakers' Lane . . . I didn't bother arguing with Anacrites. There are other ways to deal with fools. I just smiled sweetly and thanked Titus for listening to me.'

'And?'

'What would you have done, Marcus? When I left the audience, I walked down to the Forum and looked for the advertisement.'

I stopped. Nux took advantage of this to inspect a rotting half-chicken carcass in the gutter. I kissed Helena gently on the forehead, then I gazed at her with undiluted affection. No informer could want a more intelligent and trustworthy partner. I liked to think my training had played some part in her aptitude, but she gave me a stern look and I refrained from claiming credit. 'You are exceptional.'

'Anyone could do it.' Many would not have done. 'On the other hand,' Helena continued, still cruelly dismissive of the Chief Spy's stratagem, 'Veleda can have no idea she should look for a personal advertisement. She will never see it. Anyway, most Celtic tribes can't read.'

'And did you find the cunning invitation painted up?'

'Elegant lettering in dark red paint. Looks like an election poster; nobody will read the thing, Marcus. And you will hate this: Quintus is "staying with friends by the Palatine". He is the house guest of a certain Tiberius Claudius Anacrites.'

XXVIII

It was time to regroup.

Later that night Helena had a message from her father, whose interview with Vespasian had passed off in a friendly spirit. The Emperor had told him openly where his son was, and said he would be allowed to see the young prisoner. Decimus intended to visit Anacrites' house tomorrow. 'Mother can go too.'

'What about Claudia?'

'Papa and Vespasian agreed it will be better if she stays away. They don't want Claudia losing her temper with Quintus and smashing up the Spy's statue collection.'

'Anacrites collects art?'

'Cornered a niche market, apparently. Vespasian hasn't seen any, but he thinks it is rather saucy.'

'Pornography?'

'Erotic nudes, you are supposed to say, Marcus.'

'That's just typical. I bet Anacrites hasn't mentioned his rude collection to my mother!' I could tell Ma, but she would refuse to believe me.

It seemed that Vespasian was taking a benign view of the fact that in earlier years the senator's brother had been a political plotter. This dangerous past history could make a suspicious emperor regard all of the Camilli darkly. (Not only the Emperor: his advisers too. Had I not known the family well, I would myself certainly have judged them risky in the present situation.) So far, they were surviving. Even so, it might not last. I knew enough to be wary of politicians – even jolly old coves like Vespasian.

Perhaps I over-reacted, but I was afraid Justinus' connection with Veleda would cast doubts on his loyalty to Rome. That could finally crush his family. Justinus, his future once so promising after our original German escapade, was bound to be blacklisted if he showed emotional ties to the priestess. His father and brother would then be coloured politically too. None of them could expect any further social advancement.

Their disgrace might even affect me, now I was openly living with Justinus' sister. But I had been born a plebeian. I was so used to being at the bottom of the middenheap, few scandals could touch me. There were ways out of trouble for me, in any case. My work – undercover jobs that the Emperor would always need – could bleach out any grime that tried to stick to me.

Now it was urgent that I find Veleda. I wanted the kudos of beating Anacrites. Out of friendship to the Camillus family, I also wanted to show Vespasian and Titus that I was energetically assisting the state. That might just help my in-laws' position.

I had to establish whether or not the priestess had killed Gratianus Scaeva. Upon that would depend how I handled the fleeing invalid if I ever traced her. I decided to go back over the murder. The incident had led to Veleda's flight; I wanted to know much more about it.

So next morning I had another lie-in, this time planning action with Helena. It might have been a romantic occasion, but our children had managed to prise the bedroom door open, so we had two heavy toddlers jumping all over us. When the dog put her paws on the edge of the coverlet and began licking my face, I got up.

I scribbled a to-do list, which ran:

Ganna (Ma)
Zosime
Victor + Pa
Senator (lunch fixed up by Helena)
Quadrumatus house
Petro?

If I could work through that lot in one day, I would be proud of myself.

In our discussions, Helena never asked me to devise a way to set her brother free. She probably knew I thought it best if Justinus was held securely until the priestess was found. In fact, none of the Camillus family at any point suggested a rescue.

That does not mean the idea never occurred to me.

This morning, I would have the luxury of interviewing in my own home. For once, I had helpers. I sent Clemens and a couple of his lads to fetch Zosime, from the Temple of Æsculapius, and also to bring in Victor, the vigiles nark from the Saepta Julia who had seen Justinus

129

captured by the Praetorians. I told Clemens I wanted to see my father too, but he was so nosy that when he saw Victor being gathered up, he would race along to our house of his own accord.

While some legionaries – humbled by their failure to stick with me yesterday – organised those errands, Helena took a pair of the spares out for provisions. Carrying my daughter Julia, I hopped up the Hill to my mother's house.

Ma was slapping dough around in a cloud of flour, in company with Aristagoras, her neighbour. Despite his age, the papery swain was agile on his walking sticks. She brushed aside his adulation but let him into her apartment sometimes and gave him a panfried sardine to reward his faithfulness. On my arrival she always sent him packing.

'My son's here! I'll have to ask you to go.' There was no need to shelter behind me so primly but I knew better than to interfere with my mother's complicated reasoning. Aristagoras never bore me a grudge; he tottered off, with fish sauce all down his tunic. Ma's sunny social glance hardened. 'What do you want, Marcus?'

'I have brought this dear child to see her grandmama.'

'Don't expect Julia to soften me up!'

'No, Ma.' She was wrong. It never failed. Every informer should maintain a cute infant, to help him interview intractable old dames.

I hoped that Anacrites might have said more to Ma about holding Justinus, but the aggravating swine had not. I just brought down a lecture about how sad it was that the poor Spy, who had no family, would be all on his own at Saturnalia. Fortunately, Mother was sidetracked; she had learned what the girls were plotting about her gift of eye treatment.

'And what do you think?' I asked cautiously.

'I'm not having it! I don't want to be cut.'

'He'll just use a kind of needle. They gently poke the scales aside.'

Ma shuddered, with high drama.

I could have tried to persuade her, but I chickened out. My sisters had thought this up; they could deal with the obstinacy.

'What do *you* think?' Ma demanded unexpectedly, peering at me.

'It's a good idea, Ma.'

She sniffed. Still, she hated being hampered in her active, scheming life. Perhaps she would accept the operation. If it went wrong, she would blame me. She always enjoyed that.

I changed the subject, asking after the young girl I had left in her charge. Ganna had been hidden away in the back room when

Aristagoras came and was still there, so I had the chance to ask Ma in private how she was getting on with the acolyte. 'I'm knocking her into shape.' Surprise!

'You keep her in?'

'Except when we make a little trip together to a market or temple.'

'Has she said anything?'

'She fooled you plenty. There's a lot she's holding back.'

I said I thought that might be the situation, which was why I had come to interrogate Ganna now that I knew more about my case. Ma sniffed again, grabbed little Julia, and sent me in to the girl.

Veleda's acolyte looked pale and wary – perhaps from putting up with Ma, though I held back my sympathy.

Fair hair isn't everything. By daylight, I found Ganna too young and unformed to be attractive. I didn't trust her either. I must be growing old. When women gave me lies, I no longer found it exciting. I had no time or energy for game-playing of that sort. There were better games to play with somebody straightforward who was close to you. I wanted witnesses to give up their information in a pleasant voice and a direct manner, pausing at suitable moments to help me take down notes. Of course there was no chance of that.

As a neutral lead-in, I asked Ganna about any jewellery or other financial resources Veleda had. We discussed rings and necklaces, while I quietly wrote details on my note-tablet.

Without looking up, I said, 'She went straight to Zosime, but I imagine you know that, Ganna.' Then I did glance at her. Ganna twisted her hands, pretending not to understand. 'I assume there was a plan.' I kept it conversational. 'What I want from you now, please, is how did she organise her escape from the Quadrumatus house?'

'I told you, Falco –'

'You told me a load of tosh.' We were sitting in my mother's bedroom; I found it odd. In this familiar scene, with Ma's narrow bed, woollen floor rug, and the battered basket-weave chair where she sometimes nodded off in the midst of deep thoughts, I could barely bring myself to exercise tough tactics on the visitor. 'Let's be honest now, shall we? Otherwise, I shall hand you over to the Praetorian Guard. They will extract the details very quickly, believe me.'

'That man who was here the other night is with them?' Ganna demanded looking nervous.

'Anacrites? Yes. Obviously, he came because he suspects something.' Ma would never have explained that Anacrites was simply her old lodger. She liked being mysterious. 'I ask polite questions; he prefers torture.'

The young girl let out a wild, brave cry: 'I am not afraid of torture!'

'Then you are extremely foolish.' I made it matter-of-fact. Afterwards I sat and waited until terror eroded her fragile bravery.

By the time I left, I knew how the first part of the escape had been worked. An old gambit: Veleda hid in a small cart, which called daily to pick up laundry. The intention had been that Ganna would escape too. When the commotion over Scaeva's death erupted, the two women happened to be in different places in the house. Ganna said she assumed Veleda had seized her chance and hopped into the laundry cart while panic raged.

'She feared the worst? Why would she think the murder affected her?' I asked, though I half guessed the answer.

'Because of the severed head in the pool.'

'How do you know she saw it?'

Ganna looked straight at me. 'We had heard a commotion − screams and people running. Veleda went to see what had happened. She must have walked through the atrium. If she saw the young man's head, she would know at once this would be blamed on her.'

'Her reaction does seem plausible − now you have placed her in the vicinity of the crime!' Ganna was not used to interrogation; I could see she was panicking. 'From the way you spoke − ' I made it nasty − 'I could suspect you know all this for certain. So you must have seen Veleda, and discussed things, since she left the Quadrumatus house.'

'That's wrong, Falco.'

I wondered. I had never been a man who assumed all foreigners were deceitful, and their women the worst. Although plenty of provincials had tricked me, or tried to, I liked to believe other nations − taught by us − were honest and decent in their dealings. I could even pretend that outsiders beyond the Empire had their own code of ethics, a code which compared well with ours. Well, I could believe that on a good day.

Yet when Ganna gave her answers, I thought she was lying − and she was not very good at it. My work made me cynical. Plenty of people had told me tall stories, many while giving me earnest eye contact. I knew the signs.

When I first visited the Quadrumatus villa, I had inspected the remote quarters Veleda and Ganna had shared. Their rooms were a long distance from the entrance and atrium. In that sprawling house,

I doubted the two women would have heard what was happening far away in the main hallway when the murder was discovered. Even if they had, if they were frightened of the tumult, I reckoned they would have gone to investigate together. So either Ganna had then been left behind at the house deliberately – or Veleda had gone to the atrium alone. She might even have been there before the murder happened.

Why could that be? If she was visiting Gratianus Scaeva, as he relaxed on a couch in the elegant salon, with his flautist expected at any moment to entertain him with delicate music, did Scaeva know she was coming? Did they have an assignation? And if so, did the tryst go wrong? Was I to believe, after all, that Veleda did kill him?

In a house so stuffed with servants, it was impossible that nothing had been witnessed. I must have been told lies at the house too. I was starting to think that whoever could have given evidence had been silenced, presumably on orders from Quadrumatus. My planned return to the villa this afternoon was overdue.

XXIX

Victor, who acted as the Seventh Cohort's eyes in the Saepta Julia, was older than I had expected. I had thought he would be some snitch from civilian life, a double-dealing waiter or a down-at-heel clerk, not a professional. He was a pensioned-off vigiles member, bent by his early life as a slave and calloused by six hard years of fire-fighting afterwards. Thin and dismal, he was nevertheless sharpened by the training he had received. I felt his evidence would be reliable. Unfortunately, he had little to give.

He surrendered the purse Justinus had dropped when he was arrested. It contained very little money. Possibly Victor himself had raided it; I did not ask. More likely, Pa's price for Claudia's present that morning had cleaned the young man out. The present was still there: a pair of ear-rings, silver, winged figures with hairy goat legs. I would never have bought them for Helena.

Almost as soon as I sent Victor packing, Pa turned up. 'Greetings, double-dealing parent! These the baubles you sold to Quintus?'

He looked proud. 'Nice?'

'Horrible.'

'I've got a better pair – bezel-set garnets with pendant gold tassels. Want first refusal?' I liked the sound of those but even though I needed to give Helena something at Saturnalia, I declined. 'First refusal' probably meant several prospective buyers had already said no for some very good reason.

'I won't ask what exorbitant payment you screwed out of Justinus.'

'Ancient figures are at a premium. Very fashionable.'

'Who wants a leering satyr nuzzling his lover's neck? This one has no hook. How is Claudia supposed to wear it?'

'Must have slipped my attention . . . Justinus can get that fixed, no trouble.'

I wanted my father to co-operate, so I bit back my scorn. Instead I told him about Veleda's jewellery, gave him descriptive notes based on what Ganna said, and asked him to organise his colleagues at the

Saepta to keep a lookout. 'If a blonde woman with a nasty attitude offers any of this stuff around, just keep her there and fetch me quick.'

'Will I fancy her?'

'She won't fancy you. Bring this off and there's money in it.'

'I like that!' grinned Pa.

He dawdled, gawping, when Clemens brought Zosime in, but as soon as Pa heard she nursed sick slaves on Tiber Island he lost interest. Anyway, the medico was not the kind of bawdy, blowzy barmaid he liked to grapple. She was sixty, serious, and scrutinised my departing parent sadly, as if rascals were a well-known breed to her. But when Pa shamelessly asked about his haemorrhoids, she offered to recommend a doctor. 'You can have them squidged.'

'Sounds good!'

'Inspect the surgical instrument before you decide, Didius Favonius!' Over-confident as ever, Pa looked nonchalant.

'Painful?' I asked hopefully – while noticing that Zosime had a blunt sense of humour and had remembered Pa's name after I briefly introduced him. I had another good witness here – if she was willing to give.

'It's the same tool that vets use to castrate horses, in my opinion.'

Pa blenched. When he left in a hurry, Zosime sat down, but kept her cloak folded in her arms as if she did not anticipate a long stay either. Skinny and underweight, she had small hands with elderly fingers. Her face was sharp, inquisitive, patient. Thick and healthy grey hair was centrally parted on top of her head and then pulled into a clump on the back of her neck. She wore a plain gown, cord belt, openwork shoes of a workaday fashion. No jewellery. Like many ex-slaves, particularly women, who subsequently make a life for themselves, she had a contained yet competent manner. She did not push herself forward, but nor did she give way to anyone.

I reminded her of her previous interview with Helena Justina. Then I ran through what she had told Helena about visiting Veleda, diagnosing a need for rest, and being dissuaded from further visits to the house. 'I assume you treated her further when she came to the temple?'

It was a try-on. Zosime gazed at me. 'Who told you that?'

'Well, *you* didn't, that's for sure. But I'm right?'

With a hint of anger – aimed at me – Zosime sniffed. She looked like my mother poking through a basket of bad cabbages. 'She came. I did what I could for her. She left shortly afterwards.'

'Cured?'

The woman considered her answer. 'Her fever had abated. I cannot say whether it was remission or a permanent recovery.'

'If it's just a remission, how long before the trouble returns?'

'Impossible to predict.'

'Would it be serious – or fatal?'

'Again, who knows?'

'So what's wrong with her?'

'Some kind of contracted disease. Very like summer fever – in which case, you know it does kill.'

'Why would she have summer fever in December?'

'Perhaps because she is a stranger to Rome and more vulnerable to our diseases.'

'What about the headaches?'

'Just one of her symptoms. It was the underlying disease that needed curing.'

'Should I worry?'

'*Veleda* should worry,' Zosime reproved me.

She was helpful – yet she was not helping in real terms. None of this took me forwards. 'Did you like her?'

'*Like* . . .?' Zosime looked startled. 'She was a patient.'

'She was a woman, and in trouble.'

Zosime brushed aside my suggestion that Veleda had special status. 'I thought her clever and capable.'

'Capable of killing?' I asked, looking at her narrowly.

Zosime paused. 'Yes, I heard about the murder.'

'From Veleda?'

'No, she never mentioned it. Quadrumatus Labeo sent people to ask me if I had seen her, after she fled his house. They told me about it.'

'Do you believe Veleda killed Scaeva?'

'I think she could have done, if she wanted to . . . But why would she want to?'

'So, when they told you about it, why didn't you ask for her version?'

'She had already moved on.'

'Where to?'

'I cannot say.'

Could not say, or would not? I didn't push it; I had other things to ask first. I noted that 'moved on' suggested choice rather than panicked flight. 'So how long was she at your temple? And did anybody visit her?'

'Just a few days. And no one visited, not to my knowledge. But she was never treated as a prisoner while she was with us.'

So anybody could have called on her . . . Ganna, for instance. Probably not Justinus, but you never know with men who are in love with their romantic past. His parents and wife had been watching him, but any man who reaches twenty-five unscathed has learned how to dodge domestic scrutiny. 'Did she ever mention Scaeva at all?'

'No.'

This was as much hard work as moving a very large dung heap with a rather short shovel. I tried a new tack. 'Tell me about what you do at night among the vagrants. I heard you took Veleda around with you?'

'She came with me once. She wanted to see Rome. I thought it was an opportunity to test how well she had recovered.'

'See Rome? Any particular part of the city? An address?'

'Just in general, Falco. She sat on the donkey, and rode behind me while I toured the streets. I look for huddles in doorways. If there are slaves or other vagrants in difficulties I tend them there, if I can, or else take them back to the temple where we can care for them properly.'

' "Bringer of death".'

'I beg your pardon?'

I was referring to Zoilus, the ghost-man who swooped about on the Via Appia. 'Why would someone call Veleda – or you – a bringer of death?'

'For no reason –' Zosime was indignant. 'Unless he was drunk or demented.'

'The runaway slaves have seen Veleda with you –'

'Didius Falco, I am known for my charitable work. Respected and trusted. The slaves may not always accept help, but they understand the reason it is offered. I am shocked by your suggestion!'

'The other night,' I recalled, ignoring the rhetoric, 'I saw someone with a donkey approaching a man near the Capena Gate. A vagrant lying in a doorway. A dead man.'

'I go to that area,' Zosime admitted stiffly. She would not acknowledge the incident with the corpse. She had the same build as the hooded person I had seen, however. I wished now that I had waited to see what that person did when they found the body. 'If he was definitely dead, he had passed beyond our temple's help. We do arrange funerals for patients who die while they are with us on the Island, but I am discouraged from bringing home corpses.' The way she said 'discouraged' implied rows with the temple management. I could envisage Zosime as a troublesome employee. I sensed a history of conflict at the temple about her night-time good works. People there, especially her superiors who were trying to balance budgets, might disapprove of actively seeking extra patients – patients who, by definition, had no money themselves and no affectionate family or masters to weigh in with funds for treatment. 'Are you absolutely sure, Falco? Was the man you saw merely motionless, asleep –'

'Oh I know death, Zosime.'

She gave me a level stare. 'I imagine you do.'

It was not a compliment.

XXX

D istant noises intruded. Screams of delight announced that Helena's father, the senator, must have arrived and was being mobbed by my daughters. Camillus Verus understood how to be a grandfather: with uncritical love and many presents. He never knew quite what to make of Favonia, a gruff, private child who lived in her own world, but Julia, who had a more open character, had been his delight since birth. Every time he came he taught her a new letter of the alphabet. That was handy. In ten years, when she became besotted with love-poets and silly novels, I could blame him.

I let Zosime go, still feeling that she knew much more than she was telling.

It was good to see my father-in-law but we kept lunch short. He had come straight from his captive son and had yet to report on the visit to Julia Justa and Claudia.

'There's not much to say. My boys never find a problem with leisure, enforced or otherwise. The prisoner is lolling around on cushions, reading. He wants me to send Greek plays.' Justinus had had a passion for an actress once. We had all been perturbed, though compared with the mess he was in now, that seemed a normal vice. I did wonder if the current devotion to literature was a bluff, to lull the Spy into a false sense of security, but in fact all the Camilli were well-read. 'His host doesn't have much of a library. Must get bribed with other commodities . . . I didn't see Anacrites, fortunately.'

'For you?'

'For him!' growled Decimus.

'Maybe *we* should try bribing him?' Helena suggested, taking up her father's unexpectedly cynical attitude.

'No; we'll stick with the Roman virtues: patience, fortitude – and waiting for a good chance to beat him up on some dark night.'

That was supposed to be my line. It was interesting how Anacrites could so easily reduce even a decent, liberal man to a cruder morality.

*

Helena and I had plans too, and as soon as we could politely leave her father (who was enjoying his grandchildren to the extent of getting down on all fours to play elephants), we set off for the Quadrumatus villa.

'Did your father play elephants with you and your brothers, Helena?'

'Only if Mama was safely out of the house at a long meeting with the devotees of the Good Goddess.' Julia Justa supported the great female cult where men were ritually banned, and at home she kept the senator in his place. Or so he made out. Certainly his wife was a matron of the immaculate, stately kind. 'When Papa was at the Senate,' Helena then confounded me, 'Mama sometimes joined us in a romp.'

I blinked. This was hard to imagine. It showed the difference between a senator's household and the low-class home I grew up in. My mother had never had time or energy for play; she worked too hard keeping the family alive and together. My father had been one for a rough-and-tumble – but that ended abruptly when he left us.

I wondered how things worked at the Quadrumatus house. They were so rich, they probably assembled fifteen slaves just to supervise two four-year-olds throwing a beanbag around.

This sounds like daydreaming, but it could be relevant to Scaeva's death. In such a household, a young man would never be alone. Cleaners, secretaries, valets, major-domos would dog him at every step. Supposing Scaeva sought a meeting with Veleda, he would have had it among slaves bringing him snacks and drinks, water-bowls and towels, letters and invitations. Any tryst would have been watched by flower-arrangers stuffing vases with perfect winter blooms – and of course by the flute-player. If Gratianus Scaeva ever wanted a really intimate assignation, he would have had to draw attention to it by a demand for privacy.

No wonder his brother-in-law, Quadrumatus, had assured me Scaeva was so well behaved. Nobody could carry off a flirtation in such conditions. It would have driven me mad.

Perhaps Scaeva had been frustrated himself. Maybe when he called in his doctor, Mastarna, allegedly with recurrent catarrh, his sickness was really an expression of unhappiness with his love life.

'He was twenty-five!' Helena scoffed when I voiced this subtle theory. 'If he was desperate, he could have met massage girls at the baths. Or got married! Besides,' she said, 'a man like that sleeps openly with a slave girl, or several – and he doesn't think it affects his reputation one way or another.'

I gave her a look. 'Surely that depends on how good the slave girl says he is afterwards?'

'She'll just say how generous his love token was, or wasn't,' Helena disagreed. She thought of something. 'Perhaps the flute boy was his lover?'

'That would give him a reputation some would disapprove of!' But it was a good point. 'Suppose the flute boy had been Scaeva's lover; he turned up for an afternoon tootle, saw the gorgeous Veleda in his master's arms – and sliced his head off in a fit of jealous rage.'

'Is she gorgeous?' I pretended to be deaf. 'Sliced his head off with what?' Helena then asked. 'You said no weapon was found at the scene?'

'A sharp knife he used for flute-whittling?'

'Musicians in wealthy households do not have to make their own instruments, Marcus. A tiptop tibia would be purchased for him. All he would ever have to do is tune it.'

'Which is done how?' I demanded.

'By blowing a few measures to warm it with your breath. Or if it's really sharp or flat, you shorten or lengthen the pipes. Some unscrew. You adjust them to the right length, then the break can be wound with waxed thread to make the pipe airtight.'

If Helena Justina had been a plebeian, this would have told me she had once been the girlfriend of some funeral-parlour bandsman. As it was, I spared myself any jealousy and assumed she had been reading an encyclopaedia. That was also better than thinking she herself was a nymph with musical talents. I knew a girl once who played the pan-pipes. Horrendous. I dumped that one *very* quickly.

So I heard the arcane flute information calmly. Helena smiled at me. Deliberately, she failed to explain how she knew it.

When we arrived at the villa, Helena gazed around, first noting the lavish gardens then the endless indoor rooms. I could see her imagining how this luxury would have appeared to Veleda.

Her presence had got us past the door porter without trouble. I picked up with the steward and asked him bluntly which girl in the house had been Scaeva's playfellow? He said straight away it was a seamstress. He fetched her; she glanced at him for permission, but admitted she and Gratianus Scaeva had had a regular arrangement, except when she was indisposed for female reasons, when she had generally passed him on to her friend from the pot-store, but if her friend was indisposed too, the young master usually went to see the stable-hands, one of whom had a 'niece' who put herself about happily, or if she was busy, she had a willing sister who lived with the pigman –

'Thanks.' Helena was watching, so I tried to sound dour. Helena was on the verge of giggling. 'I get the picture.' A better perspective than I needed. 'Are you all upset by Scaeva's death?' They certainly were, though that seemed to be because he used to reward them decently for their services. Many a young aristocrat would not have bothered, so this showed him in a good light, and the girl rather sweetly shed a tear in his memory.

Scaeva could have dallied with Veleda because she posed a challenge, but he was far from desperate for sexual favours. Unless Veleda's golden looks had drawn him into danger, his tastes were basic. The first-choice slave girl was pretty, but inane and as common as dog dirt. She showed far too much cleavage, she had a big backside to go with it, and her conversation was tortuous. I won't say I never played around with girls like that, but I was grown up now. I became *very* grown up when Helena Justina was on observation. One thing I had learned about aristocratic girls: they were risqué – so risqué it was shocking – but only in private company. I saw it as an honour to be included, frankly.

Risking another torrent of piffle, I asked the girl if she knew anything about the afternoon when Scaeva died. 'No.' Too quick. She knew something, but had been warned to keep quiet.

Whatever she knew, the steward knew as well, but he too was lying. They both valiantly maintained that nothing odd had happened until the corpse was discovered. I then asked for another interview with the young flautist; I thought Helena, who always won the hearts of adolescent boys, might worm something out of him. Again, we were disappointed. The steward told us the flautist had upped and run off.

'Was that unexpected? He had always been well treated here?'

'Of course. This is a wonderful home. We never have people running away. Our master, a most affectionate owner, is horrified; he has had a big search organised, for the boy's own sake. He has devoted a great deal of personal time to it. The poor lad had remained in shock, terribly distressed. Quadrumatus and all the household are deeply concerned for his welfare.' I saw Helena narrowing her eyes as if she thought the degree of concern might be significant.

'No luck with the search?' I knew the answer.

'None, Falco.'

We did not meet Quadrumatus Labeo or Drusilla Gratiana. Both were in town that afternoon. But Helena, who put duty above any risk of unpleasantness, faced up to meeting the old black-clad maid, Phryne. I let her go alone.

When Helena came back, she murmured, 'Phryne was perfectly pleasant with me, Marcus. You must have lost the knack.'

'You mean she's a mean-spirited old bitch.'

Helena smiled. 'Failed to fall for your charm? All right, she is rather vinegary . . . I am sure she knows a lot more than she's told us —'

'— But she'll never reveal it on principle.'

Last time I came here, they had managed to give the impression all was openness. That story had been compacted like a mud brick. They all told the same tale. Today the careful edifice was crumbling away. Almost everyone we spoke to was patently unreliable. Perhaps the difference was that today nobody had been expecting me. No one was braced. They had lost their polish.

The steward allowed us to inspect all the relevant scenes again, so I could show Helena. He shed us, as if he was relieved to get away. A teenaged girl was deputed to escort us to the salon where the death occurred and then on to Veleda's quarters, passing the atrium as we walked to and fro. We might have picked the escort's brains — but she was apparently a new acquisition to this wonderful home, straight off the boat from Scythia and spoke no Latin.

As we took a look around the grounds outside, we commented coolly on whether it was likely such a household would buy slaves who could not communicate. Midges around the stately ornamental canals were bothering Helena, so we walked back through the topiary, towards the carriage I had hired. A man was standing beside it hopefully. 'Any chance of a lift back to Rome?' Before I could tell him to get lost, he introduced himself as Aedemon, the doctor who attended Quadrumatus Labeo. I winked at Helena, but she was already assuring him demurely that we had plenty of room for a little one to squeeze in.

Was she joking! Aedemon weighed about three hundred and sixty Roman pounds. Like many overweight men, he gave no sign of recognising that he was enormous. He hopped aboard, squeezing his bell-bottomed body through the flimsy door with a couple of sideways twists. We had to let him take one seat of the carriage, which dropped unevenly under him; we two squashed together opposite, bouncing about. But I never objected to nestling close to Helena and this was a wonderful unsought chance to interview the man.

XXXI

Aedemon was an Egyptian; he had left Alexandria twenty years before to bring his skills to bear on the putrefaction that, according to him, ran in Roman veins. I tried to look grateful as, almost uninvited, he described his history and methods. He was an empiricist; he believed all disease started in the bowels. Putrefying food created gases which invaded and poisoned the rest of the body. The only cure was purging and fasting. If purging and fasting was supposed to be the answer, it had not done much for him. He must have his tunics specially woven on a wide loom, or with several lengths joined across the body.

As this great lump made the carriage sag on its axle until the coachwork scraped the road surface, he cheerily proclaimed the Egyptian notion of bodily vessels being blocked by corrupting substances, while I tried not to imagine what would happen if his personal blockages were suddenly flushed out. Apparently you needed to use the right amulets and chants as well as medicine – so I gave fervent thanks to Mercury, god of travel, that these amenities were not in our coach.

Aedemon looked neither Eastern nor African. He had a square, dark-skinned face with lightly crinkled hair, but almost European features. His attitude had its own exotic cast. He seemed honest, and perhaps he was, yet he gave the impression he was alien and devious.

'So what brought you to the house when your patient was out?' Helena hiccuped as the carriage bounced. She was being thrown all over the place. I managed to park an arm across her and grasped the window-frame, wedging her in position.

'I had to deliver a new tincture of hellebore.'

'Quadrumatus Labeo is unhealthy?'

'He's merely rich, Helena,' I interrupted. Aedemon seemed sufficiently worldly to permit my cynical joke. 'He needs his system and his coffers flushed out on a regular basis. Rich men can't open their bowels themselves, love. They need help.'

Aedemon did give me a sophisticated smile. 'Where you would use a plate of boiled green leaves for loosening purposes, randomly selected, I give him a measured dose of an aperient, yes.'

'More scientific?' asked Helena.

'More precise.'

'More expensive,' I muttered.

'But Quadrumatus is a fit man. He has a doctor merely because he can afford one?' Helena ventured; Aedemon accepted it from her, and nodded.

Since he seemed amenable, I asked, 'Did you ever have anything to do with Scaeva?' To Aedemon's knowing lift of an eyebrow, I grinned and said frankly, 'Yes, I'm hoping that he was not strictly your patient, so you will not be bound by the Hippocratic Oath!'

'I never attended him formally, Falco. But I was once asked to examine him when Mastarna could not be contacted.'

'What did you think?'

'He had inflamed Eustachian tubes and chronic sinus blockage, which in my opinion called for detailed analysis. In my work, I search for causes.'

'Whereas Mastarna prescribes . . . ?'

'Aminean wine.' Aedemon paused, as if he was about to amplify the statement, but did not add to it.

'You disapproved?' asked Helena.

'Not at all. There is nothing wrong with Aminean wine – in moderate doses. It can cause diarrhoea, in my opinion, though its reputation is for curing that.'

'And it has no effect!' Helena scoffed. 'Our elder daughter has sore throats all the time,' she explained. 'We have tried everything.'

'Try a catmint cordial. My wife used it on all of ours. No harmful effects and a great comforter.'

'How many do you have?' Helena despised family conversations, but any minute now the shameless girl would be asking if he carried cameo portraits with him.

'Fifteen.' Either his wife, or more likely a succession of wives, really enjoyed being pregnant, or his pharmacopoeia didn't mention the benefits of alum wax when making love.

'I have heard that we could have Julia's tonsils removed,' Helena said, frowning at the thought.

'Madam, don't touch them!' Aedemon exclaimed at once. He sounded highly alarmed.

He did not expand on the warning. Helena recoiled from his

146

outburst and we were all silent for a while. The carriage was dawdling, stuck behind a heavy wagon that lumbered through the countryside about as fast as a snail who had spied his lunch ten yards ahead. The snail may have spotted the lettuce, but he wasn't very hungry yet and was gawping at the scenery.

When the chill in conversation passed, I asked whether Aedemon had been at the Quadrumatus house when Scaeva died. He said not but I sought his opinion on the manner of death.

'I welcome expert comment, Aedemon. We don't get many severed heads in domestic murders. The only one I've seen personally was the victim of a serial killer, and she had been dismembered after death, specifically for disposal. Generally in violent death, if a quarrel flares unexpectedly women are battered by husbands and boyfriends, probably with bare fists or kitchen implements; men are attacked by friends and workmates with fists, hammers and other tools, or personal knives. If loathing has brewed over a long period in the home, the method of choice tends to be poison. The wildly insane do run amok with specially obtained knives or swords, but they stab with them. And their victims are usually strangers in the street.' Aedemon was nodding. 'Is decapitation an easy way to kill someone?'

'No. A fit young man would hardly just stand there and let you hack off his head.'

'He would resist. Of course he would.'

'Violently – and there would be signs of his resistance on his body, Falco.'

'Were there any such signs with Scaeva, do you know?'

'No.' As Helena and I looked surprised, Aedemon explained that although he had not been in the house when Scaeva died, the family's doctors were sent for soon afterwards to give calming draughts – or whatever palliative they favoured – to the hysterical relatives. Poppy worked quickest, Aedemon said, though Drusilla Gratiana had been soothed with hemp by Cleander, who always had to be different. I said I preferred a stiff drink after a bad shock; Aedemon let his guard down and confessed that Drusilla consumed so much wine on a daily basis, it had little effect on her medicinally. 'Then all of us took a look at the corpse – curiosity, I'm afraid.' He was not really apologetic; in fact he looked gleeful. Doctors have their own arrogance. 'The death was, as you say, so unusual.'

'Quite.' I was still intrigued by how it happened. 'And puzzling. If you're the killer, you can't just walk up to Gratianus Scaeva while he's lounging on a couch and calmly saw through his neck. You'd have to find him asleep or unconscious – and even then you'd need to be damned quick.'

'Surely you would need to know what you were doing, too?' Helena added, wincing.

I reinforced it. 'And bring a very sharp blade for the task?'

'Extremely sharp . . .' Aedemon confirmed.

'*Surgically* sharp, perhaps?' Helena asked.

Professional caution set in fast: Aedemon pulled a face and shrugged. His mighty shoulders rose, the back of the carriage bowed outwards as he moved, then he slumped down into his rolls of fat again, to the relief of the carriage frame. The shrug was eloquent – but gurning and shrugging won't stand up in court.

'Luckily for Mastarna, he never saw his patient that day.' Watching Aedemon adopt his noncommittal face, I said, 'Or that's what he told me.' The lack of comment from Mastarna's rotund colleague continued. 'Was he summoned with the rest of you?'

Aedemon looked vague. 'I believe he must have been. I certainly saw him there when we all gathered . . .'

'Even though his patient was dead?' I demanded scornfully. 'Somebody had a high opinion of his regenerative powers!'

'Well, none of us thought he could sew the head back on to Scaeva. I dare say, the slaves were just told to fetch all the doctors quickly. But Mastarna would have to be told what had happened.'

'And that he had lost his income?' Helena dug me in the ribs. 'So what do you think of Mastarna, Aedemon?'

'A sound physician.'

'You doctors all say that about each other. Even when you're diametrical opposites in your treatments.'

'The truth. Mastarna does good work. Different patients need different cures; different people suit different specialists.'

'And what's his practice? He's Etruscan. So is that magic and herbs?'

Apparently there is a clause in the Hippocratic Oath that says no doctor shall ever criticise another. Aedemon fired up immediately: 'Oh I think Mastarna is more modern than that! Etruscan medicine of course has a long history. It may have begun with religious healing, and that in turn may have meant herb- and root-gathering, perhaps by moonlight in order to find the plants. One should never decry folk medicine; there is a lot of sense to it.'

'It certainly helps Mastarna gather in the denarii – have you seen his house?' I jibed.

A sub-clause in the Oath says that any doctor who thinks a competitor is making more money than he does, can insult him after all: 'Patients can be very gullible!' After this flash of jealousy, Aedemon recovered smoothly: 'I would classify our friend Mastarna as fascinated by theory. His school tends to diagnose using the general history of disease —'

'He's a dogmatist?' Helena asked.

Aedemon put his index fingers together and surveyed her over them as if he felt it was unhealthy for a woman to use words of more than two syllables. 'I believe so.' Since Helena was familiar with the medical schisms, he then acknowledged: 'And I am an empiricist. Our philosophical rule is, if I may say so, taking over public confidence nowadays. For very good reasons.' That was good news for laxative-sellers. I wondered if the laxative market was sponsoring the empiricist school, paying salaries for empiricist teachers and handing out free samples . . . 'I prefer to study the patient's particular symptoms, then to base my recommendations on his history, my experience and, where appropriate, analogy with similar cases.'

To me, this did not sound too different from Mastarna's approach. But Helena saw distinctions: '*You* concentrate on anatomical congestion and look to recent advances in pharmacology for treatment; *he* would be more likely to suggest surgery?' Aedemon looked startled. She carried on as if unaware he was impressed, 'I'm afraid I did upset him very much by suggesting that dogmatists approve of dissection of dead bodies. In fact Marcus and I had hoped, for selfish reasons, that as the young man's doctor Mastarna had examined Scaeva's corpse in detail. We hoped he could tell us about wounds or other significant factors that would assist us in investigating who killed the young man. Mastarna angrily informed me that post-mortem research is illegal, although he mentioned it had been carried out for a time in Alexandria.'

'Rarely.' Aedemon, the Alexandrian, was instantly dismissive. 'An anarchic, irreligious practice. I cure the living. I don't desecrate the dead.'

I saw Helena decide not to press him on whether surreptitious autopsy still took place nowadays. He wasn't going to tell us, even if he knew of it. She changed her approach: 'He had another patient too, I believe, at one point. Veleda? We know Mastarna discussed trepanation with Veleda. She was desperate to find somebody who would relieve the pressure in her skull. Did you have any views on that?'

'I never met the woman.' He was crisp. Too crisp? I did not think so; he was genuinely relieved to be able to deny involvement. Did that mean there were other subjects where his position might be more equivocal? Were our questions causing him anxiety?

We would not find out. The carriage had finally rumbled to the outskirts of the city. It lurched into the hiring stables and we all had to tumble out, Aedemon setting down one heavy limb at a time, then extracting his body from the carriage with a surprisingly lithe shuffle. As he straightened up, he was huffing alarmingly. Helena and I offered to walk with him, but he claimed he had a litter waiting nearby and was not going in our direction. Since we had not said where we were heading, either he was glad to end our interrogation because it strayed into dangerous areas – or he was just bored with our company.

XXXII

It was dark now. I walked us fast from the stables to our house. The season's misrule had begun. Barrow-wheelers and stallholders in the Transtiberina thought that meant asking women – respectable women who were promenading with their husbands – for a quickie up an alley. Helena took it in silence, but she was obviously rattled. Not as much as I was, to be put in the role of her pimp. We had hardly recovered when we were accosted by a six-foot scallywag in his sister's dress, with heavy eyeliner and rouge, and sporting a ridiculous woollen wig with yellow plaits.

'Get away from us! You look like a damned doll.'

'Oh, don't be like that, darling . . . Give us a cuddle, legate.'

'I'm not your darling, sweetheart. Compliments of the season – and take yourself off or you'll get a Saturnalia gift you won't like.'

'Spoilsport!' The burly demoiselle stopped pestering us, though not before bombarding us with festive vegetables. I threw them back, with a better aim, and he scampered away.

'I hate this festival!'

'Calm down, Marcus. It's like this in the Transtiberina all the time.'

'There must be better ways to celebrate the end of harvest and the planting of a new crop than letting slaves play dice all day and demented cabbage-sellers dress up in girls' clothes.'

'It's for children,' murmured Helena.

'What? Demanding even more presents than usual? Eating their little selves sick on cake? Learning how to put out the fire by pissing on the hearth? – O Saturn and Ops, how many burned bottoms will doctors have to treat next week? – And so much for ending quarrels and wars – there are more unnatural deaths over Saturnalia and New Year than any other working or holiday period! Merriment leads to murder.'

Helena managed to get a word in: 'Gratianus Scaeva wasn't murdered in the festival.'

'No.'

Plenty of people would have hangovers this week. Few would decide that decapitation was a reliable cure. Helena had sidetracked me neatly.

Was the timing of events at the Quadrumatus house significant? I couldn't see it. Veleda was not engaging in the spirit of misrule. She might have had the joyful feast of Saturn explained, but Roman celebrations would mean nothing to her. Did the German tribes glorify the revival of the light? Did they honour the unconquerable sun? All I knew was that those bombastic bastards loved a fight. Suspending grudges, whatever the month, was not in their character.

Veleda's gods were spirits of forest and water. She had been a priestess of the mystic presences in glades and groves. Spring and pool nymphs. They were celebrated by gifts – deposits of treasure, weapons, money – laid at sacred spots in rivers and marshes. And yes, these gods were also honoured by depositing the severed heads of enemies in water. But if there was a special season for it, other than in any time of war, I did not know when. To me, if Veleda killed Scaeva, the fact that it happened now appeared to be irrelevant.

If Scaeva's killer was somebody else, as I still thought most likely, they had hardly been overcome by the normal rages of the festival. No brooding uncle finally lost himself, driven crazy because everyone else was enjoying a good time, so he went for Scaeva. Miserable uncles, in my experience, stick it out and inflict their depression on you year after year. They never bring presents, because they 'aren't feeling quite up to it this time' (same as last year's excuse from the miser). All they are up to is swigging the best wine. They don't do anything bad enough to get themselves completely banned, though; they don't kill people.

And no disillusioned girlfriend had launched herself on Scaeva in festival jealousy; we knew the women he had dallied with accepted his attentions as a fact of life; and they liked him, at least for his generosity.

Anyway, the festival had not yet started. I could not make any of this fit . . . Well, I had a feeling I would end up being wrong, but if Saturnalia was important, it wasn't showing up on the evidence I had scraped together so far.

At home, the fun was at hand. Our two slaves, Galene and Jacinthus, had given up all attempts at work, an aspect of the festival they found greatly attractive. Legionaries were hanging green boughs everywhere. I guessed they had spent all day acquiring the foliage, cutting it to size and weaving garlands, instead of continuing the hunt for Veleda. Dinner was progressing; two of the soldiers, Gaius and Paullus, were cooking away happily, watched by our daughters. Julia was singing what I recognised, even through her half-chewed mouthful of must-cake, as a verse from the Little Mess Tin Song. Luckily it was one of the clean verses. Luckily too, Helena gave no sign of recognising the song. From evidence on their tunics and faces, both children had been tasting stuff in the kitchen all afternoon and would not want their proper food. Someone had given Favonia a *sigillarium,* one of the pointless earthenware figurines that are sold in hundreds for reasons no one can remember; she was using it as a teething device. As I entered the room, a broken piece choked her. Swift action – upending the darling with a sharp smack on the back – remedied that in time in the traditional way. Sensing terrified parents who had thought they had lost her, Sosia Favonia began screaming for more attention. The soldier Paullus remedied that, also in the traditional way: by offering her a big stuffed date. Triumphant, Sosia gobbled it with perfunctory thanks, while Julia began screaming because she hadn't been given one.

I left.

My excuse, which Helena received much too frostily I thought, was needing to see Petronius Longus about whether any civic-minded citizen had apprehended the runaway flute boy and handed him over to the vigiles. 'Seeing Petro was always on today's list.'

'Can't you do it tomorrow?'

'Could be vital. Why would the boy run away? Maybe he saw something –'

'He saw a headless body in a room full of blood, Marcus!'

'If he thinks Veleda killed the young master, he should feel perfectly safe now that she has left. I suspect he isn't only shocked by discovering the body. He is terrified by something else. This boy is a key witness.'

'Well he's a fine excuse for you!' Helena scoffed. 'Don't bother to promise me you won't stay out long.'

I did promise. I always do. I never learn. Fortunately women learn very quickly, so Helena would not be disappointed when I failed to come home.

Petro was not at the patrol house; nobody was, except the clerk. 'Give me the details, if you must, Falco – but be quick! Are you reporting him for his master? I'll need full details of the owner –'

'What for? I don't need to find the master, just the boy. He's a material witness to a homicide –'

'Was he a trained virtuoso? Exceptionally beautiful physical specimen? Did he steal the expensive flute when he ran away?'

'All you bastards care about is valuable property.'

'You get it.'

'Listen, you melonseed, he's traumatised by what he witnessed, he's a vulnerable teenager, he's lost, he's scared, and I think he can tell me something about a gory killing that has deep political overtones.'

The clerk sighed. 'So what's new? All your cases are like that. It's obvious: he saw something. Now he's scared someone may come after him – so work it out, Falco. He must have seen the killer at the scene. He knows who it is, and they either come visiting – or they even live at the house.'

That pulled me up. 'Slow down. Your job is to take shorthand notes. I'm the investigator.'

'I think like Petronius Longus, Falco. I've written up his case notes often enough.'

'All the more reason to find this boy urgently.'

'I'll do a memo tomorrow and have the lads look out.'

'Aren't you going to check if he's already in your holding cell?'

'He isn't.'

'How can you be sure?'

'I am sure,' explained the clerk meticulously, 'because the cell is empty.'

I was amazed. 'What? No arsonists or balcony-thieves? No drunks, muggers or raucous insulters of frail elderly women? Can this be Saturnalia? Whatever has happened to riot in the streets?'

'We had a bunch of house guests, Falco. I personally supervised letting them all off with a caution. In return I have a pile of promissory notes several inches high. The riot begins officially tomorrow,' said the clerk. Then he explained why he was the only person left in the station house, and why even he was about to lock up and leave. 'Tomorrow we'll need every man on the streets: no leave, no sick notes, no stopping at home with toothache *without* a sick note, and no bunking off to your grandmother's funeral for the fourth time this year. Tomorrow is mayhem, and we'll be there. Tonight, therefore, is the Fourth Cohort's Saturnalia drinks party.'

I said they would all be there tomorrow with dreadful hangovers, then – and he said, he couldn't wait around any longer, so did I want to come?

★

I should have gone straight home. I knew it. I had managed to avoid this particular event in the calendar for several years, but I was well aware of what went on. Those who attended always spent the following twelve months reminiscing about it. They would have longing looks as if they wished they could remember the best bits: what the raw recruit had innocently said to the tribune just before they both passed out and why the bill for breakages had been so high. I had been joking when I told the clerk that the troops would all be on duty tomorrow with bad heads. Most would not reappear at the patrol house for about four days, and when they turned up, ashen and trembling, it would take several hours of pep talk, stomach-settlers all round from their doctor Scythax, and a bought-in breakfast to remove the sedative effects of the stomach pills, before the situation that the innocent public know as 'on duty' could possibly occur.

I was too young for this. I had too many responsibilities. I should have run a mile from the legendary night of degeneration – but I did the same as you would have done: I let him lure me into it.

XXXIII

I was led to a large, unused warehouse. I told myself nothing could go wrong; after all, my sister – the virtuous, pompous one – was in charge of the catering.

A cohort of vigiles is about five hundred strong. Sometimes there is a shortfall, with a group on detachment to guard the corn supply at Ostia, but the Fourth had recently finished a tour of duty there. It is just like the army: on a good day, ten will be laid off with wounds (more after a large building fire, many more after a major city conflagration), twenty in the sick bay with general illnesses, and fifteen specifically unfit for duty due to conjunctivitis. The treasurer has always gone to see his mother. The tribune in charge is always present; nobody can get rid of him, whatever devious ruse they try.

The first sight to greet me, then, was Marcus Rubella, the Fourth's untrustworthy, over-ambitious cohort tribune. He was standing on a table, with his shaven head thrown back, draining the biggest double-handed goblet of wine I had ever seen. In a gathering of blacksmiths or furnace stokers, who are the world's heaviest quaffers, this would have been the final stunt of the evening, after which everyone would collapse. Normally a loner, whose men had yet to learn to like him, Rubella was just warming up in between raiding the early canapé trays. Occasions like this were when he did win the vigiles' wary respect. After a handful of quails' eggs and a few oysters, their hard man would accept some other drinking challenge, remaining vertical and apparently sober throughout. The vigiles could admire that. It deserves mention that in order to show how conscientiously he threw himself into occasions of cohort festivity, Marcus Rubella (a staid man, conscious of his dignity) was currently wearing a silly hat, winged sandals and a very short gold tunic. I noticed with a shudder that he had not shaved his legs.

Of the five hundred men who nightly patrolled the Twelfth and Thirteenth Districts, almost every one was there. The sufferers from the sick bay had bravely rallied. Even the bucket-handler with life-threatening burns from a bakery fire had been carried in on a stretcher. Someone whispered to me that he had struggled hard to last out until the party. If he died tonight, he would be smiling.

A drink found its way into my hand. I was expected to gulp it as fast as I could then have more; my elbow was jogged as encouragement. I recognised the wine as *vinum primitivum* from that night at Flora's. Then I spotted my sister Junia, red-faced and harassed as she pushed through the press. She was approaching forty and the menopause, but that hadn't stopped her pinning her hair in fat, lopsided rolls, adorning the edifice with fake rosebuds, and mincing about in her second-best stole. The effect was incongruously girlish. I felt slightly sick. 'Oh Juno, Marcus, these men are voracious – I'm never going to have enough!'

'You knew what you were taking on. You've heard Petro rhapsodising often enough.'

'I thought you and he were exaggerating as usual.'

'Not this time, sis!' Fear grew in her eyes. Grinning, I let her be dragged away by a group who were demanding their mixed platter of seafood (they knew exactly what they had signed for when the menus went round for advance orders) – what did it take to get service? they had asked four times . . . The vigiles held one party a year and were as fussy as young patricians at an expensive banquet. More so, because the vigiles paid for theirs.

When plain men who do hard jobs hold an entertainment, they like all the trimmings. Whole trees had been suspended from the rafters, until the roof space was crowded with greenery. Dropped pine needles stuck through the gaps in your bootstraps every time you took a step. Beneath the aromatic forest canopy, they had positioned enough lamps and candles to chase away the darkness of Hades. Smoke from the oil and wax was already thickening the air. Sooner or later they would set something on fire; in theory they had enough professional know-how to douse the blaze – but that assumed any of them were still sensible by then. Already they had flushed faces, gleaming with sweat from the heat and excitement. The noise level had risen high enough to cause complaints from neighbours several streets away – though if the locals had heard that this party was being planned, they had probably all left to stay with their aunties in the Sabine hills.

At one side of the room, a long table was serving as a bar. The idea was to protect Apollonius, who was penned behind it, looking unperturbed as he diligently doled out pottery cups of *primitivum* from a vast row of amphorae. The hard-bitten drinkers in the cohort had wedged themselves three deep in front of the table where they could most easily grab refills, and were set to stand there all night. Fighting fires gives men a great capacity; the vigiles were practised in working up a thirst. They had been banking contributions to the food and drink bill for the past twelve months, after which Rubella had added his customary top-up. He liked to pretend the bags of sesterces were a personal contribution, a generous thank-you to his loyal men; in fact, we all knew he fiddled the equipment budget. Still, he took the risk, and if ever the cohort was properly audited it was Rubella who would be penalised . . . Unlikely. I could see the internal auditor lapping up wine in a corner with a blissful expression that had nothing to do with discovering financial irregularities. He looked as if he had come across a crock of gold coins buried under a thorn-bush, and wasn't going to give the treasure back to its owner.

Quite a few of the vigiles were in fancy dress. They must have borrowed costumes from a third-rate theatrical troupe, the kind that drew the crowds the intellectual way: notoriety for topless actresses. The fire-fighters were sturdy ex-slaves with arms as thick as anchor cables and chin stubble a bear would be proud to own; in flimsy drapes of turquoise and saffron, the results were unspeakable. Some were throwing themselves into their feminine disguise so wholeheartedly it was sinister. Others were more restrained and had merely crammed wreaths on their greasy heads or draped themselves in strips of moth-eaten fur. Three were pretty well naked and had spent all afternoon painting one another all over with blue patterns, to look like Celts in woad – always a popular obsession in Rome. One of them had mistletoe in his hair, while a second had made himself a torque, though the 'gold' had melted and was running down over his swirly patterned chest among the curly black hairs and sweat. Attending on Rubella I saw a man dressed as a splendid five-foot carrot. His friend had come as a turnip, but had taken less trouble and didn't look so good.

Some new recruits whose mothers had sent them out cleaned up and nicely presented had used far too much crocus hair pomade. They were standing about in a perfumed little group, all very quiet. None had plucked up courage to go for a drink yet. It was their first year in the cohort and they were starting to feel overwhelmed by the promise of full-throated merriment ahead. Once they let go and began on the *primitivum*, they would be disgusting.

Women were present. None I recognised. From their dress and demeanour, it seemed unlikely they were vigiles' wives.

I was on my third beaker (though I had passed on my second to another man) when I finally spotted Petronius. He was behind the bar, helping Apollonius break off the wax bungs from a new batch of amphorae. His size and authority were helping to keep order; his only concession to fancy dress was the laurel wreath he wore. It was tied with crimson ribbons; Maia probably made it at home. Forcing my way through the press I waved a salute and mouthed '*Io!*' As soon as I could get closer, I added, 'You're in the right place!'

'Not started yet. I like to pace myself.' Even so, as there was a slight lull (comparatively), he was accepting a drink from Apollonius, whom I now saw, for the first time in all the years I had known him, holding a winecup himself.

We three stood talking cheerily, interrupted only when Junia tried to make us hand out trays of food. We pretended to help, but passed on the goodies to other people; fortunately the vigiles all have the bucket chain mentality. Petro grabbed a pie as a platter went by at eye height. 'These are not bad!'

'Maybe your sister made them,' Apollonius suggested to me; as he tried one, gravy squelched down his tunic when he misjudged the filling's consistency.

'No chance.' I knew Junia's capabilities, which were a legend in my family. 'She cooks a mean gristle turnover and her stodge polenta will fill holes in wall plaster . . . these are way out of Junia's class.' Nostalgia washed over me. 'Cassius' bakery, I'd say. Fountain Court.'

Cassius had been my neighbour and regular loaf-supplier in earlier, dreamier, more impoverished days. Petronius raised his eyes to heaven, and leaned in to refill my beaker fast. He knew I was about to hark back sentimentally. I had reached the stage of automatic swallowing, at about the level where I could reminisce without weeping. This would be a little before I began to expound theories that the Roman Empire was no longer what it used to be, nor would it ever be again thanks to the ignorance of the bovine populace and the lassitude of the governing aristocracy . . .

'The barbarians are at the gates!' Petro's apt exclamation startled me. He and I had been friends for a long time but even so he rarely read my mind to that extent. However, he was merely reacting to a lad who had come up to whisper that there was a bit of a problem on the door with some gatecrashers. The lad could have informed Rubella, but in view of the tribune's lurid Mercury get-up, he had wisely decided his chances of promotion were best preserved by reporting the débâcle to Petronius. Marcus Rubella took himself extremely seriously. If he donned fancy dress to be one of the lads, he expected the lads to keep this honour to themselves and not lure him into an unscripted public appearance looking like a tipsy transvestite. For their part, the vigiles despised the public, but still thought the public had done nothing quite bad enough to warrant seeing Rubella's hairy legs.

Leaving Apollonius to it, Petro and I set off through the mayhem. By now everyone was boasting and belching in established groups, but they let us push past if we shoved at their hot bodies hard enough. It took some time to force a passage, so when we finally arrived at the doorway, we found that Fusculus had the situation in hand. He had got rid of most of the troublemakers by telling them about 'a bloody big get-together over in Lobster Street'. The last couple, who were too drunk to take in what he had said, were being dragged away backwards by determined troopers. You may think only idiots would try to invade a vigiles celebration without tickets. You would be right. They were idiots – and I had met them before.

'Falco!' It took me a moment to identify where the bleary salutation came from, and then to remember the man responsible. His greeting filled me with foreboding. 'We want to party with you.' Oh dear. The cohort supper was hardly the exotic function Ermanus had invited me to the other day, but my eager friends from the German community had probably been drinking and fornicating for the past two nights. They were way beyond exercising judgement when they spotted a party. Had they not stumbled upon the vigiles' venue first, they were out of it enough to crash a grannies' sewing circle if the lamplight attracted them.

Ermanus and one of his large pals had gone limp in the arms of their vigiles captors, but only as a preliminary to bursting free so they could try again to rush the door. Fusculus and Petro were ready for that trick and just leaned on them, attempting to avoid physical damage. Suddenly they gave a concerted heave and threw the two gatecrashers back at the vigiles bouncers. Since one of those was Sergius, the squad's torture and beatings specialist, I shook my head sadly, warning the two Germans to give in and go away while they still had unbroken legs to take them and possessed the will to live.

Ermanus refused to take the hint. He was struggling like a bullock that had smelt blood on the altar, mainly fired up by his eagerness to discuss life and love with me. He and his friend were deeply and desperately drunk. They were now teetering on the brink of uncon-sciousness; if they did pass out, they would probably never come round again. It was better if they stayed on their feet and kept going until kindly Nature let their brains recover a little. 'Falco! – Friend!'

I wanted to escape. Petronius glanced at me and winced. He knew the score. If I did try to converse with these bonny boys it would be as difficult as wading knee deep through wet quicksand, and as pointless. They could barely remember anything for longer than three seconds. I was ready to wave goodbye, knowing that my exit was bound to result in vile curses that I was an unfriendly bastard. Then Ermanus, who could see my lack of community spirit, came up with bleary words that he knew were bound to hold my interest, 'The old fellows are going to get her, you know!'

I stopped. 'How's that, Ermanus?'

'The old fellows . . .' He wandered off into some befogged world of his own. 'Did I mention the old fellows. Falco?'

'You did, my friend.'

'They know. They know he's keeping bait . . . bait for the one we never mention. Old fellows. Going to get her. Going to get her with the bait. Clever old fellows . . . Going to get the bait.'

'Oy, oy!' muttered Petro, aware that this sounded like trouble and guessing what it could be about.

'How's that, Ermanus?' I asked, as firmly as I could.

My drunken soulmate beamed at me admiringly. 'Falco! . . . Can't tell you.'

'Oh go on,' I cooed at him, like a bad lover trying to persuade some winsome girl to take her clothes off. I dared not look at Petronius Longus or Fusculus. 'Give me a thrill, Ermanus. What are the old ones planning?'

'Go to his house. Grab her fancyman . . . She's one of ours. We should have her . . .' He passed out. Sergius and the other vigiles laid him carefully on the pavement in a neat position. Seeing this, his intoxicated German companion took the easy option and subsided with a peaceful little groan. He was lined up next to Ermanus. I bent down to check they were breathing. A gassy miasma of three-day-old wine fumes confirmed it. I reeled back, shielding my face.

Straightening, I sought Petro's gaze. This was a disaster. The last thing I wanted was those elderly social misfits carrying off a raid to capture Quintus, so they could use him to entice Veleda to them. The mere attempt was bad news for Rome. Bad news for them too, if they got on the wrong side of Anacrites.

I cursed. 'Petro, Nero's retired German guards have been unsettled since Galba disbanded them. Now they're planning a revival we can do without. If they ever get to control Veleda it will be a nightmare. If they bring this off, we're stuffed. I have to stop them.'

'You'd better get to the Spy's house before the Germans do,' said Petro, with rather too much interest. I wondered how much *he* had drunk this evening. More than I had thought, apparently. He looked ready to rob temples of their treasure, if some bright maniac suggested a romp. He was up for anything.

All the same, I had no intention of stopping him, if he was prepared to help. We thought about the situation. That is, we both thought – but only for the time it took to close our eyes and groan.

'You could just warn Anacrites.'

'And party on? How civic.' I knew 'civic' would be an insult to Lucius Petronius.

'Rats. Are you on, Falco?' You might imagine I had to beg him for help, but Petronius, that madcap adventurer, had already decided to involve himself and was checking with me.

I buried my surprise. 'Pity to miss the lads' night out.'

'Oh don't worry.' Petro appeared to do calculations. 'The night is young. We should have time to manage it: gather some back-up, break into the Spy's house, grab Camillus, hide him somewhere private – and still get back to the party before the wine runs out.'

XXXIV

Anacrites' house lay in darkness, apparently. A small group of us assembled silently in the street below the Palatine and surveyed the area. For once the Forum, behind us, seemed deserted. No lights showed at the house; the gates were barred. It looked the same as when I came here before in the dead of night, though that was no guarantee that the Spy was away from home. It was not essential that he should be out tonight, but it would be safer for us if he was.

As we walked here, I had suggested we devise a plan. No need: Petronius Longus already had one. My friend was a man of surprises. I could not even remember telling him that Anacrites was holding Justinus, and why, but Petro seemed to know all about it. When I had discussed this situation with the senator and with Helena, I had decided it was easiest to leave Justinus here, reading endless Greek plays. But since the German guards were trying to lift the prisoner, Petronius saw there was a need for radical action. His plan was: pretend the vigiles had smelt smoke at the house, cry 'Fire!', then use their legal authority to march in, conduct a search for human life, find Justinus, and haul him out.

'Rescue him like a house fire victim. Simple, eh?'

'You mean, thought up by a simpleton? It will never work.'

'Watch us,' said Petro, giving the nod to Fusculus and whistling a signal to some of his lads.

The first stage went as I expected. A couple of vigiles were given a leg-up; they climbed over the high wall, taking a covered lantern they had conveniently brought with them. Deep-throated guard dogs started barking almost at once, then abruptly fell silent. The lads returned unscathed and said they had set fire to some piles of leaves. I was puzzled by what happened next: Petronius let out a loud whistle, of the kind the watch use to signal for reinforcements when they detect a fire during their night rounds. Instead of rushing straight to the front door, we just settled unobtrusively into the shadows and kept quiet. 'Aren't we going in?'

'Shut up, Falco!'

After a while, when nothing happened, Petro muttered derisively then whistled again, louder. This time we heard swiftly marching feet. A regular bunch of vigiles came around a corner, heading for our location. Petronius stepped out into the light of their flares. 'Oh officers, I am so glad to see you. I was just on my way to a party with a group of friends when we smelt smoke. It seems to be coming from that house over there . . .'

'Have you roused the household, sir?'

'Can't get any answer. They probably think we are drunks causing trouble and don't realise we are public-spirited citizens.'

'Well, thank you. You can leave it to us now. Don't worry, sir; we'll soon have it sorted –'

Petronius grinned to me. 'Sixth Cohort. We're in their jurisdiction. There are rules, you know, Falco.' In fact I knew he was not fond of the Sixth and would cheerfully implicate them in what was to follow, rather than his own cohort – just in case things went wrong. The men he had spoken to knew exactly who he was. Somehow he had persuaded the gullible Sixth to do him a favour.

Loud bangs on the door produced household slaves, whose protests that there was nothing wrong were brushed aside in the usual kindly vigiles manner – that is, the slaves were knocked to the ground, kicked into submission, and pinned down on suspicion of being arsonists. The Sixth then rushed inside to search the building, as fire–fighters were entitled to do whenever the alarm was sounded. The household slaves were now going nuts, perhaps because they realised this would entail the customary 'check on valuables'; they may have feared that afterwards there would not be quite so many valuables in their master's possession as he had owned when the fire started. The slaves knew Anacrites would blame them for any losses and they knew how spiteful he could be.

By now there really was a fire. Apparently when Petro's men kindled a damp pile of leaves for a false alarm, it led to shutters blazing and showers of sparks in roof spaces, all in a matter of minutes. Perhaps they had been over-enthusiastic, Petronius commented gravely. At any rate, Anacrites' house was now filled with thick smoke. Heavily equipped members of the Sixth Cohort were running around with the buckets, ropes and grapplers they always carried. With commendable speed, their siphon engine turned up in the street; any owner of property would be overjoyed to receive such a fast response to his emergency – a privilege few actually receive. But we were in the Palatine and Circus Maximus sector, where many buildings are state-owned and even private houses tend to belong to men who know the Emperor personally. A cart laden with esparto mats also appeared – so laden it could hardly teeter along.

'It's almost as if the Sixth were expecting this fire!' I muttered. Petronius shot me a reproving look.

Then – was there a signal? – he grabbed my arm and ran towards the house. I followed as he dashed into the building. The smoke was real, choking us as we plunged down corridors. Ahead of us the vigiles had thrown open doors to check rooms for occupants. Coughing slaves were still being hustled out past us by members of the Sixth, who were shouting at them loudly and pushing them around; it was a tactic to subdue and confuse them. We ran on. Nobody interfered with us.

We passed through formal areas with subdued black and gold paint, a tiny courtyard with a bubbling fountain, then suddenly we were among decadent rooms in the interior, with frescos depicting intertwined couples and threesomes that would not be out of place in a brothel. We reached a narrow passageway where a vigilis was battering at a locked door while being harassed by two large baying dogs; the man kicked at them in annoyance, then hurled a hatchet at the door panels hard enough to split the wood and gain a purchase. Petronius picked up a small marble-topped table and bashed a bigger hole with that. Splintered panels soon gave way to shouldering.

The room contained a collection of the kind of art men keep in private salons with the door locked 'so as not to excite the slaves'. Thereby making secret pornography sessions more exciting for themselves.

There was less smoke in this part of the house. When we turned away in disgust from the art collection, we were able to see the young man who opened a door further down the corridor and looked out to investigate the commotion. It was Camillus Justinus.

At once, according to the vigiles' rules of duty, he was taken hold of roughly, knocked semi-conscious when he protested, then passed from hand to hand in a businesslike fashion as far as the exterior of the building where – in circumstances that were later vague – he vanished.

Among many rumours that circulated later about the fire at the Chief Spy's house, I did hear that when the Sixth Cohort came to pack up their esparto mats for return to their patrol house, they discovered someone had filched the mat-cart. And it was said, no doubt mischievously, that towards the end of the incident, Anacrites turned up and was outraged to receive a report on the damage to his house from a man dressed as a five-foot carrot. The Sixth Cohort indignantly denied all knowledge of this vegetable.

Anacrites became so angry he ordered the carrot's arrest, but it made a quick getaway when everyone was busy confronting the arrival of a suspicious group of elderly men, thought to be of German nationality, who tried to break into the Spy's house at the back, even though the Spy was standing right there at the front. The tribune of the Sixth (an officer who had been drawn to the scene by an urgent report that a VIP was apoplectic) soothed things down, and passed off the Germans' assault as a stupid escapade carried out by over-enthusiastic seasonal revellers. He ordered the bewhiskered Rhineland relics to be put in the lock-up until they sobered up. Unfortunately, when Anacrites went along next morning intending to interrogate them, someone had misunderstood the tribune's orders and released them without charge into the care of younger relatives who just happened to turn up offering to keep the old fellows out of further trouble. Sad really, everyone agreed. Ancient citizens with previously unspotted reputations for imperial service, letting themselves down by having one flagon too many . . . When Anacrites tried to find them, it was said they had all gone home to Germany for a late winter holiday.

And where was his prisoner? No idea who you are talking about, insisted the Sixth Cohort. We handed back all the slaves we found and made sure we got a receipt.

Safe. Safe and hidden.

XXXV

Anacrites' pathetic brain must be churning like a waterwheel after a thunderstorm. His first jump on the night of the fire was obvious: it did not take him long to work out that any scam involving the vigiles must relate to me and my friend Petronius. Faster than we expected, he tracked down the Fourth Cohort's party, which by then was riotous. Marcus Rubella had somehow remained sober enough to curb his antagonistic instincts when Anacrites turned up, supported by some Praetorian Guards. After all, Rubella's known ambition was to join the Guards himself. Though by now unable to speak, Rubella gravely waved them in to search the place as best they could. This would not be easy. Many of the Fourth Cohort were lying on the ground for a rest; some were upright but flopping over in all directions like weeds in the sun, others were standing rigid in their boots and offering to fight their own shadows. The Praetorians were impressed by these wild scenes; they soon forgot their orders and joined in the conviviality. I tipped Junia the wink to give them whatever they wanted.

'Anything but my body!' she giggled. I shivered at this fantastical thought.

Anacrites marched around on his own, staring at faces. Among the intoxicated this is not best practice. Several vigiles offered to floor him, furious at his attitude. Everyone he asked swore that Petronius and I had been there all night. He soon stopped asking; he was not stupid.

The atmosphere had deteriorated, to the bemusement of my brother-in-law Gaius Baebius, who never had any sense and who had turned up with his three-year-old son, aiming to wait around eating free pies until Junia needed an escort home. She had other ideas, insofar as her thinking processes still worked. Although Junia always claimed she never drank, she had reached a happy point where she saw no reason ever to leave the party (a situation Gaius may have foreseen, if he knew her better than I thought). I wanted her to leave. She was showing signs of becoming more belligerent than any of the woozy men around her, and it took the form of shouting out remarks about Anacrites and our mother which the Spy would consider slanderous. Ma would not be too pleased either. She was the important one. I wondered if killing your forty-year-old daughter would still count as infanticide.

Meanwhile some of the green boughs in the roof had been set on fire by the strings of lights. Little Marcus Baebius, who could hear none of the tumult so he was less frightened than he might have been, sat gazing around at the magical scene, and was the first to raise the alarm, delightedly pointing out to his father the flames in the dry pine boughs.

'I say!' exclaimed Gaius loudly. The vigiles' response was sillier than their fire-fighting manual orders. Of those who noticed, most took the traditional public service view that any action was the responsibility of somebody else. Some raised winecups and cheered.

'A little child is in danger!' Junia screamed, wobbling on her feet.

This only elicited guffaws of 'How many vigiles does it take to put out a fire?' To which the standard answer is: four hundred and ninety-nine to give the orders and one to piss on the blaze. Then a spark landed on Rubella, so he finally weighed in. He rounded up a group to drag out the burning branches to the street where they would only burn down houses, not the warehouse that had been so expensively hired with cash from the entertainment kitty.

When people rushed outside to watch the bonfire, a space cleared and Anacrites stumbled upon Petronius and me. He squeezed his expensive tunic through a tightly knotted group that included the man dressed as a turnip, whose friends were holding him down and pouring cups of wine into him (through his topknot of leaves) as if it was some kind of dangerous dare. Barely aware of what they were up to, the furious Spy elbowed them aside. 'I'm looking for you two!' He got no sense out of us. We were far too drunk, sitting on a platform, with our arms around each other's necks, singing meaningless hymns, while Apollonius the waiter hopelessly begged us to go home.

Anacrites was then nearly knocked face down by the man dressed as a turnip. This crackpot was bumping the Spy from behind while his companions feebly tried to restrain him. His costume was sewn on a frame of heavy wooden hoops. The Spy was picking up bruises every time he got belted. We saw that Anacrites was about to remonstrate. 'We in the Fourth Cohort know how to give a turnip a good time!' burbled Petro, with an infectious burp; he collapsed into giggles.

Safely distracted, the Spy turned back, furious with us now. I raised my arm as if to make a declaration, forgot what I had intended, then lay down and pretended I'd passed out cold.

Anacrites let out a hiss of disgust. Fortunately the fighting turnip had been dragged away by friends. Doing his best to assemble the Praetorians he came with, Anacrites made a censorious exit. Reviving, we watched his departure with cold eyes. We now knew that where most people spend their evenings with a bowl of nuts while warming their feet on the dog, or at least warming their feet on the wife, he went into a secret room alone and gloated over a statue of a naked hermaphrodite displaying its wares as if fascinated by its own array of mixed organs. The disconcerting bisexual in his private cabinet was surrounded by shelves of vases; they were painted with scenes of group sex – thrusting lovers in action, piled up in triples and quadruples like limpets, while sinister bystanders watched these antics salaciously through half-open doors.

Anacrites also owned the biggest statue group of the ripe god Pan copulating with a goat on heat that I had ever seen. And I am the son of an antique-dealer.

We transferred Camillus Justinus to a safe house as soon as it was safe. Petronius had let him come to the party first because there wasn't time to secure him while we were dodging Anacrites; it let us read him a stern lecture on playing dead before we installed him in our secret apartment. Justinus hated Anacrites; he promised to behave. Good behaviour had become a fluid concept. It was no joke getting the silly beggar up six flights of stairs to his hideaway, and there were difficult scenes when we reached the top. Only those who have tried putting to bed a man-sized, extremely drunken turnip will appreciate what Petro and I went through.

Afterwards, we two sat out on the balcony together for a while, calming down and contemplating Rome. The night was still and very cold but we had been heated by manipulating Quintus upstairs. A few faint stars appeared and disappeared through fast-moving clouds. The breeze was chilly on our faces as we breathed hard and let our hearts slow after our exertions. We shared an old stone bench and absorbed the night sounds.

From streets below came the last bursts of Saturnalia revelry, but most homes were dark and silent now. A few carts were making late night deliveries, though all commerce had slacked off for the festival period, when schools and the courts were in recess and most trades closed down. When wheels did trundle along a street, the sounds carried the more clearly because the normal background racket was absent tonight. Closer to hand, dry leaves scratched on pantiles as they bowled across surrounding roofs. Other noises came to us from far across the city. Mule hooves and dog barks. The lazy *tonkle-tonk* of rigging equipment on ships moored beside the Emporium. A gust of cheering from a fight under the arches. The occasional scream of a raucous woman pretending to resist sexual advances, amidst cackles of encouragement from her ribald friends.

Petro and I were without wine for once. There had been plenty of times when we carried on carousing on this balcony all night, but we were grown up now. Or so we said, and so Maia and Helena hoped. I thought there was a still a chance we might end up picking the locks at Petro's apartment as we used to do back in the old days, when his wife, Arria Silvia, had locked him out and I had to help him gain admittance in search of a bed. That was on nights when we didn't just fall over and lie in the street . . .

Somewhere in the city below must be Veleda. Did she sleep, tossing and moaning in fever? Or in the city of her enemies was she plagued by wakefulness, dreading the moment when her gods or ours would reveal her destiny? She had come from the endless forests, where a self-sufficient loner could ride for days without human contact, to this teeming place where nobody was ever more than ten feet away from other people, even if a wall stood in between. Here in Rome, whether a hovel or a palace was sheltering her, both luxury and poverty would be her close neighbours. Even outside the mad period of Saturnalia, noise and contention dominated. Some people had everything; many had not enough to live as they wanted; a few simply had nothing. Their struggles to live created what we who were born here called our city's character. We were all either grappling for improvement or striving to hold on, lest what we had – and with it any chance of happiness – should slip away. It was hard work and involved failure and despair for far too many, but to us, this was civilisation.

Veleda had once tried to destroy it. Maybe if the old German guards had managed to find her and control her as a figurehead, she could have tried again. Maybe she did not need them, but would try to defeat us by herself.

'What would we do, Lucius, if the barbarians really were at the gates?'

'They will be.' Lucius Petronius Longus had a morose streak. 'Not in our day, not in our children's day, but they will come.'

'And then?'

'Either run away or fight. Alternatively,' suggested Petro, sounding like a lad again, and interested in any dangerous concept: 'you become one of the barbarians!'

I thought about that. 'You wouldn't like it. You're too staid.'

'Speak for yourself, Falco.'

We remained there a while longer, with our arms crossed against the cold, listening and watching. Around us our city slumbered, except where desperate souls slunk through its shadows on unspeakable errands, or the last few fearless party-goers were making their way home shrieking – if they could only remember where home was. Petronius, who had lost two of his children to fatal disease, seemed despondent; I knew he never forgot them but Saturnalia, the damned family festival, was when he remembered Silvana and Tadia most keenly. December is never my favourite month either, but I was riding it out. It comes; if you manage to endure it without killing yourself, January follows.

Petronius and I knew how to pace ourselves, and not only with wine. Endeavour and action also have moments of high energy and recovery. We took some rest, here on the balcony of a decrepit apartment which held so many memories. This was a lonely place, a sordid place, a noisy, half-derelict, heartbreaking location – several blocks of filthy tenements around a clutch of cheating neighbourhood shops, a place where free men learned that freedom only counts if you have money, and where people who saw that they would never become citizens totally lost hope. But in this backstreet byway a man who lay low could be ignored by the world. That was our hope for Justinus. We had stashed our treasure as discreetly as we could.

I stood up, working my spine stiffly. It was time to go. Petronius stretched his long legs, kicking against the baluster with the great hard toes of his heavy boots. Since I paid the rent on this bolthole, I stood aside with a host's polite gesture to let him leave first through the wonky folding doors that led to the dreary interior. On his feet, Petronius had a last awkward stretch of his shoulders, then persuaded his tired limbs to move.

I stopped him. A sound had caught my attention, somewhere in the tangle of filthy alleys that twisted together like drab wool skeins in an old basket, six storeys beneath us.

Petronius thought I was a time-waster. Then he heard it too. Someone down there in the darkness played a few lonesome notes on a flute.

XXXVI

We never stood a chance of finding him. Whoever it was, moved off of his own accord. By the time we had careered down six flights of stairs in the dark and burst out at street level, all sounds had ceased.

'Sounded professional.'

'Bar musician going home after a night of touting around the tables for coppers.'

'Too good for that.'

'Bar musicians are bloody good. They have to be, to beat the competition.'

'I want it to be the Quadrumatus flute boy.'

'You want it too much, Falco.'

'All right.'

'That's fatal.'

'I said all right – All right?'

'No need to get nasty.'

'Well don't make so much of things.'

'You sound like a woman.'

'We're drunk.'

'No, we're tired.'

'A woman would say that's what men say as an excuse.'

'She'd be right.'

'Right.'

So we said good–night. Petronius maintained he had to stay up on duty; he would go back to the party, I reckoned. I set off for home. I was looking out for the flute boy, but I never saw him. Nobody much was about. Even the bad people were at home these nights. Burglars celebrate with their families like anyone else. Criminals honour festivals enthusiastically. There had been a rash of thefts a week ago while the old lags worked hard to obtain cash for food, lamps and gifts. If you want a good December feast, spend Saturnalia with a thief.

Now the dark entries and alleys were still. I convinced myself I was more sober than a third party would think, and on the alert for anyone who slipped through the shadows.

It was a good theory. It worked so well that when I came upon Zosime from the Temple of Æsculapius, tending a patient by a flight of steps, I nearly fell over them.

Zosime was working alone. She must have left her donkey nearby; she had a medical bag with her and when I arrived she had been bent over a motionless figure huddled on the steps. I scared her. She jumped up and almost tripped, hurriedly putting distance between us. I was shocked by her anxiety.

'Steady! It's me – Falco. The investigator.'

The woman recovered fast. She seemed annoyed by my inter- ruption, though perhaps she was annoyed with herself for jumping. She was competent and knew how to survive the streets at night so I would have gone on my way, but as she turned back to her patient she exclaimed under her breath.

'What's up?'

She straightened abruptly. 'We get too many of these . . . The man is dead, Falco. Nothing I can do for him. I am disappointed; I had been tending him and thought he was recovering.'

I moved closer and inspected the vagrant. It was no one I recognised. I doubted anyone in Rome would claim him as friend or family. 'What killed him?'

'The usual.' Zosime was repacking her medicines. 'Cold. Hunger. Neglect. Despair. Brutality. This is a terrible time of year for the homeless. Everywhere is closed up; they can find neither shelter nor charity. A week-long festival will see many starve.'

I let the rant slide to its end. 'But you think he should have got better.' I had gone down on one knee, peering closer. 'His face is discoloured. Has he been attacked?'

When Zosime did not answer, I rose to my feet again. Then she said, 'Of course it is possible. The sick are vulnerable. Lying here, he could be kicked by casual passers-by.'

'Or deliberately beaten up,' I suggested.

'There are no signs of serious violence.'

I gave her a stare. 'So you looked?'

She gazed back, openly acknowledging that she had half expected to discover an unnatural death. 'Yes, I looked, Falco.'

'You said "too many". Is there a pattern?'

'The pattern is of death by maltreatment. It is the norm for social outcasts . . . What do you want me to say?' she demanded suddenly and loudly. It was my turn to be taken aback. Then her irritation with me diminished into something sadder. 'Who would kill vagrants and runaways? What would be the point?'

'You know your business, Zosime.'

'Yes, I do,' she replied, still angry, but also despondent. It was that time of year.

I told her about the missing flautist and asked her to look out for the boy. He might trust her. It seemed unlikely he would be out and about now. The streets were cold, lonely, and pretty well deserted. I left her and walked home.

If I was lucky, I would find a warm bed with a welcoming woman in my house. My house; even the fact that it had once been my father's gave that concept extra solidity. I was now a man of substance. I had house, wife, children, dog, slaves, heirs, work, prospects, past history, public honours, roof terrace with fig tree, obligations, friends, enemies, membership of a private gymnasium – all the paraphernalia of civilisation. But I had known poverty and hardship. So I understood the other world of Rome. I knew how that man lying dead on the steps could have sunk so low he found mere breathing too much to cope with. Or, even if he had managed to continue, how other ragged men could have turned on him because his illness made him just weaker and more hopeless than they were; the perpetual victims for once finding themselves able to exercise power. The best and worst kind of power being, the power of life and death.

These were grand thoughts. Suitable for a man alone, descending an empty stone stairway among the elegant, lofty old temples on one of Rome's Seven Hills, thinking himself at that moment lord of the whole Aventine. But I had noticed that Zosime reacted to the run-away's death not with grand thoughts but tired resignation. She had believed he was recovering but she dreaded to find him dead, and it depressed her. I had seen her kind of feeling before too. She had the world-weariness of those who know that effort is futile. The city is sordid. Many people know nothing but misery. Many others cause such misery, most of them knowingly.

Whatever her personal background – which probably involved slavery and certainly poverty – Zosime was a realist. She had lived long enough to understand the harsh life on the streets. Her work with the runaways was grounded in experience. She never idealised it. She was well aware that the runaways' malnourishment and sheer despair would probably thwart her; tonight, though, she had believed worse forces were at work. I had seen that. Zosime had let me glimpse her fears.

SATURNALIA, DAY ONE

Sixteen days before the Kalends of January (17 December)

XXXVII

Dawn was approaching when I reached home. My key refused to work. I had been locked out.

I did what Petronius and I used to do at his house: turned around on the step and gazed up the deserted street as if that would make the door open behind my back by magic. As a trick, it had failed then and it still failed. But I noticed something. Not a full shape, just a hint of greater darkness in some shadows. A man was watching my house. Anacrites had wasted no time.

I sharpened up. I had my hand on the curly tail of the mighty dolphin arouser Pa had left us; before I could disturb the neighbourhood I let go again as the grille rattled, then the door slid open. One of the legionaries had been waiting up. It was Scaurus. As he stepped aside to let me enter, he nodded surreptitiously towards the place where I had detected an observer. 'We have company.'

'Spotted him. I didn't want to use the back entrance; no need to tell them it exists. Has anyone had a good look at him?'

'No, but Clemens has put a man up on the roof terrace on obbo.'

Ludicrous. Anacrites watched me and my men; we watched his. So several personnel who could be out looking for Veleda were tied up in useless pursuits.

'Some Praetorians came and searched your house,' Scaurus warned me. 'Helena Justina wants to discuss it with you.'

'Damage?'

'Minimal.'

'What did they make of you lot?'

'We were all out having a drink at the Three Clams,' the legionary confessed. 'Unfortunately, the eyes outside will have seen us rolling home later.'

'Anacrites knows you're seconded to me. And I dare say he can guess you are all reprobates and drunks. The Three Clams is a dump, by the way. If you don't want to walk all the way up the Hill to

Flora's, try the Crocus or the Galatean. Did the Guards tell Helena why they came?'

'Looking for her brother. Have you got him, Falco?'

'Who, me? Kidnap a state prisoner from the Chief Spy's house?'

'Yes, it's a shocking suggestion . . . I hope you've put him somewhere they won't look,' said Scaurus.

I went hunting for a snack, but the marauding Guards had cleaned out the pantry. Then I went to bed. The bed was empty.

I found Helena in the children's room. Favonia had a fever and had been vomiting all night. Helena, pale and puffy-eyed, was probably catching the same illness.

'What did I buy a nursemaid for? Where's Galene?'

'Too much trouble to bother her.'

I sent Helena to bed and took over. It is not in the informers' manual, but sitting up with a sick child is a good way to organise some thinking time. In between sponging the hot little head, administering drinks, finding the lost doll that has fallen on the floor, and wielding the sick-bowl when the drinks you had ticed down hurtle back up again, you can generally work out your next day's plan of action, then sit back mulling over what you have learned so far on your case.

Never enough, of course.

Breakfast was late; someone had to go out for rolls, as the Guards had raided the bread basket. Helena and I spent the wait disputing my refusal to say where her brother was. If she did not know, she could not be pressurised. She failed to see it. We ate in silence. Eventually Helena broke in with the old questions, 'So where exactly did you go last night, and who were you drinking with?' To which I gave the customary answers.

She flounced out to do the daily shop, taking two soldiers called Lusius and Minnius, together with the centurion's servant, Cattus. Lentullus tagged along with them though he was due to peel off unobtrusively. I had covertly given him a map and a money-bag, telling him how to find Justinus and saying to stick with him, if possible for a week.

'I'm sending you because you know him, Lentullus.'

'That's nice.'

'Maybe not. May be hard work. Keep him indoors. He's been told to lie low, but you know what he's like. If anyone can make him stay put, Lentullus, it's you. You fetch food and drink and anything else he needs; stick around the local neighbourhood. Whatever you do, don't come back here, in case you're spotted by the Spy's men. Here's a tunic –' The legionaries were in plain clothes, which only meant that instead of all wearing red tunics they had been issued with identical white. I gave Lentullus a brown one. 'As soon as you get there, change your togs, then go to the barber at the end of the street where the apartment is.' Plain clothes for soldiers also meant growing their hair. 'Have a close crop.' Anyone looking for a soldier in white with curls would be thwarted by this transformation into a shaven-headed civilian in inconspicuous brown. Well, anyone Anacrites employed would be fooled. 'Tell him to put the price on my slate.'

Lentullus was a big child at heart. 'I'll get a free haircut? That's great, Falco.'

'No, you'll get a long complaint about me. I used up my credit about three years ago. But he'll charge you the real price, not the stranger's special.'

'Is the tribune going to be a problem?' Lentullus then asked warily.

'I hope not.'

'Can I bop him one?'

'I'd rather you managed to control him some other way.'

'Oh thanks, Falco. I'd better not use a sword on him.'

'No, please don't!'

So Lentullus tagged along after Helena, while I stood on the doorstep talking to Clemens, offering a more interesting target in case Anacrites' observer thought of tailing the shoppers. Petro and I had warned Justinus last night that he would be given a minder. It might work. He had no clothes, other than his now battered turnip costume. No senator's son with hopes of a career wants to appear in public with roots dangling around his legs and ridiculous leaves coming out of his ears. On the other hand, there was a laundry on the ground floor of the apartment block where we had left him. Washed tunics were just hanging on lines. If he decided to bunk off, he would manage it, even though he might end up a bit damp around the armpits. We could report him to the vigiles as a clothes thief, but they had so many of those to chase, they would never get around to him.

'Stay friends with him,' I had pleaded with Lentullus. 'If he skips, make sure that you go with him.'

'When he skips.' The young legionary was cynical. He hadn't been like that when Quintus and I first knew him as a scared recruit in Germany. But it tended to happen to people who spent time around us.

Now I had to ensure that by the time Quintus did skip, I would have found Veleda and placed her out of his reach.

Easier said than done. But a breakthrough was not far away.

XXXVIII

We had reached the seven days of Saturnalia. I was almost at my deadline and now the family harassment began.

I was still on the step with Clemens (who rapidly removed himself) when festive visitors arrived: first my sister Allia, the flabby, exhausted one who was married to the corrupt road contractor, followed by Galla, who was leaner and weepier. Her water-boatman husband periodically deserted her or was thrown out by Galla, and since barmaids were extra-friendly during festivals, Saturnalia was inevitably one of the periods when Lollius went missing.

These virtuous Roman women wanted to spread the gossip that Junia and Gaius Baebius had had a tremendous row. That was unusual, since the snooty, sanctimonious couple were made for each other and doted on their harmonious image.

I looked pious. 'What's a quarrel to me?'

'You're head of the family.' Only when it suited them. Only because Pa ignored such obligations. 'Is it of absolutely no interest, Marcus Didius, that your sister was carried home across the Aventine last night by her husband – raving and uncontrollable?'

'Dear thoughtful ones, thank you. I certainly want to avoid that bore Gaius Baebius, if throwing the wine-soaked Junia over his shoulder has given him a bad back; he'll maunder on about the pain for hours . . . So it's a quiet festival all round?' I suggested hopefully.

'We are all coming to your house.' Allia had a harsh, unfortunate manner. 'You've got the space.'

'And you can afford it!' Galla assured me. All my sisters knew far too much about the contents of other people's bank chests.

'How fortunate. I can upbraid Junia with fraternal bile, like Cato the Censor . . . Good of you to tell us.' Perhaps Helena had heard about it. Probably not, or she would have made some comment this morning, when lists of my faults had formed much of her repartee. 'You don't mean tonight?'

'Marcus, don't you ever pay attention? You are doing the last

183

evening.' That gave us a week to emigrate. 'We want ghost stories and a really big log for the fire. Make sure you have enough cake too. We all agreed.' All except me. 'Tonight we're dragging out to Papa's spread on the Janiculan. He's got a tale-teller coming, with puppets, to amuse the children. Maia's refused to have anyone round to hers this year, selfish cow; she says she hasn't forgotten the unpleasantness last time . . . I blame that man she's got now. I never liked him when he was chasing poor Victorina, and I was dead right!'

'It's my best friend Petronius you're insulting, Allia.' Not to mention Maia, my favourite sister – generally the friendly one.

'Well, you never had any judgement.'

As Allia denounced us all, Galla said nothing; her half-starved, virtually fatherless children would get their only decent meals of the month at Saturnalia feasts. In thrall to a serial adulterer, Galla was feckless and hopeless – but she knew how to get free food.

'Well, if I'm hosting, I look forward to my thrilling cache of guest-gifts.'

'You are joking!' chorused my sisters, without missing a beat.

They moved off together, patrolling the street like carrion crows staking out a flyblown lamb's carcass. They were on their way to Mother's apartment, where the first cataract operation was to take place that morning. I was credited with persuading Ma to knuckle under – no doubt a prelude to piling blame on me if anything went wrong. I turned down an invitation to the eye operation, then I told Allia and Galla that if nobody had thought of a Saturnalia present for Pa yet, he was desperate to have his haemorrhoids fixed. 'Don't give him any advance warning; he'd much rather you just turned up with the doctor as a big surprise.'

'Are you sure that's what he wants?'

'Trust me. I'm your brother.'

Can they have forgotten our evil elder brother Festus, the best trickster on the Aventine? They looked suspicious, but for sharp-witted women who had known plenty of two-timing, sweet-talking, earnest-looking cheating bastards, they were easily swayed. I even gave them the address of Mastarna, the dogmatist doctor, who advocated surgery. They said they would go to ask his fees.

Bliss. Pa was in for the pile-pincers. As a lord of misrule, I had my moments.

I spent the morning helping out Clemens with the street searches. Ten men had seemed like plenty when we started, but resources were now stretched. Lentullus was minding Justinus. Minnius and Lusius were out scavenging with Helena and would be on pot duty when they returned; Gaudus was already in the kitchen, concocting treats for Favonia. Like all children our invalid had recovered fast, but she knew how to sit wide-eyed, begging to be spoiled. Titus (there is always one called Titus, generally a loafer) and Paullus were taking turns on the roof, watching Anacrites' men. Granius had gone to the Forum, to squat near the notice that Anacrites had put up for Veleda; if she appeared, Granius was to warn her that Justinus had left the Spy's house, and to bring her here. They could use the back entrance – not that it was likely. From what I remembered of the priestess, even if Granius found her, I couldn't see her meekly agreeing to come. Gaius was sick; apparently it was traditional. The only day Gaius was fit to leave his bed was payday. The centurion's servant thought most duties other than lightly brushing down a cloak were beneath him. So that left Clemens with only Sentius and Scaurus. When I joined them, he thought I was checking their methods. He was right too. They were demoralised by failure and needed pepping up.

At our mid-morning break, I made him relieve Titus and Paullus. Anacrites' watchers were tailing us, so we could keep tabs on them just by looking over our shoulders. Paullus joined us. We put Titus on rotation with Granius in the Forum, which pleased Titus, the loafer, since all he had to do was sit in the shade eating a stuffed vineleaf. Granius was less glad, because he had been chatting up a hot-pie seller, and after two hours of banter had believed he was getting somewhere. I warned him she was leading him on; he didn't want to believe it, but when he went to take over again from Titus later, Titus told him she had gone off with a man with a ladder towards the Clivus Argentarius.

'That's life!' we cried, but Granius stuck out his lower lip, still convinced he had narrowly lost the chance of a hot date.

Clemens pulled Granius off observation when we all went for lunch in a small bar at the back of the Curia. Normally I wouldn't be seen dead there, but the Curia was closed for the festival so the hang-out was empty of senators and their parasites. We were in a quiet mood. The chances of us meeting up with Veleda were slight. She had now been on the loose for over two weeks. She must have found somewhere good to hide up. I had just another six days to find her and complete my commission from Laeta, but if she continued to keep her head down, she would be safe. The legionaries were not alone in feeling demoralised.

We had been searching markets and bars between the Forum of

Augustus and the old Suburra district. It had filled in a blank on the map, where all the central areas had now been explored. Clemens and the lads had already spent five days searching the west and the south of the city street by street. Unless I ordered them to widen the circle and start enquiries in the outer districts – the Esquiline, the High Lanes, the Via Lata and Circus Flaminius, where gardens, public monuments and high-class homes tended to predominate – then it was time to admit we had drawn a blank. We raised our beakers sociably to Anacrites' men: a couple of short hairy idiots who looked like brothers – Melitans maybe – and who were sitting uncomfortably by an empty stall opposite, since our bar was too small for them unless they came and shared our table. Which they might as well have done.

Clemens and I, and Scaurus who seemed to be a man of the world, tried to explain to Granius, who was still sulking, that no pie-seller or other sophisticated Roman woman was ever going to opt for a serving soldier, who was bound to be sent back abroad soon, when she could pick up a man with a ladder. *He* was just as likely to abandon her, but if she had the forethought to chain up his ladder, he would leave it behind when he skipped. A woman who owns her own ladder is always popular. Both professional handymen and normal householders would be popping in to 'borrow her ladder' at all hours. Even if their wives saw through it.

For some reason Granius suspected we were winding his spindle. He was twenty-one, had gone straight from childhood on a farm to the navy, then the young barnacle had been plucked from the marines, still with seaweed behind his ears, to become part of the newly formed First Adiutrix legion. All he knew of adult life on land had taken place in a permanent army fort in Germany. He was a Roman legionary – but knew nothing of Rome. He had no idea of the social essentials in a hectic city neighbourhood.

'Just believe us, Granius. A big long ladder puts a twinkle in any woman's eye.'

Even Lentullus would have got that. Well, he would do nowadays.

I wondered how he was doing. There was no chance of going to ask him, with those two Melitan brothers just waiting to track me to the hideaway . . . Nonetheless, after I survived a throat-etching beaker of Campanian red at the bar, I decided life was for taking risks. I left the others to it and without looking behind me, set off across the Capitol end of the main Forum, skirted the beast market and cut around the Circus Maximus starting gates. I climbed the Aventine, where I made my way to a particular grimy alley called

Fountain Court. This dead end on the rump of society was the only street in Rome where not one building had festive decorations. It had been the haunt of my carefree bachelor years. I stopped by at the barber's for an unguent comb-through and a shave. The beetle-browed Melitans duly tailed me, kicking their heels opposite while I took my time; when I left, I dropped in at the funeral parlour. 'If a couple of losers come and ask what I just said to you, tell them I was ordering a memorial stone for someone called Anacrites.' I waved an arm to Lenia, the frazzle-headed laundress at my old tenement; the baggy hag was now so short-sighted, she just peered after me, baffled as to who had greeted her. That saved me having to listen to an hour-long monologue on her ex-husband Smaractus, and it saved Lenia from having me remind her that I had always told her so.

I did not cast my gaze up to my old apartment.

Since I was in my home area, I dutifully went to see my mother. As I arrived, I met Anacrites coming out of the building. I should have known that swine would beat me to the patient's bedside; he had probably brought grapes as well as creepy solicitude. He and I stood on the steps, engaged in meaningless chat. His watchers would be very confused when they had to report that they saw me talking to him. And he was furious when, as I went indoors, I pointed a finger at his men: 'I see you're still employing top quality!'

Maia was in the apartment, morosely pulling grapes from their stems and squashing them. I gave her a hug, but did not discuss Anacrites, with whom she had once had a misguided fling that had ended very badly. Petro and I would get even with the Spy one day. Maia did not need to know.

'Our house was full of Guards this morning, Marcus; I gather I should blame you for that.' I went cold. Maia had once had an apartment violently trashed by Anacrites, after she sent him packing. She saw my expression and said quietly, 'I was here. Lucius dealt with them.' So, fortunately, he had not rejoined the vigiles' party last night. He would have kept the Praetorians in order. Maia would have gone to pieces if she had to face a second house invasion. This mission was coming too close to home all round.

Allia and Galla had both left Mother's earlier, hysterical after the operation. It had taken five hours, during which Ma, who usually whizzed around like a demented fly, had had to sit in her basket chair and remain absolutely still. This would be hard, even without the man poking a needle around her eye. She had refused narcotic drugs. Nobody even dared suggest tying her to the chair.

Of course Ma endured it all with determination, even forgoing her customary scowl. The oculist had been amazed by her ability to sit like marble. Apparently he thought she was a dear old lady. 'Jupiter, Maia. How come you and the others found the only oculist in Rome who's blind?'

It had been intended that only one cataract should be cleared with the couching needle today, but Ma insisted that the man did both. My sister thought our mother was afraid she would be unable to find her courage a second time. She wanted to see. She hated not being able to keep a fierce eye on everyone. Besides, the oculist had said she would be the first patient who coped with both operations the same day. Well, that saved him a double visit. Ma must have been weak by then. She fell for it.

Even Maia looked strained now, but she was staying on watch overnight. Ma was resting. I looked in on her; she was lying straight on her back, with her hands neatly at her waist and her lips set in a straight line. It implied that somebody was for it. That meant nothing. She looked like that whenever she looked at me. Lamb's-wool pads covered both eyes, so someone would have to help her with everything until they came off.

'Where's —' I turned back to Maia, chilled. Where was Ganna?

'Oh we all knew your mystery woman was here,' scoffed my sister. 'Allia stormed in on her. You know what Allia's like. She couldn't bear to watch the operation, so she thought she'd cause trouble instead. Galla and Allia had got it into their head you'd stashed your tribal tootsie here so you could visit her secretly.'

'Oh yes — and Ma would go along with that liaison?'

'Do you want the story? In tramps Allia, loudly suggesting that Ganna comes out, puts some effort in, and helps us look after Ma. The girl shrieked, Allia grabbed her by the hair —' Allia had always been a bully and a hair-puller. As a child I kept well out of her way. 'So Ganna pulled free and ran out of the house. Nobody has seen her since. Well, apart from a big clump of blonde hair that Allia dragged out. Juno, I hate those mimsy little pale types!'

I swore. Maia (a vibrant, energetic girl who had a thicket of dark curls, jauntily bound with crimson ribbon) managed to look guilty about letting the acolyte run away. Then a tremulous voice came from Mother's bedroom. She had been awake and listening all the time. 'I'm just a helpless old woman, racked with suffering —

Someone must go after poor Ganna!' That order came out crisp enough.

Annoyed, I demanded a clue where to start. In a little whisper, which fooled no one, my mother named the Temple of Diana on the Aventine. Diana: virgin goddess of the moonlit groves, with the big thighs and the over-excitable bow and arrows. Well, that made sense. Any woodland priestess would feel well at home with the haughty huntress. One thing I ought to have remembered right at the start of this mission was that the Temple of Diana was by tradition a safe haven for runaways.

When pressed, Ma meekly admitted young Ganna had regularly prayed at this temple . . . 'Oh Hades, Ma; didn't you suspect something? Why would Ganna want to pray to Diana? No one from Germania Libera honours the Twelve Consenting Gods!'

A nagging recollection came to me: *'You keep her in?'*

'Except when we make a little trip together to a market or temple.'

'Has she said anything?'

'She fooled you plenty. There's a lot she's holding back.'

Stupid! I should have picked up the clue. At the very least, messages were being passed. At worst, Veleda herself had been in hiding at the temple, and Ganna had been colluding with her. If that had been true, probably neither Ganna nor Veleda would be there now.

'Why didn't you say something?'

'Oh son, I never interfere.'

Dear gods. 'I have to leave.'

'Don't rush!' cried Maia. My sister had a fast, angry way of dealing with crises. 'First off, I can read the auguries. As soon as Mother owned up what a scam the girl had been pulling, I nipped to the temple myself, Marcus. The priests denied all knowledge. They will only say the same to you. In any case –' This was the clincher; my sister knew it – 'Helena wants you back at home. She said to be there prompt, good-tempered and clean. Titus Caesar has invited you two and her parents to the official feast tonight at the Temple of Saturn. So you'll go – or you're damned to the memory.'

I closed my eyes in dread. An endless official banquet, in the presence of a god's effigy and those two stiffs, the imperial princes – gamely pretending to be men of the people while flying nuts hit their gold braid and drunks spewed on their orbs of office – was not my idea of a social life. Even Titus and Domitian would probably prefer a night in with a game of draughts.

'Look on the bright side,' Maia consoled me. 'It gets you out of

189

puppets up at Pa's house.' A thin wail of agitation came from Ma at the mention of our absconding father. Maia and I exchanged wry smiles.

Oh flying phalluses, stuff the priestess.

Since it was a festival for ending grudges, I kissed my sister tenderly, kissed my mother even more devotedly, dodged Ma's flailing arm as she tried to box my ears, and went home to take my wife out to an alfresco dinner with the ancient god Saturnus.

XXXIX

'I am sorry, Marcus. But avoiding the invitation would be impolite.'

Helena meant, it would be too political. When the Emperor called, no one was otherwise engaged. Refusal would finish us. We would not be asked again. Our public life would end. Once, I had not given a stuff about my career in public life; now I had a family.

I even had slaves to provide for. They liked to enjoy the full spectrum of Roman life. Galene and Jacinthus had now completely abandoned their duties. They were playing Soldiers on a board marked in the dust in the entrance hall. It was true the dust would not have been there if I had bought a cleaning-slave. So I might not have minded – but they were using my best dice.

'What will you do about Ganna and Veleda?' Helena fretted, as I brought her up to date on my day. I had sent all our legionaries to observe at the priestess's Aventine sanctuary. No point making too much of it; I strongly doubted Veleda was there. Helena thought the men had just gone out drinking. In case she decided I was planning some manoeuvre with the soldiers, I let her think it. I was a thoughtful husband. 'This is typical,' she said with a sigh. 'There is action at a temple – but you will be stuck in the wrong temple!'

'True, my darling.' I concentrated on fastening my party shoes.

Glancing up, I saw her expression suddenly still. For a beautiful woman with a mainly placid temperament, Helena Justina had a stare that could bore holes in stone. Parts of me felt molten. I loved her as much as a man could love anyone, but I wished that girl would occasionally consent to be bamboozled.

She had detected that I was hoping I would not be in the wrong temple for long.

The Temple of Saturn is the oldest in the Forum provided by a private sponsor. If you stand where the stairs used to come up from the Tabularium – I mean, where the Temple of Vespasian and Titus has since been squeezed in, under the shadow of the Capitol, forming that squash with the Temple of the Harmonious Gods and the Temple of Concord – that's assuming you can bear to be in an area of so much suffocating harmony and goodwill – then Saturn's antique shrine juts out straight in front of you. Clad in marble, hexastyle, adorned with Tritons, it will be blocking your view of the Basilica and the Temple of Castor. The ship's prows celebrating naval battles and the Golden Milestone with the distances to the world's major cities will be visible in front of it, if you are waiting for a friend and want a distraction to stop you attracting the notice of prostitutes.

The heavy vaults beneath the podium guard the civic treasury. The platform is high, to accommodate the slope of Capitol Hill, and the front steps are unusually narrow, to fit in against the sharp angle of the Clivus Capitolinus as it comes into the Forum, around the Tarpeian Rock. We arrived that way on foot; I glanced up as I always did, just in case any women traitors were being flung off the rock that night. With Veleda in town, it was a possibility. In the sharp night air, sounds carried; I even thought I heard honking from the Sacred Geese of Juno right up on the Arx, public birds whose official guardian I had once been, in a mad period of civic responsibility. Above, anxious crows and other birds were wheeling about the dark sky, upset by the multitude of lights that filled the Forum.

On the steps and in front of the temple, the banquet had been set out. Saturn's image, a large hollow statue, was made from ivory, so to keep it from cracking it was kept full of oil. The statue had been brought out from the interior. The ancient deity had his head veiled and was holding a hooked sickle. His feet were normally bound together with wool (no idea why; perhaps the sacred one is prone to absconding to seedy bars). The wool had been ceremonially unbound for this occasion. Oil had leaked out around the couch when he was put in position. The public slaves who moved him every year were efficient and reverent, but just you try shifting an outsize statue filled with viscous liquid. The weight was appalling, and as the oily ballast started slopping to and fro, the deity wobbled dangerously. The priests always got in the way trying to supervise, so the slaves grew ratty and lost concentration, with inevitable leakage. They would fill him up again, but not until they took him back indoors.

Helena and I, and her parents, were privileged, in theory. The whole city was supposed to attend tonight, but fitting them in would be ridiculous so hungry crowds were clustered in the darkness all around the periphery. Vespasian was a parsimonious emperor who loathed his obligation to supply endless public banquets. This feast was a *lectisternium,* a banquet offered to the god in thanks for the new harvest; Saturn's oversized, hoarily bearded, goggle-eyed image presided on a giant couch, before which were placed tables laden with rich fare. Traditionally, the fare was rich enough – and had been hanging around in kitchens long enough – to cause severe stomach upsets in the human diners who would eventually devour it (paupers, who were already queuing hopefully at the back of the temple). There were other tables, less opulently covered, where mediocre lukewarm foodstuffs in meagre quantities were available to us lucky invitees.

We had been told to come in informal Saturnalia dress. That still meant looking smart because the Emperor, Titus and Domitian would be present. They would patrol among us, pretending to be part of one giant family. So we had to concoct a reversed-rank version of formality, dressing up as we pretended to dress down. Most of the women had just borrowed their slaves' frocks then piled on as much jewellery as they could. The men looked uncomfortable because their wives had chosen their dinner robes and, according to recognised domestic rules, had chosen dinner robes their husbands hated. I had been put in blue. On men, blue is for floor designers and second-rate shellfish suppliers. Helena, who often wore blue and looked gorgeous, tonight was in unaccustomed brown, with rows of crimped hair that must have taken all afternoon to set. Unless it was a wig; I did wonder. She looked like a stranger. The ridged hair had added five years to her and seemed to belong to some impoverished orator's parchment-skinned spinster sister.

'That's certainly a disguise.'

'Don't you like it?'

'I'll like you better when you take it off,' I affirmed salaciously. If you are going to abandon a mission for an evening, you may as well get into the festive spirit and while you are at it, try to seduce a girl. Helena reddened, so I reckoned I was in there.

Camillus Verus was wearing his normal white, complete with full senatorial purple stripes. 'Olympus, I'm overdressed for this fiasco, Falco!' Nobody had reminded him that he had to play the part of a slave tonight, and somehow he had omitted to consult on his outfit with his wife. Julia Justa must have been preoccupied; she was having problems remaining decent. She had decided that playing lowborn and low budget must mean wearing low-cut. Inexperienced at flaunting, she kept fiddling with the skimpy drape across her bosom. Her husband tried to stare in other directions, pretending not to notice her difficulties. He was terrified she would ask him to assist with pinning things.

'And who have you come as, Marcus dear?' chirped Julia, bright with embarrassment. Her discomfiture inevitably drew the eyes directly to its cause.

I must have been wearing the horrified rictus of any man in danger of glimpsing his mother-in-law's nipples. 'I think I'm a back-alley debt-collector.'

'Isn't that rather similar to what you do normally?'

'I don't work in a damned skyblue tunic!'

'Indigo,' murmured Helena.

'I feel like a periwinkle.'

'Be good. It will soon be over.' Helena was fooling. It took us almost an hour merely to obtain seats. You needed to be fit. If there had ever been a table plan, nobody could find it. We squeezed in only by shoving harder than the people who were trying to climb on to benches ahead of us. 'As soon as the first course is over, everyone can get out their cloaks. Then it won't matter what you look like.' We did all have cloaks. We needed them too, dining under the stars on a gusty night in the middle of December. To do Saturnalia properly means celebrating the new crops in the wide outdoors. Helena and I were both longing for a warm brazier indoors and two comfortable armed chairs, each with a good scroll to read.

Near the temple steps, adjacent to Saturn's awesome spread, was a table for the imperial family and their courtiers. King for the Day was a public slave, but he had been carefully chosen – an elderly palace scribe who could be trusted to behave sedately. His mischief-making was forced: he kept eyeing the chamberlains to make sure he had not gone too far.

'He's a bummer. I think I ought to help him out –' That was not me, but the senator.

'You stay where you are!' commanded his wife.

Once I had thought this couple staid, but the more I knew them the more I could see where their three children had acquired eccentricity and humour. There was the senator, winking wickedly at Helena as if she was still a giggly four-year-old. Here was Julia Justa, that rigid pillar of the cult of the Good Goddess, showing more cleavage than a cheap whore in a travellers' inn; what's more, just like Ma, she distrusted food at public banquets and had lugged a hamper here. The only difference was that Julia's home fare had been cooked and packed by a battalion of slaves.

It caused a problem for me. Men of action eat or work. It is bad practice to attempt both simultaneously before a busy night. My physical trainer would have been horrified to see Julia Justa's tempting nibbles and nuggets find their way into the cheap foodbowl we had all been provided with.

Vespasian, our untroubled old ruler, tossed away his wreath happily when he progressed to his place at table. He looked jovial, but I noticed he managed to avoid any real indignities. His staff played the festive game by bowling the occasional apple at one another, making quite sure none hit the Father of his People. I recognised Claudius Laeta, plus a couple of other palace retainers I knew, and a man in a discreet moleskin-coloured tunic, who had his back to me but who could only be Anacrites. A small group of Praetorian Guards, bareheaded to suggest informality, were lounging at the back of Saturn on the temple steps; they may have shed their glittering crested helmets, but they were on duty to protect the Emperor.

Titus and Domitian, Vespasian's chubby sons, made themselves amiable by moving around the tables and sitting with ordinary folk. They both wore plain tunics, but in purple, so it was obvious they were princes being gracious. I saw Titus laughing and joking diligently, some distance from us. Domitian was working our sector of the crowd, but came no nearer than the end of our table, still out of earshot. He and I loathed each other, but I was confident he would never start anything with his father or elder brother watching.

As the noise of participants rose until it almost drowned the music of a few polite tambourinists and flautists, I busied myself attempting to acquire some of the thimble-sized cups of wine. The senator was talking to a neighbouring diner, so he could ignore the fact that his wife kept diving under the table to extract dainties from her hamper for us all. Every time she bobbed up again with new treats hidden in her dinner napkin, her dress had slipped even lower. I rather suspected the noble Julia had been plied with tots of false courage while her wardrobe mistress and makeup girl were decking her out for this occasion. Maybe the old republicans were right and it was shameful for women to drink. Meanwhile Helena Justina, that model of moral rectitude, grabbed a tot, knocked it back, pulled a face, and snaffled another one.

A sewer rat ran across the table. He thought the Forum belonged to him at night. I was the only one who noticed. Everyone else was screaming with laughter at the antics of a group of professional entertainers who were dressed as circus animals. I had never seen so many fake woollen manes or such thickly plastered artificial hide. They were rather warty. Some were going to lose a lot of skin when they tried removing their rhinoceros masks tomorrow. One frolicking jester tried investigating Julia Justa's cleavage; he got his horn stuck on her pearl necklace, without doubt purposely. *'Aah . . . Decimus, help me!'*

Now I was happy. It was worth coming, to have seen my father-in-law removing a clown from his wife's naked bosom by applying the fulcrum principle to the fellow's rhino horn. The appendage had been well glued on. The man's screams must have sounded right up on the Arx.

It was Helena, standing up so she could more easily reorganise her mother's disarray, who spotted another flurry of excitement. 'Marcus! Someone you know has had an accident . . .'

I followed her gesture. Behind the statue of Saturn a man had fallen over awkwardly on the spilled oil. It was Anacrites. Like me, he must be waiting his moment to slip away from the banquet unobtrusively; I thought I could see slaves with a litter waiting in the narrow side street by the temple. He must have tried to disengage from the courtiers' table and sneak around behind the statue, but when his foot skidded under him, he crashed against the image of Saturn and nearly pushed the god right over into his golden bowls of ambrosia. Fortunately the statue was held in position by hidden wooden bracing. As Anacrites stumbled back on to his feet, concerned slaves rushed to help him – which was what had attracted Helena's notice. They were anxiously checking that Saturn was still safe, under cover of testing if the Spy had a twisted ankle. I wished it was his neck he had twisted.

Another movement caught my eye. A helmet flashed, among the Praetorians assembled on the temple step. Oh no.

The Chief Spy had been visiting Ma just before me yesterday. She must have told him what she told me. Now Anacrites and some of the Guards were on the move, and I could guess where they were all going. They too were heading to the Temple of Diana Aventinensis – and they would probably arrive ahead of me.

XL

The senator had half risen from his seat. He liked heroics. Helena Justina pushed him back. 'Marcus, take me!'

'No.' I did not want to tell her that it might be dangerous.

'Stop shutting me out, Marcus.' She would never change. She had tamed a reprobate, settled down, borne two children, run a household – but Helena Justina would never become a respectable matron, satisfied with domesticity. We first met during an adventure. Action formed part of our relationship. Always did, always would do.

She and I shared a tussle of wills, which I enjoyed more than I should have done. As I looked into those determined dark eyes, she nobbled me as she always did, and I felt a smile twitch. I wanted her to be safe – yet I wanted her to come. Helena spotted my weakness. At once she whipped off the costume wig. Her own fine hair had been pinned up under it, but escaped in a whoosh. She wore little jewellery; with the plain brown dress under a plainer cloak, she would be anonymous on the streets. That was obviously planned.

She bent down, mouthing in her mother's ear, 'We are just going to look for –'

'Oh pee on a column, Marcus! Be like everybody else.'

Bright-eyed, Helena exploded into giggles. I grinned at the senator over Julia Justa's head, as she burrowed in her hamper again, oblivious. Camillus Verus, trapped there at the banquet, shot us an envious look. Then I clutched Helena by the hand and we left.

We ran into Titus Caesar. Youthful, splendid in the purple, famously magnanimous, the heir to the Empire greeted us like favourite cousins. 'Not leaving already, Falco?'

'Following a lead on that case, sir.'

Titus raised his eyebrows and gestured towards Anacrites. 'I thought it was in hand.'

'Joint operation, sir!' I lied. His eyes lingered on Helena Justina,

197

clearly wondering why she was coming with me. 'I always take a girl to hold the cloaks.'

'Chaperon duty!' Helena snorted, as she let Titus see her elbow me hard, correcting my cheeky suggestion. With a jaunty grin for the heir to the Empire, I dragged her away.

Anacrites had been held up. The slaves who guarded the statue were not willing to let him leave the scene until they had checked Saturn over for damage. They milled around the Spy; he was stalled, desperately trying to shake off the unwanted attention without drawing down any more on himself. The man was completely incompetent. He would be lucky to escape from his ill-timed trip on the spilled oil without a charge of insulting the god. I did not stay to watch.

We were on foot. In light leather party shoes with sloppy straps and flimsy soles, every uneven pavement tortured our feet. Still, we had no need to mill about making decisions. Our only problem was pushing through the crowds. First the banqueters, who were merrier than they should have been, given how hard it was to find any of the free wine. Then the unfed onlookers, who saw no reason to let people who had an invitation dodge their duties. *'Io Saturnalia!'* And *Io* to you, you gawking menace . . . We were elbowed and shoved – all in a cheerful spirit, of course – and only escaped after we were bruised and swearing.

I reckoned Anacrites would be heading up the Clivus Capitolinus, so we ducked the other way. I took us through the Arch of Tiberius and the Arch of Janus to the back of the temple, then turned along the dark rear portico of the Basilica. On the Palatine side it was deserted, apart from a few ever-hopeful women of easy virtue, but none tried to approach us. At the far end we took a straight run to the right up the Vicus Tuscus, a swerve as we headed for the Circus Maximus, a rush across the Street of the Twelve Gates. To climb the Aventine, I picked the first steep lane. Temple of Flora, then Temple of the Moon. A veer to the left, a shuffle to the right, and we came out by the Temple of Minerva where I had told Clemens to establish his watch-point. Flanked by enormous double porticoes, the Temple of Diana sprawled at an angle, right next door, just beyond our arrival point.

Everywhere should have been silent and in darkness, but the piazza in front of the temples was ablaze with lamps, music and excited voices.

★

We had picked a bad night. The neighbourhood was choked with a crowd of manumitted slaves, who claimed the goddess Diana as a patron. Their main celebration is supposed to be the slaves' holiday on the Ides of August, the day when the temple was inaugurated centuries before; at Saturnalia, freedmen pull their cap of liberty back on if they are tired of being sober citizens and want another chance to indulge in riotous behaviour. The singing, dancing crowd was intermingled with others whose shyness suggested they were fugitives. If these furtive souls had been hiding up at the temple, they had now ventured outside to party in the streets, thinking the festival gave them security. But I thought I recognised some from my dark adventure on the Appian Way. I certainly knew their alarming habits. A flock of them were swooping around like uninvited guests, obviously trying to unnerve other people.

'Hello, pretty boy!' Clemens greeted me, with a teasing glance at my blue tunic and soft shoes. Dropping the joke, the acting centurion helped a swordbelt over my head. Concealing it beneath my cloak, I nestled the familiar weight of the weapon under my right arm. The others were carrying too. It was illegal − but the laws for private citizens in Rome had not been composed to cover occasions when you might have to search the oldest temple recorded by the pontiffs, looking for an enemy of the state.

'This is a bit busy, Falco!'

'The night is going to be fun. I warn you, we'll be vying with the Praetorian Guards.'

'Marcus knows how to organise a good night out,' Helena told Clemens, perhaps with pride in me.

'I-o!'

We had a hard time squeezing through the crazy revellers. By the time we reached the altar court below the steep steps to the Temple of Diana, nothing was going as planned. Coming towards us from the gentle dogleg of the Clivus Publicius I now saw Anacrites' litter, presumably with him lolling inside, massaging his twisted ankle. A small armed escort marched behind. The few Guards who had peeled off from imperial duties at the Temple of Saturn would have been a manageable group for us. But I saw with despondence that a much larger force had already formed up here in the compressed outdoor altar space, waiting to rendezvous with the Spy.

Pressing forward, Clemens had seen neither the new arrivals nor their waiting phalanx of colleagues. I nudged him hard. 'Hold off!'

'Shit on a stick!' he muttered, behind his hand. He hissed an order and the lads pulled up. We edged back, hoping to hide in the crowd.

No luck. Anacrites had seen us. He had his litter carried right alongside. His sleek head appeared through the curtains. 'Falco! You were perfectly right and I should have listened. Your prescience is wonderful.' Sickened by his fake adulation, I stared around for its cause. The Spy pointed happily. Two figures approached at a fast trot from the direction of Fountain Court: Lentullus, with his ears looking big on a shaven head, loping breathlessly after my taller, faster brother-in-law. 'You warned me I did the wrong thing keeping him in custody. I should have let him go myself. If the priestess will not come to him,' Anacrites gloated, 'you knew that Camillus Justinus would come straight to her!'

XLI

The Temple of Diana Aventinensis had been built to dominate the major peak of the Hill. After centuries of isolation, it had succumbed to the crush when the Aventine became a popular living space, and it had lost its drama. The view from afar was lost. The altar court was nothing like the grand meat-slaughtering area at Ephesus, where the warm cuts from daily sacrifice feed the entire city. On the Aventine, noisy, narrow streets abutted the two long portico wings, and the front steps came down into an equally squashed thoroughfare where the altar lurked amidst normal toings and froings. It was no place to hold a riot.

The situation deteriorated rapidly. Trust a mob to sense a carnival: the frolicking freedmen immediately saw that they were unwanted obstructions to an official operation. They whooped and set out to disrupt it. Waving their caps of liberty, they began taunting the Guards, oblivious to danger.

Among them, ran a man I had seen on the Via Appia, the one who tootled a one-note pipe until your teeth gritted. I wanted to ask him if he knew anything about the boy flautist from the Quadrumatus house, but I was not free to deal with that.

The Praetorians were not only armed, but every one was an ex-centurion. Many had made it to the top: first-spear, chief centurion in a legion, hard-bitten as they come. All of them were just what you would expect from soldiers who had served out their time yet could not bear to leave the service. These types always begged to be allowed an extra stint in the legions. Then, instead of becoming veterans with provincial farms, the gnarled obsessives signed up for yet another posting, on imperial protection duty. Many had never even been to Rome before. With their special camp on the city outskirts that acted like an enormous officers' club, their fabulous figured breastplates and their immense scarlet helmet crests – not to mention their privileged position so close to the Emperor – they then thought they had been posted to be gods on Mount Olympus.

They rarely had a chance to do more than ceremonial duties. Their mood was edgy. Most of these bullies would at some period have served a tour in Germany; inevitably, some must have been there in the Year of the Four Emperors, during the bloody rebellion Veleda caused. The barbarian element in their duties tonight must be unsettling them. Grim-faced, scarred, and solid as slaughtered beef carcasses, they were keyed up to whip out their swords and fight someone. It could be anyone who offended them. These bastards had a low threshold for annoyance and once they were riled, they were not fussy whom they took it out on.

'Hold off!' I ordered my little gang. 'We can't engage with Praetorians.' The lads looked disappointed. I was not sure I could control them. Clemens, inexperienced as an acting centurion, looked as if where they led he would follow.

I had other problems. Anacrites jumped from his conveyance. Before I could intervene, Helena Justina stormed up to him. Delight at being in ascendance had healed his ankle magically, but Helena looked ready to kick his legs from under him. She had not yet spotted her brother; she was concentrating on the Chief Spy. Ever since Anacrites and I once worked together on the Census, she treated him like my junior clerk.

'This is a mess! Anacrites, I hope you have a properly thought-out public safety plan!' I doubted that Anacrites had put in place *any* crowd-control measures. In fairness, he would have thought it unnecessary. Like me, he had believed he was coming to conduct a quiet search, when the temple would be virtually closed. Now he discovered innocent members of the public milling about. From his behaviour, the bastard did not care.

My mood took another knock. As Justinus worked his way around one of the portico buildings, he had noticed the Guards and must have guessed why they were here. It made no difference. He did dodge behind a swarm of bystanders, but when they failed to provide sufficient cover, he broke free and raced straight up the central temple steps and into its colonnaded porch. We glimpsed him, but not for long. Although it was night-time, the great doors had not yet been closed but stood open as a concession to the revellers. Justinus pushed straight through a clutch of priests and priestesses, who had been watching the street party; they were too startled to stop him. He vanished into the interior. Lentullus followed. Nobody imagined they wanted to check the time on the elderly sundial fixed outside, or to consult the ancient treaty between Rome and the cities of Latium that was housed in the *cella*.

'That was Quintus!' Before Helena could take off after him, I managed to grab her.

Anacrites signalled the Guards. Hampered by the marauding crowd, the heavy troops gathered themselves for an onslaught on the temple. Clemens and I exchanged anguished glances. We reached a decision. He and I stripped off our cloaks, followed by the men of the First Adiutrix who had spotted their comrade Lentullus entering the precinct and knew he was in trouble. As one, we piled the garments in Helena's arms. 'Marcus, I did *not* come just to be the girl who holds the cloaks!'

'Do it. You're a heroine – but you can't fight the Guards. In any case, lady, you know the price of cloaks!' My grin stalled her. Staggering under the weight of heavy winter wool, she succumbed momentarily. 'Seems we should give your men a hand,' I said, very politely, to Anacrites. That simpleton looked shocked that we were armed with swords. Then we were all storming through the crowd and up the steps, trampling the big-booted heels of the Praetorians as they clambered ahead of us.

Everyone on the Aventine has a sense of being separate from Rome. It goes right back to Romulus and Remus. Our Hill was occupied by Remus; when he was murdered by his twin, the Aventine was excluded from the original city walls that Romulus completed. The Temple of Diana is the oldest and most venerable in Rome – but it was once *outside* Rome and that makes its priests reek of superiority. These indignant figures held up their hands and forbade the Guards entrance. 'You desecrate our shrine! Do not offer violence to a place of asylum!' There are precedents for requesting the return of a fugitive from the goddess Diana, but even if you are Alexander the Great and all his hosts, you are supposed to be polite.

The Guards, who reckoned they could go anywhere, were outraged. An altercation ensued. Negotiation achieved nothing, so by virtue of their weaponry, the Guards carried the motion and clanked straight indoors. They had slowed down though. Some even removed their helmets deferentially as they reached the inner precincts.

We were not wearing helmets. But like the Guards, once we crushed into the dimly lit interior, we walked more quietly. We passed through a forest of columns, to murky, incense-scented spaces. Statues of Amazons, with disconcerting friendly expressions, gazed at us from all sides. In the centre of the shrine was a lofty statue, modelled on the one at Ephesus: Diana, as a many-breasted mother-goddess, a serene smile on her gilded lips, holding out her hands, palms up, as if in welcome to fugitives.

Our hands were on our sword hilts, but we kept them sheathed. We struggled to overtake the Guards, but the overbearing bastards held us back. Some wheeled around, set themselves shoulder to shoulder, and penned us in a corner. It would be a bad idea to try and hack our way out.

Justinus and Lentullus had disappeared. Nobody else seemed to be there. A gaggle of priests and priestesses pushed in behind us. They hissed when the Guards started systematically searching. For a time those oafs tried not to cause disruption in the precinct, but their standard approach was to fling property about carelessly. Pretty soon a candelabrum went over. There was a scuffle while quacking priests doused the flames with a curtain, 'helped' by emboldened Guards plucking more draperies from their hanging-rods and tossing them aside. Votive statuettes were kicked around under needlessly clumsy boots. As priestesses shrieked and swooped protectively on temple furniture and treasure, the jubilant Guards found Ganna.

A group of Praetorians bunched tightly around her, to prevent escape. They were not harming her. But Ganna was young, female, foreign – and had no experience of defusing trouble. She screamed, and of course she kept on screaming. It was too much for Justinus, who burst from his hiding-place. Lentullus was at his heels again.

Things grew ugly. Guards finally drew their swords, so the temple staff went crazy. Justinus and Lentullus, both shouting, raced through the shrine towards Ganna, to be faced by a row of glitteringly sharp swords, wielded by brutal men who had twenty years' experience in using them. The light was bad; the space was cramped; in moments it turned into a nightmare. Justinus, though unarmed, was shouting at the Guards to free the young girl. They advanced on him, intentions clear; Lentullus, who did have a sword, flung himself between them. Clemens and I tried to exert a sensible influence, but we were all still penned in our corner by other Guards, who now decided to disarm us. As we passed our weapons from hand to hand among ourselves, to avoid confiscation, I watched Ganna being dragged outside. Breaking free, I rushed out on to the steps, only to see her carried down into the piazza, where she was bundled through the chanting crowds and shoved into the litter that had brought Anacrites. He shot me a repulsive look of triumph.

Somebody intervened: Helena Justina dropped her armful of cloaks and again accosted the Spy. The crowd hushed to hear her. She understood the situation. I knew she would be disgusted at Ganna's treatment, but she was clear and polite, with a ringing tone for all to hear: 'Anacrites, I am here to chaperon Ganna – with Titus Caesar's approval. Please be careful. You need all your diplomacy. Ganna is too young to have taken part in the rebellion – and she is *not* under threat of execution. This innocent girl came to Rome merely as a companion of Veleda – a chaperon herself. The intention now is to treat her well and make her a friend of Rome. Then we can send her back where she came from, to spread word among the barbarians that we are civilised people who should be seen as allies.'

'I know what I'm doing!' the Spy scoffed gracelessly.

'Of course. But wherever you are sending her, I shall go myself.'

Without waiting for the Spy's answer, Helena climbed into the litter with Ganna. The slaves did not wait for his reaction either. They picked up the shafts and moved off, escorted by a straggle of Praetorians. The cheering crowds divided to allow the party to leave the scene, heading down the Aventine. Anacrites had probably given orders for Ganna to be taken to some terrifying interrogation cell. With Helena on hand as an intermediary, it could be a very different occasion to the torture he had planned. For me, Helena's abrupt departure was both good and bad – but I had worse matters to deal with.

Infuriated, Anacrites came running up the steps, barging through the rest of the Guards and demanding to see Justinus. But when we all struggled back into the temple, pushing against one another vindictively and knocking priests aside, there was no longer any sign of him. In the dark interior – darker still, now lamps had been blown out in the skirmish – Clemens and most of our men were huddled around a prone figure. Lentullus lay on the ground, right in front of the statue of Diana. His left leg looked as if it was almost severed, but Clemens had it raised: Minnius and Gaudus were supporting the leg, while Paullus knelt behind Lentullus, holding his head. As Clemens struggled to apply a tourniquet, blood was soaking the tunic he had stripped off and used for this purpose. Blood was pooling all across the stone floor too. The soldiers were chivvying, calling Lentullus by name. No sound or movement came from him.

The temple attendants were useless, concerned only about the desecration in their shrine. A bunch of the Guards were pretending to be solicitous. I saw what they were up to. One of their number had done this, and they were starting to sense difficulties ahead. Most had fallen silent. Old centurions know what to do when things go wrong. They would be planning what let-out to claim, if there was an enquiry. Some approached, pretending to be helpful, offering to lift the lifeless young soldier and carry him outside.

On the verge of losing a man in his charge, Clemens went crazy. 'Leave him! Leave him to stabilise, you fools! Somebody get these murderous bastards out of the bloody way —'

I strode up. I let the Guards know from my voice how furious I was at having to sound reasonable. 'Just leave us to it now, lads. Better get lost. We were all on the same side, today. This was supposed to be a joint exercise — or hadn't anyone explained that?' Already displaying embarrassment, the Guards quickly decided to evacuate. Anacrites must have melted away from the scene ahead of them.

Kneeling by Lentullus, Clemens was still desperately trying to stanch the blood. He looked back over one shoulder, recognised me as I came to assess the problem, and yelled: 'Don't just stand there, Falco! Get some help — *get a doctor!*'

XLII

This mission was stuffed with doctors. I knew only one who might be close at hand. It was quickest to visit him. As soon as we could safely shoulder Lentullus, we rushed him to the vigiles. Their out-station was barely two streets away. Luckily, I had underestimated the Fourth Cohort's ability to recover from their Saturnalia drinks: a skeleton staff was on duty that night, and to my relief, one of them was Scythax, their morose doctor. He looked put out at the interruption, but he reacted quickly.

We lugged Lentullus in, and Scythax cleared a working space. A body was already on the table, but that was a dead man so he lost his place in the queue. The lads dumped the corpse outside in the exercise yard. At first we clustered round, but pretty soon Scythax shooed us out. He just kept Clemens to pass him equipment and take orders.

'Is there any hope?'

'Very little.' Scythax was a dour bastard.

We sat in the yard, half of us on the cold ground, some on coils of rope. I tried both; they were equally uncomfortable. Fortunately Sentius – another dismal, peculiar type – turned up with our abandoned cloaks. Two were unaccounted for. On a headcount we realised Titus and Gaudus were missing. If they went down in the fight, nobody had seen it. We just had to hope they had fled in the confusion – perhaps with Justinus.

We waited.

Young soldiers spend a great deal of time sitting around while nothing much is happening – but that doesn't mean they are good at it. Bored, Lusius took a look at the corpse Scythax had had in his cubicle. Fresh meat, Lusius said. To ease my stiffness I straightened up, and strolled over for a professional appraisal. He was fresh all right. I had seen this man alive not much more than an hour ago. It was the vagrant from the Via Appia, the musical one with the limited repertoire. He still had his deplorable one-note pipe, twisted into an indescribably filthy string he had been using as a tunic belt.

There was no indication what killed him. Lusius and I rolled him. Nothing.

Quietly I walked to the door of the medical cubicle.

Night had fallen hours ago, so the scene was lamplit; Clemens was holding a small pottery oil lamp, while the doctor carefully inserted a few animal-gut stitches to keep the flesh together on Lentullus' mangled thigh.

'How did this happen?' Scythax asked, between actions with the needle. He was no fine embroiderer. Nor was he confident at sewing; he liked a challenge, but his normal work was with burns and crush wounds. Vigiles who were cut in accidents ended up with very crooked scars.

'He tried attacking armed men when he didn't have a sword.' Clemens must have seen it occur. 'So he used his feet. He stamped them; they were not happy.'

'Drunks?' Scythax was supposing this had happened in a normal street fight.

'Oh no. They were sober.' Clemens kept it diplomatic, still not mentioning the Guards.

'You don't want to hear it, Scythax,' I added quietly from the doorway.

'Well I might have known – if you're involved, Falco.' Scythax stood up stiffly, put down the needle and flexed his fingers. Shadows from the lamp made his sallow oriental face look cadaverous, below an odd straight fringe he wore, as if he needed to keep his forehead warm or his brain would decay. He always spoke to me warily, as if he feared he was about to discover I was carrying a dread infectious disease. 'I will keep this man here; if he survives, it will be best not to move him.' He placed a soft pad over the damage, but bandaged it loosely. I guessed he would be needing access at frequent intervals. His hands were gentle as he covered Lentullus with a coarse blanket. 'I have no remit to take in strangers – Rubella won't like this.'

'Understood.' Rubella never liked anything on principle.

'You'll have to provide someone to do the daily nursing. I have my own work, you know.'

'We are extremely grateful.' Clemens might be in his first posting as an officer, but he had already learned how to handle civilians.

'I'll stay,' I volunteered. I probably ought to try to find Helena, but she might do better without me. Anacrites would accommodate her with due regard for her father's position and her own known friendship with Titus Caesar. She would not thank me for interfering. That does not mean I was not worried about her. I told Clemens to send me a message when she turned up at home, then I dispatched him and the others to their beds.

I helped Scythax tidy up and clean away the blood. I saw him put opiates ready, but our boy was still deeply unconscious. We worked silently at first; I saw the doctor relaxing. Later we sat on stools with cups of hot mulsum that someone brought us from the night kitchen. I ventured to ask Scythax about the dead man he had had on his work table when we first showed up. 'I know a little about him, that's why I'm curious.'

'He is a vagrant,' answered Scythax, as if I could have missed that. Not likely; the smell of him was reaching us from right outside.

'I know. Almost certainly a runaway slave. Lives in a homeless men's commune out on the Via Appia.'

'Musical. Is he the flautist you've been asking after, Falco?'

'No. Too old, too limited in his range of tunes – and my flautist would be new to the streets. This dead fellow has been starving under bridges for years, by the look of him.' Scythax nodded. When he volunteered nothing more, I enquired how the body came to be here.

It took him a while to respond. Still, he knew I wasn't going away – and he also knew how friendly I was with Petronius. It was either answer me, or have Petro turn up tomorrow asking the questions, by then doubly suspicious. So he answered.

According to Scythax, the corpse had been dumped beside the patrol house gates. He said this happened from time to time. He assumed people hoped there was still life in the victim, and that he might help.

The story sounded wrong. But I could think of no other reason a vigiles doctor would have fresh corpses served up to him.

' "Victim"?' I asked coolly. 'That would be as in "unnatural death", would it?'

'You tell me, Falco. There seemed to be nothing to show.'

Right. There was nothing to show why Scythax was so reticent either. But I heard voices outside, so I left it.

The new arrivals were our missing men, Titus and Gaudus. With them was Justinus, intensely anxious about Lentullus. I sent the legionaries home. Scythax stood up and went out, as if leaving us in private; I still felt he was trying to avoid talking to me about that corpse. He still feared I would not let the matter go.

I stared at my brother-in-law. He was now twenty-six or seven, a tall, slim, fairly fit man who had once had a career in front of him, though he had lost hope in that. He must have been able to keep himself clean at the Spy's house, but cannot have shaved for several days. He looked strained. It was more than his dread over the legionary's fate. Bruised circles under those dark eyes the women all fancied marred what could have been a handsome face. Among all that stubble, there was no trace of his normal wide-mouthed grin.

'We need to talk, Quintus.'

In low, level voices, we caught up. It took a while. Justinus maintained he had not known Ganna would be at the Temple of Diana; he was just hoping to find Veleda there. I picked up on that privately, but did not immediately demand how he had known her possible whereabouts.

During the mess with the Guards, Justinus had realised he was about to fall into Anacrites' hands again, so he made a bolt for it. He found a secret wooden stair that led up into the roof; sometimes the goddess made a ritual 'appearance' to the public, displayed at a window above the portico. Titus and Gaudus saw him go, knew he was vital to our task, and quickly ran after him. Later, when it was safe to descend, they had all gone to my house, but when the others returned and said Lentullus was seriously hurt, Justinus insisted on coming here.

'I keep remembering all we went through together in Germany. We all said Lentullus was hopeless – but he came good, Falco.'

'Oh I'll never forget him, swinging on the tail of that bloody great aurochs, without a fear, while the beast plunged about and I was trying to stick a tiny knife in its neck . . .'

'Heart of gold. You wanted him to keep me out of trouble – yet I ended up getting him into this. I'll never forgive myself, Marcus. He adored you and me.'

'We gave him the biggest and most exciting adventure of his life. He won't blame you.' Justinus blamed himself, however.

I let him carry on maundering over Lentullus for a while. Then I stopped him: 'So have you seen Veleda?' He looked blank. It had to be an act. 'Or had you merely been in contact with her before Anacrites had you arrested?' He tried to sustain the innocent ploy, so I shouted, *'Camillus Justinus, don't mess me about!'*

'Hush!' he remonstrated, gesturing to Lentullus. I fixed a straight glare on him. He must know I was assessing him. He must realise why. He had worked as my assistant for the past couple of years; he knew my methods. 'All right, Falco . . .' My gaze did not waver. 'I have not seen her.'

'Honest?'

'It's the truth.'

I believed him. All his family were straight. While I had known Justinus keep things to himself – his past liaison with Veleda being one – I had never known him tell direct lies. 'You will need to prove it to the world – so give, Quintus!'

'Settle down. We're partners, aren't we? There is no necessity to treat me like a suspect.' There was every need for it.

'Wrong, Quintus. And if you are fooling around with Veleda, our association ends right now.'

He cursed quietly. Then he told me. 'I knew when she arrived in Italy. You were still in Greece . . . It was supposed to be kept quiet, but Hades, everyone in Rome was talking about it. When she was at that so-called safe house, I did try to get messages to her.'

I wanted to ask how, but first I needed to know if I could trust him. So it was more important to know why. 'Were you hoping to take up where you two left off?'

Justinus looked sulky. 'There was nothing to take up.'

'I remember,' I said drily. 'I can still see you now, alleging that nothing had happened between you and Veleda, when every single one of us on that ship knew it was a load of rubbish.'

'The ship!' he reminded me. 'She gave us the bloody ship, Falco. She saved our lives by letting us escape down the river. Don't you think we owe her something in return?'

'What? Provide *her* with a ship to return her to Germany? No, it's too late, Quintus. Rutilius Gallicus has brought her here and she's stuck with her fate. We'll all have to live with it . . . How did you know about the safe house?'

'What?'

'I want to know, Quintus. How did you know where they had put her? Did she write and tell you?'

'She has never written to me, Falco. I don't even know if she *can* write. The Celts don't believe in writing things down; they commit important stories, facts, myths, histories to memory.'

'Spare me the cultural lecture! . . . Not much point Anacrites putting up a written notice to lure her in,' I commented, to lighten it.

'Not much point in anything he does.'

'How did you get on with him, when you were at his house?'

'Relations were cool.'

'Did he try to recruit you?'

'As a spy? Yes, he did. How do you know?'

'The snake tried it on with your brother in the past. What did you answer?'

'I said no, of course.'

'Happy fellow. So how did you know Veleda's whereabouts?' I reiterated.

Justinus at last capitulated, mildly enough. 'I know a man. Slight acquaintance, baths and gymnasium, nothing special. We nod to one another, but I wouldn't say I ever let him strigil my back . . . When everyone was speculating about Veleda, I happened to mutter that I had once met her. He must have been looking for somebody safe to confide in. He was bursting to share the secret with someone – Scaeva told me.'

I took a breath so hard it hurt. 'You know *Scaeva*?'

XLIII

'Gratianus Scaeva – brother of Drusilla Gratiana? Lived at the Quadrumatus villa? You know him, Quintus?'

'Only slightly.'

'*Scaeva* was passing messages for you?'

Justinus shrugged. 'He took letters *from* me. I got nothing back. Once he had given away where Veleda was, he lost his nerve fast. He was terrified of being found out. He wanted nothing more to do with me – but I kept seeking him out and insisting.'

'Did you *want* a reply from the priestess? Were you trying to resume your relationship?' Silence. 'Come on, lad. What were you playing at?'

'I don't really know.'

I believed that. 'Wonderful. Every mess in the world is caused by some idiot who can't make up his ridiculous mind about a woman who's not interested.'

I hit him with the information that Scaeva was dead. Quintus looked shocked. It could be genuine. I told him exactly how it had happened. Then I watched him work out the implications. 'Do you think Veleda hacked his head off?'

My brother-in-law blew out his cheeks. 'That's possible.' He had seen her amongst her tribal warriors, when they were baying for Roman blood; he knew that her place as a venerated leader depended on showing she was ruthless.

I liked the fact that he did not rush to defend her. Even so, his personal predicament was grim. Whatever assurances he gave, it looked as if he and the priestess had colluded.

'What can you tell me about Scaeva? This is urgent, Quintus.'

'I don't know much. Until recently I tried to avoid him. He was always snuffling and carrying on about his health. Well, that's unfair; he was fed up with it himself. He complained that he seemed to have spent every Saturnalia of his life lying sick on a couch.'

'Well, I'm afraid it won't happen this year.'

'No.' Justinus looked thoughtful. Perhaps he was considering the transience of life.

I now grilled him on how he came to think that Veleda might have been at the Temple of Diana tonight. His answer made things even more ghastly: according to him, in one of his unanswered letters, he himself suggested it as a place of refuge.

'What happened to those letters, Quintus?'

'I don't know.'

I hoped Veleda had destroyed them. If not, we had to find them. We had to retrieve and obliterate them. Another dirty task for me.

The thought crossed my mind that Gratianus Scaeva might have been killed because somebody discovered he was acting as an intermediary. If so, his punishment seemed vile. Still, the perpetrator may have deliberately set out to implicate Veleda. It was the kind of trick Anacrites might play.

'Right. Let's get it straight: Veleda comes to Rome. You think you owe her something for saving us. You offer help; Scaeva takes the letters; she does not reply.' She could have been carrying her reply along to Scaeva, the day Scaeva was killed. It was even possible Scaeva tried to wriggle out of taking her letter to Quintus, so that was why Veleda attacked Scaeva . . . Somehow I thought not. 'Even in two weeks of freedom she has not tried to contact you, apparently. So did you give up on her, Quintus?'

He looked vague, as if he could not accept that he and the priestess were past history.

'Look, you can't have seen Scaeva for over a fortnight. Scaeva has been dead all that time. Did anybody ever tell you Veleda had escaped?'

'Anacrites. At his house this week.'

'So tonight – you were just going to the temple on the off-chance of finding her?'

'Yes, but the moment I spotted the Praetorians, I went frantic. I thought they must know that Veleda was definitely inside –'

'And you know Ganna?'

'Never met the girl.' How many men had sworn that old lie to me? Justinus saw me thinking it. 'Marcus, Lentullus and I had talked, today at Fountain Court. He told me about Ganna being brought to Rome with the priestess. When the guards pulled her out of hiding, I guessed who she was . . . What will happen to her?'

'I don't know. Your big sister went with her, if that helps.' Justinus looked relieved. I felt slightly less confident: Helena would do all she could, but Anacrites was a bitter, single-minded foe. Nonetheless, Quintus and I shared a momentary smile, as we thought of Helena defying him. The first time I met him, Helena and I had yet to become lovers and she was giving me all Hades of a time. Her brother and I had bonded quickly, both overshadowed by her fierce spirit, both adoring her eccentric resolution.

I felt exhausted. I said I had to go home to see if there was news of Helena. I put Justinus on parole to remain at the station house with Lentullus – to stay there whatever happened to the injured soldier overnight. He agreed the conditions. I was almost past caring.

Just as I left, he surprised me. I glanced back from the door, raising a weary arm in salutation. Then Justinus suddenly asked me, 'How is Claudia?'

I took it as hopeful. Mind you, right when I first met him, I had noticed that Camillus Justinus had extremely good manners and a kind heart.

SATURNALIA, DAY TWO

Fifteen days before the Kalends of January (18 December)

XLIV

Positions were reversed. For once I was the one waiting among the oil-lamp shadows, when Helena crawled in at last, barely able to move from exhaustion. It was a shock to see her still in the strange brown gown she wore to the Temple of Saturn, though at some point since she disappeared in Anacrites' litter, she had plaited her loose hair into an old-fashioned bun like some severe matriarch from the Republic.

I had been sitting on a chest in a daze until I heard the litter-bearers calling good-night to her. I felt stiff myself, but managed to get to the door to open it for Helena like a uniquely efficient hall porter. 'Dirty stop-out. What time do you call this?' I took her in my arms, very gently. 'Should I check you over for bruises? Or just check how drunk you are?'

She shook her head in reassurance, as she collapsed against me. 'All we were offered was a small tray of three-day-old date fancies and some foul grape juice. Hospitality from the Chief Spy is not based on the Good Steward's Household Manual... I hope you picked up those cloaks, Marcus.'

So she was all right. I helped her upstairs, where we fell into bed wearing most of our clothes. I squirmed out of my outer tunic, hoping she had not seen the bloodstains I had acquired from Lentullus.

Helena fell asleep after me, I think, but she was up first. By the time I sauntered from our room, she had been to the baths, dressed like herself in a smart red dress and pendant garnet ear-rings, and had begun calming our household – scared slaves; disconcerted soldiers; subdued children; Nux slinking along skirting boards as if she was in trouble; Albia, equally dog-like, defiantly letting us know she was furious at us for staying out all night.

I had washed my face and put on slippers. I had decided not to shave or change my undertunic. I was master of my house. I had my own style. I wasn't a jumped-up, hidebound, establishment lackey who couldn't yawn if it was a black day on the calendar. People knew what to expect from me. I refused to create anxiety by looking too formal.

Once everyone had settled down, Helena and I were free to take a late breakfast by ourselves. After we ate, we carried warm honey drinks right up on to our roof terrace, where there was a chance we could remain undisturbed. I checked the supports on the wind-blown climbing roses while I reported on Lentullus and Justinus. 'I told your brother to remain with the vigiles. I hope he does. But I haven't the resources – or the will any longer – to hold him to it.'

'Can I go and see him?'

'I can't stop you.'

'Marcus!'

'Oh I just don't want you seeing the mess the Guards have made of Lentullus.' As Helena stared, I admitted, 'Yes, the lad could die. He may be dead by now.'

Helena slowly sipped at her beaker. 'Is Scythax a good doctor? Should we find a better man?'

'Maybe I'll ask around, see if there is a specialist for sword wounds – some old army surgeon, maybe. I don't want to appear ungrateful to the vigiles. Lentullus would have gone under last night, if I hadn't thought of Scythax.'

I told her about the incident with the dead vagrant. Helena pursed her lips. I could see her filing it away in her library of curiosities. At some point, if a link occurred, she would pull down a mental scroll case and bring out this story, making new sense of it. Meanwhile we were silent, absorbing the oddities.

'So tell me what happened, sweetheart; how did you get on with Anacrites?'

I watched Helena sorting her thoughts quietly. 'Well, to begin at the end, Ganna has been placed in the House of the Vestals.'

'Whose idea?'

Helena smiled. 'It is secure, and the Virgins will look after her. Ganna understands that nothing can be decided about her own fate until Veleda has been found.'

'And how painful was it, reaching this resolution?'

Helena said briefly, 'The man is a pig.' Seeing my look of horror, she took my hand quickly. 'Oh Anacrites didn't assault us. Nothing so direct. He deals in mental indignities. I dare say he would have tried physical mistreatment of the girl, had I not been there – '

'It's standard,' I confirmed. Without allowing the Spy any credit, I too would have done the same, faced with a tricky enemy and driven by urgency: 'In tough interrogations, even before you start beating them up, you deprive your subject of food, drink, hygiene facilities, warmth, consolation – hope.'

'Well, Anacrites certainly deprived Ganna of hope.'

'That's not fatal. Nor does it have to be permanent.'

'Are you as hard as him? No, Marcus. You have better tactics. More practical. First, you would point out the risks of her situation and the possibilities for retrieving something if she co-operates . . .' Helena was looking morose. 'I did try to persuade Anacrites that he should adopt your methods. I played on the fact that you and he are both working on this problem – working together –' I made vomiting noises. She ignored it. 'Working together now, just as you had done so successfully during the Great Census. I said, you both owe your current prosperity and your high social profile to that experience. Neither of you should forget it.'

I took the sophisticated route this time; I merely banged down my beaker hard on a garden table. 'So?' I asked coldly.

Helena chuckled. 'Oh, it worked, Marcus. Anacrites did exactly what you would do.'

'Which is?'

'He snapped, well maybe *I* would like to ask the questions then.'

We both had a chortle, then Helena admitted, 'Of course he was being sarcastic, but I jumped in and thanked him, and took him at his word.'

I allowed myself to guffaw. I was enjoying the story now. I wished I could have been a gecko yesterday in a corner of the interrogation room.

'First I suggested that I should like to get comfortable; I asked to use the facilities. Ganna had the sense to come too. A slave was supervising us, but we managed to have a few words together and I impressed on her that the more she said, the better it would look, so the easier things would go for her. And . . .' Helena paused, reconsidering.

'That "and" sounds significant.'

'No, it's nothing. So when we went back, I asked the questions and Ganna confessed pretty well everything.' I noted Helena's 'pretty well', but let her carry on with her version.

Some we already knew: how at the Quadrumatus house the two women had plotted to escape in the laundry cart, then how Veleda managed it, but went alone. How Veleda sought out Zosime, then afterwards made her way to the Temple of Diana, where a priestess gave her shelter out of sisterly fellow-feeling, while Ganna – by then staying at my mother's apartment – was able to visit the temple and leave messages of support. She was never allowed to see Veleda face to face. But temple attendants always reassured her – until yesterday, when Ganna ran there after my sisters had scared her, and they claimed Veleda was no longer with them. 'Ganna ran away because she found your sisters very frightening!' I found them frightening myself.

'So where is Veleda now?' I asked, giving Helena a narrow look.

Helena accepted my scrutiny in her serene way. 'Ganna insists that she does not know. Anacrites is all set to make pompous demands of the chief priest. A bad mistake.'

'Does he not have jurisdiction over temples?' I wondered.

'Tell that to the temples' priests! It does not do to underestimate the power of such institutions. Even the Emperor would approach cautiously. *I* think Anacrites will be roundly rebuffed – if only because of the outrages committed last night by the Praetorians in his name.'

'That was stupid.' He should have cleared the operation with the temple first.

Helena nodded. 'He has no diplomacy. But anyway, it may be that the priests really cannot help with Veleda's current whereabouts. If she sensed that pursuit was closing in on her, she may have left in a hurry and without revealing her plans.'

I was not convinced. She was sick, foreign, and probably short of funds. The Temple of Diana Aventinensis may not have liked being stuck with a fleeing barbarian, but once they took her in, they would see it through. 'So where could she go, my darling? She must be running out of options now. Where next?'

Helena Justina gave me a straight look. 'It seems nobody knows.'

I bet! I knew Helena, so I was convinced Ganna told her something in confidence when they tried the 'two shy girls have to go to the lavatory together' trick. You could tell Anacrites had no real knowledge of women, or he would never have fallen for that one.

I gave Helena a glance that told her I believed that she was holding back – and in return she gave me a smile that said she saw what I thought, and wouldn't give . . . Fine.

'So was Anacrites impressed by your help, my darling?'

Helena Justina let out an uncharacteristic snort. 'He thinks he's very clever – but the man is a fool!'

Excellent. Anacrites had failed to notice that my wife secretly possessed a clue.

Helena mentioned that she was going over to the Capena Gate later, to tell her parents and Claudia that Justinus was now free and well. She spoke idly, like any efficient wicked woman. Either she had taken a lover – which I always feared was possible – or she was up to something she thought she could bring off better than me. She might be right, but if she went out on the loose, I was a heavy-handed Roman husband: I intended to play the chaperon. During the day, I watched for indications. She spent a lot of time giving instructions about Julia and Favonia; normally she would have taken them with her to see their doting grandparents. She collected a few things, as if she might be travelling.

I gave her a couple of hours' start, using the time to shave and to pack necessities myself. I put Clemens in charge of everything at home, and I asked for a volunteer who could ride. The legionaries were still too upset by what had happened to Lentullus. Only Jacinthus whispered please could he come? Typical. I was better off when I worked alone. Still, he was a dead loss in the kitchen, he took no interest at all in cutlets or calamari, and I might well need a companion. So gritting my teeth at my usual filthy handout from fortune, I set off accompanied by my cook. Jacinthus seemed thrilled to be taken on an unknown mission. He could have been a soldier; all he wanted was to be on the move, never mind why or where.

We tailed Helena from the senator's house to the stables where I knew her father kept his carriage. Two female companions were with her, closely cloaked and followed by a slave carrying small hand luggage. They left the slave behind when they departed in the carriage like the three Graces taking their dancing sandals to a summer picnic. It was a slow vehicle, giving me time to acquire horses for Jacinthus and me.

Whether Ganna had whispered it to her, or whether Helena simply worked it out for herself, as soon as I saw that she was taking a route along the Via Appia and out towards the Alban Hills, it struck me where we were probably going. In winter it would be a long haul: we were heading for another shrine of Diana. We were going to Lake Nemi.

XLV

The carriage stopped for a comfort break after about six miles. I rode up. 'Surprise!'

'I thought we'd let you catch up,' said Helena pleasantly. Her eyes lingered on Jacinthus. The cook had no idea his presence was making me feel unprofessional.

To my surprise Helena not only had Albia with her, which I might have expected, but also Claudia Rufina, the hard-done-by wife of Justinus. Claudia was exhibiting the bright eyes and firm mouth of a wronged woman who now had her rival pinned down in catapult range. If Veleda really was skulking at Nemi, she was liable to end up buried there in a shallow grave.

When I grumbled about being excluded, Helena retorted that men were superfluous. The shrine of Diana Nemorensis had become a wildly fashionable complex for wealthy wives who needed assistance in conception. Helena and Claudia were going to Nemi under guise of seeking fertility advice.

I said a fertility shrine seemed an odd place to hide a virgin priestess.

Claudia sniffed. Albia spluttered with laughter. Helena just grinned and told me that if I had to tag along, I must keep right out of their way at the shrine. That suited me.

Since Nemi lies between fifteen and twenty miles from Rome, our late start was ludicrous. We only reached the area by the feeble light of lanterns. We were forced to stay overnight at Aricia. Aricia had been a stronghold of Augustus' horrible family, so it was full of people who took a snide view of anyone who lacked gods in their ancestry. There were inns. Any town on the edge of a famous sanctuary extends hospitality to those it can exploit. In theory Aricia was a pleasant spot, famous for its wine, its cuts of pork, its woodland strawberries. The whole place was half dead in December, however. Dinner was foul, the beds were damp, and the only consolation was that there were few Saturnalia revellers creating a din on its sour streets. At least we slept.

Helena and I slept together, and since we were so close to a fertility shrine, I made sure we demonstrated that we did not need any divine assistance in our matrimonial rites. No votive statue sellers tomorrow would be selling me little models of sick wombs or wobbly penises. In the morning I had barely enough energy to beat up the landlord for overcharging – but that was nothing to do with my exertions, just seasonal depression clamping down.

We did not linger over breakfast, since the inn did not offer any. We found a solitary bakery that condescended to sell a bag of old rolls and some must-cake. Eating as we went, in a manner that would not be approved of by snobs, we set off soon after dawn to find the sacred grove and the lake.

SATURNALIA, DAY THREE

Fourteen days before the Kalends of January (19 December)

XLVI

The Alban Hills enclose two inland lakes known as the mirrors of Diana – the Lakes of Nemi and Albanus. Of these, Lake Nemi is famously the more isolated, beautiful and mysterious. When the country road brought us three miles from Aricia along the upper ridges, nothing prepared us for what would lie below. That frosty December morning, mist writhed like abandoned laundry on the silent forest trees and hung over the lake basin in a suspended white canopy. The shrine of Diana was set apart from the world, within a perfect circle of volcanic peaks. The enclosed lake gave the impression it might be as deep again as the surrounding hills are high. Tangles of age-old vegetation clothed the steep interior slopes, ancient holm-oaks and ash, thriving amidst head-high brambles and ferns; yet somehow a road had been hacked out down inside the ancient crater. Even the presence of Julius Caesar's enormous villa, sprawled in ugly splendour at the southern end of the lake, could not spoil the remote perfection of the scene.

The narrow road led us fairly gently through the deserted woods via overgrown hairpin bends. As we descended, we passed little fields and market gardens, clearly benefiting from fertile soil, though most looked abandoned and some gave the impression they had been frozen in time since our primitive rural ancestors. There were occasional tiny dwellings, more like cowsheds than homes, with no sign of occupants. We lost our way a couple of times, but then a man in a cart came racketing around a corner and nearly ran into us. He had the haunted gaze of a husband who thought his wife was cheating on him, an obsessed cuckold who was gallivanting up the hill in the hope of catching the culprits at a tender tryst in Aricia. I bet they knew he was coming. I bet it happened every week, and they always eluded him.

Despite looking unreliable, he gave us accurate directions. We took a side road we had already passed twice, that had looked as if it led nowhere, and soon came out in a flat area close to the water, just below the levelled terraces upon which the sanctuary was built.

We were in a deep basin the eye could only take in if you turned on the spot. Ahead of us stretched the limpid waters of the lake, unmarred by fishing boats. All around, striking hills rose steeply to a sky that seemed so far away we felt like moonstruck rabbits at the bottom of their burrow.

'This place would make poets wet themselves.'

'Ever one for the fluent phrase, Falco.'

'I'm not happy. It's too sure of its own magnificence.'

'You just hate seeing that a local landowner has selfishly scarred the vista with an ostentatious holiday home!' Helena was glaring angrily down the lake to the abomination that disfigured the southern shore. She was no supporter of Julius Caesar or his great-nephew Augustus, with their boasts and empire-building machinations, let alone their crackpot, incestuous, empire-destroying descendants, Caligula and Nero.

'You said it. Filthy-rich monsters with brazen ambitions . . . Also, fruit, I am sneering at this so-called isolated shrine, which has cynically attracted shoals of élite – and loaded – so useful in gynaecology – women, whose real reason for failure to conceive is that they are all inbred to buggery –'

'I don't believe buggery would help,' Claudia Rufina murmured sweetly, as if I might not know its definition. The tall young woman (provincial, but substantially loaded herself) rearranged a stole over one shoulder, gazing around as if she feared to meet her destiny in this near-perfect place. They were all subdued. Entranced by the wild beauty of the setting, young Albia turned on me an expression she saved for when she knew indelicate issues were being discussed by adults who preferred her not to listen. Then she lost interest in being precocious and went back to admiring the grove-covered hills and the lake.

Any religious nymph from the endless forests of Germany ought to feel at home close to these graceful trees and the water. I finally began to believe that Veleda might be here.

Helena had a vague recollection of some story about horses being banned within the temple precincts. 'Wasn't Diana's hunting consort, Virbius, a manifestation of Theseus' son Hippolytus, who was torn apart by horses for rejecting the adulterous advances of his stepmother, Phaedra?'

'Sounds like a load of old myth to me . . .' I grinned. 'Families do have their troubles.'

I listened to Helena. Our purpose today would hardly be

welcomed. We could not march in and demand that a priestess who had been granted sanctuary be handed over to us. So rather than offend even more, we left our carriage and horses, and continued unobtrusively on foot. The shrine lay above us. Its main rites were in August, the birthday of the huntress goddess, when crowds of women came from Rome to celebrate the compassionate patroness of midwives, lighting up the whole area with torches and lamps. Today, we passed nobody as we walked.

We clambered uphill on a short roadway to a large walled enclosure. Albia skipped on ahead, though Claudia was breathing hard so Helena and I slowed our pace for her. Inside the walls, the sanctuary was planted with gardens. Even in December this was a pleasant place to stroll among the topiary, quiet arbours and statues, and the fine lake view beyond. Around the fane were other facilities, including an empty theatre.

'You look too virile,' Helena told me. 'We can't take you. They will know I spend a lot of time fending you off and trying *not* to conceive.' I raised an eyebrow silently reminding her that there had been no fending off last night. Helena blushed. 'Jacinthus will be acceptable as our bodyguard.' Jacinthus was tiresomely excited; he was hoping that a wild boar would thrust its snout from the undergrowth – not so he could turn it into escallops and terrine as he should do, but so he could fight it. 'He can find you when we're finished. Go and amuse yourself somewhere, Marcus, and we'll meet later.'

'How long will you be?'

'Not long.'

'Any husband knows what that means.' We could see that there were pilgrims in the sanctuary. I reckoned there would be a slow queue at the fertility shrine. The priests would keep everyone waiting, to unsettle them and make them suggestible – or as they would say, to allow the shrine's calming influence to soothe them.

'Oh don't make a fuss. Go and play in the woods, Falco – and take care!'

Woods did not frighten me.

I walked about for several hours. I searched all the small shrines, temples and recreational facilities, a task which was as fruitless as I expected, then I strolled down weedy paths among the trees. Scowling with cold and boredom, I listened to the rustles and sighs that nature devises to unnerve town-dwellers who find themselves out in the open. I remembered this from Germany. We had spent weeks

231

trailing through miles of forest, growing more and more leery; I knew how it felt to be quite alone in the woods, even for a short time. Every crack of a twig makes your heart bump. I hate that smell of old animal trails and suspicious fungi. I dread that sense, every time you enter a clearing, that somebody or something rank has disappeared on one of those damp paths moments before you – and is still close by, watching with hostile eyes.

I could understand how dark legends about Nemi had sprung up in Rome's prehistory. This spot had been sacred for centuries. In times gone by, there was always supposed to be King of the Grove, a chief priest, who came here first as a runaway slave; he plucked a golden bough from a special tree, which would only yield to the true applicant. He would find and kill in single combat the previous King of the Grove. Then he could only wait anxiously for the next runaway to arrive through the spectral mists and kill him . . . Those bloodthirsty days had supposedly been ended when the Emperor Caligula casually decided that the current incumbent had been in post too long, so he sent a tougher man to depose him and make *rex Nemorensis* a civic position, presumably with the normal terms and conditions.

Public service has its dark side. The pay is always meagre and the pension rights are rubbish. Do your job well, and some mediocrity always gets jealous, then you end up being shifted sideways, to make way for a half-baked management favourite who cannot remember the old days and who has no respect for the gods . . .

Caligula liked Nemi. He used the place as a decadent retreat. He had two stupendous barges built to float on the lake, floating pleasure palaces. I had heard that those barges were larger and even more extravagantly decorated than the gilded state barges used by the Ptolemys on the River Nile; their fabulous on-board accommodation included a full suite of baths. They had every kind of top-flight nautical equipment too, some specially invented. In the polite version, these great ships were created so that crazy Caligula could partake in the rites of Isis. The better story says that they were intended for imperial orgies.

I made my way to the shore, where I found a man who claimed he had once worked aboard the vessels. The old whelk now spent his days dreaming of past glory. He had the sense to dream out loud, in order to receive charity from visitors. Even more bored than I was, in return for half a sestercius in a rather fine bronze bucket he just happened to have handy, he was happy to talk. He admitted he had stolen the bucket from on board. He spoke of triple lead-sheathing on the hull and heavy marble cladding on cabins and the poop; lion-headed bollards; revolutionary bilge pumps and folding anchor stocks. He swore there had been rotating statues, powered by fingertip bronze bearings on secret turntables. He told me how these great ceremonial barges had been deliberately scuttled, once Claudius became emperor. I had heard about plenty of bad behaviour under Claudius, but the elderly ruler had at least claimed to clean up society. During his early days of promise, he had ordered the symbols of his predecessor's luxury and decadence to be destroyed. The Nemi barges were sunk. And then, like any King of the Grove knowing himself to be doomed, old Claudius settled down to wait for Nero's ambitious mother to serve him with a fatal dish of mushrooms. The nutty old emperor is dead; long live the even nuttier young new one.

The thought of the lost ships depressed me. I went back to walk in the woods. I wandered about despondently. Suddenly a man wielding an enormous weapon ran out from behind a nearby tree and rushed me. My assailant had a crude approach to fighting, but he was sturdy, fired up, and as he swung his big sword, I saw the panic in his eyes. I was in no doubt: his one idea was to kill me.

XLVII

I had brought my own sword, but could not immediately unsheathe it from its scabbard's cosy nook under my armpit. At first I was too busy dodging. There were plenty of trees to jump behind, but most were too slender to provide real cover. My opponent sliced through the sapling stems with all the hatred of a gardener slashing giant thistles.

Once I got my sword out, I was in a real predicament. I learned to fight in the army. We were taught to parry a stroke as violently as possible, jar the other man half senseless, then plunge in and kill him. I was happy to send this madman straight to the River Styx – but the investigator in me yearned to know first why the suicidal menace was attacking me. As we danced around and clashed blades, the effort seemed pointless. I was on the verge of ending it with one brutal stab through his ribs.

He was desperate. Every time I lunged forwards, he managed to stop me. I stabbed again: he accepted it like a gladiator who knows he won't leave the arena alive. Soon it was all defensive work; every time I attacked, he furiously protected himself. If I slacked off, he should have gone for me with renewed vigour, but he seemed to have lost his initiative.

In the end I took a chance. I let my sword dangle from my hand, point down. I held open my arms, baring my chest for a death blow. (Believe me, I was out of range and I kept a good grip on the sword.)

'So kill me,' I taunted him.

The moment seemed ageless and endless. Then I heard him whimper.

I whipped up my sword, jumped across the clearing, knocked him flat and fell on top of him. My sword point was pressing on his neck. I noticed it was slitting the complicated gold braid of a rather fine long white tunic – out of keeping with its wearer. He had a face like a milk pudding, with a dumpling where his nose should be and his body was degraded by rickets. His manner was an odd combination: bombastic authority mingled with sheer terror. The closest I had seen to this clown was a bankrupt financier when the bailiffs came – immediately before denial and self-justification set in.

'I know who you are!' the curious specimen gurgled.

'I bet you bloody don't . . . Who are you? Apart from a raving maniac?'

'I am nameless,' he wavered. This mission was full of spooks.

'Well that was an oversight on your father's part.' I released him abruptly and stood up, taking his weapon. I sheathed my own sword immediately, and stood back.

'Can I get up?'

'No. Stay there on the ground. I've had enough of you jumping around like a Spanish flea and trying to do me in.'

'I've been following you. I watched you searching –'

'I wasn't searching for you. Not unless you are a woman and extremely well disguised. Now listen to me. Whoever you think I am, my name – given to me by my mother, in fact, since my father was off buying a statue in Praeneste at the time – my name is Falco. Marcus Didius Falco, son of Marcus – a free Roman citizen.'

He gasped. By then I thought he would.

In a quieter tone I said encouragingly, 'That's right. Calm down; I am neither a slave nor a runaway. So I haven't come for you. You are the King of the Grove, I presume?'

'Yes I am.' The Rex Nemorensis spoke proudly, even though he was lying on his back in his own grove, covered with leaf litter and squashed toadstools, while being insulted by me. 'Now you know what it is all about, can I get up please?'

'You can't get up until you've answered my question.' I kept my tone rough. I was tired of my quest and ready to be ruthless in ending it. 'The woman I am looking for is a high-status German, who would have skulked here very recently. Good-looking number; sent on from Diana Aventinensis; seeking sanctuary. She may be ill. She has good reason to be desperate.'

'Oh that one! Arrived two days ago,' said the Rex Nemorensis, grateful that my demands could be met so easily. He did not care about Veleda. All he wanted was his own survival. 'Claims she is a victim of international injustice, hounded by violent elements in her own country, kidnapped against her will, due for intolerable punishment, under a death threat – the usual foreign woes. You'll soon find her moping around if you look.'

'I was looking, when you jumped me,' I reminded him.

'I thought my time had come,' pleaded the King of the Grove, his belligerent spirit now collapsed like a rotten gourd.

'Not yet,' I said kindly, gripping his arm and pulling him back on to his feet.

'Oh you have no idea what it is like, Falco, hiding behind trees all day, just waiting for someone new to turn up and kill you.'

'I thought they'd put a stop to all that.'

'So they say – but can I believe them? I took sword lessons from an old gladiator before I came, but I've forgotten all the theory. Besides, I'm not getting any younger . . .' I felt as if I was listening to some antiquated fisherman deploring how the younger generation had fished out all the mullet. 'Dead men's shoes,' he muttered. No, he was like some ghastly public scribe, anticipating the day a spotty underling with a sharper stylus finally usurped his place.

I brushed down his long priestly tunic, gave him back his sword, put him on a path with his face to the main road, and left him to his perpetual wait for death.

I quite liked him, once I got to know him. Still, the man was doomed. Being in proximity to inevitable failure is bad news. It makes you start thinking too much about your own life.

The Rex Nemorensis offered to assist me. I wanted to go on by myself, but when I set off, he came tagging along behind me like an inquisitive goat.

I was heading down to the lake again. That was when I spotted her. A woman was standing motionless, right on the shoreline, wrapped in a long dark cloak with its hood up. She had her back to me. She was quite alone, either gazing into the water or simply staring out across it. She was the right height and I thought I recognised her bearing. From behind there was no way of interpreting her mood, but her stillness and her posture suggested deep melancholia.

The King of the Grove could be useful after all. Looking back over my shoulder, I called quietly, 'One question: since she came here, has anybody died a violent death?'

He shook his head, almost sadly. 'Nobody.'

I pulled my own cloak across so it was hiding my sword again, then I walked cautiously out from the woods and crossed the low flat beach until I reached Veleda at the water's edge.

XLVIII

She was older than I expected – *much* older than I remembered. That was a shock. Although the circumstances of our first encounter may have washed my memory of her with a golden haze of romance, being captured by Rutilius Gallicus had brought about one of those abrupt deteriorations that affect some people physically. She must have aged fast over a short period; endless forests notoriously lack discreet little cosmetics shops to remedy that kind of damage.

She recognised me. 'Didius Falco.' Those blue eyes saw what I was thinking about her appearance. Mind-reading is one of the traits that mysterious priestesses always cultivate. '*You* seem unaltered by time!' It did not sound like a compliment. Rats, I was used to that.

'Don't be fooled. I'm married with two children. I grew up.' I wondered if she knew that something similar had happened to Justinus. Presumably when the fool wrote, he told her. Or maybe not . . .

Away in the forest Veleda had looked every inch a rebel leader, the brilliant inspiration of ferocious warriors who under her guidance not only took on the Empire, but took on Rome and nearly won. My companions and I had seen her walk among her people with magnificent assurance. The wiles that entrapped Justinus had been based on her physical beauty, as well as her intelligence and power (plus that talent all clever women use against men – showing an interest in him). She still was a striking woman. Tall, erect of bearing, riveting blue eyes, fair – though when her hood fell back as she turned towards me, the shining blonde had faded. If grey was not yet covering the golden braids, it would be rampant soon. None of her confidence seemed to have been sucked from her by the humiliation of capture, yet something had died – or was dying – within her. It was simple enough. The legendary Veleda was no longer a girl.

She felt no change. I could see that. The blur of a bronze or silver mirror would not have shown her those fine lines around her eyes and mouth, or the way her skin had begun to lose its elasticity. It was likely

237

the doctors who attended her at the Quadrumatus house, the men Helena had derided for instantly deciding that Veleda's problems were 'women's hysteria', had correctly diagnosed that she had hit the change of life – though looking at her, I could see signs of real illness too. But Veleda was still herself; she faced the future wanting life, influence, success. It meant she was still dangerous. I must remember that.

'Veleda. I never thought that we would meet again. Sorry; that's trite.'

'You don't improve, Falco.' Now I remembered, she had never liked me. She had taken to Camillus Justinus at once because he was uncynical, innocent and – as far as he ever could be on a dangerous mission – honest. Very few Romans would be as open in a tight situation as he was. She had convinced herself the young hero was genuine – and he did very little to disappoint her.

In contrast, she had realised I was trouble. I had been sent to the endless forest where she lived in an old Roman signal tower, guarded by a disgusting crew of hangers-on: male relatives, exploiting their relationship. I was sent specifically to manipulate her, coerce her, stop her fighting Rome. I might even have killed her. For all she knew, that had been my intention. I was not sure myself what I would have done, had the opportunity presented itself. Whenever I worked as the Emperor's agent, I was the hitman with no scruples, ordered off on dirty tasks abroad that the state would not acknowledge and could not openly condone. I unbunged the blockages in the diplomatic sewers. If elegant conversation had been enough to deter Veleda as our foe, Vespasian would never have sent me.

Last time we met, I was her captive. Now there were just the two of us, standing on a deserted lakeside, me with a sword and her unarmed. Once again, she knew what I was thinking. 'So, are you going to kill me, Falco?'

'If this were Germania Libera . . .' I sighed. Life was foul and fate was filthy. Here a swift end for Veleda was against the rules. I didn't care about the rules, but somebody might be watching us. 'I don't expect you to believe me, lady, but my version of civilisation says it would be best to kill you cleanly, rather than have you paraded on a cart like a trophy and the life choked out of you by some filthy executioner.'

Veleda made no answer. Instead, she turned away again, staring into the lake as if she glimpsed shifting images of those sunken barges in its peaceful waters.

I moved closer to her side. 'You may have met an old man who told you, there are fantastic ships lying in the lake, ships created for an emperor. I shall never forget that you gave me the precious gift of a general's ship once. You saved our lives. Your tribe must have hated you for it. So, Veleda, are you calling in favours?'

Veleda turned and raked me with a cold glance. 'If I wanted a return of my favour, I would have sent to you as soon as I arrived in Rome.'

'Who did you send to for help then?' I challenged her.

She stood straight as a spear. 'I sent to no one.'

I smiled thinly. 'No need, of course. There was a young man with a high sense of duty – and strong feelings for you that had never died. So he wrote to you.'

'If you know that, Falco, then you know I never answered him.'

I could not decide whether we were making progress, or just swamping ourselves in pointless talk. Now we were both staring into the lake water.

'I believe you, Veleda. We may be enemies, but in the past we dealt with one another fairly. I told you straight why I came to your domain, and you in turn honourably told me the fate of a man whose death I was investigating. When my companions and I left you, we went with your foreknowledge and approval. We had put our arguments for peace before you; you remained free to choose whether to continue hostile activity against Rome or to be swayed by us.' I meant, swayed by Camillus Justinus, for he had been our spokesman. He was the only one Veleda would listen to.

I dropped my voice. 'So still in the same spirit, Veleda, tell me this: was it you who killed Sextus Gratianus Scaeva?'

The priestess stepped forward half a pace and crouched suddenly at the water's edge. Leaning out, she trailed her slender fingers in the lake. Waves trickled against them as she moved her hand one way and then the other. She looked back at me over her shoulder with angry eyes in a pale face. 'And cut off his head? And placed it in the stagnant water?' I noticed she spoke as if those had been two distinct actions – and that she despised the collected rainwater in the atrium pool. She was clearly aware that blame for the atrocity had been assigned to her. Her voice sounded defiant. 'No, Falco!'

She stood again. Now she was too close to the edge of the lake, her sandalled feet actually in the water. Waves wetted her gown hem. At her flurry of movement, waves even tugged the hem of her long cloak away from her a few inches.

I wanted to ask whether she knew who did commit the murder. But I stopped. I saw from her expression that Veleda had noticed something. I glanced behind. Walking down the shore towards us, unhurried but with purpose, came Helena Justina: Helena my wife, the extremely protective sister of Veleda's one-time Roman lover.

XLIX

A s always, as soon as Helena came near enough, our eyes met and I smiled a private greeting. Jacinthus was shadowing her, looking pleased with himself as a bodyguard, but there was no sign of our two other companions, Albia and Claudia. 'Finished?'

'Unsatisfactory.'

'Claudia?'

'Waiting at the carriage. A little upset.' I saw no reason for that, unless Claudia Rufina was irritated that the priests at the shrine refused to hand over Veleda to be torn to pieces by Justinus' raging bride. Still, it was highly convenient to avoid a confrontation with Veleda at this sensitive stage. 'Albia stayed with her. Who is your friend, Marcus?'

'Introductions – Veleda, this is my wife, Helena Justina.'

Helena went right up to her and grasped her hand formally. 'I was hoping to meet you. Can you understand me?'

'I speak your language!' declaimed Veleda, in the crushing tones she liked to use when proclaiming her knowledge of Latin. It had impressed me the first time. Now she and Ganna were overplaying the act. 'I believe I knew your brother,' stated the priestess then, in belligerent mode.

At that, Helena leaned forward unexpectedly, embraced the other woman and kissed her cheek as if they were sisters. Veleda looked startled. 'Then thank you for what I know you did five years ago to return my two men back to me.'

Released from the embrace, Veleda could only shrug. The motion had disturbed her cloak. Now I saw that below it she wore Roman clothing. Her ears had piercing-holes, but no ear-rings. If she had had to sell her treasures, that was good. I wanted her to be without resources. No jewellery glinted at her slender throat – though I did see she wore a soapstone amulet, carved with a magic eye.

I knew that. It had been given to me by a friendly quartermaster at Vetera, who pitied me for my suicidal mission into Free Germany. Later, I had tucked the thing around Justinus' neck, when he went alone to see the priestess in her tower. He had come out alive, though the amulet had not protected him from misery. Our young hero had carried loss with him wherever he went after that night. I always thought he must have given away the mystical token as a love-gift. Now I was sure. Veleda, presumably, had worn it ever since for the same reason.

Helena was watching me; she had seen me scrutinise Veleda's ornament. In the swift way she had, she turned to the priestess and asked the direct question: 'Will you return to Rome with us?'

'Do I have any choice?' snapped Veleda.

Helena remained patient, her tone courteous and tinged with dry wit. 'Well, you will have to give up your flight, you know. Your *choice* is either to come willingly and have us help you if we can – or to be very efficiently carried back by my husband. You may know that although he is charming and can be a sensitive companion, he is brutally practical. Marcus Didius will be undeterred by priests' protests or a woman's screams.'

'I imagine that would add to his sense of importance,' Veleda scoffed, joining in the humour. I could not tell if these women were forming a friendship, though I knew they had assessed one another as high quality opponents. 'How could you help me?' For a woman of mystery, Veleda could be quite direct.

'I really don't know,' admitted Helena, ever frank herself. 'But I can promise to try.'

'Is she good?' Veleda then asked me, with a hint of true amusement in her eyes.

'Superb. You can trust her to get the best bargain in the marketplace – if any bargain is available for you. But I suppose you know how bleak it looks.'

'Oh yes!' replied Veleda in a drab tone. 'I know what happens. When the magnificent Vercingetorix was captured and brought to Rome by Julius Caesar, he was kept in a deep pit for five years – then paraded, derided and executed.'

'Crude,' I said. 'But didn't you admit to me that a Roman legate who had been captured by your people was first earmarked as a gift to you and in fact died horrendously – tortured, garrotted and drowned in a bog?'

Stalemate. Veleda made no comment.

'Generals still have their Triumphs,' I told her. 'Your prospects are grim. Simon, the scapegoat for the war in Judaea, died on the Capitol only a few years ago to enhance Vespasian's glory.'

'Cleopatra and Boudicca cheated your crowds their own way,' the priestess reminded me.

'Don't expect me to bring you asps in a basket of figs.'

'Do you know Rutilius Gallicus?' she asked. 'He wants fame and high position. He invaded Germania Libera and captured me so my sordid death can give him an honoured life.'

'I do know him. Clearly he has upped his expectations of personal reward. He was a mediocrity when I met him.'

'I did no wrong,' Veleda said, not interested in Rutilius or my assessment of him. 'I fought for my people. I hate Rome for stealing our land and our heritage.'

It was Helena who agreed and sympathised. 'Your society is as fine as ours. Before Rome imposed itself on mainland Europe, the Celtic empire flourished just as strongly as our own does now. You had magnificent art, skilled metalworking, networks of roads, gold coinage —' It was the gold we went for, naturally. They could keep their naturalistic art; we preferred to steal design ideas from Greece. Our great men wanted their fat faces glittering on golden money. 'You enjoyed trade throughout the known world,' Helena continued. This was our way in interviews; she was tolerant and fair, I was the rude bastard. 'You were moral, civilised people with a rich spiritual culture where women were respected, children, the old and the sick or disadvantaged well cared for —' While the men were drunken braggarts, as famous for starting fights as for collapsing or dispersing in disorder before a war finished. 'You may well ask,' said Helena, 'why should our nation take precedence? And I have no explanation.'

'I do.' I spoke levelly. 'Face it, Veleda. It is our time now.'

'You said that before, Falco.'

'And you did not believe me. But since then, as I have heard, the Bructeri, your tribe, have turned against you. Now here you are, a captive in a foreign land, ill, penniless, without supporters, on the run — and in dire need of assistance. Your one good fortune is that here are two people, who both owe you a great deal, offering you help.'

Veleda stepped away from the lake waters, which had continued to swirl around her skirt hem. She shook her garments, holding the wet cloth away from her ankles. Her chin was up. 'I have been granted sanctuary.'

I laughed. 'How are the dear priests treating you? — I bet they hate you. They may have felt bound to take you in, just because once, according to a legend, Diana gave houseroom in Tauris to a bunch of homeless Amazons. But believe me, your claim is already faltering.

When the Emperor asks the priests to give you up, they will. Don't tell me it would break the rules of sanctuary. The only rule that matters will be this: the Emperor will promise to build a new temple or theatre here, then the priests will find they have absolutely no conscience about you.'

Of course this did mean that if I could lure Veleda back to Rome of her own accord, it would save Vespasian the price of endowing a new temple. That was the kind of benefit the gruff old codger loved. He might even express minor financial gratitude to me.

'Why is your man doing this?' Veleda stormed to Helena. 'Will it bring him renown if he hands me back?'

'No,' replied Helena smoothly. 'This is his job.' She did not directly mention payment. 'But his ethics include moral courage and compassion. If Marcus returns you to the Emperor, he will do it in his own time, and decidedly his own way. So, Veleda – bearing in mind that you will be sent back to Rome anyway – it would be better to come with us now. Marcus has a deadline of the end of Saturnalia; he will find it pleasing to complete his mission on the last possible day. So for a short time we can look after you. We will bring Zosime to attend to your health problems. I promise that I will personally speak to the Emperor concerning your predicament. Please do this. Please come and spend Saturnalia with our family at our house.'

The priestess thought Helena Justina was mad. I was none too confident myself. But that was how we persuaded Veleda to return to Rome.

There were logistical niggles.

Since Veleda was coming voluntarily, it would be impolite to put ropes or chains on her, even though I had in fact brought a coil of rope on my saddle-bow. Nor was I letting her loose on one of our horses; the last thing I wanted was to see her gallop off to freedom with a carefree Celtic wave. I ordered her to travel in the carriage – after a tense moment when she first encountered an icy Claudia Rufina.

We did not need to introduce them. Their face-off was brief. The dark Baetican Claudia glared down her nose at the golden Veleda, who stared back. I recalled that Claudia had once lost her temper and lashed out at Justinus; it seemed quite likely that if we let her she would attack the priestess. Her eyes flashed; I wondered if she had practised, while her maids held a hand mirror. For a mad moment I was expecting a cat-fight here on the lake shore. There was no chance of reconciliation between these women; not even Helena attempted her usual role of peacemaker. Each loathed the other fundamentally. Veleda saw Claudia as a pathetic Roman collaborator from a subjected people, Claudia saw the priestess as feral. Curiously, my fostered daughter Albia, who could be British, or Roman, or some half-blood mixture, gazed at them with her most quizzical expression, as if she thought they were both barbarians.

Claudia wrapped herself tightly in her stole and hissed loudly that she refused to be anywhere near this woman. Veleda, looking scornful, shook out her cloak and cooed that she would ride outside the carriage with the driver. Claudia at once responded, 'Oh Marcus Didius, this prisoner of yours is supposedly unwell. I am Baetican. We are tough; *I* shall ride outside, enjoying the fresh air and the countryside.'

It was a moot point whether Veleda saw herself as my prisoner. But Claudia clambered up beside the driver, showing more leg than she may have intended, and prepared to freeze for twenty miles. I saw Helena and Albia exchange glances for some reason, then they climbed inside the carriage and placed blankets on the sickly priestess.

I told Jacinthus it was his big moment. He and I would escort the carriage and it would be his duty to guard the priestess when I was otherwise engaged. He looked puzzled; he knew how to play the simpleton. I explained that on a journey this length I would sometimes have to take my eyes off Veleda while I organised food or accommodation, drove away country peasants trying to sell us Saturnalia nuts, or hid behind a tree to relieve myself and enjoy some private peace from him.

'Can I have a sword?' It was a sick reminder of Lentullus.

'No, you can't. Slaves don't carry weapons.'

'What about the King of the Grove? I'd like to have a crack at him, Falco!'

I seriously thought of letting him. Helena put a stop to that crisply. 'You cannot allow it, Marcus. This is the situation when you own slaves. Jacinthus is now part of our family – and our family is civilised. You will show him kindness and a good example, please, not permit him to go off into a grove of oaks, looking for a bout of fisticuffs.'

'You heard her, Jacinthus. End of story. Don't ask me again.'

Our over-eager slave looked downcast. Veleda put her head out of the carriage window; she asked me who he was. While Helena and Albia smiled at my discomfiture, I then had to tell my famous, high-class prisoner what quality of escort she would have on her re-entry into Rome. She sneered at my hopeful explanation that this was a ploy

245

to deter suspicion. Veleda was showing signs of regret that she had capitulated. She knew what she thought of being taken to her fate in Rome by me and my kitchen staff.

I hadn't even told her that Jacinthus couldn't cook.

L

We spent the rest of that day travelling.

By the time we reached the Capena Gate, we were all wrecked. Soon I was even more anxious. The mood in the streets seemed ugly, if not as angry as the mood between Claudia and Veleda. When we finally parked outside the Camillus house at the Capena Gate, I could hardly wait to escort my young sister-in-law into the house. Though stiff and bruised after a long ride on the carriage box, she still managed to mention her baby loudly, an obvious put-down for the priestess. Baeticans were certainly tough.

The senator managed quickly to pass word to me that Justinus had been home, though after cleaning up he had returned to the patrol house to stay with Lentullus. Lentullus had recovered consciousness a little, but his survival was still touch and go.

With the odd formality he had, Camillus Verus came out to the carriage with me and introduced himself briefly to Veleda. He did not say he was her lover's father. For him, that was irrelevant. He represented the governing body of Rome and she was a national figurehead from outside the Empire. He saw it as a senatorial duty to mark her arrival in our city (even though she was a captive, and being brought here for the second time). So this sturdy old pillar of noble values stomped out to the street and gave her a polite greeting. He even put his toga on to do it.

Don't ask me what Veleda made of this, but Helena Justina jumped out of the carriage and hugged her papa proudly. She had tears in her eyes. Seeing that, a lump came to my own throat.

We carried on home. Fortunately it was after curfew, the streets were clear because of the festival, and now we had shed Claudia we could all travel in the carriage. Helena kept the window curtains well fastened. Nobody had to know that we were bringing home one of Rome's most terrible enemies.

SATURNALIA, DAY FOUR

Thirteen days before the Kalends of January (20 December)

LI

I had sent one of the soldiers to tell Petro I was home, and ask him about the situation in the city. He whizzed straight around to our house. I should have remembered he rarely worked in the day so would be free to socialise. Anyone would think the bounder knew he would walk in on me just as I sat down for a private interrogation of the priestess.

Petronius had a black eye. 'What happened to you?'

'Forgot to duck. Pelted with a festive nut.'

'Some street urchin?'

'No, Maia.'

Petronius Longus took one look at Veleda and announced that she was too gorgeous for me, so he had better stay to lunch. Since it was only mid-morning, that put an end to any hopes I had of a session alone with her. Alone apart from Nux, that is; for the dog was lying asleep at my feet, re-establishing her rights after my two days away from home; she treated the forest *femme fatale* as if she wasn't there. Helena had had to go shopping, urgently needing to replenish the store cupboard, which the soldiers had emptied while we were away. Albia was helping Galene keep the children quiet. The legionaries had been posted on protective guard around the house and on the roof terrace.

Hoarse with curiosity, Petro assured me I would be safer having a witness if I was prying into state secrets. The priestess gazed at my brazen old tentmate as if he was the kind of tree-trunk snail her tribe ate mashed up on crusts at feasts. He had not changed since we were lads; female disdain only encouraged him. 'Falco's all right,' Petronius confided with his friendliest manner. 'But a famous lady deserves respect; you need an interview with a professional.'

'Lucius Petronius Longus lives with my sister,' I warned Veleda. 'The suspicious, hot-headed one.'

'Are you related to everyone in Rome, Falco?'

'It's the only way to be in this city.'

Petronius sprawled in Helena's armchair, and happily beamed at both of us.

I tried to put him off by abandoning my interview and grilling him on why the mood on the streets had seemed so angry last night. Petro told me that Anacrites had caused the dismay. In a wayward ploy that was typical, the Spy had openly let it be known that Rome's loathed and feared enemy was a fugitive at large – making sure he included the detail that she had taken flight after horrifically murdering one of her aristocratic Roman hosts. He was now leaving it to the mob to turn up her hiding place and hand her over.

'Or tear her to pieces, of course,' Petro suggested. 'Oh sorry, sweetheart!' Veleda produced a wan smile. She had passed beyond insults.

Anacrites had seen fit to offer a reward, though given the constraints of his budget, it was a ludicrously small one. However, it had made partying in the streets assume a violent trend. To enhance the air of menace, the Praetorian Guard were openly conducting a stop-and-search of any unaccompanied women; ugly stories had circulated about how they did it. Anybody German, or with German connections, had left town if they knew what was good for them. Foreigners of all flavours were hiding indoors; naturally there were some who had not been told about the problem, had not understood the implications, or just did not speak the right language to grasp the danger to them. Many had discovered the situation when they had been beaten up by 'patriotic Romans' – most of whom were foreigners by birth, of course. The people who were keenest to look patriotic were the ones who originated in Upper and Lower Germany.

Petronius cursed this development. He said the vigiles already had their hands full, without beatings on every street corner. Saturnalia meant a big increase in fires, due to the enormous number of festive lamps in feckless homes. There were fights everywhere, arising from friends and family fall-outs, even before this new rash of anti-barbarian feeling. Petro was glad that the vigiles could at least stop the searches he had set in hand for me; I asked him to tell the cohort commanders this was because of poor results, without mentioning that I had in fact found Veleda. I wanted to avoid bounty hunters turning up at my house.

'Quite right!' exclaimed Petronius, managing to imply I was a bounty hunter myself.

Still seeking to distract him, I asked if the vigiles searchers had come across anything unusual to do with dead vagrants. He gave me a sideways look, but slowly admitted there might be a problem. 'We have been aware of an increased unclaimed-corpse count for some time.'

'Does Scythax know about it? Or is he somehow mixed up in it?'

'Of course not. Crazy suggestion, Falco.'

'Hear my words: he had a *very* fresh cadaver of a runaway slave laid out on his workbench when we took in Lentullus. According to Scythax, someone dumps them outside the patrol house, but that story sounds fishy.'

'Reminds me: my tribune wants you to shift Lentullus off our premises.'

'Tell Rubella to stuff a festive garland where it hurts. And answer my question, please.'

Petronius shrugged and admitted there had always been a high death rate among the homeless, as long as he had been in the vigiles. Recently numbers had increased; they blamed the winter weather.

'So why does your doctor involve himself?'

Petro looked shifty, so I kept probing until he stopped wriggling and owned up feebly, 'Scythax takes an interest in why the vagrants die.'

'An interest – how?'

'I believe,' said Petronius, looking shy, 'he has been known to dissect the corpses.'

I presumed that information had to be kept confidential. 'Using the dead for autopsies is illegal, I'm told.'

'Too right, it is! We don't want unnatural practices in backstreet morgues.'

'No, much better to have them right in your patrol house!'

On my promise of discretion, Petronius said what I already knew, that Scythax was occasionally allowed to take away the corpses of criminals who died in the arena – so long as he carried out any scientific research in his spare time and it was all kept quiet. The excuse was that what Scythax learned could help the army repair wounded soldiers. In any case, post-mortems only happened when the executed criminals had no family to complain, and when Scythax could pay enough bribes to sweeten the arena staff.

'So when his supply from the arena dwindles, he encourages the dumping of dead runaways on your doorstep. Does he advertise this service? Jupiter, Petro, does he *buy* the bodies? And if so – you need to think about this – is somebody killing off vagrants deliberately for Scythax?'

Petronius Longus sat bolt upright. 'Nuts, Falco. Scythax would

253

never countenance that. Besides, there are far too many runaway slaves being found dead!'

'So it's really a problem? You think you have a serial killer?'

'I think it's possible.'

'Because the targets are vagrants, does nobody care?'

'I care, Marcus.'

All this time, Veleda had been sitting quiet, listening to us pretty blank-faced. She had a basket chair, like the one Petronius had commandeered, and was wrapped in shawls, with her feet on a small footstool. Had she had a wool basket at her feet, a child on her chair arm and a pet bird in her lap, she could have been a classic Roman matron. You might say she was too blonde – but a lot of married women I knew had turned mysteriously golden-haired, once they got their hands on their husband's income.

The intent way she was listening to us had attracted my attention. I doubted she was merely entranced by our talented oratory. 'Veleda, you went out on the medication run from the Temple of Æsculapius. They find a lot of these bodies. Anything you can tell us about it?'

'*Did* she?' exploded Petronius. Assuming he was upset at the thought of her wandering loose on the streets that his cohort patrolled, I ignored him.

'I never saw anything like that.' Veleda disappointed me. Even if she had seen something, gratitude to the temple kept her silent.

I decided it was time to pick up my original intention and tackle her about the death of Scaeva.

Petronius Longus crossed his booted feet on a low table, linked his hands behind his head, and watched me proceed. His stare was supposed to unnerve me. I had known him a long time and just ignored his attitude.

I explained to Veleda that one reason I had agreed to Helena's suggestion and let her come to my house was that I hoped to use this period before I handed her over to justice – whoops, took her back to the authorities – in an attempt to discover what had really happened at the Quadrumatus house. If she was innocent of beheading Scaeva, I proposed to clear her. She seemed less impressed by this handsome offer than I thought she should have been. Maybe when you are already indicted for the deaths of thousands of Roman soldiers, one more murder makes little difference on the charge sheet.

'I like to know the truth, Veleda.'

'I remember.'

She should do. I had, after all, once trekked for days to ask her, amongst other things, about the fate of a kidnapped army legate. It was nearly ten years now since that man disappeared in Germany, but if ever relationships became too friendly with this woman, what happened to the legate ought to be remembered. Veleda had not killed him (in her version), nor even ordered his appalling death by drowning while trussed up and pressed under a hurdle in a bog. Still, the devoted tribes who followed her had thought a kidnapped Roman army commander was a suitable 'gift' to send to her. Whether they expected her to eat him, rape him, kill him herself, or keep him on a perch in a golden cage and teach him to tweet nursery rhymes had never been entirely clear, but it was certain that even if his fickle captors had not finished him off before he ever reached her, Veleda herself would have sacrificed the legate to her gods and stacked his bones in the kind of shoulder-high ossuary that I and my companions saw in the forest. That was what this woman now sitting quietly in my home had once been. Perhaps she still was. In fact, since she showed no sign of repentance, make that 'perhaps' a 'probably'.

'You told me that you did not kill Scaeva.' Five years ago Veleda had assured me she did not kill the legate either; she may have been lying. She certainly was responsible for his death, through firing up her followers' bloodlust.

She could be lying about Scaeva. 'Do you know who did kill him? Or why?'

'No.'

'Were you there when he died?'

'No.'

'But you saw his severed head lying in the atrium pool?'

Perhaps Veleda hesitated. Petronius certainly winced as he imagined it. 'I did *not* see the head, Falco.' At my irritated growl, Veleda added quickly, 'I never passed through the atrium that day; I left by way of a tradesmen's exit on the side of the house. But I knew that Scaeva's head was there. Ganna had seen it. She ran and told me.'

This did not fit the facts Ganna had fed to me. I wondered if, in some way I had yet to discover, Ganna was trying to protect the priestess.

'So tell us,' Petronius leaned forward with his 'trust me' look. 'What exactly happened on that afternoon. Let's start with why your – maid, is she? –'

'Acolyte,' I said tersely.

'Oh nice! We'll start with why your acolyte was walking thorough the atrium, shall we?'

Veleda told him without arguing: 'I had some letters that I could not read.' That was good. Whatever mad, romantic pleas Justinus had made, Veleda had never been able to read them. Excellent. 'At first I did not want to read them –' Even better. This was too important for scoring points, but Petro did enjoy a smirk at me over the way she was confiding in him. 'I became so unhappy I changed my mind. The only person we could trust there was the man who had delivered the letters to me: Scaeva. I was constantly being watched – that terrible old woman who attended on Drusilla Gratiana –'

'Phryne.' I scored no points for sounding knowledgeable.

'Phryne, of course. Phryne had always made it clear she hated me. She knew every move I made. So Ganna was going to ask Scaeva what the letters said.'

'She never managed it?' asked Petro. Veleda shook her head.

Now the story went that Ganna only made it as far as the atrium that afternoon; she saw the head, then raced back – with the letters – to inform Veleda of the murder. They realised at once that blame would be piled on the priestess, so with no chance for further conversation, Veleda made her escape in the laundry cart.

'So why didn't the young lady go with you?' asked Petro, with what he probably imagined was a winning smile. Veleda's eyes were shadowed; I reckoned she felt patronised.

'We thought there would be an investigation.'

'There is an investigation. Didius Falco is conducting it now.'

'No, we thought there would be an investigation at the house, straight after the murder. Ganna says nothing ever happened.'

I interrupted quietly to explain that Quadrumatus Labeo had refused to have investigators on the premises until the nine days of formal mourning for Scaeva had finished.

'What's he hiding?' Petronius asked me.

'Did it to "spare the distressed relatives further upset".'

'Beautiful! Didn't these relatives want to know who killed their boy?'

'You said it!'

'Ganna did not understand what Quadrumatus was doing.' Veleda showed no emotion at our angry exchange. 'She despaired of justice, so she made her escape too. But initially we hoped she would be able to exonerate me. Ganna stayed behind in order to tell the enquiry officer what she had seen.'

Petronius Longus, practised as he was, managed not to sound

startled. 'And what was that?'

Veleda, equally intelligent, was clearly enjoying the suspense. 'Ganna had seen someone positioning the head in the pool.'

Of course we demanded to know who it was. According to Veleda, Ganna had never told her.

Petronius could see no problem with this. We would go and ask Ganna to name the culprit. That was before I explained that Ganna had now been placed for safe keeping in the House of the Vestal Virgins, where no men are allowed.

'You've been there, Falco!'

'In the first place, as you so often tell me, I am an idiot. Then, it nearly got me executed. If anyone is breaking into the Vestals' House, dear Lucius, it's your turn.' He declined the offer. 'So what happened to the letters from Justinus?' I asked Veleda.

'I left them behind in my hurry. Maybe Ganna still has them.'

We would probably have put Veleda through some even more intense questioning, but at that moment Helena came in. Our daughters were clinging to her skirts, ruining the fabric while they gave the priestess the hostile toddlers' silent stare treatment. Stooping and prising little hands free, Helena announced that Zosime had come to the house as promised, so she was taking Veleda away from us for a consultation in private. Julia and Favonia made a break for safety, and rushed across the room to me. Petronius casually captured Favonia as she tumbled over in her haste.

Just as the priestess reached the door, Petronius stopped her. He always favoured the routine where a witness was allowed to think they had been released, then he flung an extra question at them. As my daughter hid her face in his tunic then peeped at the priestess, Petro called out: 'So, Veleda, when Zosime took you out among the homeless, did you ever suspect she was harming them, not healing?'

Veleda looked surprised, then denied it. Helena then shepherded her out.

I asked Petronius if there was a real suspicion that Zosime was behind the deaths of the vagrants. Ever cagey about vigiles business, he merely confirmed that he had the woman on a watch list.

I was glad that Helena was supervising the consultation here. I could not see Zosime as a killer – but if she was, I did not want her working any fatal magic on Veleda. Having Rome's famous prisoner die before the Triumph would be bad enough. Having her die at my house would finish my career.

257

LII

The consultation seemed to be dragging on, so Petro and I had lunch together, with my children and some of the soldiers.

Before he left, Petronius invited us to a festival dinner that night at his house. He jauntily extended this to include the priestess. I told him that Anacrites' narks had turned up again outside. I had barred her from leaving the house; the legionaries would stay in and guard her tonight during my absence. 'And, Lucius, you are too old to be playing with fire, especially right in front of Maia! I thought you had grown up.' He loved Maia, there was no doubt of it. In his view, that freed him to keep looking around.

'I'm growing up about as fast as you!' he scoffed. Whatever that meant.

Well, I knew what he meant. I told him that anyone who had seen Veleda five years ago would be disappointed now. To which Petronius Longus answered sadly that he only hoped Quintus Camillus Justinus would see it my way. 'If she went for Camillus, you're not her type, Falco. She likes them clean and intellectual.'

Detecting a wistful note that I remembered from his wicked past, I scoffed, 'Dear Lucius, she gave you the bum's rush too, and you know it.'

We sounded as if we were eighteen again. The legionaries watched us curiously.

Still weary after the Nemi trip, I was fast asleep on the part of a couch I had wrestled from the dog, when Helena tickled my nose.

'I'm awake!' To prove it, I grabbed her and pulled her down with me, shoving Nux to the floor. The elegant antelope legs of the reading couch were protesting, but would probably support us so long as we didn't try anything athletic. With a house full of nosy people that was unwise in any case, so we talked.

'You were a long time closeted with Zosime.'

'She's still here. In return for a large donation to the temple this morning, I obtained agreement to keep her here while Veleda stays with us.'

I suggested that if Zosime was involved in killing the vagrants that could be dangerous; Helena brushed my fears aside. On consideration, I thought she was right. 'Luckily for your bankbox, you'll be paying for four days at most.' I felt myself tense. Three days to deadline. It was starting to prey on my mind. 'So what's the verdict on our guest's health?'

'Zosime suspects just a bout of marsh fever. Epidemics are usually virulent in summer, but people can get the fever any time – especially strangers to Rome, before they are used to our climate.'

'Hmm. The Quadrumatus villa isn't in a marsh.'

'No, but Marcus, I remember the gardens are full of water – canals and other ornamental features. The miasma, or whatever it is that carries the disease, could be lurking there.' Helena looked optimistic. 'Zosime thinks there is an improvement since she saw Veleda at the villa, although Veleda may never quite recover. People don't; once struck down, they remain vulnerable to new attacks. Zosime is prescribing rest and good food: frequent small meals, no wine – and fresh air.'

'Veleda is not allowed out to go walking in parks. She'll have to make do with our roof terrace. And if she goes up there, two of the legionaries are to be in attendance at all times.'

Helena dug me in the ribs. 'Don't be so gruff, Marcus. She's hardly going to light a signal fire. Who would she contact, in any case?'

Good question. I was not taking any chances.

That afternoon, Helena and I had a pleasant winter stroll together through the city. At the far end of the Forum lay the Vestals' House, where we made an application for Helena at least to be allowed in to see young Ganna. This was rejected outright.

Annoyed by failure, Helena and I had an irritable discussion about one of the younger Vestals, a kind-hearted and rather lively gem called Constantia, who had been helpful to me in a previous enquiry. Despite the strict conditions under which the Virgins live, I suggested I contact Constantia again. Helena responded that if I wanted to stay married, that idea was a non-starter. I sighed regretfully. Constantia's willingness to help me had been wonderful.

We went to see Helena's mother. Julia Justa had heard from Claudia all about us finding Veleda. I had to endure a shriek about whether having Veleda at our house was *wise* – where 'wise' had nothing to do with cerebral efficiency and everything to do with me being an idiot. I managed to hold back the information that the scheme originated with Helena, but since she was an honest, ethical girl, she confessed. Her mother said I must have put her up to it.

Once she had worked out her anxieties, Julia Justa settled down. I explained that the accusation of beheading Scaeva was uncorroborated, and that Ganna might be able to prove the priestess was innocent; Julia brightened up. For the sake of her lovestruck son and her unhappy daughter-in-law, she was clearly hoping that Ganna's evidence would do the opposite. She promised to contact her friend, that very much older and plainer Vestal Virgin than the charming one I knew, and request an interview with Ganna herself. As a respected matron who could demonstrate that she had a good reason, in Julia's case it might be allowed.

'The important thing,' I told her, 'is to find out who Ganna saw laying the severed head in the water. But if you have the chance, you might like to pose one other question.' Before my mother-in-law could formulate her indignation at being treated like my junior assistant, I got in pointedly, 'Ask if she knows what happened to some letters Veleda received at the Quadrumatus house.'

'What letters?' snapped Julia Justa. I smiled at her sadly.

'Oh the fool! – He didn't?'

Until now I had not even mentioned Justinus' letters to Helena. She and her mother instantly colluded and swore never to tell Claudia. (Claudia was in the nursery with her baby son and did not know we were visiting.) From what I knew of the daft relationship between Claudia and Justinus, he would probably confess to his wife himself. They had never had secrets. A cynic would say that explained their problems.

Helena and I walked home via the Aventine. We visited Ma, who was holding court among her neighbours as a pitiful invalid; the operation must have been successful because I caught her casting a very sharp eye over their dainty offerings of fruit and pastries. Although we told her Ganna had been sent to a place of safety, we had decided not to risk Anacrites finding out that we were giving houseroom to Veleda. We kept quiet about that. Ma thought she could always tell when I was hiding something, but I had lived at home until I was eighteen; I knew how to bluff.

Once my mother had made free with her instructions on child care and household management for as long as we could bear, we left.

'I hear your father had his piles attended to,' was her gleeful parting shot. 'Apparently it was *very* painful!'

Only an impious Roman son would rejoice that his father was suffering – but the thought of Pa lying face down in agony while the pile-crushing gadget savaged his posterior was boosting my mother's recovery. Happy for her, I gave Ma my best grin.

'That's the wicked grin she says reminds her of Geminus,' Helena remarked. I let her have a share in it.

Strolling in an affectionate mood, we made our way to the patrol house and dropped in to see Lentullus. I had snaffled some of my mother's treats to bring him – the titbits Ma had judged not good enough – but he was still far too ill to eat. Quintus volunteered to see nothing went to waste. While Helena mopped the sick soldier's brow, I warned Justinus that Anacrites and the Praetorians were marauding through the city with increased desperation. He should remain inside the patrol house. So long as Petronius kept his promise of not mentioning Veleda, I hoped Quintus would never learn she was at my house. He asked about my search, of course; I just said I had a few leads to follow.

Lentullus kept bleating that he was sorry to be such a trouble and would hurry to get well and rejoin his comrades. Quintus privately shook his head at me. We went into the yard and he let me know quietly that the lad was unlikely ever to be fit enough for the army. Clemens and the others would be going back to Germany without him. If he survived, eventually somebody would have to tell Lentullus that his days in the army were over. I could see it would be me. Knowing his innocent joy in legionary service, I saw no way of consoling him.

His survival still hung in the balance. Being realistic, he was more likely to die than live. It would be some time before we could be sure he had avoided a fatal infection. Gangrene lurked ever closer. The doctor was daily reviewing the need for amputation, which would probably kill the patient. Lentullus had lost huge quantities of blood and was unable to take much nourishment. He now had an enormous pad of wadding bandaged on to the injured leg, which Scythax said was too badly damaged ever to bear his weight properly again. A large bottle of pain-killing medicine had been left for when he needed drugging – which Quintus said was frequently.

Scythax was not here, so Quintus was in charge of the soporific. His duties as a nurse must include more intimate attentions too; the calm, kind-hearted way he was getting on with it all reminded me why his men had so admired him as an army tribune. Although he had a sensitive nature, he was not afraid to get his hands dirty. At his best Quintus Camillus Justinus was practical, competent – and completely decent. At his very best he had applied those qualities to his marriage. Then, there had seemed a chance he and Claudia could survive together. As Helena and I walked back home slowly together, she cursed Veleda's presence in Rome, which had put her brother's future in jeopardy.

Helena had not yet made good her promise to beg for clemency for the priestess. After seeing Justinus, she confessed to me, 'I half wish I could forget that noble offer!' Being who she was, I knew she would honour the promise. The only reason she had not yet tried approaching Vespasian or Titus was that we wanted to be able to prove that Veleda was innocent of murdering Scaeva. With the charge hanging over her, especially with the killing here in Rome, no plea for leniency stood a hope.

We still had three days. I told myself that if Ganna really had seen the killer in action, three more days should be ample to establish our case.

LIII

We spent a good evening with Maia and Petronius. This was mainly achieved by Maia pretending it had nothing to do with Saturnalia but was a simple family meal. My daughters were well behaved, as often happened in the presence of much older children; in the company were Maia's four, plus Petro's daughter and Albia, who all got on together.

I would normally have avoided breaking off in the middle of an investigation merely to socialise, but at that point I was stuck, waiting on other people. I managed to relax. Well, Lucius Petronius always had a good wine to hand, and was liberal with it. Maia could cook too.

My mother had been invited, which at least kept her out of the clutches of Anacrites. Apparently he was paying her a lot of attention, grilling her about my activities. She claimed she always told him I was a good family man, devoting myself to giving my children a wonderful festival. 'And what have you bought for Helena as a present, Marcus? Oh don't tell me; you're just like your father. I don't suppose you've given it a thought.'

I claimed it was a secret. Maia muttered that that was always a good way to buy time. Helena said she would be happy with a surprise, so we all roared the traditional reply that her surprise would come when she received nothing. Some younger children who had never heard this one before collapsed in hysterical laughter.

Helena had never been demanding in that way. Her soft brown eyes were telling me she would not mind – while I felt my heart lurch guiltily because I had still not arranged anything.

Ear-rings. Pa had mentioned unsold ear-rings . . . 'What have you got for Maia?' I muttered to Petronius.

'A neck chain.'

Why did I ask? He had always bought neck chains, whatever woman – or women – he was buttering up. That way, the philandering rascal never got caught out in conversations afterwards.

★

Although they were not invited, we were joined just after dinner by my other sister Junia and dreary Gaius Baebius. They always knew when someone else was entertaining. To demonstrate that Junia's slip-up with *vinum primitivum* was all forgotten and they were once again the devoted couple, they made a big fuss of jointly issuing invitations to their house the next day. Abruptly, Petronius stood up and left, saying that he had to be on duty. This left Maia with the task of refusing the invitation for them (Petro loathed Junia and Gaius Baebius). Maia, who was always blunt, just said, 'No thank you, Junia.'

'Oh I suppose you busy people must have other plans!'

Maia bared her neat little teeth in what could be either smile or snarl.

I tried to bluff by saying we had a house full of soldiers, so Junia countered quickly that we would be glad to get away from them – as we had obviously done today. I then assumed it was Helena's turn to cover for us, but she had gone into some dream of her own, so we ended up with no escape.

'We are having ghost stories. I shall be giving you a perfect night!' Junia oozed, with the self-satisfaction we all hated.

Junia and Gaius clung on like rock anemones. They were still there swiping the leftover food from Maia's serving dishes when a message came for me from Petronius, so I was able to abandon the party and go over to the patrol house. I assumed the call was merely a courtesy on his part, but it turned out to be genuine: another body of a vagrant had been found.

The dead man was laid out in a cell, since Lentullus was still occupying the doctor's treatment room. I found Petronius and Scythax bending over the corpse, a weightless, grey-faced vagrant who could be anywhere between forty years and sixty. If I had seen him walking around, I would have kept my distance in case he harboured an infectious lung disease. Petro said he had instructed his men to give all rough-sleepers a kick to ensure they were alive. After zero response to their greeting, a vigiles patrol had brought this one in, just after twilight.

'Not dumped for Scythax then?' I gave Scythax a forbidding glance. He refused to look shifty.

Petronius said, 'I sent to the temple to have Zosime questioned, but I gather she is still at your house, Falco?'

'Right. Helena wants her for something . . . Time of death,

Scythax?' Only a couple of hours earlier, he said; the body still had traces of warmth. It was a mild night for December, and the vagrant had wrapped himself in many dirty layers. We joked gently that the dirt alone would have kept him warm. I frowned. 'We know for sure this one wasn't done in by Zosime. I've got ten daft but honest legionaries and a centurion's servant who can all give her an alibi tonight.'

'Could be a damn copycat killing.' After dear Junia's invasion of his home, Petronius was in a dour mood.

'Think so? So far, the authorities haven't commented,' I put to him. 'You normally have a problem advertised and a loud public outcry, before the crazy emulators start. I'd say there is an original serial killer prowling out there – hitherto unnoticed.'

Reluctantly, Petro nodded. 'We have absolutely nothing on him.'

I turned to the doctor. 'Scythax, come clean about the corpses that are dumped for you. This one was left on the streets. So what do you know about your little presents – and do you suspect Zosime from the Temple of Æsculapius is connected with them?'

For a moment Scythax looked unhelpful. Chin up, Petronius stared at him, though my pal said nothing. 'The ones we find at the patrol house,' Scythax finally admitted, 'are brought here by the woman.' He seemed to cringe, knowing that Petro would be annoyed.

'By Zosime?' I said quickly. 'I assume you can explain that?'

Scythax let himself be drawn out by me, where he was obviously wary of Petro. For one thing, I did not have the power to set Sergius on him. Sergius was the muscle-man who beat criminals into confessions. Well, sometimes they were criminals, sometimes they had just been arrested by mistake – but they all confessed. The vigiles were one happy family; if anyone upset Petro, he believed in traditional paternal chastisement. When he was feeling particularly conservative, he would rave that it had been a bad day when fathers of families lost the power of life and death. 'Zosime was the first to suspect something,' Scythax admitted nervously. 'She came and discussed it with me. Her temple won't take any action, so she has to rely on the vigiles.'

'Why not mention this to me?' snarled Petro.

'Nothing definite to go on. Zosime brings me the corpses, when she finds them, so that I can say whether they are natural or unnatural deaths.'

'*Unnatural*, I take it?' I asked.

'I am starting to think so. Sometimes we get one who has genuinely died of malnutrition or disease. But most display the classic sign of manual strangulation – a small bone in their throats is broken.' It seemed best not to ask how a doctor would discover that. Presumably not by pressing down a tongue and ordering the corpse to say *ah*. 'It is as if,' said Scythax, with dry distaste, 'they are birds who have had their necks casually wrung.'

'Anything else we should know?' demanded Petronius, becoming more intrigued.

'Anything sexual?' Scythax knew the vigiles' preoccupations in murder. 'Nothing that seems connected. Many vagrants have been abused at some time prior to death, it goes without saying. In those who are clearly runaway slaves, indications of long-term brutalisation are practically generic.'

'Are the corpses all men?' I asked.

'Occasional women. And, sadly, a few children.'

I looked at Petro. 'Isn't this wide spread of victims unusual from repeat killers?'

He nodded. 'Yes, mostly they go for one consistent type – male or female, adults or children.'

Scythax volunteered, 'I believe the common factor is that the victims live on the streets. They seem to be chosen for punishment because of their indigent lifestyle. Someone finds them sleeping under arches or in doorways, and ends their existence. He – or she – may justify murder as a kindness to end their misery.'

'Putting them down like worn-out horses?' Petronius was shocked and angry.

'Unless,' said Scythax, with his odd dispassionate attitude, 'this killer hates them – sees them as a kind of human vermin. Eradicates them for the greater good.'

'Even more delightful. How will I find this self-appointed Fury?'

'Look for someone who is convinced cleaning up the streets is a decent motive. Of course,' said the doctor diffidently, 'you need to know where to start looking.'

'*Io*,' replied Petronius glumly. 'Happy Saturnalia!'

SATURNALIA, DAY FIVE

Twelve days before the Kalends of January (21 December)

LIV

The fifth day of the festival brought a turn of the winch.

It started well: we were at breakfast when a message came for me from Petronius. He had obviously buckled down last night to reviewing reports. Among a pile from other cohorts he picked out that the Third had discovered a runaway slave, a teenaged musician. Petro sent a runner over to the Third, who rapidly returned confirmation that they had banged up the Quadrumatus flautist. He did not confess, but when he was rounded up he was carrying a flute. The Third were not bright, but they could add I and I to make III. (According to Petro, III was the only number they knew.) They had chucked the flute away; their tribune hated music in the cells.

I was in my cloak and about to set off for the Third's patrol house to interview the recaptured slave, when a huge litter with gold knobs on the poles turned up on the windy embankment outside my house. The gold was wearing thin and the eight bearers were a lop-sided, shabby set who could not march in time. The conveyance was government issue: some tatty leftover from the imperial transport pool, downgraded from when Claudius or Nero were dragged around in it. Twenty years later it was due for a bonfire. Equally senile, the bearers lurched and dropped it heavily. Out staggered Claudius Laeta and under compulsion I greeted him. He was fetching me to a meeting. Laeta said it was urgent. I knew that meant two things: it wasn't urgent – and the pointless blather would drag on for hours. This was my day ruined.

'I'll fetch my toga.' Helena caught me in the unusual activity, so I lured her into the expedition. That was not hard. After our late night with Maia and Petro, the children were over-tired and squabbling fretfully. Both Helena and I could have coped with the children, but their nursemaid, Galene, was screaming in a hideous storm of foreign frustration. Albia had refused assistance. Currently she was locked in her room. She was a teenaged girl; Helena let her act like one. Nux was in hiding with Albia. We tapped at the door and called out that we had to go somewhere. 'Get going then!' snarled Albia from within. Well, it was better than 'I hate you', and much better than 'I hate myself'. In about six months we would be facing both.

We sent Galene to the kitchen, telling her to make good use of it and cook something. Jacinthus was there, but unlikely to be productive. Galene bounced off happily. Helena looked rueful. 'Maybe we should just accept this, Marcus.'

'Right. First step to degeneracy: be ruled by your slaves.'

We put our daughters into cute little matching tunics with bows in their hair and took them with us. Anyone who wants to offer a better solution can just keep quiet.

'What extremely advanced parents!' Claudius Laeta hooted with disdain.

'Your soldiers have disrupted my quiet household routine,' retorted Helena.

Laeta said he would be happy to remove the soldiers – when I earned my fee and found Veleda. Feigning anxiety, Helena and I relaxed. Julia and Favonia sat on our laps as good as gold, fascinated by riding in the litter. If Laeta took us anywhere with slaves, we were sure of a welcome for these deceptively sweet cupids.

I had assumed the conference was in the Palace. Instead, I soon realised we were going down the Via Aurelia; Laeta admitted we were going to the villa of Quadrumatus Labeo.

'One of his Saturnalia guests needs a progress report.'

'We answer to Quadrumatus?' I snorted with astonishment.

'Not him.' Laeta lost some of his pomposity. 'Out-of-town is more discreet, Falco.'

I let Laeta deal with the bloody-minded Lusitanian doorkeeper.

While he struggled to declare his invited status and the porter sneered at that idea, Helena wiped up Favonia's dribble. Although I had kept a close grip on Julia, she had managed to get black door-hinge oil on her; I dealt with that by the time we carried them indoors, where entranced slave girls fell on them. After hardly any training from us, my children both knew how to gaze at strangers with big appealing eyes. 'Don't give them any food!' I ordered sternly, as Scaeva's ex-girlfriends carried them off in delight.

They took the hint. 'Oh the dear little things must have some must-cake to celebrate the festival!' Good. It was bound to be made properly here, with wine-lees from the estate. After running around the peristyles playing hide-and-seek with the sewing girls, mild intoxication would work magic. Our little monsters would be fast asleep when we collected them.

There were plenty of grand ladies on whom Julia and Favonia could practise their techniques of begging for jewellery and toys, for the place was full of stiffs, and since it was Saturnalia, the stiffs had brought their stately wives. The Quadrumati were bravely putting bereavement behind them and going ahead with their annual house party. 'Invitations will have been sent months ago,' Helena sneered. 'And the hospitable Quadrumati would not want to disappoint their many friends.'

'I seem to recall Quadrumatus asserting *"We are a very private family"*! Yet half the Senate have congregated, in the hope of blood on the marble.'

'Marcus, I bet most of them will slip a servant a denarius to sneak them into the crime scene.' Apart from the fact they looked a mean bunch who would think a whole denarius was too much, Helena was bound to be right. Snobs are the worst gawkers. It explained why the Quadrumati had tried to hush up what happened.

Laeta bustled off importantly to see where the meeting would be. We moved among the milling groups of notables, marvelling that none of the family was anywhere in evidence.

'Entertaining the fashionable way,' Helena enlightened me. 'You invite hordes of people, whom you know only slightly, then you keep out of sight but let them wander at will admiring all you own.'

'Giving them a good shake-down for stolen silverware when they leave?'

'I suppose the message is that the hosts have so much money, Marcus, that even if everybody steals something, they won't miss it.'

We worked out that the gathering was mixed, in fact. We identified various off-duty hired entertainers, and Drusilla's troupe of dwarfs were stomping about being offensive. They were all drunk. Perhaps they knew where Drusilla kept her wine stash. The men the dwarfs were insulting seemed to be tradesmen. Although it was still mid-morning, they were digging into trays of pre-lunch snacks and aperitifs; perhaps it was the only way they could guarantee themselves a Saturnalia bonus. Of course the senators ignored them, and the tradesmen were even more snobbish about sticking together and not conversing with the senators. While such a *mélange* could appear egalitarian, Helena and I thought that the groups had just been bunged together in a perfunctory and rather tasteless manner.

'It makes you wonder what they would have done with Veleda,' said Helena. 'I suspect they would have let everyone know they had her – and made her a sideshow.'

Among the retainers who had gathered to grab festive gifts, we found a knot of medical specialists. Aedemon's bulk made him instantly visible; he was talking to a man I remembered as Pylaemenes, the Chaldean interpreter of dreams in his shabby robe. I would have ignored them, but I spotted Anacrites nuzzling up to them. He must be here for the same meeting as me. When I walked Helena over to see what he was up to with the physicians, I also recognised the third man. He was Cleander, who on my previous visit had turned up for a consultation with Drusilla Gratiana. He had an oval face, round eyes, and a restrained manner which probably meant he could be savage if he fell out with anyone.

'Name's Falco. We passed in a doorway. You look after the lady of the house.'

'And you're the bloody sleuth.'

Cleander looked too busy to speak. His bedside manner must be brisk. He made it plain he had no time for meaningless socialising. Nonetheless, the others treated him as a respected colleague.

'Anacrites!' I gave my own colleague a brush-off nod.

'Falco.' He was equally indifferent.

'Dear Anacrites.' Helena forced him to acknowledge her.

'Helena Justina!' When he clasped her hand, greeting her formally, he bent his head obsequiously, showing the grease he always lathered too thickly on his hair. He was wearing a heavy tunic, with a sweaty nap like a mushroom, in a shade of ochre that reflected off his face and made him look bilious.

'So you're all here, to receive your rewards for a year's hard work!' Helena exclaimed to the doctors, trying to dissipate the heat between the Spy and me. She must have worked out that Mastarna, the goatee-bearded consultant who used to attend the deceased Gratianus Scaeva, was absent. 'It's rather hard on him to lose out on his Saturnalia bonus, just because his patient happened to have had his head lopped off.' The others were silent, not meeting each other's eyes.

Turning to Cleander, I tried the friendly chat which is an informer's trademark: 'We haven't had an opportunity to get to know each other.' He despised the offer. 'As I remember, I was informed you are a "Hippocratic pneumatist"?'

'He's a good doctor despite that!' Aedemon joshed him, while Cleander himself merely inclined his head snootily. He thought it degrading to discuss his craft with me. 'All his patients will tell you how wonderful he is,' Aedemon continued. 'I'm hanging around trying to poach them, but they all adore Cleander far too much.'

'As I understand it,' Helena joined in gamely, 'the Hippocratic approach is a sensible, comfortable regime, encouraging health by diet, exercise and rest. I know someone who is being treated that way,' she told Cleander. It was Zosime's prescription for Veleda. Since he himself was not the favoured physician, Cleander obviously didn't care if the patient was Helena's favourite donkey. She noted it, and changed the subject: 'Of course, any treatment must be very difficult when some patients refuse to help themselves.' Still playing dangerously, this was a veiled reference to Drusilla's alleged habit of over-imbibing wine.

Unwilling to talk about his patient, Cleander made a sudden excuse and left us.

'Sometimes gruff ones are the best doctors . . . Is he a bit of a loner?'

'Married with children,' Aedemon disabused Helena.

'You mean quite normal?' I laughed. 'Horrible to his wife, and distant with his offspring?'

'I expect he blames his work, darling! He is a loyal physician,' Helena commented disingenuously. 'He didn't like me criticising Drusilla.'

'Drusilla Gratiana foolishly blames the gods for her misfortunes,' Aedemon replied. 'Cleander won't have it. He rejects all superstition – irrational assignment of causes – shamanism.'

'He hates me, of course!' giggled Pylaemenes, the dream therapist.

'And what do you think of him?' I asked, keeping it light.

'I would like to know that man's dreams,' exclaimed Pylaemenes, with feeling.

'He's a tortured soul?'

'He has his dark side, I suspect.'

'He is bloody rude,' snarled Aedemon. 'He gave me all Hades, just for supplying Quadrumatus with a scarab amulet. A patient who is drinking his own urine as a laxative deserves a comforter!'

The Chaldean patted the fat man's knee. 'Oh that was a misunderstanding,' he soothed. 'Quadrumatus had a nightmare in which your scarab was eating him –' A nightmare seemed natural, if the man had been drinking his own water. Quadrumatus took a sharp downward lurch in my estimation for submitting to it. 'He gave away the scarab to his cheese-server, and Cleander happened to see the boy with it.'

'So what's wrong with that?' wailed Aedemon. 'The cheese-server needs help. He is permeated by gas. Classic bowel putrefaction. Every conduit in his body must be blocked.'

'I fear you are right,' agreed Pylaemenes gravely. 'His farts are legendary.'

I cheered up. At last we had encountered someone attending the Quadrumati who had a sense of humour.

'I'd like to get access to that boy and give him a thorough empty out with wild cabbage,' Aedemon exclaimed.

At that moment Cleander returned. The man had no social skills. Overhearing Aedemon, he scoffed, 'He's just a slave, man; he'll get over it!' We were only discussing flatulence, but this would clearly have been Cleander's attitude whatever the boy suffered from. He then charged in with: 'You're chasing Scaeva's death, Falco? Can we assume you've got nowhere?'

I had met his type before. Some know the effect of their rudeness. Most are just so arrogant they have no idea. I did not need to justify myself to him. Aware of Anacrites watching me, I declared that I would identify the murderer publicly in the next few days.

'*Someone* had better look out then!' muttered Cleander in his low, gruff voice. I glanced at Helena but with the Chief Spy standing alongside, neither of us elaborated. I felt the Spy's intense tingle of curiosity. He as good as fetched out a note-tablet and made a memo to himself.

Once again, Helena attempted to improve the atmosphere. 'How are your headaches these days, Anacrites?' He jumped. He had been listening in, with the unobtrusive silence that was his favourite technique, a slight smile on his face as he followed everything the rest of us discussed. He hated being made the centre of attention; I guessed Helena knew that. She turned to Cleander: 'Our friend here had a bad head injury and still suffers side-effects. I wonder if one of his humours may be a little out of balance?'

Surprisingly, this tactic worked. Cleander was at once drawn into a discussion with Anacrites about his famous headaches. He even seemed to be offering cures. Before I could suggest blood-letting from a main artery, Helena pulled me and the others off to one side.

'So Cleander won't let Drusilla Gratiana get away with believing she hits the amphora because she's fated?' Helena asked Aedemon. 'I don't suppose she enjoys being warned off wine – but she puts up with it? It confirms that Cleander's patients think he's marvellous.'

'The rest of us suspect they love him because he's a hot dispenser of poppy juice . . . Drusilla is in Cleander's pocket because he never seriously insists she dries out. He loathes slaves and freedwomen, so he sees Drusilla even without that scowling maid of hers present, and has complete control. Husband doesn't help,' Aedemon informed us, happily insulting his own patient, Quadrumatus. 'Says "a drop never hurt anyone". He only has to observe Drusilla after a hard bout to know how wrong that is.'

'I don't suppose he does see her tipsy,' suggested Helena. 'This seems like a house where they may well lead separate lives much of the time – and when Drusilla is unfit for society, I expect the scowling Phryne keeps guard.'

While Pylaemenes just winked at me, Aedemon muttered, 'Too much is concealed behind closed doors in this house. Abominations. Quadrumatus is a good judge and has a mind of his own, sure – but that's useless if nobody ever takes notice of his instructions.' It was unclear what abominations had upset him.

In a pause, Helena asked, 'So where is Drusilla, our hostess, today?'

'Rumour is, she had a complete nervous breakdown. Swallowing more wine than ever – never got over her brother's awful death.' Aedemon then raised himself upright like an uncoiling reptile and swanned off, following a slave who had a huge tray of seafood bites.

I could see the dream therapist was about to move away too, but I made a last effort: 'So what has Quadrumatus been so lax about?'

Pylaemenes just shrugged.

He sidled off, so we shifted further from Anacrites and Cleander. We managed to position ourselves beside one of the three-foot silver salvers. It seemed to be wielded by the cheese-server Aedemon and Pylaemenes had mentioned, but I had to leave Helena at risk of his fabled gaseous emissions because Claudius Laeta was gesticulating from a doorway. Helena waved me off to my meeting. I left her discussing Gallic cheese with the server: was it best pounded with pine nuts, hazel nuts or almonds?

She had the best bargain. At least she could pick out a cheese and the flatulent slave boy would cut her a sliver. He looked like a reprobate who would give a handsome woman more than a sliver, in fact. I heard him begin chatting to her; he was full of cheeky quips.

I meanwhile was made to halt by a valet, whose purpose in life was to irritate men by fiddling with the folds of their togas. A sponge-slave grabbed me by both hands and cleaned any grease from my fingers and palms, then a boy almost tripped me up, scrabbling round so he could dust my boots. I had endured less attention when visiting Vespasian.

Emperors can afford to relax. This manic preparation told me that inside the room I was trying to enter was someone dull, but highly aspirational.

Too right. An ingratiating major-domo whispered the good news. His duty was to set people at their ease with terrifying lists of VIPs. 'You are entering the presence of Marcus Quadrumatus Labeo, who is hosting and chairing the convocation. Also present are Tiberius Claudius Laeta and Tiberius Claudius Anacrites, who are both highly placed imperial freedmen. The guest of honour is –' The creep nearly wet himself – 'Quintus Julius Cordinus Gaius Rutilius Gallicus!'

Rutilius had enough names already but I invented a few more for him: 'Old Grovel is here, is he? Bonanza Boy! Domitian's Ovation Sparkler. I'm Falco,' I said as the major-domo gasped at my irreverence. 'If you need a mnemonic, give me a piece of brazier charcoal and I'll write it on your wrist for you.'

LV

'Didius Falco!'

The triumphant, pretty nearly triumphal, great general Rutilius remembered me! Could it be I had impressed him with my talent when we first met out in Tripolitania – an event made the more memorable for both of us when he ordered my brother-in-law to die in the bloody jaws of arena lions? Could he even be recalling with nostalgia that long hot summer evening when he and I, the most mismatched of literary entertainers, hired the Auditorium of Maecenas and gave a cringe-making poetry recital?

I did not fool myself. A flunkey would have whispered my name in his ear. In any case, Rutilius Gallicus knew who I was because he was expecting me.

He was in his early fifties, the kind of provincial senator who could pass for a market trader. A couple of generations back, his family were probably not much better than that; still, it meant the man was sharp. His career progress confirmed how well he could schmoose. Consul, priest of the Augustan cult, imperial legate, governor. Top of the tree – and looking at the sky.

'This is a pretty mess, Falco!' Too right. He caused it – though you might think, from the easy and companionable way the general spoke, he was making Veleda's stupid escape our joint responsibility.

Never trust a member of the aristocracy. Rutilius was as close to benign as they come. But if he had driven all the way back from Augusta Taurinorum at Saturnalia – after returning to Italy specifically to spend Saturnalia with his family – he must be desperate to cover his back. Old Grovel had decided that being young Domitian Caesar's buddy might not be enough.

It was an interesting meeting, if you liked watching an empty potter's wheel. Round and round and round again they went. Quadrumatus Labeo made a capable chairman, as I had always suspected, but the rest sidelined him. I could see why one of the family doctors had said nobody listened to him; worse, Quadrumatus accepted it. Laeta had produced the agenda; he steered progress. Rutilius Gallicus listened regally. He had the air of a man who will be reporting back to higher life forms. I could guess who.

As the 'official' trouble-fixer, Anacrites was invited to summarise progress. He waffled as far as the abortive operation at the Temple of Diana Aventinensis, then he tried to force my hand: 'Apparently Falco has new evidence about the Scaeva killing.'

'Just a lead.'

'You said –' He had slipped up. He realised I was deliberately undermining him.

'Misunderstanding?' I grinned at him. 'As soon as I have hard evidence, I'll produce it.' He was furious.

'So.' Quadrumatus tapped a stylus end a few times. 'The priestess went to the Temple of Diana Aventinensis after she absconded from here, but left four days ago, and the priests have no knowledge of her subsequent movements. It's a start.'

No, it was useless. The lard buckets all sat there until one of them thought to ask, 'Anything you want to add, Falco?'

I leaned my chin on my hands. 'Couple of points. First, before she moved on to the Aventine, Veleda was at the Temple of Æsculapius. They say her illness may be marsh fever or similar. So she is likely to suffer relapses, in the usual cycles of recurrence, but if she survives the first bout, she won't die on you.'

They had forgotten they could lose her simply through disease. Laeta looked impressed, Rutilius grateful – mildly.

'Second – a minor correction – she left Diana Aventinensis *five* days ago.'

'Who told you?' Anacrites burst out.

'Can't reveal my sources.' I glanced at Laeta, who made a gesture to the Spy in support of me. 'Third – major update, this one: the priests of Diana *do* know where she went next; they sent her there.'

They all looked at me. I kept it quiet and polite. Some of these idiots might offer to employ me on another occasion. I needed the money, so I was daft enough to humour them. 'I have seen her. I have spoken to her.' That made them sit up. 'The situation seems to be containable – I mean, not simply that Veleda can be forcibly recaptured, but that she may surrender peacefully. Which would be *much* better for the Empire.'

At the mention of the Empire, they all looked down at their nice clean note-tablets and assumed pious expressions.

'I'd just like to go right back to before she ever took to her heels,' I told Rutilius. 'She was said to be greatly distressed when she learned she would be part of a Triumph. You had never said what fate awaited her – am I right?'

'Maybe I should have done, Falco.' Rutilius paused. 'The reason I did not, frankly, is that it would be wrong to anticipate that my Ovation would be granted. Such an honour must be voted by the Senate. Even if it is thought appropriate, I must first complete my task as Lower German governor.'

'Your modesty commends you.' In retrospect his caution was even more wise. I reckoned Veleda's bungled captivity could well lose Rutilius his Ovation. The man was bright enough to know it too. 'I was told originally that Veleda overheard her fate from "a visitor". Quadrumatus Labeo, can that be right? You were providing a safe house, where she was to be kept in conditions of absolute secrecy. Did you really permit your visitors to communicate?'

'I did not. Of course I did not.' Quick to defend himself, Quadrumatus looked put out. Then, in his normal direct way he confessed what he had previously fudged: 'It was one of my household who revealed what was planned for her.'

'You know who?'

'I do know. The person responsible has been reprimanded.' There was awkward shuffling among the others. I gazed at the crestfallen householder. He had intended to withhold the truth, but weakly confessed: 'It was my wife's freedwoman, Phryne. She took against the priestess and committed this very spiteful act.'

'Your wife cannot control her?'

'My wife is a . . . benevolent disciplinarian.' His wife was a lush, and the freedwoman controlled the keys to her wine cupboard. 'How does this help, Falco?'

'Maybe it helps *you,* sir, to reconsider just how you govern your household.'

Laeta pursed his lips. They all knew about Drusilla, and while none of them would have been so blunt they remained silent through my rebuke.

Anacrites was rubbing his forehead, a sign that stress had brought back his headaches. He could no longer contain himself. 'You're wasting time, Falco. If you know where the priests sent Veleda, I demand to be told!'

We were colleagues in this, so I answered his question. 'They sent her to the sanctuary at Nemi.'

279

Then I sat back and let the fool rush from the room, intending to apprehend her at the shrine, taking all the credit. If he dashed all the way there, he would be gone for two days. My guess was, somewhere along the crazy ride, he would realise I gave him the information too easily; he would suspect I had misled him and turn back. It would do me no good in our tortured relationship – but it bought me, and Veleda, precious time.

LVI

Helena and I did remember our children. We were going home in a hired chair, one of a row that had been thoughtfully ordered up in case the house-party guests wanted to go out. We had shed Laeta, who was lingering to make himself useful to the great Rutilius. We had not even reached the gate at the property boundary when we both gasped guiltily. We turned the chair around, and our daughters never knew how close they came to being given up for adoption in a very wealthy house.

At the Probus Bridge, Helena went on with our two sleeping nymphs, while I climbed out and set off to the patrol house of the Third Cohort of Vigiles.

It was a wasted journey. The Third told me proudly that as soon as Petronius had alerted them to the flautist's owner, they notified the Quadrumati. Someone had been from the villa to pick up the missing boy already.

'Had you interviewed him?'

'What about, Falco?'

I hired another chair, and returned down the Via Aurelia. It was late afternoon and at the onset of darkness, the villa had been trimmed with half a million lamps. Everyone had been eating and drinking all day now. One of Drusilla's dwarfs had been chosen – or had elected himself – King for the Day; he was causing havoc. It took me an hour to find anyone who knew about the flautist and even longer to persuade them to take me to him. He was locked in a cell-like store-room.

'This is harsh.'

'He's a runaway.'

'He fled because he was witless with terror – terror of somebody here.'

'It's for his protection then.'

As protection it had failed. When they opened up for me, the young boy I remembered cowering in shock nine days ago was stretched out, face up on a mattress, dead.

Word of my furious return must have gone round. Quadrumatus and Rutilius appeared in the doorway as I straightened up from examining the lad. I had found nothing to explain his death. It was classic: he looked as if he was asleep.

'He has been back in this house less than three hours – but someone got to him. He was trapped in here; he must have known he was doomed. Whoever came and killed him, it's a certainty they also killed Gratianus Scaeva. Your flautist,' I told Quadrumatus fiercely, 'saw your brother-in-law's killer. I won't ask if you knew that all along – you're a patrician and I'm not stupid. But I tell you this: others in your household did know; they arranged a cover-up. I sensed it when I first came here and if I had been given true information then, this boy would be alive.' He would have been a witness, but that wasn't what was making me so angry. 'He has been murdered to silence him. Don't tell me he is just a slave. He was human; he had a right to life. He was *your* slave; he was one of *your* family. *You* should have defended him. Call this a safe house? I don't think so! You run a house of riot, sir!'

Disgusted, I turned on my heel and left.

I went back.

I cleared the store-room and locked the door. I kept the key.

I found Quadrumatus Labeo: 'This house is outside Rome and theoretically beyond the jurisdiction of the vigiles. By the authority conferred on me by Claudius Laeta in the Veleda affair, I am ordering that your flautist's death be referred to the city authorities. We will not have the same appalling mistakes that were allowed when Gratianus Scaeva died. This time the crime scene and the corpse will be meticulously catalogued, and witnesses who fail to co-operate will be taken into custody. *You,* sir, will be responsible for ensuring that members of your household tell us the truth. Someone will be sent to examine the body professionally. Until then, the room is to remain locked. Take the name of anyone who attempts entry, and detain them for interrogation.'

Petronius Longus would give me that rueful look of his. Still, Marcus Rubella was already collecting for next year's Fourth Cohort drinks party. Given a large cash contribution, which could be suitably disguised on my mission's expense sheet, he would agree to help. I wanted a doctor to look at the dead flautist. This house was full of medical creatures, but I trusted none of them. I wanted Scythax. I was going to find out how the flute-boy died, even if we had to conduct an illegal autopsy.

LVII

I barely made it back in time to be smartened up and hauled out to dinner with my sister Junia. I tried telling Helena I was too tired, too gloomy and too tense to go. I received the response I expected. All over Rome unhappy lads were being forced to attend parties with uninspiring relatives. To avoid it needed very careful prior planning.

It was a perfectly good evening – if you ignored the fine detail: Junia couldn't cook; Gaius Baebius had no nose for wine; their overwrought son Marcus – King for the Day – had no idea what was going on; my precocious little girls knew exactly what they wanted – to be princesses who behaved badly; and wonderful Junia had invited Pa. Helena asked him to tell us about his operation, knowing that would cheer me up. It did. Better still, prim Junia was thoroughly offended by the ghastly details. That was even before my father offered to show us all the results.

He drew me aside at one point, and I thought I was to be favoured with distasteful tunic-lifting, but he just wanted to croak that he had brought the ear-rings he was trying to flog me. I bought them. Then I refused to humour his proffered demonstration of his wounds.

He must have found a taker, because soon we were subjected to an hour of three-year-old Marcus Baebius Junillus running around, showing everyone his bare little bottom. 'We can't stop him!' gasped Junia, horrified by her predicament. 'He is our King for the Day!' Little Marcus might be deaf and speechless, but he had a flair for misrule.

Notwithstanding his rights, Helena eventually grabbed the excited child, plonked him on her lap and made him sit quiet for the ghost stories. All the children were far too young for that. Things became tricky.

Pa, Gaius and I made the traditional exit to the sun terrace, where we stood around with half-empty winecups, shivering and discussing chariot teams. I supported the Blues, while Pa supported the Greens (that was precisely why, many years ago, I had chosen the Blues).

Gaius never went to the races, but ventured that if he did he thought he might fancy the Reds. At least that gave Pa and me something to talk about, as we massacred the mad idea that *anyone* would ever support the Reds. 'You two bastards always gang up together,' complained Gaius – which gave us both something else to get annoyed about loudly, while we were angrily denying it.

This was a true family occasion. We walked back indoors for another drink – Pa and I both extremely keen to open up the amphora he had hospitably brought, rather than Gaius' vinegar. Junia's hired ghost had arrived.

'*Whoo-hoo?!*' he went, spookily gliding around in a white garment with his face hidden. Silent children cowered against their mothers, thrilled. Helena and Junia were equally thrilled, now the children had calmed down. We men stood and applauded, pretending to be brave. Only Gaius Baebius was quaking, since I had just muttered to him to keep a check in case the spook stole something. Pa couldn't care less so long as it was over quickly; he was too busy shifting from foot to foot as the red hot pain flared up in his damaged posterior. I was stunned: I knew this ghost, though he did not remember me. It was Zoilus.

He might be crazy, but as Saturnalia entertainment that could only help. I had thought when I met him on the Via Appia that he must have had theatrical training. Actors are often paid too little to lead decent lives, and Zoilus had the air of being too unreliable to obtain steady work. Even so, he was on some good contacts list. Junia had obtained him from the Theatre of Marcellus, a snooty monument built and named for a nephew of Augustus, but not above providing acts for private homes. Intellectual aesthetes employed small teams to give them masterpiece-theatre all to themselves, on rickety stages in their chilly villas. Children's parties in fine mansions had little entertainments where the spoiled brats threw food at the performers. Stage donkeys were popular. And there was always a demand for sexy charades at degenerate banquets. The stage donkeys, and sometimes stage cows, featured in those too – usually having a really good time with some stage virgin.

'They offered me a stage donkey,' said Junia, unaware of the effect she caused in some of us. 'But I didn't think we had the room.'

'Very wise!' intoned Pa seditiously.

When Zoilus had finished his turn, I cornered him. 'That was a good haunting – though not as frightening as when you jumped me on the Via Appia!' I backed him up against Gaius and Junia's petite but decorative Greek urn display stand. Their four *alabastra* and their *kylix* (which had one broken handle, but Pa thought it was reproduction anyway) wobbled disconcertingly. 'Now before you get paid, you will answer me some questions.'

'Marcus, mind my precious red figures!'

'Just shut up, Junia. This is men's talk. Talk, being the big word, Zoilus.'

'I am just a restless spirit –'

'I know, I know; drifting about eternity like a dried leaf . . . Why did you call Zosime a bringer of death? – Don't go all vague on me. My sister's going to give you a big bowl of her deep-fried sesame balls as thanks for this evening, so there's no need to be ethereal. You'll need a strong stomach. Why did you say it, Zoilus?'

'I don't know-ow – *Ow!*' He might be a spirit but he knew when his privates were kneed. This was my first time putting the persuaders on a ghost. His ectoplasm had more substance than he pretended. After a couple of winecups, I was not gentle; my sudden jerk produced a satisfactory shriek.

'Stop messing about, or you'll really be dead and I won't bother to bury you.' I had no time for finesse. 'Look here – Members of my family, some of whom are young and sensitive, are gathering to see what's going on. I'll have to beat you up fast and *very* hard . . .' Zoilus understood. He had roamed among vagrants long enough to know about impatient men and the pain they could inflict.

He caved in and answered me sensibly. He knew about the runaways who died in the night even though they were fit, or halfway fit. I asked if he had seen any being killed. He moaned a bit, which I took for an affirmative. I asked if the killer was a woman or a man; to my surprise, he said a man. It was one of the few statements I had ever heard him make with firmness.

'Are you sure? So what had Zosime to do with it?'

'*Woo-oo* . . .' This tremor was barely audible.

'Oh stop it, Zoilus. Brace up, you ghoul! If I brought him in front of you, could you identify this man?'

But Zoilus collapsed. Hiding his head in his spectral robe, he just writhed about and moaned more. Eventually I foolishly loosened my hold on him as Junia interrupted again, bringing a tray of dubious-looking bites. Zoilus made a sudden run for it, through a set of double doors and away across the home-built sun terrace that was the pride and joy of Gaius Baebius. My hands were too greasy to stop him; my will was flagging too. As he fled, he snatched the purse with his agreed fee from Junia, but ignored her snacks. Maybe he could tell that my sister's famous over-salted, under-spiced deep-fried sesame balls were as hard as Pluto's heart in Hades.

SATURNALIA, DAY SIX

Eleven days before the Kalends of January (22 December)

LXVIII

The sixth day of Saturnalia often sees revellers reviving. Those who had been out of their heads for the past five days either die of drink and debauchery or learn to live with their condition. I felt I was enduring the worst aspects, with no chance to enjoy myself. I missed the good events because of my work, and was sober for the grim ones.

Junia's layered cheesecake was repeating on me acidically when I climbed out of bed. Helena rubbed my hunched shoulders and crooned sympathetically.

'I'm depressed about that flautist.'

'I know you are, love. Maybe today Mother will manage to get into the Vestals' House. She knows we are going to them tonight –'

'Are we?'

'I'm sure I told you, Marcus.'

'I'm sure you thought you did!'

'Oh please be good about it. Mother is trying to create a normal festival for Claudia. She will do her best for you; she realises you're bound to ask has she talked to Ganna.'

Being 'normal for Claudia' might be Julia Justa's aim, but her eccentric daughter threatened to jeopardise that: Helena had a bad conscience about leaving the priestess on her own for the past two evenings, so she proposed taking Veleda with us this time.

'That's risking trouble! Ulterior motive? – You think if Claudia hits her hard enough, Veleda will be done for and my problem will be over?'

'Desperation! Somehow, Marcus, we have to resolve issues.'

I said I wanted to resolve what I would have for breakfast first. It ended up being honey on a brown roll, but I ate it on the hoof. Petronius Longus sent me a message to come to the doctor Mastarna's house. It wasn't to help Petro face up to a medical consultation: Scaeva's physician had killed himself.

I walked to the place by the Library of Pollio, musing on how many times I had been called out at first light by the vigiles. Suspicious deaths often occurred at night. Either that, or nosy neighbours informed at the patrol house last thing, so they could go to bed with a clear conscience. Sometimes the watch simply found the corpses while they did their rounds.

When I reached the house, processing was virtually complete. 'Your name came up,' Petro informed me dourly. Whenever he found me involved in a case, he disapproved.

What had happened looked obvious. Mastarna had been found by his housekeeper, the lop-sided midget I had seen before busying herself around his smart apartment. She was now pretty shocked. Sometimes if she had backache Mastarna would give her a 'tonic' so she slept well and the pain eased. She must have known that he had a habit of dosing himself with mandrake too, but she had not expected the jug of poison.

'We know he did himself in,' Petronius confirmed. 'It's classic. He left a note.'

'Don't say that's where my name cropped up?'

'Bright boy. *"There is no way out. Falco knows everything. I apologise."* So what's that about?'

I sat down to think. His despair could be because I had announced yesterday that I was on the verge of identifying Scaeva's killer. Petro and I gazed at the Etruscan lying on his reading couch. The toga he had worn so fastidiously when Helena and I visited now lay in a crumpled heap on the floor, one of the signs that he had roamed about the room in anguish before he stretched out on his couch, with a jug of dark liquid. There was a clean cup on the tray, untouched. He had swigged straight from the jug. Then he tossed the valuable article across the room. Drips followed its progress. One of the vigiles rubbed at a spot on the floorboards; Petro kicked him just in time as he went to lick his finger and taste the stuff.

Petronius knew more than he had at first revealed, even to me. Mastarna had died yesterday evening. Before that, he had been visited by a colleague who had greatly upset him. The housekeeper was bad with names but she said the fellow-doctor was a Greek.

'Must be Cleander. He has a spiteful attitude. And he gave the impression he knew something – must have concerned Mastarna.'

There had been a short argument, then Cleander left. Mastarna went out a couple of times, seeming agitated and saying he wanted to seek advice from friends, but he returned forlorn because they were out. He asked for writing materials and sent the housekeeper to her own house; she lodged elsewhere. She said he was a very private man; Petro and I exchanged glances. Uneasy, the loyal biddy had got up very early and came to check on him. When she could get no answer, she panicked. Thinking the worst, she sent for the vigiles.

'One of his friends turned up to see what Mastarna wanted yesterday – apparently he went around banging on doors like mad. The fellow is co-operating.' Petro had closeted the witness in another room, to which he now took me.

I was surprised to see Pylaemenes. The dream therapist said that he had not known Mastarna well. He had been surprised that the man had been trying to see him so urgently last night. 'Bit of a shock – Aedemon says Mastarna was after him too.'

'You both know something that explains Mastarna's suicide?'

'*Everybody* knows,' Pylaemenes exclaimed. 'After we saw you yesterday, that bastard Cleander must have come here, crowing that the game was up – they were always on bad terms. Mastarna tried turning to Aedemon and me but then he despaired . . . Somebody is going to tell you now, so it may as well be me. This is what I know, Falco. I had a slight involvement because there had been a family argument. Quadrumatus needed me to interpret a dream and tell him whether he was right to take a stand.'

'Quadrumatus Labeo,' I told Petro, 'is a man of enormous wealth and power, apparently incisive – yet he can't jump unless this starspangled Chaldean tells him what to do.'

'What was the problem?' Petro asked Pylaemenes.

'Scaeva. Scaeva was always sickly. He wanted to be well for Saturnalia, when they had a big programme of events planned. He and his sister –'

'Drusilla Gratiana. Wife to Quadrumatus,' I spelled out to Petro.

'They were keen that Mastarna should carry out an operation on Scaeva's throat. Mastarna claimed he could remove Scaeva's inflamed tonsils and cure him. But Quadrumatus has his own doctor – Aedemon – who strongly warned against it. Aedemon wanted to purge the patient of the impurities that he said would be causing the infections. As you know Falco, Cleander attends on Drusilla; he also is a huge opponent of surgery – that's his beef against Mastarna. But Drusilla was dead set on her brother trying anything.'

'So young Scaeva is in misery, the doctors are all squabbling and the relatives are slogging it out at top volume; you get called in to tweak a dream or two as the beleaguered master's last resort?' Petronius looked askance. 'And you helped him decide what he thought, did you?'

'Quadrumatus forbade the surgery,' agreed Pylaemenes coolly.

I saw it all now. 'The others ignored him? Mastarna egged on Scaeva; Scaeva and his sister secretly arranged to have it done. So what happened? Was the operation on the same day Scaeva was found dead?'

Pylaemenes nodded. 'He bled to death during the surgery. Mastarna admitted afterwards that it was a known risk.'

It took me a moment to grasp the nuances. 'It was a throat operation! Unless Mastarna was the most brutal surgeon in history, or so drugged up he was floating on the ceiling, however could he slip with the knife so badly that he lopped off Scaeva's entire head?'

This time Pylaemenes just shrugged. 'Unbelievable. That's doctors for you.'

It explained why no weapon had ever been found. After the débâcle, Mastarna would have taken it away in his medical bag. Even if we now found a surgical implement drenched with blood, that would prove nothing. We could not say it came from Scaeva. Mastarna probably cleaned up the knife afterwards in any case. Most surgeons are that hygienic. Well, their patients hope they are.

'So who removed the head?' mused Petronius. 'And why, then, did they put the head in the atrium pool?'

'As a cover-up,' I said carefully. 'Drusilla still didn't want her husband to know that his orders had been countermanded. They organised a vindictive little enhancement, to disguise the bungled surgery and place blame on an innocent party.' Petro knew who I meant, of course.

'There was panic,' said the Chaldean. 'Drusilla was distraught at the death of her brother – blamed herself. Still blames herself, in fact, and frankly she's going to pieces over it. Her staff were running around in circles, wondering what to do. They all knew this was more than Quadrumatus would take. Drusilla herself found the head before they could warn her.'

'Does Quadrumatus know the truth now?'

'He suspects. His nightmares have been indicative.'

'You could interpret them,' Petronius suggested. 'Might be for the best. Man deserves to know.'

'The mind is a sensitive organ,' murmured Pylaemenes. 'He needs to work it out himself. So much more healthy!' The bastard thought that whoever told Quadrumatus the truth of this tawdry episode might end up being dismissed.

Petronius looked at me. His vigiles training had come to the fore. He was working out how to avoid documentation. 'There has been no crime, Falco. What they did with the head was an act of desecration – but that's for Quadrumatus to take up with his wife. Woman sounds troubled enough already. Her brother's death was stupid and avoidable, but that's her punishment. I'll put that death down as an accident. Mastarna's a suicide. Must have hated the thought of losing his reputation.'

'And his business,' I said. 'Who would ever hire him after hearing he lost Scaeva that way? Besides, there might have been a whopping compensation claim. If Quadrumatus employs as many lawyers as doctors, one of them was bound to spot the potential to screw Mastarna for professional negligence.'

Petronius whistled, thinking of the possible sums involved.

For him, it was neat. I still had one preoccupation. 'Pylaemenes, what was the involvement of Scaeva's boy flautist?' Petro looked at me quickly. Unsure whether he knew yet that I had asked Marcus Rubella to authorise further investigation by the cohort, I told him, 'The flautist must have known something. I think he's been killed to stop him speaking out. I want Scythax to look at him.'

'The flautist was supposed to be *there*,' interrupted Pylaemenes. 'He knew all about the operation. Scaeva used him for music therapy. So he was meant to be in the room all the time, playing soothing tunes to help relax people. Unfortunately he's a dozy soul – well, maybe he was scared of watching the surgery. I heard that he turned up too late. Mastarna had completed the operation – as far as it went, before the patient haemorrhaged everywhere. Drusilla and her maids were screaming. Scaeva was dead – that must have been obvious – and the child witnessed his master in pools of blood, in the very act of having his head cut off . . .'

Petronius cursed, brutally. 'Killing the boy was pointless. Accidents happen. If there was no crime, there was no need to silence the little beggar.'

'But since they did kill the flautist,' I barked back at him, 'there *is* a crime – and we are damn well going to solve it!'

Petronius patted my shoulder. He knew about my deadline. 'You've got your own worries. Leave this to us, Falco.'

LIX

I took Petronius Longus at his word.

While I was out and about, I went to see Julia Justa. At the senator's house the door porter consented to say that my mother-in-law had gone that morning to the Vestals' House, though she had not returned. Typical: Mastarna killed Scaeva and presumably he then decapitated the dead patient. I no longer needed an explanation, but I was obligated to Julia Justa anyway . . . I would not have made her beg favours from her Vestal friend unless it was unavoidable; next time we needed the Vestal it was bound to be more difficult, and who knows what emergencies lay in the future?

The senator was out. Gone to the gym. Perhaps to escape the stress at home. He and I were both members of Cassius' gymnasium by the Temple of Castor, so I thought I might drop in and find him there. Unfortunately, someone had reported my presence in the house to Claudia Rufina. She came flying downstairs, green stoles fluttering like yacht pennants, and accosted me. She was a good mother, and her arrival was punctuated by alternate wafts of a very expensive perfume and baby milk. One of her pendant pearl ear-rings was sitting askew; Claudia had a devoted Baetican maid and plenty of polished silver hand mirrors, so it had probably been playfully yanked by nine-month-old Gaius Camillus Rufius Constantinus.

She grabbed at my sleeve. 'Marcus, don't go!'

'Ah Claudia – don't hit me!'

She lowered her voice swiftly to a quieter register. 'Don't ever joke about that, Falco.' Teasing was what this highly anxious young woman needed, in my opinion. She needed to hand it out too. If she had let Justinus think she didn't give a damn, he would have come skipping home weeks ago. Still, not all women were like Helena Justina; that was why Helena had been inescapably my choice. I was still being surprised by her. Whereas this one had had her fiery moments and was generally viewed as temperamental, to me she would always be straightforward and predictable. I knew what she thought of my talents, for instance: 'You are never going to sort it out, are you?'

'Claudia, don't be so pessimistic. Events are moving fast. Have you seen Quintus?'

'I don't care if I never see him again.'

'You do care – and, Claudia, you have to contact him. You and he must talk.'

Claudia fiddled with the bangles on her wrist. 'Well he knows where to find us. He could come home. He could visit the baby, at least.'

'Claudia, he really can't come at the moment. He is generously caring for a young soldier who is terribly wounded. Quintus and I are both fond of Lentullus, and he is perilously close to death. He saved your husband's life getting his wounds. Besides, I ordered Quintus to stay put. I had to. I'm trying to keep him out of Anacrites' clutches.'

Claudia stared at the floor. 'That man came to see me.'

He was back from Nemi then. 'I hope you didn't tell him anything.'

Claudia's face clouded. She had talked. Rats. At least she was now feeling guilty about it. That meant she was vulnerable to pressure.

'He's a bastard. Poor you. Was it awful?'

'Oh Marcus, I told him Quintus was hiding with the vigiles. Was that very wrong of me?' Just very, very stupid.

I sucked my teeth. 'Well, whatever comes of it, I'm sure Quintus will forgive you.' I let it sound doubtful. 'Given how much he loves you, Claudia . . .'

Claudia Rufina burst into tears. Oh, excellent. Or as Helena scoffed later when I told her about it, 'You swine, Falco!'

LX

I was still trying to escape from Claudia when Julia Justa was brought home. The bearers carried the dilapidated Camillus chair into the hall, and she descended stiffly, looking weary, just as I was saying, 'Some men find it hard to show their true feelings, Claudia.'

Shedding her cloak, Julia Justa gave me a narrow look. She was as shrewd as Helena and would have spotted at once just how I was working on Claudia's feelings. My deviousness would not surprise her. The noble Julia had always seen me as unreliable.

We all moved to a frescoed salon. Then followed a delay while slaves – who were already getting into a slapdash holiday mood for the dinner that evening – were prevailed upon to provide pre-lunch snacks to revive their mistress. Julia only toyed with the food, so I weighed in. Nobody should make a big fuss about obtaining service, then not use what they have demanded. Slaves take against that, and who can blame them? Julia, who was a strict, good-mannered woman, even nodded her approval as I munched.

The news was interesting. 'I saw Ganna as you asked, Marcus. She is well cared for and fairly content. The Vestals are taking the opportunity to teach her Roman ways.' This would be another side of Rome from that Ganna saw at Mother's house. 'Unfortunately –' I had to concede, my mother-in-law did have a sense of humour – 'they have taught her to read and I suspect that she has read the letters my foolish son wrote to the priestess.' Julia was telling me this in a hurried undertone while Claudia made a temporary foray back to the nursery.

'Ganna has the letters?'

'Not any longer. I persuaded her that it was best for all concerned if we destroyed them. My first thought was to bring them away with me, but the Virgins are very much concerned with the confidentiality of documents, as you know.' Elevated citizens gave their wills to the Vestal Virgins for safe keeping. 'It is apparently improper for a mother to see love letters written by her son!'

'Well, I think most sons would agree with that.'

'So they were burned. And good riddance.'

Claudia returned, so without missing a beat we made the conversation more general. 'Were the Vestals present for your interview?'

'My friend supervised. It was a condition, Marcus.'

'Fair enough.'

Julia did take a small almond cake from the tray of titbits. She was allowing herself a moment of reflection. After six or seven years, I now knew her well enough to trust her instincts and let her dictate the rhythm of conversation. For me, talking to my mother-in-law was always eerie. She and Helena were enough alike for it to feel like familiar territory – yet Helena took after her father in more ways, so Julia remained worrying.

Claudia, who seemed even more jumpy than usual, could not wait patiently, but burst out, 'So what did this Ganna have to say? I don't know her, but I think I hate her.'

By contrast, Julia Justa seemed increasingly rational. Unlike the night of the feast for Saturn, when her garments got the better of her, she was now stonily calm and in charge. Julia finished her cake, wiped away a few tiny crumbs, and leaned back in her basket chair. 'She is just a frightened girl, my dear. You have no need to be defensive. Marcus, with regard to your business, the person Ganna saw placing the severed head in the atrium pool was a freedwoman called Phryne.'

'What? Not the doctor, Mastarna?'

Julia looked as surprised as I was. 'Apparently not. How could a doctor be involved?'

'He killed his patient during an operation. Still, the freedwoman may have taken part in the cover-up, trying to protect her mistress.' I now wondered whether it was Phryne or Mastarna who actually cut off Scaeva's head. Phryne had showed enough hatred towards Veleda. She could have grabbed the doctor's knife and done the deed. 'The mistress had let the operation go ahead, even though her husband had forbidden it.'

Julia nodded. 'Drusilla Gratiana.'

'You know her?'

'No, but my Vestal friend does, naturally.' The Vestal Virgins know all the senior matrons in Roman society, where 'senior' normally means rich, with powerful husbands. Julia commented coolly, 'Apparently the woman is in poor health.'

'She drinks.'

'Oh Marcus!' This was from Claudia.

'True – fact of life.'

'Please! She has just lost her brother in appalling circumstances.' Back in Baetica, Claudia had lost her own brother to murder; she had obvious reasons for sympathy.

'Forgive me.'

'Well, those were my commissions.' Julia thought it time to shoo me off home. 'But I am the bearer of a good suggestion. Marcus, will you put this idea to Helena, please? I know she is intending to ask the Emperor to extend clemency to Veleda. My friend suggested we make a formal, old-fashioned deputation of Roman matrons. She even volunteered to accompany us. If Helena wants to do this, I will certainly join with her.'

'You mean, a group of respectable women in black, covering their heads, and confronting Vespasian with noble pleas to save the priestess?'

'I do,' said Julia. It sounded historic, but the last time this classic political ploy had been used, the full trick with a Vestal Virgin to the fore, had been as recently as the civil war that brought Vespasian to power.

Now Julia showed why she had hesitated earlier. She turned to her daughter-in-law. 'My dear Claudia Rufina, this is a lot to ask, I know. To be effective, the Vestal Virgin felt that the deputation really needs you to be a part of it with us. Veleda once saved the lives of both Marcus and Quintus, so both their wives should be seen to plead to save her.'

I was glad I did not have to suggest that.

Claudia took it well. That is, she refrained from hurling furniture. Her tone was acidic: 'My husband wants to leave me for this flagrant enemy of Rome – and I am to make such a selfless gesture?'

'That would be the point.' Julia managed to sound diffident.

'The sacrifice would be too cruel!'

'Then don't do it,' replied Julia briskly. 'I told the Vestal you could not be expected to. Marcus, we shall see you tonight, I hope?'

I said she would, and on cue began to take my leave. When Julia rose and kissed my cheek (a formality that always chilled me) I could see Claudia behind her, biting her lip as she reviewed her dilemma. I went over and kissed her too, bending down as she remained seated. 'Veleda will never be a free woman. Just think about saving your marriage. You could demonstrate to Quintus that you trust him, while showing your own generosity of spirit. Seems to me, it would put him in a position where his love and respect for you would then take precedence –'

Claudia jumped up, nearly knocking me over. 'And would that work with you? – Marcus Didius Falco, I *don't think so!*'

I grinned. 'Oh I'm an informer. I'm famous for hating upright women. You're quite right – do as Julia says, lady. Tell them just where they can put their great idea! That could work too; Quintus did marry you because you were adventurous and forthright.'

'He wanted my money.' That was the first time I had ever heard Claudia say it. She sounded wounded, wan and defeated.

'He wanted the package,' I told her. 'The money was good, but the woman was better.'

Claudia was not having it. She drew herself up; she was at least my height. Then she stalked from the room. Her despondency suggested she was off to pack her bags and leave for Baetica with her young child immediately.

I made a conciliatory gesture. Julia Justa stilled me with an oddly casual little shrug, as if Claudia was better left to reach her own decisions. I thought Julia was wrong, but I told myself my mother-in-law was a wise woman. Besides, there would be other chances to plead with the young woman. We still had to get through a Saturnalia feast tonight.

LXI

'Anacrites is back!' Had it not been so serious, Helena would have been giggling. 'He didn't go to Nemi. He rode about seven miles then he decided you had sent him on a fool's errand. He came here to search the house.'

I gulped. 'Where's Veleda?'

'*Now*,' said Helena, 'she is sleeping on a couch. At the time, she had gone out in the chair with Albia and Zosime to take some air in Caesar's Gardens.'

'How come? I gave strict orders she was to stay in at all times.'

'Don't be pompous. If I took any notice of your orders,' Helena told me, 'you would have lost her to Anacrites.'

'The stricter my orders are, the quicker you defy me.'

'That's right, darling. Do you want me to describe how enraged the Spy was when he went all over our property and could not find her? He had been *so* sure! I just stood in the hall with my arms folded and waited for his men to finish. That should have told him I was not afraid of discovery. The longer it lasted, the more he was sweating as his mistake dawned on him. All the soldiers stood to attention, with disapproval painted all over them. Julia and Favonia clung to me and cried their eyes out. We made a wonderful picture of an outraged matron and her children, offered grave offence – *in her own home, where she should be safe from insult* – moreover, while the father of the family was absent. I asked Anacrites icily whether he had obtained your permission to enter and search our house. I swear he blushed. When he left, his apology was so sickly I could hardly bear it.'

I had calmed down. There was no way I would ever make Helena Justina a submissive partner who followed my rules. She knew how to handle a crisis. I myself would have tied Anacrites to the filthy underside of a manhole cover and left him to hang there in the dark with rat-bait in his boots. This way, he had put himself in the wrong, he must be scared that Helena or her father would complain to the

Emperor – and he had failed to find the priestess even though he guessed I had her.

Helena continued, still enjoying her narration: 'After he apologised, I asked him about his headaches, implying I hoped they were unbearable. He's going to that man Cleander, for some treatment. Marcus, you'll be glad to hear it involves putting cups on him, with lighted herbs against his skin, and what sounds like quite a lot of blood-letting.'

I said it was time to get dressed for dinner. Helena told me it was too soon yet. I let her know that I was planning on getting undressed first, and staying undressed for quite some time.

Later, in a private part of the house, at an inappropriate moment:
'There's another thing, Marcus – we had a busy morning. Petronius popped in to discuss the flute-player. Scythax seems confused, and has left him a message, showing that he thinks he was brought in because the boy was killed on the streets like the vagrants. Petro said he has to speak to Scythax and straighten this out. He will talk to you about it when he can.'

'Damn Petro. And damn talking . . .'

Some time afterwards:
'Sweetheart, I ought to tell you . . . Your mother wants to organise a formal deputation to Vespasian, headed up by her old Vestal Virgin, when you go to beg for clemency for Veleda.'

Silence.

Suddenly, one party sitting up abruptly:
'Oh Juno and Minerva, you are not serious. I don't have to plead for the priestess with my *mother* there?'

'The crabby Virgin too, dear one. Plus, if they can force her to be so magnanimous, poor Claudia Rufina . . .'

Startled party collapses and hides her head under the pillow. Other party lies prone, recovering, and thinking about the frightening power of mothers . . .

'Claudia might just do it, Marcus. She really needs to win Quintus back. I haven't told you yet why the sanctuary priests at Nemi were so unpleasant to us. We were pretending to seek fertility treatment – but we were unmasked when they detected that Claudia was already pregnant.'

I choked. 'So the authorities at Nemi would say the treatment works!'

'It's ironic, because she was hoping to avoid this. Everyone wondered why she wouldn't try to wean little Gaius. Poor Claudia had been told she would be safe, so long as she kept breast-feeding.'

'Your sweet-looking brother doesn't mess about. Their first is not yet a year old.'

Slight embarrassed pause.

'And Marcus darling, there is something I should tell you . . .' Olympus! What was this about? 'I know it is not what we planned –'

Any fool could work this one out. 'You mean, the priests were upset because *neither* of you needed the expensive ritual baths and the votive-sellers? You are *both* expecting?'

'Yes. Me too, sweetheart.'

I kissed Helena ruefully. 'Life is getting expensive. If your deputation to the Emperor fails, I'll have to drag Veleda to the Capitol and strangle her myself. We'll definitely need the mission fee.'

Pause.

'So are you pleased then, Marcus?'

We already had two children. Like every father who knows what a pregnancy means in short-term and long-term trouble, I had learned from practice how to lie well. 'Helena Justina, you do me an honour. I am delighted, of course.'

The senator sent his carriage to fetch our large group to the Camillus party. Praetorian Guards, looking nervous, did a stop and search, but only found Helena and me, our two over-excited children, and Nux, who bit a Guardsman. The Guards pretended they had a routine road block to monitor all traffic on the Aventine embankment, but I guessed that the Spy had ordered them to check anyone who left my house. Too bad they never noticed that a carrying chair with Albia and Veleda had crept out via the back exit while they were occupied with us, and sneaked the other way up the Embankment under cover of a passing high-piled empty-amphora cart. (I can't bear to think how much it had cost to bribe the driver of that cart.)

We arrived first at the Capena Gate. We were able to witness, therefore, the moment when the priestess was greeted by Julia Justa. She looked Veleda up and down. It was a simple gesture, but killing. I don't know how Veleda felt, but I had sweat crawling all over me.

'Welcome to our house.'

'Thank you.'

Claudia Rufina stood at her mother-in-law's shoulder, holding the baby in her arms. 'This is my son's wife.'

'We have met.'

'Welcome to our house,' repeated Claudia, making it sound like a death threat.

As we moved to the interior, towards sounds of music and revelry, Helena squeezed my arm and whispered, 'I'm starting to wonder if it was wise to bring Veleda for food and drink here!'

'Don't worry. Poisonings are my favourite kind of case. The descriptions of the death agony are always so colourful.'

Veleda already sported a spine taut as a bow and a rictus, though it had nothing to do with anything fatal in her foodbowl. Claudia, who had been wearing her legendary emerald parure, disappeared and rejoined us after adding extra gold bangles.

Julia Justa ran a Saturnalia feast on surprisingly traditional lines. Her slaves were in charge. King for the Day was a terrified boot-boy with sticky-out ears and a regal display of pimples, who waved his mock-sceptre bravely but never uttered a word. A battalion of slaves were lounging in the various dining rooms, including a few brave souls outside on the garden couches, where they were ceremonially served by the noblewomen of the family. The senator and I were deputed to be wine-waiters, with muttered instructions to make sure anything consumed was well watered. I joked with Decimus that more slaves were here than I realised they owned; he said he had never seen half of them before either. As soon as he could do it surreptitiously, he was planning the male householder's traditional role at this festival: hiding by himself in his study, while the merrymakers got on with it. I said I might join him; he said I was welcome, but only if I helped him barricade the door. We set about choosing which wine to take with us.

After a certain amount of enforced obedience to the slaves, who gave us impossible orders with a fine imperial manner, things relaxed (the slaves were now too busy eating their unaccustomed banquet to do much, and some were suffering biliousness because of the rich food). We managed to fill our own bowls from the laden comports. Julia and Favonia had learned their roles as inferiors and were scampering to and fro, delightedly trying to clean everybody's shoes for them. Claudia was showing what a wonderful maternal type she was by allowing my insistent daughters to keep running back with squeals of laughter to buff her gold sandals. Veleda watched snootily. 'I suppose even the girls among your tribes are so busy learning to be warriors, they have no childhood,' sneered Claudia. 'In Rome we would regard warmongering as a little unfeminine.'

'Your women sound rather feeble!' countered Veleda, venomously.
'Oh we Baeticans know how to fight back.'
'Surprising then, that you allowed your country to be overrun!'
Helena and Julia separated them.

Great bowls of nuts were carried in by the senator. Then, as the almonds and hazelnuts began to fly, we were joined by an unintended visitor. The jollity was at its height, which made the sudden silence more dramatic. The happy slaves all settled back, thinking *'Wey-hey! This is where the real party starts!'*

In a doorway stood Quintus Camillus Justinus. He looked like any family's dopy son who had just come home and was slowly remembering that his mother had informed him three times that the Saturnalia dinner was tonight. He lived here: the no-good son of the house – vague eyes, rumpled tunic that had not been changed for days, bristling chin left unshaven for even longer, floppy hair uncombed, slouching and relaxed.

From his expression I guessed that nobody had yet told him that Veleda would be here.

Surprisingly, he appeared to be sober. Sadly, both Claudia and Veleda had drunk quite a lot of wine.

LXII

For a moment they all stood, in a stricken triangle. Justinus was horrified; the women took it better, naturally.

Justinus straightened up. Veleda had last seen him dressed in a keenly-buffed tribune's uniform, five years younger, and fresher in every way. Now she looked stunned by his casual domesticity. He addressed the priestess formally, as he had done once before, in the depths of her forest. Whatever he said was again lost on the rest of us, because he used her Celtic tongue.

'I speak your language!' Veleda inevitably rebuked him, with the same pride and the same contempt that she had used to our party then: the cosmopolitan barbarian, showing up the inglorious imperialists who could not even bother to communicate with those whose terrain they invaded. It was a good trick, but I was tired of this.

He was staring at her, taking in that she looked so much more worn by time and life, and the despair of capture. Veleda's eyes were hard. Pity was the last thing any woman needed from a handsome lover. Quintus must already have struggled to cope mentally with the fact that the love of his young life was doomed to ritual killing on the Capitol. Would he turn his back on the Roman world – and if so, would he do something really stupid? We could see it was a hard shock to find the priestess here in his home, swaying very slightly from Roman wine in the cup that she still gripped unknowingly – a small silver beaker that Justinus must have known since his childhood, from which he may have drunk numerous times himself. He had found her being entertained among his parents, his sister, his wife and young child. He was not to know – or not yet – just how strained relationships had been.

In the silence, his baby son gurgled. 'Yes, it's Papa!' crooned Claudia, nuzzling his soft little head. I wondered if anyone had told Quintus yet that a brother or sister was expected. The little boy stretched his arms out towards his father. The traditional gold bulla his uncle Aelianus had given him at birth swung against the soft wool of his tiny tunic. He was a delightful, highly attractive child.

At once Quintus, the great sentimentalist, turned and smiled. Claudia thumped home the battering ram. 'Let's not bother Papa. *Papa doesn't want us, darling!*' Despite being tipsy, she produced one of her well-practised stalking exits, heading off for her kingdom, the nursery. Once there, some women would have burst into tears. Claudia Rufina had a sturdier spirit. I had talked her through past moments of decision and anxiety; I thought she would simply sit there by herself, quietly waiting to see whether Quintus came to her. If he did, she would be difficult – and who could blame her? – but as on previous occasions, Claudia would be open to negotiation.

Veleda looked as though she knew now that Justinus was too inhibited to abandon his Roman heritage. It was clear what she thought of that. She tossed the silver cup on to the mosaic floor, then with a broody glare she too swept out to take refuge in another room.

Quintus was left facing up to his tragedy. This was no longer an issue of whom would he choose? Neither of *them* wanted *him*. Suddenly he was looking like a boy himself, who had lost his precious spinning-top to rougher, ruder characters who would not give it back.

When the doomed man went first to follow Veleda, nobody stopped him. I moved closer to the double door he had closed behind them, but did not interrupt. Quintus stayed in the room for a short time only. When he came out, he looked agonised. His face was drawn with misery, perhaps even tear-stained. He was grasping a small object tightly in one hand; I could not see it, but I recognised the dangling strings: she had given him back the soapstone amulet.

When he reached me, he made an impatient movement, wanting me to step aside. I grasped him and embraced him anyway. Apart from Veleda, I was the only person present who had been with him in Germany, the only one who fully knew what she had meant to him. He had lost the love of his life not once, but twice. He had never got over it the first time; he probably imagined it would be even harder now. I knew better. He had had plenty of practice in bearing his loss. Grieving a second time is always easier.

Camillus Justinus was a young man. Now he knew that his fabulous lover was an older woman, growing ever older than his treasured golden memories. Whatever he had said to her, from the short time she spoke with him it was clear to all of us that she had cut short any grand protestations. What was there to say? He could plead that his wife was young and needy, a mother; perhaps Claudia had told him she was again pregnant. Veleda would see the situation. Justinus had lost his innocence – not that starry night in the signal tower in the forest, but in the instant when he chose the Roman life he had been born into: when he turned and smiled instinctively at Claudia Rufina and his little boy.

Perhaps Veleda had also noticed that when it came to women, Justinus was an idiot.

He continued resisting contact. I released him. Without a word to anyone, Justinus began his lonely walk to find his wife and tell her the hard decision that maturity and good manners had now thrust upon him. None of us envied the couple their coming struggle to regain some kind of friendship. But he was by nature easygoing and she was bitterly determined; it was feasible. For now at least, the Baetican emerald set would stay in Rome. Justinus and Claudia would get back together, although like all their reunions it would be bittersweet.

SATURNALIA, DAY SEVEN, THE FINAL DAY

Ten days before the Kalends of January (23 December)

LXIII

I know the historians will not record how the priestess Veleda's future came to be decided. I am debarred from revealing it, for the usual pretentious 'security reasons'.

What occurred in my own house is my own to reveal or conceal. In the circumstances, Helena said it was understandable that the priestess was bad-tempered at breakfast. She had been deeply withdrawn since the moment the previous evening when Helena kissed both of her parents gently, leaving them to oversee whatever transpired between her brother and Claudia. The senator and Julia were sympathetic in-laws. I myself was intending to suggest to Quintus that since Claudia did have so much money, it was time they acquired their own house where their tantrums – which would probably continue – could take their course, unobserved by relatives.

We had gathered up the children, Albia and Veleda and come quietly home. Anacrites seemed to have called off his useless spies. This morning everyone rose promptly. The Vestal Virgin had sent word to Julia that she had arranged an appointment at the Palace. She had made it clear this had not been easy. Although Claudius Laeta had given me this day as my deadline, most imperial business was suspended during the festival.

When it was time to leave, the Virgin sent a *carpentum* – the two-wheeled formal carriage used only by empresses and Vestal Virgins, which can be out on the streets even during the wheeled traffic curfew. This unusual arrival caused a traffic jam on the Embankment as all my neighbours rushed to gawk. Julia Justa had already been collected; she leaned out and indicated, by that screwing of the face all women understand, that we were not to show amazement – but she had after all brought Claudia to take part in the deputation. This made it a squash, since the *carpentum* is not designed to carry three. Clad in black from head to foot, Helena pushed her way in anyway. We had a chair ready, with Veleda inside but heavily curtained, which then followed the carriage to the Palatine. It was flanked by Justinus and me, and escorted by Clemens and the remaining legionaries, all in burnished gear and, as far as I had been able to ensure, minus hangovers.

We had left Lentullus at my house. Helena and I now knew why her brother had appeared at dinner: Marcus Rubella had finally kicked them out of the vigiles' patrol house, so we had acquired the invalid. His condition was much improved, though he did have a setback when I had to tell him he would have to leave the army. Lentullus rallied, however, when he knew that 'the tribune' was offering him a home.

So that Clemens did not return to Germany short-handed, I had suggested that I should formally free the appalling Jacinthus (he would have to lie and say he was thirty), then we would take him before a recruiting officer (to lie again and say he was twenty), enrolling him in the legions. Jacinthus was thrilled. So was Galene, who had convinced Helena that she should be moved to the kitchen as replacement cook. Once again we would be lacking a nurse for the children, but we were used to that. Once again we would have a cook who couldn't cook – but at least Galene would be interested in learning.

All these issues had been debated and resolved that morning, while Helena and I tried not to disturb Veleda's gloomy reverie. By the time the Vestal Virgin sent transport, we had been running out of bright ideas. Veleda had been dumped by Quintus and was returning to captivity. She hated all of us.

At the Palace, the women stepped down from the carriage. Helena led her mother and Claudia in a stately procession, in through the great roofed Cryptoporticus, along many corridors, to an anteroom, where Julia Justa and her Vestal friend met and exchanged dry kisses. I noticed that Claudia had managed to wear quantities of jewels, which drew disapproval from the Vestal. Claudia tossed her head defiantly.

We had brought the carrying chair indoors with us. Still guarding it, we men remained outside in a corridor. I kissed Helena. She shook out her skirts, straightened her stole, firmed up the pins holding her veil on her fine hair and led the formal deputation into a major receiving room. We had been told Vespasian was on his usual festival pilgrimage to his grandmother's house at Cosa, where he had been brought up. We could have been lumbered with Domitian, but we were in luck: Titus was imperial caretaker, dealing with emergencies.

They were a long time. I was sweating. Flunkeys were anxious to depart for lunch. It was clear that ours was the only business being thrust before Titus that morning. It might be dealt with briskly and casually. I cheered myself up thinking that if Berenice really had been sent packing to Judaea, Titus would have no calls on him during the festival and might welcome work.

Rubbish, Falco. Nobody welcomes work when all of Rome is playing. Titus would rather play solo draughts all day than be tied to the office.

Just as I braced myself to barge past the flunkeys and invade the audience, things became even trickier. Word of what was afoot must have reached the Chief Spy's office. Suddenly Anacrites appeared and demanded that we unload the chair and give him Veleda.

At the same moment, ten-foot double doors with gilded handles silently swung open and the women reappeared. Titus was graciously escorting them out. He always looked fetching in purple, and today was bedecked with an extra-large Saturnalia wreath. His hair, normally barbered to a crisp, had been allowed to grow shaggy as a sign of being broken-hearted at the loss of Berenice, but even so a careful valet had spent time positioning the wreath fetchingly on the curly mop.

'You've lost the game – hand her over, Falco!' the Spy was commanding, as he dragged open the half-door and started pulling Veleda from the chair.

He was stopped in his tracks by the frigid tones of the elderly Vestal Virgin: 'Tiberius Claudius Anacrites – *Unhand that woman immediately!*'

Titus Caesar had an eye for a beautiful foreigner. At once I saw him sizing up the priestess. As she recovered from the Spy's mauling, she gave a rapid assessment to the imperial prince who controlled her fate. In view of her reputation, Titus thought better of flirting, though he inclined his head politely as far as a heavy wreath allowed. Perhaps Veleda looked more hopeful for the future – though I could see she thought Titus a typical, sexually voracious Roman male. Behind everyone's backs, Helena Justina winked at me.

Her mother had noticed, and smacked Helena's wrist playfully.

The Vestal was in charge. 'You are to be sent to a shrine at Ardea,' she told Veleda. Thirty miles from Rome, Ardea was close enough to supervise yet far enough away to be secure. I thought it had been used as an exile for political prisoners before. 'Your life will be spared. You will live out your days as a temple cleaner.'

Veleda bridled. Helena grasped her hand and muttered quickly, 'Do not despise the honour. Being housekeeper to the gods is a worthy occupation – the Vestal and her colleagues traditionally have that role. It is neither onerous nor demeaning.'

Titus came forward. 'These three noble women – Helena Justina, Julia Justa and Claudia Rufina – have pleaded for you most movingly, Veleda. The Vestal Virgins, who see you as a sister, support them. Rome is pleased to accept their request for clemency.'

I stepped forward. I could see Claudius Laeta hovering. With Justinus at my elbow, I formally asked, 'Priestess, Helena Justina promised she would do her best for you. Do you accept these terms? Will you live out your days at Ardea quietly?'

Veleda nodded her head, in silence.

Then Justinus and I formally completed my mission. We handed over Veleda into imperial control. Giving her up must have been as hard for Justinus as pleading had been for Claudia. I had insisted that Justinus accompany me, in his normal role as my assistant. I hoped this would reinstate him in imperial favour. Perhaps it would even impress his wife. We knew Claudia would make it a condition of their marriage that he never went anywhere near Ardea. As far as I ever knew, Quintus promised her, and he stuck to the promise.

When Veleda was taken away by the Guards, she kept her gaze cast down and did not look at him. Justinus stood quietly and sadly as she left. Only a cruel cynic would have pointed out that he had the air of a condemned man.

LXIV

I had all of my sisters, and some of their husbands, and most of their children, in my house for the last night of the festival. We were also entertaining Zosime and the soldiers. To help Quintus and Claudia mend their marriage, we had asked them too. Helena had invited my mother, though fortunately she did not stay long; invited by me inadvertently, my father turned up, but he was late as usual. They must have passed in the street. At least we escaped having their first confrontation in twenty years in our dining room. Who wants violent recriminations over the must-cake at a feast dedicated to reconciliation?

There were complaints. 'Everyone else had puppets or ghosts, Marcus. Couldn't you have made an effort to fix up some entertainment for the last night?' The troops had made plenty of must-cake, however. Nux thought it was wonderful and spent the day trying to steal pieces. We had a large log in a hearth, filling everywhere with smoke and threatening to burn down the house, plus green boughs shedding pine needles and dust. My lamp-oil bill would take about three months to pay off. By a deft sleight of hand, I arranged that our King for the Day was my nephew Marius – a lad with a dry wit, who accepted the bean with a wink that suggested he knew he had been chosen on purpose for his discretion. He enjoyed the role, but kept the antics within acceptable limits.

It was a decent night. A night for generosity of spirit. Gifts appeared at appropriate moments, and nobody made too much fuss if their gift cost less than they had hoped. The men were allowed to come dressed as they liked; the women wore their newest jewels. Claudia was showing off the satyr ear-rings Quintus bought from Pa; Helena kept her more tasteful ones for another occasion so as not to upset Claudia. Everyone was comfortable. Everyone ate just enough, and drank only a little more than sensible. None of my family would ever remember it; there were no fights and nobody was sick on Junia's dog.

My dog Nux spent most of the time hiding in the little room that I was turning into a masculine study. As soon as I could, I joined her.

We were both there, doing nothing much, when Helena looked in, threw a nut at me, and said Petronius had just arrived. He had been invited with Maia, who was still being stand-offish, but had come with Ma and had stayed on. After he grabbed food and drink, Petro took me aside. He told me what he thought of my wine; it did not take long.

'It's leftover *primitivum* I cadged from Junia. And before you say it belongs to the cohort then, this will pay me back for the bribe I handed over to Rubella for help at the Quadrumatus house.'

'Oh we drank your cash up yesterday!' grinned Petro.

'That was for next year's party.'

'Nuts. As a bribe it didn't cover the aggravation that you've handed us at that villa.'

We settled in for a discussion. 'Look, Petro, it's all very well saying there's no crime. My view is that Mastarna let Scaeva die – genuine accident, maybe – but then Mastarna is unlikely to have decapitated the corpse. For one thing, if he did, he's just a hired man and the Quadrumati would have had no compunction in exposing him. No, they are trying to shield one of their own. I am sure the freedwoman, Phryne, was malevolent enough to grab a knife and do the deed – and then she carried the head to the pool.' I remembered now, how she had looked when I asked whether weapons or treasure were found in the atrium pool with the head: *Should there have been?* 'Even if that's all she did, somebody needs to tell Quadrumatus to stop looking away and deal with the woman. I thought I might write to Rutilius Gallicus and make him responsible for stiffening up his so-called friend.'

Petronius shrugged. 'Well you do that, and I'll get Rubella to ram home the message too.'

'I think there was more to it, Petro. I think that the poor flute boy saw what she did. The family covered it up but he was terrified of her. That's why he ran. When he was brought back to the villa, he may have become hysterical; Phryne killed the boy to keep him quiet.'

Petronius looked troubled. 'It's not her.'

'Alibi?'

'Her mistress vouched for her . . . Surprised? I'm still baffled by this flute boy death, Marcus. Scythax is being a menace over it – he is sticking to his theory, that the boy was killed like the street vagrants. The freedwoman can't have been constantly out of the house at night, killing runaways. I've explained to Scythax that the boy was found dead by you, indoors, and it just doesn't fit. Scythax wants to do more work on the corpse, but the Quadrumati won't allow it –'

'I told you; they are covering. They don't want a scandal.'

'Well, Scythax is rambling. There can't possibly be a link between that villa's household and what's happening to runaway slaves on the streets of Rome. We're stuck, Marcus.'

I had reached the mellow stage by then. I told him we could think about the flautist tomorrow, when everything returned to normal. Most likely, since there was nowhere else to go with the case, we would have to forget about it.

The night went on. Pa and some of my sisters went home. Zosime returned to her temple. 'Will you continue your work with the homeless?' Helena asked her as we bade farewell.

'Oh yes. I've been doing it ever since I was first trained.'

'Well, good luck to you!'

A few favoured people remained and we would probably stay up for hours yet; it was the soldiers' last night with us and they were melancholy to be losing domestic comforts. I sat fairly cheerfully among my family, waiting for the next angrily slammed door, the next whining child with a sore throat, the next tipsy woman to tread on the dog's tail...

I thought I was cheerful, but melancholy thoughts came drifting through my brain. I found myself thinking about the runaway who had told me his life story on the Via Appia – the ex-architect with the long tale of woe. I had learned that man's whole history, yet never even knew his name. I would never see him again, never know his fate. He had been sickly and could by now have died of December cold. His run of bad luck could even have ended with a final gasp, strangled by the unknown killer who bent over sleepers in doorways and choked the life out of them. I wished I could have asked him if he had ever seen the killer at work.

Then, as the oil lamps flickered and wine wafted me halfway to oblivion, the truth hit me: Scythax was right. There *was* a link between the villa and the dead runaway slaves. The flute boy may have been killed at Phryne's instigation yet it was not one of the household who took his life, but somebody who came in from outside. One of the doctors employed by the Quadrumati had let a patient bleed to death by accident. That was nothing; another was far more menacing.

I ordered Justinus to stop smooching Claudia and come with me after Petronius, who had left to go on duty at the patrol house. Once there, I asked Petro if his famous lists of undesirables included doctors. Since medicine is akin to magic, he had a list all right. He would not let me see it, but he found the address we needed and we set off to apprehend the man whom I was now convinced must be the killer.

'He hates all slaves. I've heard him disparage them – Hades, he even sneered at me when he supposed I was one – and people have been telling me about his attitude ever since I first met him. He follows the same broad Hippocratic doctrine as Zosime and the doctors at the Temple of Æsculapius. Zosime, or maybe it was someone else, told me a long time ago that he trained her. She calls the way they work, "softly, safely, sweetly" – but he has foully perverted that . . .'

We were going to see Cleander.

The streets were a nightmare, full of revellers who could not understand our need to pass through the crowds quickly. Petro had brought a few men, but most were too busy attending fires that night. The smell of smoke hung on the air, as thickly as the noise of merriment. We found the house. It seemed to be in darkness, but after muted knocking by a vigilis who pretended to be a patient, Cleander himself opened the door.

Petronius Longus led him back inside and began to interrogate him. In response, Cleander only glared haughtily. We were all beneath him. He treated the charge of murdering the runaways with chilly contempt. Soon he began refusing to answer any questions at all. Petronius eventually had him taken away to the patrol house.

'Seen it before, Marcus. He will never confess. I can put Sergius to work on him, but this man is so arrogant he will think it a challenge to withstand the pain.'

'Maybe his slaves – or his patients – will give up information.'

'I bet they'll protest his innocence just as much as he does.'

'All his patients thought he was wonderful.'

'And his household won't admit that they should have seen what he was doing.'

'Well, keep at it, lad. If you let it be known among the vagrants that he's in captivity, you may just find more witnesses. His activities were known among the runaways, but fear kept them silent. Even Zosime should help. He trained her, but I never had the impression she was particularly loyal to him. She hates what has been done to the runaways, for one thing. Shock her with the facts; she'll give evidence.'

Petronius was called away. He left a man to guard the house, ready for a full search of the property next day. Justinus and I cast a quick eye over various rooms, and were about to leave ourselves. Then the vigilis called to us; he had found a locked closet. We could not discover a key to it; Cleander must have taken it. For half a beat we nearly left it for the lads to search the following day. But in the end, Justinus put his shoulder to the door and forced it open.

The interior was in darkness. As we crashed in, a faint groan alerted us to human presence. We ran for lights. Then we saw that Cleander had left a patient, or a victim, strapped to a pallet. He was gagged, and blood trickled inexorably from his arm into a by now very full bowl.

We could have left him there. Sometimes afterwards, I wished we had. But even when we recognised the patient as Anacrites, our humanity won. We removed the gag. We held his arm in the air until the blood flow stopped, then the vigilis, who knew basic bandaging, swathed his arm in torn cloth.

'I thought Cleander strangled his victims, Marcus.'

'He did normal doctoring as well, Quintus. Mastarna letting Scaeva die may have given him the idea. Perhaps Cleander hated Anacrites as an ex-slave, but thought a spy should die slowly . . . Drip, drip, drip – softly, safely, and sweetly over the Styx to the Underworld . . .' Anacrites was reviving enough to glare at me. We sat him up. He fainted, but we soon revived him. We were not gentle.

'There is always the chance of getting the bastard next time,' I told Quintus drily, letting the Spy overhear me. Anacrites hated having his life saved by me. Nothing good could come of it.

But for now, my assistant was overcome by kinder feelings. Since Camillus Justinus had left Claudia Rufina throwing herself into revelry at our house, he was returning there with me. Perhaps he felt that his time as Anacrites' house guest had given him a host/guest bond of duty; perhaps he wished to explain about the turnip. Whatever the reason, everyone else in Rome was indoors with happy friends and relatives. Anacrites had no friends and probably no relatives. So I heard Justinus issue a good-natured invitation to the enfeebled Chief Spy. He asked Anacrites to come home with us and share our family celebration on the last night of the festival . . .

Io, my dear Quintus. *Io*, Saturnalia!

AFTERWORD – 'ALL POSY POSY ON THE VIA DERELICTA'

'Words are real,' says Falco to Albia in Chapter XVIII of this novel, 'if other people understand their meaning.'

'Is this,' enquires my editor in the margin of the manuscript, 'your defence for your many neologisms?' (most of which he has singled out with underlining and exclamation marks). I pacify him with a promise of an Afterword and talk of lunch.

I write about another culture, where people spoke another language, one which has mainly survived either in a literary form or as tavern wall graffiti. Many an argot must have existed in between. People sometimes discuss whether the Romans would really sound as I portray them – forgetting firstly that the Romans spoke Latin not English, and that on the streets and in the provinces they must have spoken versions of Latin that did not survive. I have to find my own ways to make narrative and dialogue convincing. I use various methods. Much of it is done by 'ear', and is difficult to describe even if I wanted to reveal the secret. Sometimes I merely deploy metaphors and similes, but even that can cause difficulties; I treasure the conversation with my Swedish translator who was puzzled by Thalia referring to male genitalia as 'a three-piece manicure set' and who had gone so far as to consult a medical friend . . .

Sometimes I invent words; sometimes I am not even aware I have done it, but through nineteen books my British editor has diligently challenged me when he believes I have erred. Some years ago we reached an agreement that each manuscript might contain one neologism, or *Lindseyism*.

For a time I stuck to that. Once, there was even a competition where readers could identify the invented words. It foundered rather, because many American readers suggested perfectly good items of English vocabulary and in any case I could no longer remember what some of the allowed Lindseyisms were; however, I feel that 'nicknackeroonies' was identified at that time as the word some of us would most like to see absorbed into real life. (Let me credit my late Auntie Gladys with providing the inspiration.) A movement to establish 'nicknackeroonies' in current idiom began in Australia, where delicate finger-food is of course a speciality.

Then there was Fusculus. He loves words as much as I do. It has always been clear to me that there must have been Roman street language, specialist underworld cant in Latin and vigiles' slang expressions, all of which are so far lost to us but all of which Fusculus would know. It is no use hoping that the carbonised papyri from Herculaneum that are now being so painstakingly unravelled by scholars will produce clues; so far they are all Greek to me, and indeed to everyone. If Calpurnius Piso, thought to be the villa's owner, owned a Slang Thesaurus, we have not found it. I am on my own with this. I cannot use the rich seams of English and American equivalent terms from the Sixteenth to the Twentieth Centuries, for the secret languages of coney-catchers, spivs and drug barons are tied too closely to their periods. So when Fusculus speaks, odd words appear.

It will be noted by bean-counters that Chapter XVIII of *Saturnalia* contains more than my strict allowance of neologisms. Chapter XVIII is a celebration of the tolerance and understanding that have always been shown to me by my editors. Literary novelists, fuelled by booze and their own pretensions, are customarily permitted to write gobbledegook yet to be praised for their highflown inventiveness, but in the field of the light page-turner, it is generally assumed that nothing offered by an author will offend a publisher's standard spell-checker. Time and again I have been allowed to deviate. Apart from the lady who felt 'The' was 'too heavy' for her readers in the United States (a severe prescription that I constantly bear in mind, I promise), my editors have been models of restraint in the face of heartless prose misrule. In this Afterword, I salute them. In particular I salute Oliver Johnson, who is a serious, cultured Englishman and in his heart does not want flighty bits of author messing him about with funny stuff. This man has spent nearly twenty years patiently training me in plot development and chronological description, listening to my prejudice against Chardonnay, and crossing out distasteful sex. He knows I can't spell 'alter', when it's 'altar'. He accepted the one-word chapter. He let me kill the lion. He himself devised 'tribute plagiarism', which we hope will become recognised legal terminology for bandit usage of another author's material. (Of course I know 'bandit' is improper adjectival use of a noun. Still – good, isn't it?) I am rightly devoted to my editor, and this is where I get the chance to say: don't blame him!

I would also like to apologise to all my translators and to acknowledge their ingenuity in their constant battle with my vocabulary. It will take real woozlers to devise graceful equivalents for 'fragonage' and 'ferrikin' in Spanish, Turkish, Japanese and all the other languages in which Falco novels are published; the special use in the Fusculus context of 'nipping' and 'foisting' – though real words in theory – won't be easy either. Sometimes one of you honest men and women is drawn to approach me diffidently about a really impossible word or phrase and I want to say thank you for the courtesy with which you do this – and for not gloating when it turns out that the answer is, 'That is not a Lindseyism; it is a previously undiscovered typing error.'

'Wonk' is real, by the by. My new American editor used it, then defined it for me, and it is here to fulfil my promise to try and 'get it past Oliver'. (He saw it. He exclaimed at it, but he has not crossed it out, so it stays.)

Chapter XVIII was a deliberate bit of fun. There is an official Lindseyism in another chapter. I know my rights.

I think very carefully about my choice of words – even when I make them up. When I do, I think they work. Try them out if you like, though do heed Falco's caution: it is not necessary to know these words to be a Roman and you don't want people thinking you are eccentric . . .

MARCUS DIDIUS

FALCO

FOR ALL DISCREET ENQUIRIES
GOOD REFS
CHEAP RATES

If you have enjoyed *Saturnalia*, see the Official Lindsey
Davies website for up-to-date news and discussion:
work-in-progress, author talks, radio programmes,
translations, audio and other editions
www.lindseydavis.co.uk